MURDER BY THE MILLIONS

The Literary Dining Mystery series
Murder on the Page
Murder by the Millions

The Aroma Wellness Mystery series
Essence of Foul Play

The Fairy Garden Mystery series
A Sprinkling of Murder
A Glimmer of a Clue
A Hint of Mischief
A Flicker of a Doubt
A Twinkle of Trouble

MURDER BY THE MILLIONS

DARYL WOOD GERBER

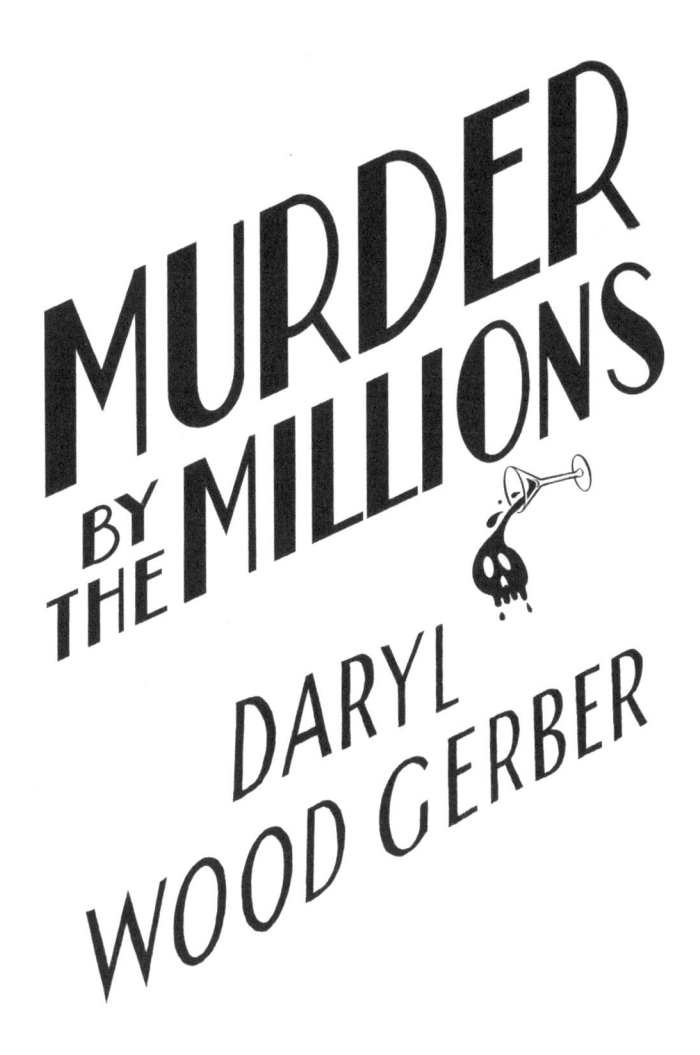

KENSINGTON PUBLISHING CORP.
kensingtonbooks.com

This book is a work of fiction. Names, characters, businesses, organizations, places, events, and incidents either are the product of the author's imagination or are used fictitiously. Any resemblance to actual persons, living or dead, events, or locales is entirely coincidental.

To the extent that the image or images on the cover of this book depict a person or persons, such person or persons are merely models, and are not intended to portray any character or characters featured in the book.

KENSINGTON BOOKS are published by

Kensington Publishing Corp.
900 Third Avenue
New York, NY 10022

Copyright © 2025 by Daryl Wood Gerber

All rights reserved. No part of this book may be reproduced in any form or by any means without the prior written consent of the Publisher, excepting brief quotes used in reviews.

Without limiting the author's and publisher's exclusive rights, any unauthorized use of this publication to train generative artificial intelligence (AI) technologies is expressly prohibited.

All Kensington titles, imprints and distributed lines are available at special quantity discounts for bulk purchases for sales promotion, premiums, fund-raising, educational or institutional use. Special book excerpts or customized printings can also be created to fit specific needs. For details, write or phone the office of the Kensington Special Sales Manager: Kensington Publishing Corp., 900 Third Avenue, New York, NY, 10022. Attn. Special Sales Department. Phone: 1-800-221-2647.

KENSINGTON and the KENSINGTON COZIES teapot logo Reg. US Pat & TM Off.

Library of Congress Control Number: 2025937912

ISBN: 978-1-4967-4820-1

First Kensington Hardcover Edition: November 2025

ISBN: 978-1-4967-4822-5 (ebook)

10 9 8 7 6 5 4 3 2 1

Printed in the United States of America

The authorized representative in the EU for product safety and compliance is eucomply OU, Parnu mnt 139b-14, Apt 123 Tallinn, Berlin 11317, hello@eucompliancepartner.com

To all those dreamers who want to write a novel but were told to not even try, may you continue to aspire. May you hope. May you study and apply yourself.
Believe you can and you will.

"A rock pile ceases to be a rock pile the moment a single man contemplates it, bearing within him the image of a cathedral."

—Antoine de Saint-Exupery, *The Little Prince*

Cast of Characters

Allie Catt, caterer
Brendan Bates, police detective
Candace Canfield, singer
Chloe Kang, bookshop clerk
Evelyn Evers, head of theater foundation
Fern Catt, Allie's mother
Finette Fineworthy, town council president
Helga, housekeeper at the Blue Lantern B&B
Ignatius Luckenbill II, developer
Jason Gardner, developer
Jenny Armstrong, owner of Jukebox Joint
Katherine Fineworthy, Finette's great-aunt
Lillian Bellingham, Puttin' on the Glitz shop owner
Magda Bellingham, Lillian's grandmother
Noeline Merriweather, owner of the Blue Lantern B&B
Ott, hiker
Patrick Hardwick, renovator
Pinkie, aka Pearl, neighbor
Reika Moore, museum curator
Shayna Luckenbill, Iggie's wife
Stella Burberry, accountant
Tegan Potts, bookstore owner
Ulla Karlsson, friend of Shayna Luckenbill
Vanna Harding, caterer and Tegan's half sister
Wallis, waitress at the Brewery
Zach Armstrong, police detective
Zorro Vega, hiker

Chapter 1

I was within and without, simultaneously enchanted and repelled by the inexhaustible variety of life.

—Nick Carraway in F. Scott Fitzgerald's *The Great Gatsby*

"Allie, I love *The Great Gatsby*," my best friend, Tegan Potts, said as she did a two-step through Feast for the Eyes, the bookshop she'd recently inherited from her aunt Marigold. "Love, love, love it."

"Glad to hear it." I'd just finished straightening up the reading nook located at the back left of the store, because the beanbags and comfy armchairs had all been askew. Now I was intent on organizing the items on the pegboard behind the sales counter. That was where we posted notes to one another, like "Out of *The Mystery of the Blue Train*" or "Need three copies of *The Diva Goes Overboard*." Once the issues were handled, the notes were tossed in the trash.

"I love the history." She skirted the year-round book tree decorated with miniature book ornaments and disappeared down the mystery aisle to pull books from the shelves. Though the bookshop wasn't huge, her voice became muffled. "And the glamour."

"What about the story?" I teased.

"The story's good."

Though my full-time career was working as a caterer and

baker, delivering tasty treats to the good people of Bramblewood, I had inherited a small percentage of the bookstore, so I helped out my pal whenever my baking and deliveries were done. The tragedy of Marigold's demise still brought tears to my eyes. She had been like a beloved aunt to me. But at least her murderer had been caught and imprisoned—the silver lining in an otherwise sad tale.

Tegan reemerged with a stack of books, which she deposited on the sales counter, already overflowing with others. On Sundays, before the bookshop opened, she was adamant about gathering all the preordered titles.

"The story is excellent when it comes to painting a picture of a tragic hero." Tegan spread her arms wide, which made the bat wings of her oversized anime shirt expand. She reminded me of a bird about to take flight. A very tiny bird. She was a good three inches shorter than me. "After all, Gatsby brings about his own downfall."

"True." I began to tag the books using the list Tegan had prepared. "Fitzgerald tried to portray Gatsby as a perfect person, but his imperfections were clearly evident. And let's face it, Gatsby shouldn't have cared for Daisy so much. He shouldn't have built his whole world around the possibility of her return."

"But he believed she couldn't possibly love her husband and would come running back to him because he was so rich."

A man's wealth wasn't a good enough reason for a woman to fall for him. Character mattered, as did kindness.

As if reading my mind, Darcy, my tuxedo cat, emerged from the office, which abutted the storage room, leaped onto the shop's desk beneath the pegboard, and swished his tail.

"Yes, my sweet boy. A man must also be a lover of animals." I kissed his nose.

At first, when I'd started bringing him to Feast for the Eyes, he had been shy and had remained in the office. Other than liking me and a few of my friends, he wasn't much of a people person. However, lately, he had grown bolder and made occasional appearances. His movement stirred the screen saver on the tabletop computer, and it came alive with magical swirling books.

I tickled him beneath his chin, and appeased, he bounded off the counter, trotted to an endcap and, using it as stairs, bounded to the top of the bookshelf closest to the front door for a snooze. I caught a glimpse of myself in the office window—the slats were drawn—and I frowned. My curly red hair was a mess. The scoop collar of my white T-shirt was uneven. I righted it and patted my hair into place.

"The book party for *Gatsby* is going to be such a success, don't you think?" Tegan continued.

When Marigold died, Tegan and I landed on the idea of having a book-themed memorial for her. Marigold had loved the classic *Pride and Prejudice*. At the memorial, we'd served food from the Regency era, and lots of people had worn time-appropriate costumes. Following the memorial, which had been widely attended, we decided we should have book-themed parties a few times a year—and no more memorials, if we could help it. If readers desired, they could wear costumes. I wasn't a fashion guru. I preferred jeans or leggings and solid-colored T-shirts. However, although sage green was my signature color, for *The Great Gatsby* event a week from Saturday, I'd selected an emerald-green flapper costume with silver spangles, a sexy V-neck, and shoulder fringe trim. *Ooh la la.*

"Lots of townsfolk will attend," Tegan said. "And tourists, too."

Bramblewood, North Carolina, was a serene community northwest of Asheville, the nearby metropolis, which, in addition to being the brewery capital of the country, boasted the famous inn on Biltmore Estate, a University of North Carolina campus, and a vigorous art scene, one that was rebuilding itself after a horrific hurricane. Our town drew a lot of visitors, but nothing like Asheville. However, the rustic allure of the Blue Ridge Mountains made Bramblewood extra special. Hotels, rental homes, and bed-and-breakfast inns were constantly filled. Most were within walking or biking distance of Main Street, where Feast for the Eyes as well as Dream Cuisine were located.

"Isn't it amazing the response we've gotten?" Tegan went on. "Readers are coming out of the woodwork. I've ordered fifty copies of the book. Fifty!"

Tegan and I had been best friends for over twenty-one years, ever since kindergarten. We both loved reading, though she liked fantasy, sci-fi, and comics, while I preferred mysteries and suspense. Her soon-to-be ex-husband also enjoyed fantasy—one of the few reasons they'd stayed together as long as they had.

"I'm telling you, these parties are going to put Dream Cuisine on the map." She knuckled my arm.

"Ahem." I cleared my throat mock-haughtily. "My business is already on the map."

"Sure, sure, but did you have a clue when you gave up becoming a teacher and moved back to Bramblewood to open your business that you would become this big a hit?"

"Well, I'd hoped."

Though I'd graduated Davidson College eager to introduce young minds to the classics, no teaching jobs were available, so I went to work for a caterer in Charlotte. I'd learned to cook at the tender age of five because my mother and father wanted me to be self-sufficient. The skill helped me get the job. Then when my ex-fiancé dumped me for a younger model, I decided to move home and parlay my cooking skills into a business. Now a number of restaurants and other businesses ordered my baked goods or hired me to cater their soirees. For some souls who were averse to cooking, I provided personal meals.

"How about you?" I asked. "Look at the success you've become, going from wannabe librarian to bookshop owner."

"Which would not have happened if my aunt hadn't died."

"Yes, it would have. She was seventy and ready to retire. If fate hadn't intervened, I'm positive she would have brought you in as her partner. You are the best salesperson I know." At one time, Tegan had wanted to become a librarian, but when she fell in love with selling books and interacting with customers, she abandoned the dream. "Now let's talk décor for the party." I perched on one of the ladder-back chairs by the sales counter. "I've discussed it with Reika and Lillian."

Reika Moore was the president of the Bramblewood Historical Preservation Society and the curator at Bramblewood History Museum. Lillian Bellingham was a contemporary of Tegan's and mine and the owner of Puttin' on the Glitz, the high-end clothing boutique next door. In addition to running a top-of-the-line retail business, Lillian donated her time as the costume designer for the community theater. Both Reika and Lillian were regulars at Feast for the Eyes.

"Reika thinks we need to focus on the art nouveau aspect of the era," I said. "She's trying to lay her hands on a few items, like gold lamé drapes and tablecloths. She says black and white feathers would be apropos. She's already rounded up gold candlesticks and Prohibition beverage glasses."

"Cool."

"Lillian has acquired strands of pearls and a bunch of flapper costumes and men's suits, because the theater did *Anything Goes* two years ago. I picked out one of the dresses already, and I saw another that will be perfect for you. Navy blue and silver, with exquisite floral beading." I fluttered my fingers in front of my chest.

"*Ooh*. I love beading." Like me, Tegan wasn't a fashion junky, although she did have a tendency to impulse shop when she was in a funk.

"It's sleeveless, of course."

"That will be perfect in this heat. Man, has June been hot! It wouldn't surprise me if we started to see tempers flaring. Bramblewoodians don't do well with the heat."

I snickered. *Bramblewoodians*. What a mouthful, but over the years, all other demonyms had faded away. Bramblewoodite sounded like a bug. Bramblewoodese sounded fussy. Bramblewooders was plain silly.

"Hot, hot, hot," she repeated.

She was right. The temperatures in the Asheville area were typically moderate. In March the low might be in the midthirties. In June we rarely inched above eighty-two degrees. But this week, we were close to ninety. Whew!

"I saw a couple of guys going at it down the street on my way in this morning," Tegan went on.

"Fistfighting?"

"Finger-pointing."

"Finger-pointing can be sooo dangerous." Laughing, I aimed my index finger at her.

She playfully batted it away.

The door to the shop opened, and Vanna Harding, Tegan's half sister, sashayed in. "Allie!" Vanna didn't enter a room without making a statement. In her pencil skirt, silk blouse, and stiletto heels, her blond hair swooped into a chignon, she looked ready to go to court. And win. "There you are."

Six years older than Tegan and me, Vanna had been the premier caterer when I'd moved back to town. As my business ticked up, she got ticked off. However, because she was actually the one who came up with the idea of hosting future literary dining parties, we mended fences. A month ago, when I asked her to help out at Dream Cuisine so I could expand the business, she said yes. Color me surprised!

"I've been searching everywhere for you." Her voice was

abrasive and sounded something akin to the bugle call of a whooping crane.

A voice coach could help, I was certain, but far be it from me to suggest it. I'd mentioned the idea to Tegan, but she'd said, "No way will I stick my nose into my sister's business," after which she'd clucked like a chicken.

"You look nice," I said.

Vanna had dusted her eyelids with a sparkly shadow, and her lips were ruby red. I couldn't remember the last time I'd put on lipstick. I was a lip-gloss kind of girl.

"Thank you." After her aunt died, Vanna softened a tad. I think she began to realize life was short and she needed friends, in particular her half sister and me. Also, though she had inherited a tidy sum from her aunt and didn't need money, she had a healthy ego. Partnering with me by providing baked goods to Bramblewood and nearby towns meant she would have a wider reach and could grow her clientele. "Now let's talk about the email you sent me regarding the menu for the *Gatsby* party." She wrinkled her nose and waggled her cell phone.

Uh-oh.

"Why are you so gussied up?" I asked as a diversion.

"I had a meeting."

Though Vanna and I worked together, she still had her own clients, as did I.

"Ahem." Vanna cleared her throat. "Anybody home, Allie? The menu?"

Her attitude occasionally rankled me. I fought the urge to hurl a sassy one-liner at her, a defensive tactic I'd acquired while growing up. "Yes." I smiled. "What about the menu?"

"You've got to be kidding." She consulted her iPhone. "Pineapple upside-down cake? How prosaic."

"It was big during the Roaring Twenties." I'd done my research. "Around 1925 the Hawaiian Pineapple Company held a contest, and many entries featured pineapple upside-down cake. Judges from Miss Farmer's School of Cookery, *Good House-keeping*, and *McCall's Magazine* chose the winner."

Tegan added, "Twenty-five hundred of the sixty thousand entries, to be exact!" A history buff and trivia nut, she'd enjoyed doing a deep dive into the era with me.

"What about this one?" Vanna referred to her cell phone. "Tomato soup cake? Ugh. How pedestrian."

"I know tomato soup is an odd ingredient for a cake, but no one will guess what the secret ingredient is," I said. "In the late 1920s or early 1930s the Campbell Soup Company created the recipe using their condensed tomato soup. Canned foods were all the rage."

"Fine." Vanna made a dismissive gesture. "Next! Deviled eggs. Totally plebeian."

"Everyone loved them back then," I said, "especially when Hungarian immigrants helped popularize paprika."

Vanna sniffed. "And small plates of pasta pomodoro? Pedantic."

"Gee, Sis, do you know only adjectives starting with the letter *p*?" Tegan teased.

Vanna's gaze shot daggers at her. Tegan did not cower. She had pluck in spades.

I said, "All Italian food grew in popularity during that time, because it was considered exotic and cultured. The simplest way for people to enjoy pasta is with a pomodoro sauce." I loved deglazing tomatoes and adding something as fresh and lively as basil. My mouth was watering contemplating it. "What would you like to serve?" I asked.

"Oysters Rockefeller."

Tegan snorted. "The oysters will spoil sitting out on a buffet and will make our guests sick."

"Fine. Then a Waldorf salad made with julienned Granny Smith and Fuji apples, halved red and green grapes, and candied walnuts. I'll emulsify a mixture of Dijon mustard, olive oil, champagne vinegar, egg yolk, and white truffle oil for the dressing." She twirled her hand with a flourish.

I bit back a smile. Vanna couldn't help herself. A perfectly good *simple* salad, in her opinion, always needed tweaking.

"As for our other business," Vanna said, pressing on.

Our? She meant *mine*, thank you. I was including her as a favor.

"We need a larger ghost kitchen."

"The one we . . . *I* . . . have is fine." A ghost kitchen, or virtual kitchen, was a place where chefs could cook for delivery or pickup. I rented my modest space on a month-to-month basis. "We're rarely in it together."

"We need to double the space."

I hated how pushy Vanna could be. When she wasn't partnering with me, she cooked at a well-known restaurant that leased her a corner of its kitchen. "If you help me double the business, we'll talk."

She huffed and started for the door but halted when Chloe Kang, the twenty-something junior clerk at the shop, who could be as energetic as a toddler experiencing a sugar high, rushed in.

"Stop the presses!" Chloe yelled. "He's here. Jason Gardner is here. In town. He's, like, wow." She wagged her hands frantically. "You know who I'm talking about, right?"

I shook my head. So did Vanna and Tegan.

"He's been on magazine covers and everything." Chloe sounded like she'd been dashed with stardust.

"Is he an actor?" Tegan asked.

"No. He's not an actor, silly." Chloe's almond-shaped eyes sparkled with impishness. "He's a builder. A really famous builder."

How famous could he be if none of the rest of us had heard of him?

"He's purchasing the lots across the street from the Congregational church," Chloe added.

The Congregational church was the first church built in Bramblewood and the one I used to go to with my grandmother before she passed away. "There are no vacant lots across the street," I said.

"Not *lots* lots." Chloe twirled to place her purse beneath the sales counter and whirled back around, smoothing the skirt of her fluted red dress. "The properties. The houses."

"Those aren't for sale."

"Yes they are, Allie."

"No. They're historic landmarks," I stated. "The preservation society has plans to include them in its tour of the town, once they get the funding to complete the sale. They want to show life as it was when Bramblewood was initially settled."

"The town council has approved Mr. Gardner's bid," Chloe said.

"You're kidding." I exchanged a look with Tegan, who raised her shoulders, clueless.

"Mr. Gardner has a few permit hurdles to jump over before the sale is final, of course, but . . . oh, oh! That's him." Chloe bounced on her toes and jutted an arm toward the street. "Outside. There. See him? He's walking this way. He's coming into the shop!"

Seconds later a decidedly handsome man pushed through the front door. He reminded me of someone—an actor—but I couldn't drum up the name. "Are you open for business?" His voice was warm and refined.

"It's Sunday," Tegan replied.

"Is that a yes or no?"

"Hello, Mr. Gardner," Chloe said, waving demurely. "I'm Chloe Kang."

"Hi." Jason Gardner had wavy hair, which he had swooped off his face and wore longish, cut above the collar of his brown linen jacket. His jaw was strong, and his eyes, though narrow, held a glint of humor. Two lines, like double parentheses, bracketed the left side of his mouth, hinting that this was the side he favored when he smiled. If not for the furrows between his eyebrows and the way he was nervously fisting and unfurling his left hand, I would think he'd lived a carefree life in his forty-something years. "Yes or no? Open?"

Tegan glanced at me for a response to his question.

"No," I replied, "we're not open yet, but we will be after noon. You're free to browse now and reserve books to purchase then."

He grinned, confirming my deduction about which way his smile would go. Chloe drew in a quick breath. So did Vanna. Both were clearly smitten.

"You met Chloe," I continued. "The one in the anime shirt is Tegan Potts. The other is her half sister, Vanna Harding." I pointed to them. "I'm Allie Catt."

He let out a laugh. "Really? You're not pulling my leg?"

"No, and yes, it's a funny name, but I come by it honestly. Catt, C-a-t-t, is an English name derived from Catford, which initially meant 'a ford frequented by wildcats.'"

"I'll bet you heard a lot of jokes growing up." He sauntered toward the thriller and mystery section of the store.

"Of course. Here's one. Knock, knock."

"Who's there?"

"Fur."

"Fur who?"

"Fur heaven's sake, open the door."

"You poor kid," he said.

I supposed to him I was a kid. I was a good fifteen to twenty years younger.

He pulled a hardcover off an endcap and opened the book to read the blurb on the jacket.

I said, "I heard you're planning on buying property here."

"To build a mall," Chloe chimed.

I gawked at her. Why hadn't she led with that? A mall? In Bramblewood? We took pride in the fact all our stores were independent concerns. Our streets were lined with antique shops, jewelry shops, novelty shops, and more. Even the cafés, restaurants, and inns were small and intimate. We did not need a mall. Shoot.

"Malls are classless," Tegan declared.

Vanna hushed her.

"But they are."

Jason arched an eyebrow.

"Tegan isn't wrong," I said. "Malls attract people who are looking for bargains, not people who are interested in the history or the serenity of the town."

"They're also places where some people are looking to meet other people," Vanna argued.

"She's right." Jason replaced the book, loosened the knot of his paisley tie, and shoved a hand into the pocket of his trousers.

I nearly shouted, *Ryan Gosling*! That was who he reminded me of. The famous film star posing for the front cover of *People* magazine couldn't have come across more casual yet stunning.

"I assure you it will be classy," he said.

One couldn't rely on assurances, I mused. Personal history had taught me so.

"It'll be a mecca," he went on enthusiastically. "Like its own Main Street, and in keeping with the architectural style of the town. It will be located at the west end of Main Street, where everyone enters town."

"Or leaves," I said. "Our roads go both ways."

"It'll bring quality tourism, I assure you."

"We get plenty of excellent tourists," I countered.

"I'm sure you do."

"How long do you intend to be in town?" I asked. "Will you build the mall and split? Or do you plan to stick around and make sure it maintains its level of supposed quality?" I made air quotes to highlight the word *quality*.

"I intend to establish roots here." He pulled his hand free from the pocket and strolled toward us with a self-assured gait. "I'm having a summer party soon to show my designs for the mall. I'll be inviting lots of people. Why don't you all come? It'll be at the estate I'm renting."

"Which estate?" Chloe asked, starry-eyed.

"The Sugarbaker estate."

The Sugarbaker estate was a gorgeous spread built in the nineteen hundreds and owned by Thomas Sugarbaker, one of Bramblewood's greatest philanthropists and a patron of the arts. Annually the art guild would stage the house and open it for tours. All proceeds went to funding budding artists' careers. In addition to the grand house, the grounds featured an open-air pavilion, an elaborate swimming pool, and miles of walking trails. The babble of Bramblewood Creek could be heard from the back porch.

"Once I pin down the time and date," Jason said, "I'll let you know. First, I need to hire a caterer for the soiree."

"Allie's a caterer," Tegan said. "Hire her. Here's her card." She seemed to whip one out of thin air.

I shot her a look.

"Allie and I are partners," Vanna said, digging in her purse for a business card. "We'd love to give you ideas for your event."

"She's Allie's sometimes partner," Tegan countered. "Not full-time partner."

"Full-time for now," Vanna said with a grunt, still struggling to produce her business card as she stepped toward Jason.

Chloe said, "I'd love to help with the party, if you need me."

Rushing around the sales counter, she caught her toe on a runner and tripped into Vanna.

The two pitched forward and collided with the endcap. Display books went flying. The shelf beyond the endcap teetered. Vanna screamed with horror.

Darcy, disturbed from his nap, yowled and leaped off the bookshelf.

"My cat!" I yelled.

Jason tried to catch Darcy. The two got tangled up and fell to the floor.

Chapter 2

[His smile] understood you just as far as you wanted to be understood, believed in you as you would like to believe in yourself, and assured you that it had precisely the impression of you that, at your best, you hoped to convey.

—Nick Carraway in F. Scott Fitzgerald's *The Great Gatsby*

Unscathed, Darcy scrambled free of Jason's grasp and bounded through the shop to take refuge in the office.

Chuckling, Jason scrambled to a stand and dusted himself off.

"I'm so sorry," Chloe cried. "My fault—"

"No, it was mine," Vanna cut in. To be fair, she wasn't appeasing Chloe. She looked absolutely mortified by her erratic behavior. She presented Jason with her business card. "I have my own business. I'm not merely Allie's partner."

"Sometimes partner," Tegan repeated.

"I'm a professional through and through," her half sister added hastily and, red faced, hurried out of the shop.

"Well, that was fun," Jason joked. "I hope your cat doesn't hate me as much as you do, Allie."

"I don't—"

He winked sassily.

Apparently, I wasn't deft at hiding my aversion to his mall. "Darcy was scared."

"Darcy, as in Mr. Darcy?" Jason asked. "Nice literary reference. Your cat looks like a Mr. Darcy with his classic tuxedo markings."

Was he trying to butter me up, so I'd approve of his cockamamie plan?

"Do you have an effect on all women, Mr. Gardner?" Tegan asked.

"Call me Jason," he said. "And what effect?"

"Having women throw themselves at you?"

"Women threw themselves at me? Gee, I hadn't noticed."

I had to admit I did like his sense of humor. It gave him an air of humility. I glanced at my watch. "Oh, my! I'm late. I'm sorry, Tegan, but I have to meet Reika. She's going to show me photos of everything she wants us to use at the *Gatsby* party."

"What *Gatsby* party?" Jason asked.

"We're putting on a *Great Gatsby* literary dining party." Tegan beamed. "Complete with food from the era. You can attend if you read the book. Many will dress in period costumes for the occasion."

"I've read *The Great Gatsby* a number of times," Jason said. "It's one of my favorites. Fitzgerald was brilliant, the way, through the character of Gatsby, he captured the belief that every individual, regardless of their origins, can pursue and achieve their desired goals."

Knock me over with a feather. He understood the theme?

"The book is truly the literary expression of the concept of America being the land of opportunity." He started for the door. "I'll return during normal business hours to purchase some books. If you have a copy of *The Great Gatsby*, set one aside."

Tegan said, "Will do."

"And, Allie"—he flicked my business card—"I'll call you regarding the soiree. I intend to win your approval of me."

I felt my cheeks flush and wanted to kick myself. His charm was starting to get to me. Drat.

I retreated to the office, grabbed my purse, told Darcy I'd be back soon, and headed to Ragamuffin, a coffeehouse located in one of the connecting courtyards between Holly Street and Elm.

The bistro tables on the exterior patio were filled. Inside, all the tables were occupied, as well. I spotted Reika at the standing-only bar. Amira, her emotional support animal, or ESA, a bulldog named after a dog in *The Serpent on the Crown* by Elizabeth Peters, stood beside her. I'd met Reika at a book club event at Feast for the Eyes. She often proclaimed she was a devout Peters fan. Though she was in her sixties, Reika, who had donned a square-shaped blazer and a knee-length skirt, looked as muscular and energetic as her bulldog. Her pixie-style salt-and-pepper hair didn't dissuade me from the comparison.

"Good. You're here. I worried I got the time wrong." Reika didn't wear a watch, saying she hated how one felt on her skin, but she loathed referring to her cell phone all the time. Therefore, she invariably showed up early for events so she wouldn't be late.

"What can I get you?" I asked her. "Mocha? Cappuccino?"

"An Irish cream latte, please."

Ragamuffin's baristas were gifted when it came to their coffee beverages, adding all sorts of house-made syrups, like lavender, honey-maple, and Irish cream.

"Extra sweet," Reika added. The bulldog barked in its throaty way. She hushed it and tugged lightly on the dog's leash, which was loose around her wrist.

"And to eat?" I asked.

"Nothing." Reika waved a hand. "I'm watching my figure." She winked. "That's all I'm doing. Watching it. Not minding it." Though the curator had a stubborn streak, which made her a force, she also had a self-deprecating wit, which I appreciated. The history museum was in good hands under her leadership.

The bulldog yipped again.

Gently, Reika tweaked the dog's nose with her finger. "Shh, you silly beggar."

I got in line behind Patrick Hardwick, a home renovator in his late thirties. Rugged and lean, with unruly dirty-blond hair, he reminded me of the kind of guy who could climb Mount Everest with one hand tied behind his back. He also appeared to have been stomping through a filthy area recently. His work boots were caked with dried dirt.

"Hi, Allie," he said over his shoulder, before shoving a wad of gum into the hollow of his cheek. "Nice to see you. I'm on my way to Tegan's mother's place to pin down the details about how she wants me to renovate her office."

Tegan's mom owned the Blue Lantern, a lovely bed-and-breakfast in Montford, an enclave at the north end of Asheville.

"In those?" I indicated his boots.

"Oh, geez, bad on me. I forgot to clean them up. I had a minor snafu with yesterday's rain. It washed out my gravel driveaway. Don't worry." He grinned. "I'll switch shoes for the meeting. Had to stop here first. I'm getting muffins for me and my crew. They're finishing up another job and love the poppyseed ones."

"I'm glad you like them. I make them." Ragamuffin was one of my many customers. "When do you start working at the Blue Lantern?"

"It's a go Tuesday, as far as I know." He paid for his purchase and said, "Say hi to Tegan for me."

"Do it yourself. The copy of *Dune* you ordered came in."

"Cool. I've carved out an entire reading day next Sunday." Like Tegan, he enjoyed the fantasy, sci-fi, and supernatural genres. He raised the bag as a good-bye salute and exited the coffeehouse.

Minutes later, I rejoined Reika with two lattes and a dog biscuit for Amira. I bent to scratch the dog behind her ears. "How are you, Princess?" A while back, Reika had told me the dog's name translated to *princess*, so I'd begun using the moniker as a greeting. She let out a low, raspy bark of joy and salivated for the treat. I made her sit before giving it to her. Watching a bulldog sit made me laugh. Because of their short legs, they hunkered down like a human.

"She's spoiled rotten," Reika said of the dog, "but I couldn't live without her. She keeps me calm. Ever since . . ."

She didn't continue. She didn't have to. She had confided on another occasion that in her thirties she'd been attacked by an intruder and had owned an ESA ever since. Amira was her third dog.

"The doctor says my heart . . ." Reika stopped mid-sentence again and sipped her beverage. "My heart can't take any more surprises." Her mother had died suddenly a month ago. Her father, last year. Not from anything untoward. They'd been in their nineties. Even so, losing a parent could be daunting. Reika withdrew a manila envelope from the tote bag she'd hung on one of the standing bar's purse hooks. "Let's get down to business. Take a gander at these beauties."

I pulled photographs from the envelope. "You didn't have to print them. I could've viewed them on your cell phone."

"Bah. It's important to touch things. Tactility matters."

"Always the museum curator."

"That's right. Cameras capture memories, but they don't provide the joy of a physical photograph. The feel of the paper. The brilliance of the colors."

I spread the photos on the standing bar and oohed with excitement. "The pearls in the oversized champagne glass are gorgeous. And these feathers?" Two-foot-tall black as well as white plumes sprouted from the tops of gold-flecked candlesticks. "Stunning."

"By the by, I need you to supply two dozen assorted cookies and two dozen muffins for my Thursday morning meeting at the museum. I prefer chocolate, but do include those fabulous apple muffins you make. My assistant adores them."

"Got it." I logged the order on my cell phone. "Before I forget, have you heard a man named Jason Gardner wants to purchase the historic properties opposite the Congregational church?"

"I heard, and I'm not happy about it. It's all Finette's doing."

Finette Fineworthy was the president of the town council.

"Speak of the devil incarnate," Reika muttered.

I pivoted, expecting to see Jason, but instead I saw Finette sauntering into the coffee shop.

"Too bad she can't Photoshop her ugly personality," Reika said under her breath.

I snickered and stored the quip in my brain for future use.

Finette was a handsome woman in her late thirties who always sported a skirt suit. I'd seen her wearing the white one she was wearing on numerous times. She thought her legs were her best feature and liked to highlight them. In addition, she regularly slipped on a slew of bangles and an infinity bracelet. Trailing her was Ignatius Luckenbill II—Iggie to his friends—a real estate developer.

The twosome passed by us without glancing in our direction.

"I was reading Burt's blog the other day," Finette said.

"Burt the Cyber Buddy?" Iggie asked.

"The same."

Neither Finette nor Iggie ever spoke in a dull whisper. They always wanted to be heard, as if by forcing people to pay attention, they raised their status.

"Love the gadgetry tips he shares," Iggie said. "What's new?"

Finette pulled a pen from her tote. "See this? It's a digital pen that records whatever you hear, say, and write. It pairs with audio recordings or your mobile phone's Notes app."

"Love it."

"I'll send you a link."

I said to Reika, "Why did you call Finette the devil incarnate?"

"She's boastful. Her last exchange is a perfect example. I peruse Burt's blog, and I get all sorts of tips, but I don't brag about them. And I don't buy everything he thinks is cool. Who has that kind of free cash? I think Finette does, hoping Iggie and others will be impressed. *Pfft.* She's not hot stuff."

Recently, I'd gotten to know Finette, because I'd attended a few town council meetings, plus she'd come to a neighborhood watch gathering I'd thrown at my house. She lived around the block from me. Generally, she was nice, but yes, she could be a braggart. I recalled a conversation at the neighborhood gathering where she told me how she'd come up through the ranks in the political sphere, working on real estate projects first as an assistant and then as a project boss. According to her, her tech savviness had given her a leg up. After she'd made a name for herself, she ran for office. I wondered if heading up the town council was as high as she aspired to go. Maybe she would set her sights on becoming mayor.

"Look how she swishes her tawny hair about." Reika fingered her tight gray curls. "It's vain."

How do you really feel? I mused but didn't voice the words.

"And don't get me started on Iggie," Reika continued. "He's rude and crude and reminds me of Homer Simpson, with his florid cheeks and his rotund belly. How he can be as good at golf as he claims to be is unfathomable. And his thinning hair! He's always patting it into place." She mimed the action. "As if it'll help. Ha!"

"Having good looks or a fit body doesn't guarantee you can

swing a club," I teased. "However, I will agree with you about his character."

I didn't know Ignatius Luckenbill II well. He wasn't a reader, and I'd never catered an event for him. Even so, he had a reputation for being a puffy blowhard with a kiss-my-tush attitude. I'd read accounts of him in the news. He'd made his mark as a real estate developer by putting many of his competitors out of business. Whenever he could, he'd maligned them. My father had once opined that Iggie's father, from whom he'd inherited Luckenbill Construction, had been equally shrewd, with a take-no-prisoners approach.

"If only the police had proved he burned down his last project," Reika said. "But, alas, the arson inspector couldn't find any evidence. If I were a betting woman, I'd guess he's wooing Finette so he can make a bid for the properties Mr. Gardner wishes to purchase."

"I got the impression Jason had sealed the deal."

"Jason?" Reika arched an eyebrow. "You're on a first-name basis?"

I hooked my thumb over my shoulder. "We met a bit ago, when he stopped into Feast for the Eyes while Tegan and I were doing inventory."

"Uh-huh." She smirked. "Well, don't call him a property owner yet. He still has permit hoops to jump through. If he doesn't qualify, the properties will be back on the market, and I'll do a full-court press to convince the preservation society donors to scramble up the cash to make the highest bid and preserve the properties, as we'd intended. If you'll excuse me, my aging bladder calls. I must use the loo." She took Amira along.

I eyed Iggie and Finette again. They'd joined the line of people ready to order.

Iggie was fiddling with the cuff link on his right sleeve and bumping into customers without apology. "We don't need another developer in town," he said, loudly enough for the entire place to hear. "If anybody is going to design the future of Bramblewood, it should be me."

"You," Finette said, disdain dripping off her tongue.

"All my properties are premier. As you well know, the community surrounding the golf course is top notch and in demand." He'd upgraded the area about three years ago. The houses were expensive. The club memberships were costly, as well. "What do you know about this—Dang it. Help me with my cuff link." He held out his arm to her.

She slipped her cell phone into her tote and did as asked; then she pushed his arm away. "You're welcome."

"What do you know about this guy named Jason Gardner?"

"I know he's smart. Talented. Wealthy—"

"Admit it, you know next to nothing," Iggie interrupted. "He's got money. Big deal."

"He's originally from Bramblewood but relocated to California when he was ten."

Why hadn't Jason mentioned his roots at the bookshop? Vanna hadn't seemed to recognize him or his name, but then she was a number of years younger.

"Do you have an appointment with him?" Iggie asked. "Is that why you're all dolled up?"

"Don't be ridiculous," Finette hissed. "I always dress for success."

When Iggie reached the head of the line, he ordered a black coffee. "What do you want to drink, Finette?"

"A caramel macchiato with two pumps of vanilla syrup."

He pulled his cell phone from the inside pocket of his jacket, flicked a finger across the screen, and displayed the phone to the barista. She rang up the purchase. I noticed he didn't leave a cash tip. Conceivably, he'd added one via the app. "Give me a reason why you passed on my bid," he said to Finette as he shuffled to the spot where completed drinks were placed. "You used to be my best cheerleader."

"Once upon a time you were brilliant, with cutting-edge

ideas and a vision for Bramblewood. Now? You're stale. A hack."

"Take it back."

Finette shook her head.

"Is Gardner paying you?" Iggie demanded.

"Paying me?"

"Yeah. With jewelry? I've got eyes. I see you've got a new infinity necklace and ankle bracelet. I happen to know you're stretched for funds, having to take care of your great-aunt. So, fess up. Is he bribing you? Otherwise, how you can afford the bling?"

"You . . . you . . . I'll have you know I've purchased everything I own myself. I've had this necklace and these"—she aimed a finger at her ankle bracelet and the bangles on her arm—"for years! I wear the infinity symbol because it fills me with confidence and radiates a sense of sophisticated style. It bestows upon its wearer a reminder of her potential and of the impactful relationships that shape her life."

"Bullpucky. Sheer, utter rot! Why, I should press the town council to dismiss you."

"Don't take a tone with me, Ignatius."

"Are you sleeping with Gardner?"

"Enough! Scrap the coffee. May you burn in hell, you . . . you . . . snake." She turned on her heel and stomped out of Ragamuffin.

Reika exited the restroom at the same time, eyes wide. She'd heard what everyone else had. "Oh, that man!" She stomped past me to Iggie. "You imbecile."

"Huh?" He looked dumbfounded.

"You're mad because the town council didn't grant you the rights to the properties and now you're taking it out on Finette. Not fair. You're slime. A boor. I don't know what your problem is, but I'll bet it's hard to pronounce."

Holy heck. For someone who, minutes ago, had referred to

Finette as the devil incarnate, Reika was certainly going to bat for her. On the other hand, who better than her to do so? She was a vocal women's rights advocate who'd led numerous marches for a variety of causes.

"At least Mr. Gardner promises his mall will replicate the historic look of the town," she went on. "Unlike whatever you might construct."

"Hogwash," Iggie said. "The guy has all of you wrapped around his finger, but I promise you, he'll make the mall as gawdy as the one he planned to build in Santa Monica, California, but abandoned. Do you hear me? It. Never. Got. Off. The. Ground."

"I heard he was quite the celebrity in Hollywood."

"He was until he wasn't. 'Why?' I ask you. Because he's a poser. A deadbeat. He lost interest in his last project, and wham! He hit the road."

Why had Jason abandoned it? What was his story?

"Face it, he's a flake," Iggie continued. "A ne'er-do-well." He took his beverage from the barista, told her to dump Finette's order, pushed past Reika, and exited the coffeehouse.

I shuddered, recalling how Tegan had claimed tempers were flaring in the heat. In view of Iggie's sketchy history of possible arson, I certainly hoped that was all that would flare up.

Chapter 3

"I didn't want you to think I was just some nobody. You see, I usually find myself among strangers because I drift here and there trying to forget the sad things that happened to me."

—Jay Gatsby in F. Scott Fitzgerald's *The Great Gatsby*

At four p.m. I arrived with Darcy at Dream Cuisine. I loved cooking there. Following strict health guidelines, I'd arranged it so I could also fill orders at home, if necessary, but there was something about baking in the ghost kitchen that made me feel free and ultra-creative. It was three times the size of the kitchen in my cabin and outfitted with dozens of pans, utensils, counter space, a pantry, and a walk-in refrigerator. Plus the location, not far from Feast for the Eyes, was superconvenient.

Darcy meowed from inside his cat carrier. I never allowed him to leave the bag when I was cooking, which didn't make him happy—cat hair in the food I made was a no-no—but given the alternative, he'd rather be with me than home alone. I rested the bag on the desk to the right of the front door, tossed my keys beside the bag and, after thoroughly washing my hands, slung on an apron.

For the next few minutes, I arranged mixing bowls on the stainless-steel counters, pulled two blenders from the shelf beneath the island, and removed a number of utensils from the magnetic strip affixed to one of the walls.

"I'm here," Vanna trilled, entering through the rear door. She was wisely dressed in a loose-fitting blouse, leggings, and flats. Like me, she parked her personal items on the desk, washed her hands, tied an apron over her clothes, and tucked her hair beneath a mesh-style chef's cap.

"We need two dozen scones," I said.

"For?"

"Legal Eagles." The law firm was one of my most prestigious clients. "Plain."

"Why not spruce them up with ancho chiles and paprika?"

I wrinkled my nose. "Heavens, no. They don't go for anything frou-frou." Vanna was the kind of chef who thought micro whatever was chic. "Also, we'll need two dozen raspberry scones for Perfect Brew. I'll get started on the apple-rosemary muffins for Blessed Bean. Then I'll frost vanilla cupcakes for Milky Way. I have four dozen in the freezer, which will work perfectly." On light baking days, I often made extra muffins and cakes and froze them, in case I needed them in a pinch. "I'd like to wrap up everything in a couple of hours. I have a big day scheduled tomorrow. Deliveries. Meetings. Helping out at the bookshop."

"Why don't I make all the deliveries and free you up? I'll arrive at seven sharp."

"Perfect."

Surprisingly, with no chatter about the incident between her and Chloe making a dash for Jason Gardner, Vanna got to work.

Despite our differences, in the short while we'd been working together, we did seem to move around a kitchen as if choreographed. We never bumped into one another. Vanna started to hum a Swifties' favorite. I joined in. No lyrics. Singing lyrics might make us miss a step in a recipe.

A half hour later, the rear door opened again. Tegan tapped the frame as she sauntered in. "Knock, knock."

I groaned. "No jokes."

"I was merely announcing my arrival, but since I can tell you're dying to laugh . . ." She winked. "Dying."

I motioned for her to continue. She would taunt me until I caved.

"Knock, knock."

"Who's there?"

"Cat."

"Cat who?"

"Allie Catt you take a joke?" She chortled.

"Ha ha. Groan. What's up? Why are you here?"

She perched on a stool beside the island, shifted her crossbody purse to the other side, and pulled her cell phone from it. "I did some digging."

"About?" I regarded her.

"Jason Gardner."

Vanna was mixing dough by hand. She paused, her curiosity piqued. "What did you learn? Did you find it on the Internet? You know you can't believe everything you read there."

"No." Tegan tapped the cell's screen. "I'm referring to my phone because I made notes. Patrick Hardwick filled me in."

"Patrick?" I waggled my eyebrows. "When did you run into him?"

"He stopped by the shop for the copy of *Dune* we put on hold. A little birdie told him it was in."

I said to Vanna, "I'm the birdie. I bumped into him at Ragamuffin." I turned back to Tegan. "So . . . fill us in. Don't keep us in suspense."

"Until recently, Jason was living in California."

I said, "I overheard Iggie Luckenbill say Jason was a bigwig in Hollywood, but then he reneged on building a mall and came here."

"True. Partly."

"What happened? Did he run out of funds? Come up against an adversary?"

"Nope. It seems he was in love with a woman named Delilah Brenneman, but she married someone else thirteen years ago." She swiped to a page in her notes and showed it to me. "This is her."

Delilah had beautiful blond curls, a Cupid's-bow mouth, and arresting eyes.

"She's quite pretty in a delicate way," I said.

"Yep. Apparently, he was so heartbroken, he abandoned all the projects he had in the works."

"Thirteen years later?" I shook my head. It didn't make sense. I could see how losing the love of one's life in the present might make one's interest wane . . . but thirteen years later? Something didn't add up.

"Patrick didn't have an answer," Tegan said.

"How much of the mall had been built?"

"The foundation and framing."

"So it's a shell."

"Yep."

"How sad," Vanna said. "Why did the woman Jason loves marry someone else?"

"Patrick wasn't sure."

"Why does he know so much about a newcomer to town?" I asked.

Her mouth quirked up on one side. "Because Patrick is miffed Jason is here, so he did a deep dive into his past."

"Why is he miffed?" I started scooping the apple-rosemary muffin batter into the pans I'd lined with cupcake liners. "It's not like his renovation business is competitive with a builder who creates malls."

"He says he's worried the mall won't be eco-friendly. He

loves Bramblewood and doesn't want to see the landscape tarnished."

"How silly," Vanna said as she inserted a tray of scones into one of the oversized ovens. "A mall doesn't necessarily ruin the landscape. Some are quite beautiful. Have you ever seen the mall in Melbourne, Australia? Stunning architecture. It features faceted gold ceiling panels and travertine flooring. And Palm Court in Miami, Florida, is breathtaking with its blue glass façade."

Tegan gawked at her sister.

"I subscribe to *Architectural Digest*," Vanna said. "I find it relaxing to browse." She switched on the oven light and peeked at the scones. "You heard Jason. He said it's going to be classy, and he promised he'd keep the town's heritage and current architectural style in mind."

"We'll see." I inserted the filled muffin pans into another oven, set a timer for eighteen minutes, and took the mixing bowls to the sink. "By the way, Tegan," I said over my shoulder, "I think Patrick has the hots for you."

"He does not."

Vanna joined me at the sink and deposited her dirty items on the drainboard. "I liked Patrick for a nanosecond, until I found out he's a raw-food omnivore. Can you imagine?"

I chuckled. "There's nothing horrible about it. It means he eats raw fish, meat, dried meat, and plant-based foods."

"But nothing is cooked. Spare me!" Vanna wriggled with displeasure. "Also, he didn't go to college. Straight out of high school he started working for the family business."

"Lots of people wind up working in a family business," Tegan stated.

"It's a farm." Vanna made a face like she'd smelled something rotten.

"A family farm," I clarified, "with over two hundred acres.

They grow farm products and also offer a farm stay in their opulent barn. Plus they have classes and events to teach people about organic living."

Tegan's eyes widened. "How do you know so much about them?"

"Because I consulted them when I wanted to find the best places around Asheville to buy eggs and fruit. They told me Patrick gave up farm life eight years ago to become a home renovator."

"To his credit, he reads a ton more books than you do, Sis."

"Pfft." Vanna fetched another mixing bowl. "I must say I'm intrigued by Jason Gardner." She disappeared into the walk-in refrigerator and reemerged with a colander of rinsed raspberries. "He's my style, right down to his adorable grin. And the way he dresses? Pure class."

Tegan hopped off her stool, plucked a raspberry from the colander, and popped it into her mouth. "Allie, how's it going with you and Zach?"

Zach Armstrong was a detective for the Bramblewood Police Department. He and I first met at Feast for the Eyes, and I'd been instantly attracted to him. He had a strong jaw, mesmerizingly dark eyes, and a dry wit.

"You haven't spoken about him for a few weeks," Tegan went on, "so I've been afraid to ask."

I ogled her skeptically. Tegan was never afraid to ask about my love life. Ever. Why, almost every time I'd slept over at her house while growing up, she'd wakened me from a sound sleep to pelt me with questions about this or that boy. To be fair, I had been reluctant to discuss Zach of late. "Dating didn't work out."

"Why not?" Tegan squawked. "You two are perfect for each other. The girl next door and the policeman? A match made in heaven."

I wasn't a girl next door by any stretch of the imagination. Yes, I had an easy smile—nothing sensual about it—but I had ample curves. Plus I had sage-green eyes, which my ex-fiancé had told me were smoldering.

"Well?" Tegan tapped the counter.

"We . . ." I crinkled my mouth.

"Out with it."

"We kissed."

"Woot!"

"Once."

"Once?" Vanna echoed. "On the lips or the cheek?"

"On the lips. It didn't click. For either of us."

The memory was still etched in my mind. I'd been looking forward to our first kiss. During the initial weeks of seriously dating, we'd gone to the theater and hiked and talked about myriad subjects. We'd never argued. I knew our first kiss was going to be amazing. But then it wasn't. It had felt like our lips were made of sandpaper. I figured, when the truth hit the pavement, he still missed his first wife. They'd married right out of high school, and she died a year later from complications of COPD. They'd known she was sick when they said their vows. Her death wasn't a surprise. But he'd loved her with all his heart. Now, fifteen years later, I got the impression he still wasn't ready to move on.

"Oh, come on, Allie," Vanna said, adding raspberries to the batter she'd prepared. "One kiss does not make or break a relationship."

"It didn't feel right." I was unwilling to educate them about Zach's past. It wasn't my story to tell. "We're still friends. I'm fine with the arrangement. We play heads-up poker occasionally."

"What's that?" Vanna asked.

"It's a game two people can play," I said. "Both have to be

aggressive, to a point. It's a lot of fun. As a matter of fact, he's coming over tonight for a penny-ante game."

Vanna made a dismissive sound. "Poker is not in the least romantic. You should kiss him again. Take him by surprise. Throw yourself at him. See if it'll change the chemistry."

"No you should *not* do that. Sis, get real. It's the reason why you lost you-know-who."

"I didn't throw myself at—"

"Yes, you did, and he bolted." Tegan petted my shoulder. "If you're sure it's over."

"I'm sure." Engaged at twenty-two and unengaged months later, I'd been gun-shy about dating ever since. I really liked Zach, and I'd jumped at the chance to date him, but I knew now we weren't meant to be.

"There's someone else out there for you," Tegan said.

"Is there?" Vanna quipped. "She's now in the second half of her twenties. Men don't exactly fall off trees once a woman reaches a certain age."

Tegan snorted. "In that case, why aren't you in a relationship?"

"I'm discerning."

"Back to Jason Gardner." I was desperate to change the subject. "I'm concerned about him destroying historic properties for a mall. Reika is worried, too. She really wanted the houses to be preserved for a tour."

"Reika is a stuffed shirt," Vanna said.

"She is not. She loves our town and its history." An idea came to me as I fetched a new mixing bowl. "You know what? As much as I like Jason . . ." And I did, I realized. A man with a well-tuned sense of humor was a rare find. "I'm going to make signs protesting the project. Maybe it'll be a way to get the town council's attention, and they won't grant the permits, and he'll move on."

"Allie, that's not a good idea," Tegan warned.

"I agree," Vanna chimed. "Nothing good can come from inserting oneself into politics. I should know."

"What're you talking about?" I asked.

Tegan sniggered. "My sister wanted to add speed bumps on North Mountain Road. Bikers came out in droves to object. They TPed her house. They smeared her car with petroleum jelly."

Mountain Road had two designations. North Mountain Road was a twisting road running north of Main to the Blue Ridge Mountains. South Mountain Road was straighter and headed toward Asheville. Bikers, most of them Harley lovers, enjoyed speeding along the northern stretch and wouldn't tolerate being bossed around.

"The worst offense," Vanna said, "was when they iced up my sidewalk last winter and I fell."

Tegan scoffed. "You survived."

"With a bruised hip."

"A bruised ego, you mean. Allie, my sweet friend, please don't protest." Tegan folded her hands in prayer. "You don't know how Jason Gardner or anyone in his camp might retaliate."

"In his camp? Does he have a camp?"

"Who knows?"

"Fine." I sighed. "I'll bide my time. But if his plans prove to be bad for the community . . ."

"Vanna and I will demonstrate with you."

"Speak for yourself," Vanna gibed.

By the time Darcy and I returned home to my mountain retreat, which was a mere mile from the center of town, I wasn't in the mood to eat. However, knowing Zach would need a snack, I threw together a cheese and salami platter, added olives, cornichons, and a mound of cashews, and arranged a separate plate of sugar cookies. Then I filled Darcy's food bowl with his favorite tuna dinner and kibble, shifted my to-be-read pile of books from the rustic dining table to the coffee table in the living room—the topmost book being one I couldn't wait to sink my teeth into, Tess Gerritsen's latest Martini Club suspense—and fetched a couple of decks of cards.

Mission accomplished, I took a moment to survey my place. "I love you, house," I murmured.

Darcy leaped onto the top of his barrel-shaped llama, a cat-scratching station near the dining table, and mewed for attention.

"Yes, I love you, too, cat."

The house wasn't mine. It belonged to my parents, but they were world travelers and rarely returned to Bramblewood. I'd been renting from them for the past five years. I loved the cabin flavor and all the comfy décor the previous owner had ceded to them, right down to the photographs of mountain vistas, the collections of gemstones and native artifacts, and the wood-carved sculptures. The eagle was my favorite. I'd added a rocking chair and a number of plaques with sassy literary sayings, like one by actress Emma Thompson: *I think books are like people, in the sense they'll turn up in your life when you most need them.* Skylights allowed in a lot of daylight. The stone-faced gas fireplace was inviting. Darcy particularly liked the bench by the south-facing bay window abutting the kitchen. When not snoozing on the llama, he chose to soak up rays there.

I changed out of my work clothes into a loose-weave summer sweater over leggings, ran a brush through my hair, and was pouring myself a glass of chardonnay when the doorbell rang. Zach usually knocked. I set the bottle and glass on the dining table and went to open the door. I was surprised to see Lillian Bellingham, the owner of Puttin' on the Glitz, with her grandmother Magda. A fashion horse, Lillian rarely ventured anywhere without being outfitted to the nines. Today's ensemble included a romantic fascinator hat adorned with yellow flowers, a yellow chiffon dress, and strappy heels. She was carrying a relatively heavy-looking dress bag. Though Magda was wearing espadrilles, she was so petite the top of her head didn't reach my chin. She was an avid reader of all genres, and she never missed a book club meeting. Like her granddaughter, she liked to dress up, today's outfit being no exception. I could do without the lacy blouse, but the designer jeans were top-notch and studded with rhinestones.

"What a surprise." I invited them in.

"I would've phoned ahead," Lillian said, "but I saw you making the turn onto your street as I was finishing up with a client, and thought it would be best to drop in to show you a few more of the outfits I scored at the theater department for the *Gatsby* party. Am I interrupting anything?"

"My first sip of wine." I motioned to the bottle. "Would you like some?"

"Would I ever." Lillian's voice was a breathy mix of Marilyn Monroe meets Sharon Stone, with a tinge of a Southern accent. For a brief moment, she had lived in Hollywood and had starred in a couple of B movies. Inside of two years, she had tired of beating the pavement and, like me, had come back to the Asheville area to be close to family. Her parents were the ones who'd fronted her the money to open her shop. They, like Magda, were well-to-do, thanks to investments they'd made over the years.

"Magda, wine?" I asked.

"I'll pass, dear," Magda said. "I'm not much of a drinker. At my age, liquor can make me unsteady. Heaven forbid I trip over my sweet Baboo."

"Her schnauzer," Lillian confided.

While she moved to the living room and draped the dress bag over the back of the sofa, I poured her a glass of wine and carried it to her. Magda followed.

Darcy leaped off the llama and whizzed past us with his catnip toy. He swatted it under the sofa, pursued it and, like a talented hockey player, batted it across the room, straight between the legs of the armchair to the right of the fireplace.

"Cat, stop!" I ordered.

Darcy didn't obey. He chased it and began clawing the underside of the chair.

"Stop. C'mon. I know I need to get the webbing fixed. Come out." He obeyed, whacking his toy into the Plexiglas kitchen door. Why was it Plexiglas? Because I'd wanted to earn a positive Cottage Food Operator health rating, so on the rare occasion when I couldn't bake at Dream Cuisine, I could do so at home. To comply with the rating, I'd installed the see-through door to keep the kitchen separate from the rest of the house. Darcy was pretty much hypoallergenic, and I groomed him often enough to remove his undercoat, but I wouldn't allow him into the cooking area. Ever.

Lillian took a sip of her wine and set the glass on the end table beside the sofa. "He sure is a devil."

"I don't have a clue what's gotten into him," I said. "I mean, I know spring fever is a thing. Is there such a thing as summer fever?"

Lillian laughed. "Don't ask me. I never had a pet."

"Yes, you did, sweetness," Magda said. "You had a turtle."

Lillian howled. "A turtle that did nothing but sit on a rock, Nana. Allie"—she unzipped the dress bag and removed a gold-and-black number from it—"the first dress I want to show you is another flapper costume."

"Look at the embroidered sequins," Magda said. "Aren't they incredible?"

Lillian swiveled the dress on its hanger so I could inspect it.

"Gorgeous," I said.

"I think I might wind up slinking into this for the party," Lillian added. "I wanted your approval."

"With your coloring and blond hair, it will look exquisite."

"Lillian, dear . . ." Magda cleared her throat and motioned with her chin at the dining table.

"Oh, my," Lillian said. "You're having guests over to play cards. Why didn't you say so?"

"Just Zach."

"Ooh." She fluttered her eyelashes. "How's it going with you two?"

"Is she talking about Detective Armstrong?" Magda asked. "Hubba-hubba."

I laughed. "We're friends."

"Uh-huh." Lillian winked. "You keep telling yourself that." She eyed her grandmother. "You should see the way he looks at her." She pressed a hand to her chest and swooned. To me, she said, "Did you meet the newcomer? Jason Gardner?"

"I know Jason," Magda chimed.

"You do?"

"I knew his parents, I should say. He was a boy at the time." Magda didn't live far from the Sugarbaker estate. "His parents often asked your mother to babysit him. He was quite a renegade, running hither and yon. I bet he turned into a looker."

"He did," Lillian said. "He came into the shop to purchase a tuxedo."

Given his wealth and such, I couldn't imagine he didn't own a tuxedo, but perhaps when he left California, he'd arranged for a moving company to bring all his worldly goods, and to date nothing had arrived.

"Although, if he's still a renegade, this would be a better choice." Lillian pulled a striped men's suit from the bag. It reminded me of something a gangster might wear. "I have to say he's very natural and warm. Not at all what I'd pictured after hearing the gossips wagging their tongues."

Like any town, Bramblewood did have its share of rumormongers.

"What have you heard?" I asked.

"He's running from the law. He's as broke as a skunk. He's leveraged to the hilt. And"—she paused for effect—"he murdered his parents."

Chapter 4

Angry, and half in love with her, and tremendously sorry, I turned away.

—Nick Carraway in F. Scott Fitzgerald's *The Great Gatsby*

"Yipes," I exclaimed.

"Yipes is right, if any of it's true," Lillian agreed.

Magda clucked her tongue. "Which most likely it is not."

Jason's supposed history made me think of Jay Gatsby and how many lies had been told about him. What was truth, and what was fiction?

Someone knocked loudly on the door. Magda gasped.

"It's me," Zach yelled from the porch.

Lillian said, "Relax, Nana. It's Allie's guest. We should go."

"Come on in," I called.

"'Come on in.' How neighborly." Lillian tittered. "Yes, darlin', you keep telling yourself you're just friends." She reinserted the suit and dress into the bag. "Swing by the shop this week so I can show you the rest."

"Don't rush out on account of me, Lillian," Zach said, emerging from the foyer.

"Me rush, Detective? A lady never rushes." She blew him an air-kiss, slung the dress bag over her arm, and sauntered out of the house, deliberately swinging her hips.

Her grandmother gave Zach a once-over, said, "Have a nice night, Detective," and followed Lillian out.

Zach laughed. "Lillian is such a character."

"Yes, she is."

"And her mother is a hoot. According to her, she knows everything about everyone in town."

"I'll bet she does." I moved toward the kitchen. "Would you like a glass of wine or a beer?"

"Beer, thanks. Got any Holy Grail?"

Monty Python's Holy Grail was a hoppy and nutty English pale ale, and as it humorously stated on the bottle, it tasted as if it had been "tempered over burning witches." A month ago Zach had discovered it and loved it, so I always had it on hand.

I fetched a bottle and an opener and handed them to him. He popped the top and took a sip. Darcy abandoned his playtime beneath the chair and scuttled to Zach. He scooped up the cat in one hand and kissed his nose. Like me, Zach was an animal person. Unlike me, he'd had a menagerie while growing up: cats, dogs, and rabbits. His mother was a soft touch.

"Mom says hello," he said.

His mother owned Jukebox Joint, or the Joint, as locals had dubbed it. It was a hip and happening diner and one of my newest clients. Sadly, Zach's father, whom I had never met, had passed away from a heart attack when Zach was in high school.

"I see cards on the table," he said, settling onto a chair, which he dwarfed due to his six-foot-four frame. He mounded a pile of pennies on the table, after which he began to shuffle a well-used deck. "Got your losings ready?" He swooped a lock of dark hair off his face, a move that made the muscles beneath his short-sleeved polo bulge. "You're going down."

"No, you are." I fetched the mason jar of pennies I'd labeled *my winnings* from the fireplace mantel, plunked it on the table, retreated to the kitchen for the snack plates I'd arranged, and returned. "Cheese and salami, a few accoutrements, and cookies."

He took a sugar cookie, which I knew he'd go for first. He loved sugar cookies . . . or any cookie, for that matter. "Things good?" he asked.

"Good enough. Busy." I sat at the table and had a sip of wine. I didn't eat anything. Lillian's gossip about Jason Gardner had thrown me for a loop. Were any of the rumors true? Was he running from the law? "Have you heard about the guy who came to town to build a mall? His name is Jason Gardner."

"Nope."

I filled him in on what I'd learned at the bookshop as well as from Reika. "So, there she and I were, sipping coffee, when Finette Fineworthy came into Ragamuffin with Iggie Luckenbill. And get this, they were arguing about Jason's intentions."

"Neither keeping their voices down, I imagine."

I chuckled. "Right. Iggie said he'd wanted to bid on the mall project. He demanded to know why he hadn't gotten the gig. Finette, in no uncertain terms, called him a hack."

"Whoa!"

"I know. She added that Jason promised to tailor the project in keeping with the town's designs, implying Iggie wouldn't."

Zach sipped his beer.

"Jason is originally from Bramblewood," I went on. "It turns out Magda Bellingham knew his parents. But he relocated to California when he was young."

"I can always count on you to get the skinny."

Zach dealt cards, two each facedown and one up. I had the lowest upcard, a three—he drew a six—so I paid the bring-in of one penny. He matched it and dealt another upcard to each of us. A four to me. A five to himself.

"Go on," he said.

I peeked at my down cards. An ace and a jack. Not a pair. Even so, I added another penny to the pot. I wasn't rash. I was confident.

"Big spender," Zach teased.

"Iggie got quite steamed and asked Finette if Jason was bribing her."

Zach whistled. "That must've gone over well."

"Like a sledgehammer. She put him in his place and stormed out."

"She's a tough nut. Her father was equally robust."

I hadn't known the man, although his reputation as a fireman was epic. He'd saved many people, homes, and kittens from near disaster. He passed away ten years ago, and her mother, a year after that from a broken heart, if the stories were correct. The remaining relatives Finette had were her sister, who lived in Arizona, and their great-aunt, who was childless. According to Finette, her great-aunt had declined in recent years.

"By the way," I said, "I've seen Finette eyeing you at council meetings."

"Nah."

"Oh, yeah. She likes you."

"Get out of here. I'm young enough to be her little brother." I chuckled.

He dealt another upcard. A four for me, meaning I had a pair showing, and a seven to himself. With his down cards, he might have the beginning of a straight, but my hand was better for now. I bet another penny.

"I see on Instagram you and she still join in the Hikers Rule meetup group."

"We hike. End of story."

I waggled my eyebrows. "She's quite attractive."

"Cut it out. Not interested." Soon after his wife died, he joined the army, after which he moved home to Bramblewood, went to college, and subsequently joined the police force. I was the first woman he'd dated since his return. "Tell me more about this Jason guy."

He dealt a fourth upcard. A ten for me and an eight for himself. My pair was still the best hand. I added another penny.

"He says the mall will be a mecca, a place where everyone can gather and be a community."

"Did you like him?"

"Sure. He's nice enough. But I hate to see historic property destroyed." I sipped my wine. "I was hoping those houses would be part of the preservation society's tour for years to come."

"Yes, me, too." Zach offered a supportive smile and a casual shrug. "We can't fight progress sometimes."

"Is a mall progress?"

"Some in town will be thrilled they don't have to go all the way to Asheville to shop. Mall stores will offer lower prices."

"Making mom-and-pop shops struggle. Ugh." I heaved a sigh. "I wanted to create protest signs, but Tegan and Vanna talked me out of it."

"I'm glad they did," he said. "Demonstrations don't get results and often garner resentment." He dealt the last upcards. A four to me and an eight to him.

Three of a kind was a good hand. I added five pennies to the pot.

He matched the bet and raised me two more pennies. I saw the bet and flipped over my ace and jack. Slowly, painstakingly, he turned over one card, a ten, and then the next, a nine. He had a straight, five to ten.

"Rats!" I muttered.

He gathered his winnings, took another cookie, and shuffled the deck. After we played ten more games, he yawned, which of course made me yawn.

"It's late," he said, rising. "I'll get going." Darcy sped to him for a goodnight caress. Zach obliged and walked to the door. He rested his hand on the doorknob. "You know, Allie..." He looked like he wanted to say more, but he didn't.

"I do know. A lot."

"Yeah, you're a know-it-all." His grin was easy, warm. "Sleep well."

After he left, I leaned my back against the door. What had

he wanted to say? Had he wanted to talk about our friendship? The kiss? How I wished I was good at reading men, but I wasn't. It wasn't a fatal flaw, but it sure didn't make life easy.

While cleaning up the dining table, I stumbled over Darcy's catnip toy. Frustrated, I kicked it across the room. Darcy startled and leaped into the barrel of the llama cat-scratching station to hide. I peered in at him. "Don't worry, my sweet pal. I will never hurt you. Your toy? There's a chance. You? Never." I reached in and stroked him beneath his chin. The action soothed me and helped him chill.

The next morning after loading up Vanna's vehicle at Dream Cuisine with the goodies she would deliver—she owned a Nissan NV Cargo van, so I didn't need to lend her my Ford Transit—I headed to Feast for the Eyes. Tegan was already at the shop, behind the sales counter, unpacking a sizable delivery of copies of *The Great Gatsby*. She'd ordered the deluxe hardbound edition, which featured an Art Deco drawing of an elegant couple standing in front of a snazzy car and a huge mansion. The house reminded me of the Sugarbaker estate, and I thought about Jason Gardner. He hadn't called me yet about catering his soiree. Had he merely been polite in asking for my card? Had he reached out to Vanna instead? No. She couldn't have held such juicy news from me. It was against her nature. She'd have wanted to boast.

"Let's tag this stack. Here's the list of preorders." Tegan provided a printed copy.

"First, coffee." I'd awakened a few minutes late and barely had enough time to feed Darcy, let alone eat a bite or make a pot of coffee. Fortunately, I'd convinced Tegan to buy a Keurig machine, so we would never need to rely on Chloe making the coffee. Chloe was a terrific salesperson, but she couldn't boil water. "I brought some homemade protein bars."

"I was hoping for an apple-cinnamon bun."

"Those are midmorning-type treats. Always start the day with protein."

"Yes, Mom," she said snottily.

While we were tagging everything, Chloe arrived. At times, she moved as fast as the Energizer bunny. She swooped past us, deposited her sweater and purse in the stockroom, and whisked back out. "Can I help?"

Tegan nodded and asked her to stack the books, alphabetically by recipient, on the counter.

Around nine, Vanna ventured into the shop. When she'd come to pick up the baked goods for delivery, she'd worn jeans, flats, and a sweater. Now she was dressed for success in an aqua-blue sheath, a chunky necklace, and heels. I wondered if she'd thrown on the getup hoping she'd run into Jason. She looked like a million bucks.

"Can we discuss the menu for the party again? I have some thoughts." She took a seat on one of the ladder-back chairs by the sales counter and pulled her iPad from her tote bag. She opened the Notes app and consulted it. "I did some research about what food was served during the Roaring Twenties. You're right about the deviled eggs and the pineapple upside-down cake, but I'm spot-on about the Waldorf salad. Meatballs were all the rage, too."

"You would serve meatballs, Sis? I mean . . ." Tegan exaggerated a gasp. "How plebeian."

Vanna stuck her tongue out at her. "Not just any meatball. They'll be gourmet, made with basil and garlic. Divine." She kissed her fingertips like a chef. "Also, chicken à la king was popular. We could serve it as the filling in vol-au-vents."

Under her breath, Tegan muttered, "Heaven forbid we serve it on regular bread."

"I have the best recipe for puff pastry," Vanna said. "It's buttery and melt-in-your-mouth delish. Cross my heart. As for entertainment, we will have a band, won't we?"

"In the shop?" Tegan asked.
"Big bands were all the rage."
"Um, no room. I was thinking of piping music through the speakers."
"Couldn't we ask the town to allow us to move the party into the street? Wouldn't that be fun?" Vanna clapped her hands. I'd never seen her so enthusiastic. "It doesn't have to be a big band. An octet would do."
"Too expensive," Tegan countered.
"I know a group that will play for free," Vanna said in singsong fashion. "The pianist has quite a thing for me. Have you heard 'Jazz Baby'? It's a great song. So much fun. Perfect to Charleston to." She placed her iPad on the sales counter, hopped off the chair and, to my surprise, did a quick step with flair. "Oh, how I love to dance."
Tegan regarded me, pleading with her eyes.
"I'll see what we can do." I wouldn't, but the fib seemed to please Vanna.
"Yay! Perfect! Must run." She retrieved her tote bag, adjusted the strap of her tote, and hurried toward the exit. "Ciao."
As she left, Reika stepped inside, wheeling a large suitcase and carrying a torchiere lamp with a bronze base and body. Her bulldog, Amira, trailed her on a leash Reika had looped around her wrist to free up her hands. "Hello, ladies. You must use this for *Gatsby* décor."
She asked Amira to be a good girl and sit by the sales counter. She released the dog's leash, and the dog trotted to a safe spot. Reika set the lamp by the table in the far right corner of the shop, an empty area Tegan was still contemplating how to utilize. Coffee bar perhaps?
"Are you okay?" I asked.
She looked tired. Her skin was sallow. "Wipe that look off your face, Allie Catt. I had a bout of indigestion last night. I'm fine." She gestured to the lamp. "This is perfect for the period,

don't you think? You won't believe where I found it. In the museum's attic. It was covered in dust, but I could tell it would be perfect."

It was still dusty and would need a thorough cleaning.

"Honestly, how my predecessor could allow such a beautiful item to be doomed to the shadows is beyond me." Amira barked in agreement. "Shh, Princess," Reika said and laid the suitcase flat on the floor. "Look at these goodies, ladies." She unzipped the case and opened the lid. From within, she withdrew dozens of plumed feathers, copious strands of pearls, gorgeous pillar candles, and more.

"Where on earth did you find all those items?" Tegan asked.

"I asked the employees and friends to pitch in. You know, back in the late seventeen hundreds, when Asheville was an outpost, Bramblewood was a flicker in the minds of our forebears. Around 1820 is when the vision for the town came together. By the 1920s, we were quite hip and raring to dance the night away."

I tamped down a laugh as I mentally pictured Vanna doing the Charleston "bee's knees" step, bent at the waist, hands on her thighs.

"Many of us have ancestors who enjoyed the dances of the day and donning the latest fashions," Reika said. "My grandmother was one of the first women to show her ankles."

Chloe whistled.

"Keep these and ponder which you'd like. I'll be back with more." Reika left the suitcase, gathered the dog, and departed as quickly as she'd entered.

I told Tegan and Chloe we'd review the items later; then I packed up the suitcase, took it to the stockroom, and returned.

The door to the shop opened, and two women, regulars to the shop, stepped inside.

"Morning!" Tegan cried.

The women responded with a breezy hello.

"I received a new batch of Percy Jackson novels your boys will love," Tegan added.

"Thanks," the taller of the two said as they headed for the YA aisle. Their kids were avid readers.

Right behind them appeared Evelyn Evers, the head of the Community Theater Foundation. She was a dynamo in the African American world and had been one of Tegan's aunt's best friends. Her coiled updo made her look eons taller than she already was. "Tegan, I have all sorts of items to lend you for the *Gatsby* event. I simply can't wait! My people have been amassing them for days. I brought a list." She waved it.

I said, "With Reika and Evelyn's help, our cup runneth over."

Tegan beamed. "No kidding."

"Chloe, honey," Evelyn said, "before I continue with Tegan, tell me, do you sing?"

"Sing?" Chloe froze, looking like a kid who was going to be punished. "Why?"

"I'm curious."

"Um, yes. I sing. In the shower. And I used to sing in the choir at church."

"I knew it. Your speaking voice is so lovely," Evelyn said. "I want you to audition for our new production."

"Audition? To act? In a p-play?" Chloe sputtered.

"To act and sing."

"I've never acted."

"There's always a first time," Evelyn said. "I think you're perfect for a role in *Miss Saigon*."

"I love that show," Chloe effused. "I never saw the play. I was a girl when it closed on Broadway, but I've seen the twenty-fifth anniversary film production ten times."

"Excellent. Then you're familiar with the story."

"Yes, ma'am, but . . ." Chloe looked between Tegan and me.

Was she hoping we'd say we couldn't spare her, so she could opt out? When we didn't, she addressed Evelyn. "I'm too shy."

"Shy, *schmy*." Evelyn batted the air. "I've seen you in action here. You are not a wallflower. You love being attentive to others. That's what acting is. Focusing on your fellow thespians. Let the lines provide your dialogue and allow the music to carry you away." Evelyn petted Chloe's cheek. "You'll shine. I can see it now. Auditions are tonight. Seven p.m."

Chloe pulled Tegan and me aside. Her cheeks were rosy red. Her eyes were glistening. "I'd like to try, but I won't unless one of you accompanies me. I'll be too nervous."

Tegan squeezed her arm. "Sure, I'll go. It'll be a lark. You'll have fun. I never acted. I used to be frightened of public speaking. I mean petrified, but my dread has eased up a tad."

She had emceed her aunt's memorial and had done a bang-up job.

"Allie acted years ago. She's talented," Tegan added.

Evelyn eyed me, and I waved a dismissive hand, meaning the stage was no longer calling to me.

Tegan said, "Give her some tips, Allie."

"The most important thing"—I rotated a hand in front of my chest and up to my mouth—"is to breathe. Always breathe."

The door to the shop flew open, and Finette raced inside. "Help! I can't breathe!"

Chapter 5

"And I like large parties. They're so intimate. At small parties there isn't any privacy."

—Jordan Baker in F. Scott Fitzgerald's *The Great Gatsby*

I dashed to her. "Do you need CPR? The Heimlich?"

"Relax." Finette guffawed. "I was being melodramatic. I can breathe. Has it ever been a day!" She fanned her face with a pink envelope, her bangles clacking. "'Always make an entrance,' my father used to say. 'People will remember you that way.'"

I glanced at Tegan, who was pulling a face.

Finette swept her long locks over her shoulders. I noticed she'd added attractive highlights, and I wondered when I might need to do the same. At my age, I didn't have a speck of gray, but my mother said she turned prematurely gray at thirty. Something to look forward to?

"Allie . . ." Finette frowned. Without asking, she flicked my hair. "You had a lock out of place."

Peeved by her audacity, I said, "What's new?" My curly hair had a mind of its own.

"Ahem. What do you think mirrors are for? One must always present one's best face. You don't want to look a mess."

I knew I didn't look unsightly, but I let her dig slide.

"Anyway, back to me," Finette continued. "It really has been a whirlwind today, which explains why I'm finding it hard to breathe. A meeting here, a phone call there, talking to loan officers, chatting up citizens. Have you ever been faced with too many challenges all at once?" She didn't wait for a response. Instead, she made a beeline for the sales counter.

I followed. So did Tegan.

"I'd like a copy of *The Great Gatsby*," Finette stated.

"These are all spoken for." Tegan waved a hand to the stacks of books. "But I've placed a new order, which should come tomorrow."

"Hold a copy for me. May I take a peek at one of these?"

"Feel free."

"I'm so excited to take part in the festivities." Finette lifted a book and flipped through the pages. "I've read this book many times, as a teen and again in college. I always wanted to own a copy but never got around to it. I love the hardcover version." She made a swooning sound. "Do I need to sign an agreement for the preorder?"

Tegan smiled. "I trust you."

"Perfect." She regarded me again. "Allie, I'm so glad you're here. I've been meaning to ask . . . " She paused.

"Yes?"

"Would you share the recipe for the mini quiche you served at the neighborhood watch gathering? They were so yummy."

I squinted. Was that really her question? "Sure," I replied. I wasn't proprietary about recipes anyone could find online. Lots of sites provided instructions on how to make broccoli and cheddar quiche. Mine included finely chopped broccoli, cream of chicken soup, and tons of cheese. "I'll email it to you."

"Thanks. Also . . . " She fluttered her eyelashes. "I've been meaning to ask why Zach Armstrong didn't come to the party. Don't Bramblewood police try to attend all the neighborhood watch parties? Are you two no longer an item?"

Aha. The truth will out. She was interested in him, despite the difference in their ages.

"We're not dating, if you're curious. We're friends." I was still concerned about the way he'd left last night without saying what was weighing on his mind, but I pushed the niggling feeling aside. "Yes, Zach does come to some of the gatherings. So does his partner. But not all. If they're too busy solving crime—"

"Does Bramblewood really have that much?"

For heaven's sake. She ran the town council. How could she not know the statistics? "We have more than we'd like, for sure."

The door opened, and two more women—regulars in their fifties—entered the shop. They hustled to the reading nook, unloaded their carryalls, and headed to the sci-fi and paranormal aisle.

Vanna rushed into the store behind them. "I almost forgot my iPad. Can you believe it?" She hurried to the sales counter. "I can't live without it."

Before the door swung shut, Jason Gardner stepped in. I debated whether we needed to invest in a revolving door.

"Hello, ladies." He was clad in an outfit right out of *The Great Gatsby*—a three-piece cream-colored suit with a double-breasted vest, a pocket scarf, a black tie, and a handsome onyx jacket chain lapel pin. "What do you think?" He dragged an open palm down his togs.

"Wow, Jason!" Tegan exclaimed. "You look great! The costume is perfect."

"Very dapper, Jason," I chimed.

Vanna swiveled. An ooh escaped her mouth.

He chuckled. "Precisely the reaction I was hoping for. Lillian said it was a traffic stopper."

"She's right." Finette crossed the store, studying him with admiration.

"Hello, ducky, old sport," he said to her in a British accent. She laughed and swatted his arm. "Stop!" Over her shoulder, she said, "It's an inside joke. When he and I first met, he mistakenly thought my last name was Duckworthy."

"I knew a guy in college with the surname," Jason explained.

"Did I ever set him straight," Finette said. "I'm a Fineworthy of *the* Fineworthys."

"*The* Fineworthys," Jason repeated. "The ones who are known for donating time to feeding the homeless, building Habitat houses, and cleaning up hiking trails." He ticked their attributes off on his fingertips. "What else did the altruistic Fineworthys do?"

"I heard her father saved a schoolhouse from burning down," I said.

"He rescued one of my favorite restaurants," Tegan added, "from a near-fatal oil fire."

"He also salvaged a church and the YMCA, if I'm not mistaken," Jason said. Having recently arrived in Bramblewood, he sure knew a lot about Finette and her family. Was that her doing, or had he done oppo research so he could sweet-talk his way into a contract with the town?

"What you don't know is my mother's pet project was acting as a book fairy," Finette said. "She'd buy books from the library, and she and I would hide them in places for people to discover."

"Aw," Tegan said. "What a nice memory."

"I still do it, but I miss doing it with her."

Jason gently chucked her chin and said, "Buck up, old sport." He sidled past Finette and over to me. "Allie, yesterday I'd only sensed your dissatisfaction with my plan to build a mall, but now I've heard for a fact you are not happy with me and my proposal."

Tegan shook her head, meaning she hadn't spilled the beans. Zach certainly wouldn't have mentioned a thing. Vanna's face was stony. Had she contacted him to ask for the catering gig and told him my plans in an effort to turn him against me? She wouldn't dare. Not when we were getting along so well. We'd chatted about it at Dream Cuisine, so a bookshop customer hadn't overheard. Possibly Chloe had mentioned it in a public place.

"Why aren't you happy with the mall, Allie?" Finette asked. "It is going to be wonderful. Jason and I have been working closely for weeks to make this a superior project."

"You've been in town for weeks?" Tegan asked. "And yet yesterday was the first day you came to the bookshop?"

"He's been so busy." Finette pulled her cell phone from her tote and swiped the screen. "Applying for building permits. Getting the designs approved by the town council. He hasn't had a spare moment. It's all calendared." She flashed her cell phone at us. It displayed a lengthy to-do list. "This mall is going to be a feather in all our caps. And don't you worry, Allie. Jason promises to make it a boon for Bramblewood. Don't you?"

Jason nodded. "I do."

"You know how much I love our town, Allie," Finette went on. "After all, that's why I ran for town council. To have my finger on the pulse. To steer the ship."

"The way I hear it, ducky," Jason said, "you joined the council so you wouldn't have to be a lowly project manager again, forced to wrangle with all the contractors."

"Oh, stop teasing." She thwacked his arm a second time.

Jason turned to me, his smile genuine. "By the expression on your face, Allie, I'm still getting the feeling you're wary."

"I'm—"

"Jason, let it go. She'll get on board. I'll make sure of it." Finette gave his arm a tug. "Let's grab a coffee and catch up."

"In a sec." His gaze at me intensified, which sent shivers down my spine.

To my surprise, they were the good kind of shivers. Out of eyesight, I pinched my arm, urging myself to snap out of it. Jason wasn't the enemy, but he certainly wasn't dating material, either.

"Allie, how about you and I have dinner?" he went on. "It's not a date. Purely for business."

I felt my cheeks warm. Had he read my mind?

"My domestic helper is off for the night," he said. "I need to eat. We'll discuss the details of my soiree, and I'll show you the architectural plans for the mall. Say, seven? The Brewery. I've heard it's great."

"It is." I loved the Brewery. Tegan and I often went there to hang out. The selections of beer were great, and the food was homey and substantial.

"I've also heard it's casual."

"Ultracasual."

"My kind of place."

I doubted that, considering his choice of attire.

"I'll meet you there," he said.

"Coffee now," Finette reminded him.

"Sure, sure, but first, I've got to go back to Puttin' on the Glitz to return these fancy duds."

They left the shop chatting, and Vanna descended on me.

"How dare you, Allie! What were you thinking?" Her voice could cut ice. "I should come to dinner with you."

"Sis—"

"Don't 'Sis' me, Tegan." Vanna swatted the air. "Allie and I are a team. Partners."

"Sometimes partners."

"Vanna." I maintained my composure, even though, seeing the way her hands were flailing, she looked like she might claw me. "At the outset, we said we'd work together with the baking end of my business, but if we drummed up individual gigs, we were free to take them."

"I'm regretting ever saying yes to you."

"Hello." It was my turn to slash the air. "You jumped at the chance." I wasn't usually so forceful, but I would not let her bully me.

"Because . . . because . . ."

"Because you wanted to grow your business, and you thought working with me would expand your reach."

She chuffed like a horse.

"Right?" I asked.

"Fine. You always need to have the last word. Be selfish." She stomped out of the shop, iPad under her arm, and slammed the door.

The glass and the wood rattled, mirroring how I felt.

An hour later, after the last customers had gone and only Tegan, Chloe, and I were in the shop, Vanna swanned in with a huge tray of baked goods. Her mother, Noeline Merriweather, trailed her. Noeline, who was just shy of sixty-one, turned heads. Attired in a frilly floral frock, her bobbed hair gently curled, she reminded me of Blanche DuBois in *A Streetcar Named Desire*.

"I'm sorry, Allie, about earlier," Vanna said. "I was in the wrong."

In all the years I'd known her, I couldn't remember her ever saying the word *sorry*. Certainly not to me.

"Go on," Noeline said. "Tell her you were being a diva."

"I was being a diva."

I didn't disagree. Chloe tamped down a snort. Tegan elbowed her.

"I'm working on this aspect of my personality with my therapist," Vanna added.

I mentally palm slapped my forehead. She was in therapy? I exchanged a look with Tegan, who looked as shocked as I was.

"Auntie encouraged me to go, but I never did. When she

died . . ." Vanna's gaze skated toward the ceiling, as if she was trying to stem tears. She lowered her chin. "I'm going to honor her."

Noeline smiled. "And to help yourself."

"Yes." Vanna placed the tray of goodies on the sales counter. I caught sight of the macarons and her specialty, petits fours, and my mouth began to salivate. I snagged a pink macaron and bit into it. "Delicious. You're forgiven."

The compliment made her smile.

"What can I do for the event, girls?" Noeline asked. Twice a widow, after her second husband—Tegan's father, the true love of her life—passed away from a rare blood disease, she'd pieced herself together and invested wisely. The B&B was a huge success and was constantly filled with happy travelers.

"You've done enough, Mom," Tegan said. "You emailed all the invitations."

In this day and age of online *everything*, we didn't send formal invitations. The cost was prohibitive. E-vites worked perfectly well.

"But I want to do more," Noeline said. "I want the event to be thrilling. After all, *The Great Gatsby* is one of my favorites. I can quote so many lines." She intoned, "'I was within and without, simultaneously enchanted and repelled by the inexhaustible variety of life.' Dear sweet Gatsby." She sighed. "He was so incredibly forlorn, don't you think?"

"Mom, Nick, the narrator in the book, says that line."

"I know, darling. It's neither here nor there. We're not competing in a comparative literature contest." She raised a finger in the air. "I was merely commenting on the character of Gatsby. I think he is to be pitied."

All of us agreed.

"How about if I take on the chore of having quotes printed like you did for the memorial?" Noeline asked. To honor Marigold, we'd chosen selections from *Pride and Prejudice*. "It was such a lovely touch."

"Yes, please do," I said.

Chloe cleared her throat. "But—"

I shot her a look. Granted, she was in charge of printing and posting the quotes, but Noeline looked earnest and in need of a project. I was sure I could find more for Chloe to do. The décor alone was going to require a lot of hands. We hadn't adorned the shop for Marigold's memorial.

"Oh, by the way, daughters," Noeline said, "since you're both here, I'd like to tell you the news. I'm considering purchasing another bed-and-breakfast."

"And selling the Blue Lantern?" Vanna cried.

"No. I'd own two."

"Mom, that's too much," Tegan protested.

"No it's not. I've easily got the ability to leverage the one and snag the other, and if I need to pay all cash to get it, I can. I'm flush. It's also in Montford and so adorable. A pink Victorian with white vergeboard trim. The garden needs work."

"But, Mother, you're—" Tegan pressed her lips together.

"I'm what?" Noeline jutted a hip. "Too old? Too feeble? Past my prime?"

"Don't put words in my mouth."

"You're in your sixties," Vanna said without thinking. "Near retirement age."

"Tosh! I'm not going to retire until death do I part."

Good for you, I thought. Her sister Marigold would be thrilled with her energy and enthusiasm.

Noeline clapped her hands once. "I'm excited for the challenge. I've hired a great contractor to do the renovations."

"Patrick Hardwick," I said.

"Yes. How did you—"

"I ran into him at Ragamuffin yesterday, and he mentioned he's going to start by renovating your office."

"He has all sorts of clever ideas for the rest of the place."

"I'll bet he does," Tegan said. "To drive up his paycheck."

"Nonsense. He's quite attentive to cost. Everything is written in a proposal, with no possibility of going more than ten percent over the estimate."

"I like him," Chloe said. "He reads across genres, is very eager to please, and is so handsome."

"Speaking of handsome men," Noeline said, "have all of you met Jason Gardner? He's new to town. I ran into him earlier at Blessed Bean. He's going to—"

"Build a mall," Tegan cut in. "Yes, we met him. He's going to join the *Gatsby* event."

"Isn't he extraordinary looking?" Noeline said. "His square jaw and blond hair. He reminds me of Ryan Gosling."

"I'll wager he hears that a lot," I said. "Those eyes. The wicked smile."

"Yes." Noeline tittered. "You know, Tegan, with Winston out of the picture, you should—"

"Mom, thanks, but no thanks. I'm not interested in Mr. Gardner. Besides, Vanna has set her sights on him."

"I have not," Vanna said, but her pink cheeks belied the statement.

"Allie is going to a business dinner with him tonight," Tegan said.

Vanna lasered Tegan and then me with a lethal look.

"Whichever of you wants him, go after him," Noeline said. "I'm all for it. He's polite and charming and well read. We were talking books while standing in line. He's quite a Dashiell Hammett fan, with a penchant for *The Thin Man*." She snapped her fingers. "But if he's not to your liking, Tegan, then Chloe's got a point. Consider dating Patrick. He's a catch."

"Patrick?" Vanna exclaimed and wagged her head. "No, no, an emphatic no."

I laughed and explained to Noeline how Vanna thought Patrick was nuts because he was a raw-food omnivore. "FYI, he eats muffins, Vanna, so he might be a quasi–raw-food omnivore."

"You like muffins, Tegan," Noeline said.

"Isn't he a little old for me?" Tegan asked.

"Oh, darling, men mature slower than women. Give it a think. I'm off." She pivoted and wiggled her hand overhead as she swept out of the shop.

"My mother wants to buy a new B&B?" Tegan murmured to me. "Why, for heaven's sake?"

"To keep busy," I replied.

"But the Blue Lantern keeps her plenty occupied."

"Are you sure? Her accountant manages all the finances, and Helga seems to have the food and housekeeping well in hand." Helga was a devoted employee with a quick wit and a heart of gold. She had started working at the B&B at eighteen and had stayed on after Noeline purchased it.

"Mom has her hands full. She sets the menus. She does the meet and greets." Tegan ticked the list off on her fingertips. "She tends to the nightly cocktail soirees. She loves chatting up the guests."

"Relax." I petted my friend on the arm. "Don't work yourself into a tizzy. Let's see how it pans out."

Vanna agreed and departed to run an errand. Chloe excused herself and went to the stockroom so she could spruce up her makeup before her audition. Tegan and I resumed organizing the sales desk.

Minutes later, the door opened, and Patrick strode inside. "Hello!"

Tegan muttered, "What is he doing here? Did my mother . . . ? *Ooh.*" She blew frustration out of the side of her mouth.

"Chill," I ordered. "I'll bet he's here by chance. After all, he does love to read." I smiled at Patrick. "Welcome! Were your ears burning?"

"Should they have been?"

"Your name came up in conversation. Noeline is very happy you're doing the work at the B&B."

"Glad to hear it," he said. "It's such a cool place. I've already recommended it to a few people who have family coming in for the holidays." He addressed Tegan. "You look nice today."

"You don't," she replied.

"Ha!" He didn't falter. In fact, his eyes were twinkling with humor. He offered a lopsided grin. "Do I need to wear my Sunday best to come into the shop on a Monday?" He eyed his clothes, which were covered with sawdust. His boots were yet again caked with dried dirt. "Want me to stand outside?" He ran his fingers through his tousled hair, which, if I was honest, gave him a bad boy look . . . in a good way.

"No. You can stay."

"Care for a piece of gum?" He pulled a pack from his shirt pocket and offered her a square. "Spearmint. No sugar. Your favorite brand."

He was right. How did he know? Kudos for paying attention.

"No thanks. Why are you here?" Tegan asked rather ungraciously.

"I ran into a few people who'd picked up their copies of *The Great Gatsby*. I'm here to buy one. I didn't know you had them in, or I would've bought it yesterday, when I stopped in for *Dune*."

She studied him. "Do you really want to read it?"

"Absolutely. I missed out in high school because I got mono in my senior year. I was home in bed for a full month."

"Mono," she scoffed. "The kissing disease."

"Yeah, usually, but no, that's not how I contracted it. I drank from my buddy's soda using his straw. He came down with it thanks to his girlfriend. Not a very sexy story, is it?" He made an amusing face with googly eyes but quickly reverted to his rugged, handsome self. "Also, I came to tell you I've already read half of *Dune*."

"Since yesterday?"

"Yeah. I'm not much of a sleeper. All I need is four hours. But back to *Dune*. It is such a cool story, about Paul and his family and the mélange spice which enhances mental abilities. There are days I wish I had some. Except it's a drug. And I don't do drugs." He hooked his thumb over his shoulder. "Hey, may I use the restroom?"

"Of course," Tegan said. "It's for our customers."

He strode through the reading nook to the bathroom on the left.

At the same time, Jason strolled into the shop, looking elegant in a light gray suit, gray-striped shirt, and smoke-gray tie. Whoever was his stylist knew what worked. On the other hand, he'd probably look good in a potato sack.

"Why are you back?" I asked as he approached the sales counter. "Are you changing our dinner plans?"

"Nope. I needed to return the costume I'm renting from Puttin' on the Glitz—I've decided on another—and decided I'd pick up my copy of *The Great Gatsby*." He inserted one hand into his trouser pocket. "I'd also like the latest Grisham novel, and I'll let you suggest another."

I fished through the stack of *Gatsby* books labeled *e* to *h* and withdrew one tagged with his name. "Here you go."

"Thanks."

"If you like Grisham, you might also like Michael Connelly's *The Lincoln Lawyer*."

"Read it. Enjoyed it."

"How about David Baldacci's *Absolute Power*?"

"What's it about?"

"A vicious murder involving the US president and a cover-up."

"Say no more. Deal."

"It was written a number of years ago," I added.

"Sounds current to me."

The door to the restroom slammed, drawing our attention.

Patrick approached and, seeing Jason, drew to a halt. "You," he said, venom in his tone.

Jason's expression soured.

"Gardner, you shouldn't be building in Bramblewood," Patrick said.

"Why not, Hardwick?"

Whoa. Jason knew Patrick's last name?

"New construction causes water and air pollution," Patrick stated.

"New construction brings trade to a waning town," Jason countered.

"Bramblewood isn't waning. It's thriving."

"It is thriving," I concurred, hoping to tamp down the heat between the two men.

"It is," Tegan chirped.

Jason said, "The town council's latest findings don't show that. Bramblewood needs a shot in the arm. I intend to provide it."

"Your people will leave trash everywhere," Patrick said.

"Not on my watch."

"You'll be clearing vegetation and excavating." Patrick fisted and unfisted his hands. "Such actions can destroy wildlife and habitats."

"We're building where houses already exist. No wildlife harmed."

"I know all about you, man," Patrick said between tight teeth. "I've done my due diligence. I know about the mess you left in California."

Was he referring to the unfinished project in Santa Monica?

"Back off, Hardwick, because two can play this game. I've done some digging, as well. For instance, I know you wanted to get your hands on the properties but you couldn't scrape together a bid. Why wouldn't the banks lend you the cash? Are you deep in debt?"

Double whoa. Jason had done opposition research on Patrick?

"My finances are fine."

Jason continued, "FYI, I make it a habit to learn about the builders and contractors in a town where I intend to invest time and money, Hardwick, and you, my friend, better hope people don't get a load of your past. Memories of one's mistakes rarely fade." He turned to leave.

Patrick skirted around him and poked him in the chest. "Don't you dare threaten me."

Quick as a flash, Jason seized Patrick's arm and yanked while kicking out with his left leg, knocking Patrick to the floor, chin first. Patrick scrambled to gain purchase but faltered and landed on his knees.

"Hardwick," Jason said, his gaze steely. "Stay down and listen up. I don't mean anyone harm in this town. I intend to build the best mall I can with as little impact on the environment as possible. This is a passion project of mine."

"Why do you care?" Patrick snarled. "Do you think if you build it, she will come?"

Was he talking about Delilah Brenneman? Why on earth would Jason think a mall would lure her here? Why not build a home with magnificent grounds, like the Sugarbaker estate? Or a beautiful villa with a view of the Blue Ridge Mountains?

"She's not coming," Patrick continued. "She's never coming back to you. De—"

"Don't!" Jason aimed a finger at Patrick. "Do not utter her name."

Patrick's eyes blazed with anger.

Jason caught sight of Tegan and me and registered our shocked faces. Civilly, he said, "I'm sorry you had to witness the fracas, ladies. I promise it won't happen again." He neatened his tie and jacket and strode out the door.

Tegan knelt beside Patrick. "What were you thinking?"

He rubbed his chin. "Sorry. I'm not typically a bruiser. I don't get into fights. I'm not sure what came over me. But there's something about the guy—"

"What was he referring to in your past?"

"It's nothing."

But he refused to make eye contact, meaning it was clearly something.

Chapter 6

"Can't repeat the past? . . . Why of course you can!"
—Jay Gatsby in F. Scott Fitzgerald's *The Great Gatsby*

Though the Brewery was a casual place, I decided to dress to impress. After all, my dinner with Jason was business. In keeping with my understated style, I chose a pair of black linen pants, sling-back flats, and a simple white silk blouse. Plus I spruced up my makeup with a dab of lip gloss and a dash of mascara. Nothing too dramatic.

When I was ready to leave the house, I checked myself in the mirror, centered my gold Celtic knot necklace at the hollow of my neck—I'd opted not to don stud earrings—and then I added kibble to Darcy's bowl, kissed him on the nose, and said I'd be back soon. Walking out the door, I reminded him to be a good boy, and he mewed. I didn't speak *cat*, but I figured he was agreeing.

After a long day, the walk to the Brewery was heavenly. There wasn't a hint of a summer breeze. The air was delicious. The vista of the Blue Ridge Mountains to my left brought a smile to my face as I remembered my last hike there with Zach. How we'd enjoyed the spicy aroma of the pines.

I approached the restaurant, gripped the door handle, and braced myself for noise before venturing inside. Like many restaurants in Bramblewood, the place was rustic and not very big, meaning it could get crowded and noisy. High ceilings plus stone floors amplified the sound. The TVs hanging on the walls as well as from suspension rods were playing a Charlotte Knights game, which was making the clamor even louder. The Knights were a minor league baseball team beloved throughout North Carolina. The six-seat bar, where Tegan and I usually sat, was filled to capacity. The two bartenders were feverishly manning the dozen beer taps affixed to the wall.

In addition to the three rectangular bar-style tables fitted with stools and a couple of tall tables sans stools, for diners who preferred to stand, the owner had added six tables for two, each abutting the far wall. Next year, he promised, he was adding a rooftop bar. The small tables were usually difficult to score for a reservation, but Jason had. So had Reika Moore, who was seated at the nearest one.

I nodded to her as I passed by. She raised a bottle of sparkling water in response.

"Sorry I'm late," I said to Jason, taking my seat.

"You're right on time. I was early. What would you like to drink?" He handed me the beverage menu.

"I'll take Oly's pale ale."

"Is it good?"

"All the beer here is excellent."

I noticed Jason was tapping his foot. He was also fisting and unfurling his left hand, as he had yesterday. Nervous habits, I decided. I used to chew my lower lip, until my ex-fiancé mentioned it. A therapist I saw on occasion had recommended securing a rubber band around my wrist and snapping it whenever I caught myself doing the lip thing. The resulting pain of snapped rubber striking flesh had driven the habit from my life.

"Oly, who happens to be the owner, makes it himself." I hoped idle chatter would put Jason at ease. "Tegan likes to drink Ugly Pig. I hear Spruce Goose is good."

Our server, a petite blond woman with a winsome smile, greeted us and set two glasses of water on the table. "Hi. I'm Wallis," she said, "but Allie knows that. You are?"

"Jason Gardner."

"You're the developer."

"Word travels fast."

"Sure does. 'Gossip is as gossip does,' my mother always says." She winked. "Know what you want to drink?"

Jason gave her our order.

"Gotcha." She handed us dinner menus. "Allie, before I forget, I scored a second job at Blessed Bean on my days off." By day, Blessed Bean was a coffeehouse. At night, the place could now serve wine and beer. The owner had secured a liquor license, hoping to grow her business. "It's sure going to help pay the rent." Wallis's father had walked out on the family a year ago, and ever since, she'd been helping her mother and younger sister cover expenses.

"Good for you."

"I'll be back in a flash with your drinks."

Jason watched Wallis go, and his expression grew wistful. Wallis looked a lot like Delilah Brenneman, based on the photograph Tegan had shown me. Was he thinking about her now? I reflected again on the dustup between him and Patrick, and Jason warning Patrick not to utter Delilah's name. Did he truly hope she would walk back into his life?

"You're staring at our server. Does she look familiar?" I hoped Jason would speak frankly.

"No." He wiped the nostalgia from his face and fidgeted with his place setting. "Tell me about you. Where did you grow up? What do you like to do?"

"You didn't do oppo research on everyone in town?" My tone was light, playful.

"Ha! Not on a bet. Purely competitors." He folded his hands on the table and leaned forward. "Back to you . . ."

"I grew up in Bramblewood, went to Davidson College, earned an English degree, thought I'd teach, but life took a different turn, and I came here to start my catering business. When not working, I love to read or exercise or play with my cat."

"Sounds like an online dating profile. Do you do that?"

"No way." I blurted the answer so fast I shocked myself.

He chuckled. "Taboo subject?"

"Tegan's mother . . . she . . . Never mind. It's not important."

"I don't do it, either." He sat back in his chair. "Teaching and catering seem like opposite ends of the spectrum."

"I've always loved to cook. I learned when I was five."

"What did you make? Mud pies?" His mouth quirked up on one side, triggering the double dimple.

"Three-cheese mac 'n' cheese was my specialty."

"Wow."

"And cookies."

"I love cookies."

His eyes twinkled with interest, and I decided they were his best feature. The rest of him wasn't bad—the aquiline nose and devilish smile—but his eyes were studious yet heartfelt and imploring. To my dismay, I found myself attracted to him and wanted to know if he had this mesmerizing effect on all women.

I gave my mind a mental kick to stay on track and said, "I heard you're originally from here. Where was your childhood home?"

"North of the golf course, not far from where I'm staying now."

"Was it one of the estates?" Forty populated that part of town, including Magda Bellingham's. They weren't properties set miles apart, like you'd find in England. They were half-acre and one-acre lots.

"One of the smaller ones. We had a tennis court."

"You moved away when you were young, I heard."

"Yes. My father was interested in growing his wealth by investing in real estate. He figured California was booming. Why not go where the action was? It was a worthwhile move."

"When did you become a developer?"

"After high school my father wanted me to go to college and earn my MBA so I could join his investment group. However, doing something so boring wasn't in my plan. Instead, to irk him, I joined the army."

I was surprised he'd taken a similar path to the one Zach had followed. Had his choice been due to heartache, as well? I was reluctant to ask.

"In three years I became a sergeant," he continued.

My eyes widened. "You must have been exceptional."

"I'm a hard worker. I also took leadership courses. A few years after that, I bowed out and opted to go to college. I earned an MBA and became the man my father wanted me to be. With a twist."

"A twist?"

"I became an independent developer, not a group investor. I've always been a maverick."

"When did you meet—" I jammed my lips together, angry at myself for speaking before thinking.

"Who?" He eyed me warily. When I didn't answer, he said, "My ex-fiancée? I'm sure you've heard about her. As Wallis said, rumors abound in a small town. Her name is—"

"Delilah Brenneman."

"*Aha.* You have heard of her. Yes, we're no longer a couple. She's married now, but . . ." He went quiet and ran a finger along the rim of his water glass, his gaze following the motion.

But *what*? Did he hope she'd leave her husband? Did he pray the marriage wouldn't last?

"How did you meet?" I asked.

He raised his gaze. After a long pause, he said, "We hooked up in college."

"Where'd you go?"

"UCLA. She was quite a bit younger and an art history major who aspired to be a curator of MoMA in New York."

"A big aspiration. Did she achieve it?"

"She got a gig at a small museum in Los Angeles, where she met her husband." His chest rose and fell, as if he was burdened with regret. "He's a vintner and a renowned art collector."

"Do you keep in touch with her?" It was a bold question, but I was dying to know.

"No. I should . . . Maybe you could . . ."

He should *what*? I could *what*? His unfinished sentences were driving me nuts.

"Do your mother and father still live in California?" I asked, switching gears.

"They passed away ten years ago." His expression grew grim.

"I'm sorry." My cheeks grew warm as I recalled the rumors Lillian had mentioned in regard to Jason, one being he'd murdered his parents. Could the rumor possibly be true?

"Can't fix fate." He shrugged. "They were helicopter skiing in Canada. The snow was too wet, which triggered an avalanche. The crew looked for them for days. When they located them, they were long gone."

So they hadn't been murdered. *Phew.*

Wallis returned with our beverages, and Jason raised his beer glass in a toast. "To happier memories."

I mirrored the gesture.

We took a moment to order dinner, and when Wallis left, we resumed our conversation.

"You've got to visit my place," Jason said, veering the conversation away from maudlin subjects. "Seeing it should help you fashion the perfect soiree. I want champagne flowing and a chocolate fountain and the constant delivery of appetizers. The whole affair should be artistic and passionate." He painted a picture with his left hand. "There's a beautiful terrace overlooking the grounds and the swimming pool. I'd like six or seven food stations out there. Pasta. Stir-fry."

"A seafood bar. A cheese and accoutrement table."

"Yes, you've got the idea."

I thought of the lavish parties Jay Gatsby threw. Was Jason channeling the man because of the upcoming Feast for the Eyes event? Or had he come to town hoping a big bash might make news in California and alert Delilah as to his whereabouts and, despite Patrick's taunts, lure her here?

"How about I give you a tour tomorrow?" he continued. "In the morning a decorator is swapping out a number of furniture and art pieces. You shouldn't see the place until that's completed. Say, four o'clock?"

"Sure."

"Answer me this." He slung an arm casually over the back of his chair, which made him look decidedly rakish. "How many men's houses have you toured in your lifetime?"

"Plenty," I joked. "I am a caterer, after all." It dawned on me I'd never seen the inside of Zach's house. Why not? He'd promised to barbecue for me sometime. I guess he'd changed his mind.

As if I'd summoned Zach with my musings, he took a seat at the bar, along with his partner, Detective Brendan Bates, who was taller than Zach and meticulous about his appearance. I couldn't remember ever seeing the man without his Afro and goatee neatly trimmed. Both men were in jeans and polo shirts, suggesting they were enjoying a well-deserved night off. Zach caught me looking his way, and I averted my eyes, but not before I saw his gaze narrow. With what? Jealousy? Confusion? I considered waving in greeting, but I kept my hands on the base of the beer glass and made a mental note to talk to him tomorrow. We had to clear up whatever was coursing through his mind. We were friends. We owed each other an honest chat.

Our dinners came. Jason bit into his "everything" burger

and hummed his approval. "It's better than the menu claimed it would be." He put his burger on the plate, propped his elbows on the table, and tented his hands above his plate. "What kind of events have you thrown so far?"

"You name it. Themed parties. Kids or adult birthday parties. Recently I served eighty people for a couple's fortieth anniversary. And I cater events at law offices, fire stations, and the like."

"Fire stations?"

"Yep. Last year they threw a party for residents who lived near the station. After all, fire trucks create a lot of noise. There's no better goodwill gesture than free food. I offered a buffet with all the best finger foods you could imagine. The biggest draw was the three-alarm-fire chicken wings."

"Three-alarm fire. Clever." He chuckled. "My soiree should be about five hundred people. Can you handle something that size?"

I tempered the urge to let my mouth fall open. "I'm sure I can." I'd have to hire every server in town, as well as a few from catering outfits in Asheville and possibly beyond. "What date are you thinking of?"

"Next Sunday. The day after the bookshop's *Gatsby* event."

Whoa! So soon?

"Can you handle it?" he asked and once again attacked his burger.

"Of course."

I spotted Iggie Luckenbill following the hostess to one of the six tables by the window. He was with another developer, the one who'd done the update on the rec center and the library. Iggie glanced our way, and his mouth curved down in a frown. He wasn't a reader, so he wasn't upset with me for messing up a book order. Was he still ticked at Jason for putting a bid on the historic properties? Couldn't he let bygones be bygones? I studied him, wondering again whether he had had feelings for Finette Fineworthy at one time and was upset Jason was getting buddy-buddy with her. Sure, he was married, but many men had affairs or previous lovers. Women too. Before taking his seat, Iggie straightened his tie, fussed with the cuffs of his shirt so a perfect half inch of cuff would show beneath the sleeves of his jacket, and smoothed his thinning hair.

"Who are you staring at?" Jason swiveled in his seat. "Oh, him. He's got a chip on his shoulder the size of New Jersey."

"He said you . . ." I hesitated.

"Go on." Jason tilted his head, those dreamy eyes of his pleading for honesty.

"He mentioned you started a project in California but abandoned it. Was that the one Patrick was referring to?"

Jason considered the question for a long moment. "Yes. It wasn't the right one to complete."

"Did you give up because you lost interest?"

"Sort of. It lacked style and substance. I returned the investor's money plus interest."

"But you began construction. The foundation and framing are still there."

"I put money in an escrow account to cover the cost of tearing it down and restoring it to the bare parcel of land it was, but it's taking time due to a lot of red tape. My lawyer is handling it. Trust me, I'm not a sluggard. I'm not heartless when it comes to the needs of a community." He sipped his beer. "Don't give Mr. Luckenbill or Mr. Hardwick another moment's thought. Now, back to the soiree. What do you think it will cost?"

I did the math in my head for liquor, dining tables and prep stations, food, and servers' wages. "I would think a hundred and fifty per person. It depends on the presentation and the variety of dishes you're hoping to provide, as well as the availability of the ingredients."

He downed a French fry. "What will you need as a deposit? Will twenty-five thousand cover it?"

I swallowed hard. I'd never received such a large deposit.

"Yes, it'll do." I'd have enough to buy all the liquor and provisions and then some. I wondered if Vanna would help or if she'd still hold a grudge against me because I hadn't insisted she join this dinner meeting? I might have to win her over by promising she could make frou-frou appetizers.

"Swell. Glad we've agreed. We'll review a menu tomorrow." After he polished off his burger, he said, "I hear you work out of a ghost kitchen."

"I do."

"Is it nearby?"

"It's four blocks away."

"I'd love to see it," he said. "If you feel comfortable letting me in, just the two of us."

"I'm fine." I didn't get the vibe that, one, he meant me harm, or two, he had any personal interest in seducing me. Perhaps it was because he had spoken freely about Delilah and had revealed, without saying the actual words, he still loved her.

"Do you have any desserts on hand for me to sample?"

"As a matter of fact, I do."

"Lead the way." He threw a couple of crisp one-hundred-dollar bills on the table and rose to his feet.

Wallis closed in on us. "I'll be right back with your change, sir."

Jason said, "No need. Whatever is left is for you."

"Thank you!" she gushed.

I unlocked the door to Dream Cuisine and switched on the lights.

Jason entered, taking it all in while nodding. "Nice. Everything in its place."

"If I didn't keep it organized, I wouldn't be able to accomplish anything." I switched on one of the double ovens to preheat it before fetching some premade tart shells from the walk-in refrigerator. "Do you like blueberries?" I asked.

Jason was peering at the flowchart hanging above the desk.

The chart held the names of the clients I needed to bake for in the coming week, plus all the private meals I had to prepare. I had a duplicate list on my Notes app. "You're busy."

"I am. Um, blueberries?"

"Love them."

"I'll make blueberry tarts for you to sample. I think your guests will appreciate them." I arranged a few of the tart shells on a baking sheet and popped them into the oven. While they baked for ten minutes, I mixed blueberries, cornstarch, a dash of salt, and a squeeze of lemon juice in a saucepan on the gas stove. I switched the burner to high to make a quick syrup. "I have cookies if you're hungry right now."

"Snickerdoodles?"

"Yes. I also have sugar cookies."

"Snickerdoodles only, please. They're my favorite. My mother made them. I love the flavor of cinnamon."

I opened a tin and arranged a few snickerdoodles on a plate. I always had some on hand because they were Tegan's favorites, as well.

Jason nabbed a cookie and took a bite as he settled onto one of the stools by the prep counter. "Perfection."

I tapped the button on my Bluetooth speaker, paired it with my iPhone, and pulled up a jazz playlist on my music app. I loved to bake to music. The strains of Dave Brubeck's "Take Five" filtered through speakers affixed to two upper corners of the kitchen. "Coffee?" I indicated the Cuisinart Coffee Center.

"Just cookies. Until the tarts are done."

"Ready in about fifteen minutes."

"You said you made mac 'n' cheese as a girl. That's cooking, if I'm not mistaken. When did you learn to bake?" Jason rose from the stool and stepped closer to me.

"At the same age. My mother was a mathematician and inept in the kitchen. If I wanted to eat something other than peanut butter and jelly—she made a mean PB and J—I needed to do it myself. I adore fresh baked bread, and I have a sweet tooth."

"You're industrious."

"I've been told."

He drew so near I could feel heat wafting off his body, and I wondered if I'd been wrong in my assessment. Was he making a move? He reached out and brushed a stray hair off my face. The gesture made me shiver.

"Shouldn't you put on a hairnet?" he asked.

"Ye-es," I sputtered, feeling silly for my concern. "When I'm cooking for my clients. Do you want me to do so?"

"Not on my account."

Call me crazy, but it wasn't proper even to contemplate romantic feelings for someone who was hiring me for a huge soiree.

The timer for the blueberry concoction buzzed.

Saved by the bell, I thought and hurried to the saucepan to stir.

A couple of minutes later, I removed the tart shells from the oven and spooned the blueberry filling into them. While they firmed up, I reviewed tomorrow's orders, and Jason sat down again to scan messages on his cell phone.

When the blueberry filling was fairly firm, I topped the tarts with freshly whipped cream, and we ate them warm.

"Delicious," Jason said when he had finished. "You absolutely must serve them at the soiree." He rose to a stand. "Would you like a ride home? I parked behind the Brewery."

"No, thanks. I'll clean up before I leave, and I can walk. It's not far. You go on."

"This was lovely." He leaned in, pecked me pristinely on the cheek, and exited quietly.

In a flash I washed and dried all the dishes and was soon strolling up the path to my place.

"Here, Darcy," I called as I unlocked the front door. He didn't race to me, which didn't alarm me. He could be a sleepyhead. I stepped inside. "Darcy! I'm home."

The sound of mewling alarmed me. I rushed to the cat-scratching station and peeked inside. Darcy was in the llama's barrel-shaped belly, curled into a ball.

"What's wrong?" I lifted him out. "Oh, no! Darcy."

His front right paw was bleeding. Not the paw pads. One of the toenails.

"What happened? What did you do?" I whirled and spotted blood on the floor by the fireplace. I held the cat's face to mine and said, "Did you scrape it on the hearthstone? I can't fix it. We have to see the vet."

Darcy wriggled. He understood the word and was having none of it.

"Sorry, buddy." I held on tight. "You need expert attention." I wrapped his paw with a towel, deposited him in his cat carrier, and raced to my Ford Transit, which was parked in the carport. I phoned the vet on the way.

When we arrived at her office, she was already there, because she lived upstairs in a two-bedroom unit. Seeing as she was the sole vet in town, her living arrangement made it super-convenient for emergencies. I had to assist her since her staff wasn't available. As expected, Darcy tried to wrench free of my grasp, but I wouldn't let him. The vet gave him a small dose of sedative, then trimmed his nail, cauterized it to stop the flow of blood, applied antibiotic ointment to prevent infection, and expertly bandaged his paw.

A half hour later, as he and I were walking into my place, my cell phone pinged. Jason had texted.

Jason: **Need to talk. Really important.**

I dialed his number, but he didn't answer. Another text materialized.

Jason: **Please come to the estate now. I've got to talk to you in person.**

Now? What could he need to discuss at half past eleven? He hadn't made a pass at me earlier. I doubted he wanted to pounce on me. Had something happened to his house? Had someone broken in? If so, why not call the police? Was he being overly dramatic?

A little weirded out by the tone of the message and loathe to go to the house of a man I'd recently met, I texted back that if he needed to talk more about the soiree and pin down details, I could come earlier than planned tomorrow morning.

Jason: **Please. Come. Urgent.**

Okay, I was losing it, big-time. *Urgent?* I should at least check on him. He could be in trouble. Perhaps someone who, like me, was against his plans of building a mall had trashed his place.

Me: **On my way but not staying long. My cat is hurt.**

In fact, Darcy was so drowsy from the sedative, I decided I couldn't leave him home alone. I'd take him with me.

A few of the estates in Bramblewood were hidden behind gates or fences or stands of trees, but the Sugarbaker estate wasn't one of them. Located at the top of a winding road, it was a sight to behold, all lit up with a gorgeous array of lights. A travertine fountain in a quatrefoil shape stood in the middle of the circular drive. Exquisite Doric columns buttressed the entry of the two-story home. Sprinklers—armed by timers, I guessed—were spraying the lawn to the right. Puddles bordered the gardens that had previously received a good watering.

I parked and trotted up the front steps, with Darcy in his carrier. The front door was ajar. I didn't push on it. Instead, I yelled, "Hello! Jason? Anyone home? It's Allie. I'm here." I waited for a few seconds, but he didn't reply.

I thought I heard a door close, but I didn't detect the sound of footsteps. I recalled Jason saying his domestic helper was off for the night. "Jason, hello?" I glimpsed my phone. He hadn't sent another text message, canceling his request. In fact, the messages were gone.

What the heck? I hadn't imagined them. I was certain I hadn't.

I pressed the doorbell. A melodious tune rang out. Still no response.

"Jason!" I knocked on the door, prepared to leave if he didn't respond.

Someone moaned inside. Darcy roused and mewed.

I hushed him. "Jason? Are you all right?"

Another moan.

I inched open the door and gasped. Jason was lying on his side in the foyer.

Chapter 7

So we drove on toward death through the cooling twilight.
—Nick Carraway in F. Scott Fitzgerald's *The Great Gatsby*

I raced in while pressing 911 on my phone. It didn't connect. I checked the bars for a signal. Weak. I put the cat carrier on the floor and bent on one knee to inspect Jason. His eyes were closed. His breathing was labored. His arm was outstretched, as if he had been trying to grasp the cell phone lying on the marble floor beyond his reach.

"Jason, are you okay?" I asked. I noticed blood pooling around his body and gagged. Had he tripped on the Persian rug runner and fallen? Had he struck his head? "Jason?"

"Duh . . . ," he rasped.

I shook my head. I didn't understand.

"Duh . . . she . . ."

"Are you trying to say Delilah? Did she reach out to you? Is that why you needed to see me? You texted it was urgent."

He inhaled sharply and wheezed.

"No, Jason. Stay with me!"

He slumped forward. I gasped when I saw a crystal quartz spearpoint jutting from his back. I grasped the butt of it before recalling that if someone pulled a knife from a wound, a victim might bleed out. I released it as if it was on fire.

"Oh, Jason." Unable to roll him onto his back because of

the spearpoint, I couldn't administer mouth-to-mouth. Tears sluiced down my cheeks as I pressed 911 again on my phone. This time a dispatcher answered.

"What is your address?" she asked.

I provided it and gave her my cell phone number, in case we got disconnected.

"What is the nature of the emergency?"

Adrenaline pumped through my veins as I informed the woman that Jason Gardner was injured. "He's been stabbed. Come quickly. We're in the foyer. The door is open."

"Did you see who stabbed him?" she asked.

"No, ma'am." I could've sworn I'd heard a door close before I entered. Had his attacker stolen out the rear of the house? "Please hurry. I don't want him to die. Please."

I stared at Jason, and my chest tightened. His skin was ash gray, and there was no longer the rise and fall of his chest. Whatever I wanted, hoped for, was of no concern. More tears spilled down my cheeks.

The dispatcher warned me not to hang up and gave me instructions on how to proceed when help arrived.

Nodding mindlessly, I rose to my feet and surveyed the foyer. I noticed small clumps of mud on Jason's shoes as well as on the floor and runner. Given the glorious evening weather, if he'd gone outside to view the night sky but spied a trespasser, he might have dashed through the recently watered gardens to escape. Had the intruder followed Jason through the mud and tracked some in? Could the remnants help the police discover the killer's identity?

Though it creeped me out to do so, I began clicking photographs of the foyer with my cell phone. I hadn't documented the crime scene when Marigold died, and, though I had good visual recall, I had regretted it. I started with Jason and the floor around him. Then I aimed the lens at the oversized front door and sidelights. The door had been ajar. Had the killer entered that way? Would there be traces of footprints outside? Might he, *or she*, I thought, revising myself, have clods of mud on the soles of his or her shoes?

I took pictures of the velvet bench to the right of the door, the Italianate foyer table to the left, the gilded mirror above the table, and the beautiful porcelain vase filled with fresh flowers resting on the table. The ornate chandelier provided ample light. The photos were crystal clear.

Squatting, I steadied the camera on the floor to snap photos beneath the scalloped lower edge of the foyer table. I didn't see any telltale clues. I swung around to capture the area under the bench, although I could clearly see it was bare. The gaudy Art Deco piece of art on the right wall looked out of place. The Miró on the left was more in keeping with the grandiose style of the house. Idly, I wondered if the decorator Jason had hired would've chosen more contemporary furniture.

I refocused on him, and as gruesome as it sounded—*and it was*—I took photographs of the spearpoint in his back. It seemed familiar. When I realized why, I moaned. It was nearly identical to one of the spearheads the previous owners of my parents' mountain retreat had ceded to them along with all the furniture.

A siren bleated. Tires screeched on the driveway. Flashing red light pierced the sidelights and ricocheted off the chandelier and mirrors. Two doors slammed. A second vehicle arrived, and two more doors closed. I swiped the camera app to remove it from the screen and shoved my phone in the pocket of my pants. I didn't think the police would appreciate I'd taken pictures.

Seconds later Zach pushed open the door, announcing himself as he did. His gun was drawn. Right behind him came Bates, also armed. They were still in jeans and polos, but they hadn't come from the Brewery. I'd seen them leave minutes before Jason and I did. I happened to know they regularly attended a poker game. Perhaps they'd gone together.

Two emergency medical techs paused in the doorway. "Sir, may we enter?"

Zach summoned them inside. They made a beeline for Jason.

"Sir," the taller of the EMTs said, "permission to inspect the body?"

"Permission granted." He eyed me. "Allie, what are you doing here?"

"Jason . . . I mean Mr. Gardner texted me." I thrust my arm at Jason's lifeless body.

"Use his first name. You had dinner with him."

"A business dinner." I wondered why I felt the need to clarify. "He wanted to hire me to cater a soiree. When we were done, I went home. I mean, first, we went to Dream Cuisine to taste some desserts he might want for the party. Then I went home. Alone."

Zach shifted feet.

"A while later, he texted me. He said he needed to talk to me. I phoned him, but he didn't answer. A second text came through. I replied that we'd meet in the morning. But then I received a third text. He said it was urgent. I worried he might be in trouble, so I—"

"Came on your own and didn't call a friend to accompany you?"

"No, I—" My voice cracked. "When I got here, the door was ajar. I called his name. He didn't answer. Neither did the domestic helper. That's because he . . . or she . . . I don't know which gender . . . I didn't ask . . . has the night off. I thought I heard a door close, but I didn't detect footsteps. It could have been the wind, or it could've been the killer fleeing. I don't know." I hated that I was rambling, but I couldn't help it. I wrapped an arm around my torso to steady myself.

The taller EMT stood and nodded to Zach. "He's dead."

"Thank you." Zach dismissed both EMTs and asked them to wait outside.

Bates slipped on latex gloves and crossed to Jason. He felt for a pulse, as the emergency technician had. "Definitely dead," he said.

Hadn't he believed the EMT?

Zach slipped on a pair of gloves. "Go on, Allie."

My throat felt thick, like I'd swallowed talcum powder. "Then I heard someone moan, so I entered and found Jason like—" I shot out a hand.

Darcy yowled, reminding me he was in his carrier. I cooed to him that everything was okay, even though it wasn't, and said to Zach, "Jason . . . he wasn't facedown when I entered. He was on his side. And he was still alive. I bent to help him. But he pitched forward, and I saw the spear. Actually, it's a spearpoint."

"A Clovis spearpoint, to be exact." Bates rose and continued speaking while making his way around the foyer, snapping pictures with a cell phone, as I had. "It's presumed Clovis points were first used over thirteen thousand years ago in Chatham County, outside of Raleigh."

"And you know this how?" Zach asked.

"History buff." In addition to reading thrillers and suspense, Bates was an avid nonfiction reader. Like Tegan, the more time I spent at Feast for the Eyes, the more I learned about the reading habits of the bookshop's customers. "The Clovis culture hunted big game. They fancied crystal quartz."

"Um, Zach—" A chill cut through me. "I touched the spearpoint."

"You what?"

"I'm sorry, but Jason was alive. I thought if I pulled it out, I could roll him on his back and give him mouth-to-mouth, but then I remembered I shouldn't remove it. He'd bleed out. My fingerprints—"

"Are on it."

I felt my cheeks warm with embarrassment. "One other

thing. The spearpoint. It looks like one from the plaque in my living room." I explained how I'd inherited it.

Zach mumbled under his breath as he bent to study the weapon.

"Of course, it could be from the history museum," I went on, "and I'm sure others in town have some. They are collectibles. I haven't paid attention to my collection in ages." Although my gaze had grazed over the array when I'd told my house I loved it. Had the spearpoint been missing then? "If the weapon—" Saying the word made me gag. Jason had been killed. Murdered! "If it is mine, someone stole it from me."

"How? Aren't you locking your door, even after what happened?"

"I do lock it. All the time." I wasn't stupid. In April somebody had entered the house without my knowledge and swiped a spare key to Dream Cuisine. Since then, I'd been diligent.

"Allie's right," Bates said. "It could be anyone's. Amassing ancient relics like spearpoints from the area is a common hobby for North Carolinians. I have a few at my place." He circled the area to document the scene.

"Zach . . ." My voice trailed off because my insides were quivering with anxiety. *C'mon, Allie. Buck up.* "Jason said something before he died. He said, 'Duh,' and he added the word *she*. He was engaged once. They broke up, and she married someone else. Apparently, he was heartbroken."

"What's her name?"

"Delilah Brenneman. She lives in California. Do you think he wanted me to call her for him? He was reaching for his cell phone, but it was too far away." I motioned to where it rested on the floor.

"We'll never know."

"I got here as fast as I could after he texted. I didn't see anyone on foot or driving away, but there's plenty of property out back where someone might have escaped."

The other homes near the Sugarbaker estate were sizable, but their perimeters bled into one another.

Bates said, "Uh, Zach, I think you should see this." He held something gold and shiny in the palm of his hand. "I found it by a leg of the foyer table."

I couldn't make it out from this distance and wondered if the picture I snapped had captured it.

Zach took the item from his partner and said. "Go outside. Call for backup."

Bates followed the directive.

Zach regarded me, his mouth screwed up in an unappealing way. "Why would you say yes to catering a party for Jason Gardner?"

"I'm sorry. I'm not following."

"Yesterday you said you wanted to oppose the mall he was building. You were very upset."

"Yes, I was, but I got over that."

He gazed at Jason's lifeless body. "Did you?"

"Did I what?"

"Get over it?"

I tilted my head. "What are you implying? Are you accusing me of murdering him? Zach, get real."

"You said the spearpoint could be from your collection."

"If it is, I didn't bring it here. Are you going to accuse Bates, since he owns a few? One could be missing from his place."

"Can you explain this?" Zach opened his fist. In his palm lay a gold Celtic knot dangle earring. "Look familiar?"

My insides snarled. "It's not mine, and you'll notice . . . no earrings." I cupped a hand behind one ear.

"You're wearing your necklace."

"As well as the Celtic knot ring Marigold bequeathed me." I had Celtic heritage on my mother's side, which favored the more talkative Irish nature than the direct and economical English personality. "No earrings."

"Maybe you had them on, but you and Gardner struggled, and your earring fell off. You couldn't retrieve it before we arrived, so you slipped the matching earring into your pocket."

"Want to pat me down?" I asked testily, turning sidewise and motioning to my pants pockets. "Feel free to probe."

"Don't take an attitude."

"Look, a week ago I lost an earring similar to the one you're holding while I was making deliveries. I haven't worn the other since."

"Uh-huh."

I glowered at him. "You don't truly think I killed him, do you?"

He didn't reply. I could see he was weighing the possibility. The evidence was mounting. The earring. The spearpoint. Me rashly coming to the house alone.

After a long moment, he said, "No, I don't."

"Thank you for your reticent vote of confidence. I swear I came because Jason texted me to come over."

"Let me see your phone."

Pulling it from my pocket, I remembered the text thread had mysteriously disappeared, and my gut wrenched. Zach would think I'd lied. *Shoot!*

"Zach," Bates said from the doorway. "A few neighbors are outside wondering what's going on."

Zach strode to the front door and came to a stop just over the threshold. Granted a brief reprieve, I followed him and peeked around his torso. At least ten people, some in jackets and pants, others in robes or pajamas, stood facing the house.

"I heard a scream!" yelled a woman younger than me. "It was faint but shrill." In her pink jumper, her hair swooped into a messy bun, she reminded me of Pinkie, a cuddly stuffed bunny my nana gave me when I was six.

"Was it a man or woman, miss?" Zach asked.

"Woman. I'm sure of it."

"It wasn't me," I whispered.

Zach cut me a look.

"I didn't scream." Or had I?

"I heard a dog bark at eleven thirty," said an elderly man in overalls. He was barefoot. Glasses perched atop his balding head.

"We hear dogs barking all the time," a younger man said.

"Not at this time of night," the elderly man said.

Zach said, "What kind of dog, Mr.—"

"Smith. Ed Smith. A medium-sized dog is my guess. You know, it sounded like this." He imitated a throaty bark. "Sort of muted, I suppose, but anything from this distance would sound muffled."

"Folks, did any of your animals bark?" Zach asked the crowd.

They all shook their heads.

"Did any of you scream?" he asked.

A chorus of noes followed.

I said sotto voce, "Zach, I got a series of texts from Jason, the third at eleven thirty-five. I remember the time because I was so tired after going to the vet."

"Why were you at the vet?"

"Darcy hurt himself." I gestured to the foyer, where I'd left the cat in his carrier.

"Is he okay?"

"He'll survive. Thanks for asking. But back to . . . this."

This. Jason Gardner . . . dead. I couldn't wrap my head around it.

I pressed on. "Like I told you, when I received the text saying it was urgent, I came right over. I arrived within ten minutes."

"Mr. Smith, are you sure of the time?" Zach turned back to the elderly man.

"Yup. I was watching the nightly news. There's a whole lot going on in the world these days. Not safe, you know. Lots of upheaval. Gotta watch the news to stay on top of things."

I hadn't heard a dog bark, but I'd arrived after the time frame Mr. Smith outlined.

"Thank you, sir." Zach held up a hand. "Everyone, please give your statements to Detective Bates."

Bates strode down the steps to the neighbors. The EMTs were standing beside their vehicle, awaiting further instructions. I imagined the police would have to release the body before they could transport it to wherever they needed to take it.

"Allie, let me see your phone," Zach said for the second time.

"Yeah, that's the thing. The text thread is gone." Quickly, I added, "I didn't erase it. It just vanished. Jason must have deleted it."

"He could erase texts off his phone," Zach said, "but he couldn't off of yours. The texts would still be there."

"I'm not making up the exchange. It's the reason why I phoned him. To ask what was wrong." I pulled my phone from my pocket and swiped the screen to access my recent calls list. It showed I'd dialed Jason's number. "Here's my response. Time-stamped eleven thirty-six."

"Doesn't prove anything," Zach said.

His curt tone irked me. Was he, yet again, questioning my veracity? That said a whole heck of a lot about our friendship.

"I want to believe you," he said, as if reading my mind.

"Then do."

He pivoted to return inside.

I trailed him. "See the mud on the floor and the runner? Jason has mud on his shoes."

"So?"

"Maybe he went outside. It's a beautiful evening. He could've gone to look at the stars, spied a menacing trespasser, and raced through the gardens to escape. If the killer followed him, there might be footprints in one of the flower beds. The soil should be wet. The sprinklers were on when I arrived."

"My team will check it out."

I eyed Jason's phone. "Could you please review his phone for the texts?"

He lifted it and was unable to open it. "Password protected."

Swell. I glanced at the foyer table. If the Celtic knot earring was, indeed, the mate to mine, how had it gotten here? Only one explanation came to mind. The killer found it the day I lost it, and, seeing the matching one dangling from my earlobe, knew it belonged to me and brought it to the scene. Where could that have taken place? Ragamuffin? Blessed Bean? Big Mama's Diner? I had been furiously making deliveries and hadn't noticed it missing until dinnertime. I'd run into just about everyone I knew at one place or another. Even Zach.

I bent down to look beneath the table, hoping I could divine the answer.

"Allie, don't touch anything," Zach cautioned.

"I haven't." *Other than the murder weapon*, I thought glumly. "I won't," I added, revising my answer. I spotted something glistening beneath the table, close to the wall. It looked like another piece of jewelry. "Zach, what's that?"

"What's what?" He crouched to have a look.

"See it?"

He rose, shoved the foyer table away from the wall, and retrieved the item. It was a cuff link with a cursive letter *J* on it.

Jason's. Not the killer's. *Dang.*

Chapter 8

"They're a rotten crowd . . . You're worth the whole damn bunch put together."

—Nick Carraway in F. Scott Fitzgerald's *The Great Gatsby*

After the evidence team arrived, followed by the coroner, who officially declared Jason dead from a stab wound, and after Zach asked me each question two more times to see if I would change my answers—I did not—he released me on my own recognizance, adding I was a person of interest and not to leave town.

As if.

On the drive home I went over every detail of the crime scene. Had the killer staged the clues? Had he or she tossed my earring under the furniture to make Zach think Jason and I struggled, and I killed him? Why frame me? I'd just met him. My motive to want him dead was weak at best. Big deal if I didn't want him building on the historic properties. I had no say. All I could do was carp about it.

Way past midnight, I carried Darcy into the house and released him from his carrier. Despite his bandaged paw, he scampered toward the fireplace, but I intervened. "No, sir." I scooped him into my arms. "You may not play here until I've made it cat friendly. For now, it's bedtime."

My gaze landed on the collection of spearpoints hanging on

a plaque to the right of the fireplace. I teetered. There had been five. Now I counted four. One was, indeed, missing.

No, no, no.

Resigned, I immediately dialed Zach. While I waited for him to show up, I inspected the front door lock. It didn't look like someone had tampered with it. How had the thief gotten in?

Zach arrived within thirty minutes, leaving Bates to manage the evidence team at the Sugarbaker estate.

I showed him inside, relocked the door, and ushered him into the living room. "I'm not sure when it went missing. It's not something I look at every day. It could've vanished months ago."

He pulled his cell phone from his pocket and snapped pictures. Darcy butted his leg. Zach bent to pet the cat's head and said, "Sorry, pal. I'm busy."

Darcy retreated to the belly of the llama cat-scratching station, probably hoping I wouldn't notice he'd already stripped the bandage off his paw, the sneaky Pete. The vet had said he might do it and not to worry. Infection was her main concern. As long as I inspected and reinspected the toenail and determined it was healing, I could let him be.

"The plaque isn't dusty," Zach noted.

"The housekeeper comes every other week, on Fridays."

"She could pinpoint when it disappeared."

"I suppose." She wouldn't have taken it. She was sweet and kind and devoted to all her clients. "I also had a handyman fix the shutters and a few loose cabinet doors in the kitchen, but he's as honest as the day is long. I'm sure he didn't swipe it." I fought back an edgy yawn. "While I was waiting for you to arrive, I checked my front door lock. It doesn't look like it was jimmied."

"Do you keep a spare key outside, like in a fake rock?"

"No. I have one in my van."

"Do you secure it?"

"Yes. I have a ton of paraphernalia in there."

He examined the plaque again. "You hosted a neighborhood watch party a few weeks ago."

"I did. I also held a book club when the bookshop was dealing with a leak in the plumbing, and I invited a few friends for a wine tasting."

"Okay." He heaved a sigh, rubbed the back of his neck, and headed for the door.

I followed and startled when he swiveled abruptly. I almost bumped into him but didn't move away.

"Allie . . ." He held my gaze for a long time, but he didn't continue, in the same way he'd faltered after our poker game. What did he want to say? Why couldn't he spit it out?

I murmured, "Please find the killer."

He promised he would and left.

Though it was late, after I washed my face and changed into pajamas, I texted Tegan about the situation. Jason, dead. Me, a person of interest. The spearpoint missing from my living room. She didn't reply, which probably meant she and Chloe were still at Chloe's theater audition. A month ago Lillian had confided that they often ran late, because the director was a stickler for reading each actor multiple times.

Relieved that Zach hadn't arrested me, I crawled under the comforter and nestled into a ball. Darcy liked to sleep on the pillow to my right. He paced in a circle to get comfortable and regarded me with soulful eyes.

"Yes, it's a good thing Zach doesn't think I'm guilty." Sure, clues pointed to me, and my being on the premises when Jason died made me look culpable, but I wasn't, and Zach had to know in his heart of hearts that was the case. I peeked at Darcy's toenail. He withdrew his paw quickly, but from the brief appraisal, I didn't think it was infected. I tapped his nose. "I'm checking again in the morning."

He meowed.

When the alarm on the cell phone rang at five a.m., cobwebs

were fogging my brain. Even so, I clambered out of bed. I had a lot of baking orders to fill and deliveries to be made. Darcy didn't budge, but I couldn't leave him home, where he might further injure himself, so I dressed in work clothes, packed him a breakfast, deposited him in the cat carrier, and took him with me. On my way out the door, I peered at the fireplace, searching for what Darcy might have snagged his toenail on. I didn't see a thing.

"Figure it out later, Allie," I murmured.

My gaze fell on the plaque with four, not five, spearpoints. Though I got nauseous thinking about the possibility that a killer had stolen one of them to use as a murder weapon, I texted my housekeeper and asked if she could remember the last time she'd seen the spearpoint in question. She responded in an instant that she'd dusted the plaque Friday morning and all of them were accounted for, meaning whoever had swiped it must have done so between then and now.

Minutes after I entered Dream Cuisine, I heard a fist pounding the front door.

"Allie!" Tegan bellowed. "Open up."

I did. "It's early. What're you doing awake?"

"What am I . . ." She barged past me and stopped by the prep counter. "Why didn't you call me? How could you text me?"

"I thought you might still be at Chloe's audition."

"It wouldn't have mattered. Honestly, you're a goon sometimes. I would've come over in a flash. As it was, Chloe and I left the theater around eleven and went to her place to rehash her audition until around two, and I didn't see the message until I left her house." She yawned.

"Why didn't you call me then?"

"I didn't want to wake you." Though it wasn't cold out, she was bundled in a bulky sweater and pajama bottoms adorned with bunnies. I recollected numerous sleepovers as girls where she'd worn equally ridiculous ensembles.

"Nice of you to dress up," I gibed.

"Give it a rest. I'll go home and change before heading to the bookshop. Back to you. Is Zach nuts? It's ridiculous for him to think you could be a killer."

"As ridiculous as when he thought you were?"

"I've had nefarious thoughts from time to time. You? Never."

"Oh, yes, I have." My desire to eighty-six my ex-fiancé had been so powerful I'd seen a psychologist to work through the anger. I still touched base with her every few months. Heaven forbid I reveal that tidbit to my parents. They were dead set against anybody picking apart another person's brain.

Tegan grasped me in a bear hug and released me. "Tell me everything."

"As I bake."

I referred to the flowchart on the wall and awakened the laptop computer on the desk—the business one. I had a personal one at home. I reviewed the orders I'd jotted on my Notes app. "Big Mama's needs lemon muffins." I opened the recipe I'd stored in a Word file as I recited the other orders. "Milky Way wants four dozen oversized chocolate crinkle cookies. Legal Eagles is expecting a vanilla cake with coconut frosting for the receptionist's birthday. Jukebox Joint wants scones."

I paused. I hoped Zach's mother wouldn't press me for information when I showed up. We weren't well acquainted. I'd been supplying scones for only a month. I pushed the thought aside and reviewed the order chart. "And I'm going to make a dozen poppy-seed muffins for Patrick and his crew." Ragamuffin wouldn't suffer if Patrick didn't purchase muffins from them. They sold out daily. "He's starting the renovation at your mom's B&B today."

"Helga won't be happy about you popping in with goodies."

"She'll be fine. In fact, she'll be over the moon. She'd begrudge having to provide sustenance for the workers." Helga was devoted to Noeline and wouldn't dare cut into her bottom line to give treats to the workmen. *Let them feed themselves,* I could hear her say.

I donned an apron and reminded myself to breathe. I had plenty of time. I didn't need to start deliveries until at least nine a.m.

The rear door opened, and Vanna hurried in, appropriately attired for baking. No high heels, her hair swept into a chef's cap. "What are you doing here, Tegan?"

"Good morning to you, too, Sis," Tegan replied.

"You're never up before eight."

"Allie texted me."

"Allie"—Vanna addressed me, dismissing her sister—"I had a dream to beat all dreams and came up with so many ideas about how to expand the business." She flung her purse on the desk. "I was thinking we could deliver flyers to every refined business in town. You know, lawyers, accountants, and the like." She slipped on an apron and viewed the recipes I'd pulled up on the computer. "Want me to make the cake?"

"Yes."

She placed a mixing bowl on the prep counter. "We can also reach out to nearby communities, like Black Mountain, Swannanoa, Leicester, and Woodfin. Think of all the inns and B&Bs we could approach. Oh, and art galleries. There are so many. They're always having gatherings."

"Not a bad idea." Many of the towns surrounding Asheville were similar in size to Bramblewood.

"Vanna, time-out." Tegan formed a T with her hands. "Allie's in a pickle. I'm here to help."

"Do you need me to do a grocery run?"

"Not that kind of pickle. She's a person of interest in the murder of Jason Gardner."

Vanna gasped. "He's dead?"

"He was stabbed," I said. "Last night."

"Oh, no!" Tears sprang to her eyes. A sob caught in her throat. She covered her mouth. "Oh!"

The memory of Jason mumbling, "Duh," and expiring directly afterward caught me up short. Should I try to track down Delilah and let her know he'd been killed? Would she care?

Doing my best to maintain my calm, I went into the walk-in refrigerator and emerged with two dozen eggs and four cubes of butter. I dumped the butter into a large glass bowl and placed it in the microwave to melt. Then I began cracking eggs into two other bowls—eight for a double batch of cookies and eight for the poppy-seed muffins.

"Stabbed?" Vanna repeated.

"In the house he was renting," I said.

She slumped onto a stool beside the prep counter. "What happened? Why are you a person of interest? Because you met him for dinner?"

"Because around eleven thirty, he wrote me three texts and asked me to come over. He said it was urgent."

"Urgent?" Vanna screwed up her mouth. "Since when is a booty call urgent?"

"It wasn't a booty call!" I snapped. "We did not have that kind of relationship. He wanted to hire me . . . us," I added judiciously, "to cater his soiree next Sunday."

"Us?"

"It was going to be huge. We'd scheduled an appointment to discuss the menu today, so I thought he was texting me about it. Anyway, I phoned to find out what was so vital, but he didn't answer, and I got worried, so I went there, and . . ." My breath caught in my chest. "He was still alive, but he died within minutes."

"Who do you think stabbed him?" Tegan asked.

"I don't know." I told them what I'd relayed to the police, and once again wondered if the killer had left through a rear door and escaped across the backyard. Had the police searched for footprints?

"Allie," Vanna said, her voice thin, "if we'd both gone to dinner with him, we could've saved him."

I gawked at her. "He didn't choke to death."

"I mean he would've stayed out later with both of us to entertain," Vanna said. "He wouldn't have been there when the thief was robbing him."

"I didn't say he was robbed." Had he been? Was the killer simply an opportunist? No. Whoever it was had stolen the spearpoint from my house, indicating premeditation. One didn't go around town carrying a spearpoint on one's person.

Tegan crossed to the Cuisinart Coffee Center and switched it on. "Who wants coffee?"

"Me!" I'd fed Darcy, but I'd skipped my morning cup of coffee. Caffeine was a must to help me get through the day.

Vanna fetched a tissue from her purse and blew her nose. "Jason, Jason. Now I'll never be able to date you."

"Sis, can it!" Tegan hissed. "This is not about you."

Vanna had the decency to blanch. "I'm sorry. You're right. Allie, what was he stabbed with?"

"A Clovis spearpoint."

"What's that?"

I described it.

"It's from a collection hanging in Allie's house," Tegan explained.

"What?" Vanna's eyes widened. "It's yours?"

"The previous owners who sold my parents the house were collectors," I explained. "My parents bought it furnished."

"And the killer stole one from you?" Vanna shook her head, incredulous. "Who knew you had a collection?"

"Lots of people."

"What else do the police have?" Tegan asked.

"Detective Bates recovered a Celtic knot earring from under

the foyer table. Zach theorized that Jason and I fought, and my earring fell off in the scuffle. I'm not convinced it's mine, but it could be." I positioned the canisters of sugar and flour by the mixing bowls and began to measure out the amounts for the cookies first. "Remember how I lost one a week ago, while making deliveries?"

Tegan jumped on that. "What if the killer got his hands on it and planted it at the crime scene to frame you?"

"Exactly what I think."

"Meaning the killer would've needed to see you lose it," Vanna said.

"It's a safe bet, but why set me up?" I asked. "Who hates me so much?"

"As far as I know, only my sister has it in for you." Tegan smirked. "Are you the killer, Vanna?"

Vanna stuck her tongue out.

"What other clues did you notice?" Tegan asked.

I fished my cell phone from my purse and opened the Photos app. I showed them some of the pictures I'd taken—not of Jason's body, of course—gave them a recap of what I'd noticed, and told them that I'd theorized Jason was reaching for his phone because he'd mumbled the syllable *Duh* and the word *she* right before he died. "He might have wanted me to reach out to his ex-fiancée, Delilah."

Vanna said, "How heartbreaking."

"Hey." Tegan raised a finger. "What if she's in town, and she killed him?"

I hadn't considered the possibility. "Why would she? I mean, she's married. Happily, he told me." Actually, he hadn't said she was happy, simply that she'd married well. Why had she and Jason broken up? Had she ended it before meeting her husband, or had he been the catalyst?

"In *The Great Gatsby* Daisy came to him when bidden," Tegan said. "It was the beginning of their downfall."

I revisited Patrick taunting Jason, saying even if he built the mall, she wouldn't come—she meaning Delilah. Why would Jason have believed she would?

I texted Zach and asked if he'd reached out to her. To my surprise, he reminded me immediately that it wasn't my investigation. *Snarky*, I groused to myself and didn't give him the pleasure of a reply.

Vanna took my phone and clicked on the Photos app. She gasped. "Is this him? Dead?"

I snatched the phone back. "Sorry. My bad." I'd forgotten I'd captured a few shocking images. On the other hand, she'd been the curious cat.

"What's the mud from?" she asked.

"I think Jason might have gone outside to look at the night sky, seen the killer, and raced through the moist gardens to escape." I tapped a spoon on the rim of a bowl. "The texts."

Tegan squinted. "Huh?"

"Zach didn't believe Jason texted me, because they were erased from my phone, but I didn't remove them."

"Jason must have deleted the thread," Vanna suggested.

"Zach said it was impossible. Unfortunately, we couldn't open Jason's phone to see how anything might have happened."

"Look at us"—Tegan motioned to the group—"theorizing like we're Allie's clue crew."

"Clue crew?" Vanna scoffed.

Tegan offered a sly smile. "I heard the term on a kids' TV show—clue crew. Hey, we could make it go viral. Hashtag"—she mimed the number sign—"AlliesClueCrew. No apostrophe. The three words smooshed together. What do you think?"

"Be serious."

"I'm deadly serious."

When the baking was done, Vanna and I packed up everything in white pastry boxes with Dream Cuisine's signature sage-green labels, and she and I headed off in separate directions. She would focus on Bramblewood deliveries. I would drive to Montford, specifically to the Blue Lantern.

After Noeline had purchased the bed-and-breakfast, she'd fixed it up to be one of the best inns in the area. It was designed in the Gothic Revival style, a variation of the Victorian architectural style, with steeply pitched roofs and lancet windows. The peacock-blue exterior color was a lovely contrast to the extravagant white vergeboard trim along the roof. Multiple lanterns hung from shepherd's hooks. The springtime azaleas had shed their flowers, allowing summer blooms like petunias, zinnias, and black-eyed Susans to shine.

The temperature was still cool, so I left Darcy in his carrier in the van, a window open, and told him I'd return soon. Then I carried the box of poppy-seed muffins into the inn.

Helga, clad in her pale blue uniform fitted with broad white lapels and white cuffs, stopped dusting the foyer furniture and fixed me with a frown. "What is in the box?"

"Muffins. For the workmen. Where are they?"

"Allie, I can bake very well."

"But you wouldn't want to give them free muffins and cut into Noeline's profits, would you?"

Helga chuffed. "You are incorrigible."

"So my parents tell me."

"Mr. Hardwick is in the office." She waggled her feather duster. "The others, I do not know."

I blew her a kiss and traipsed down the hall. "Yoo-hoo." I rapped on the office doorframe and peeked in.

Like the guest rooms, the office was decorated in white and blue, its wallpaper featuring antique lanterns, but it appeared Noeline was making a serious change. The bookcases that lined the walls had been removed, and all the furniture pieces were covered with tarps. Patrick was facing the far wall, removing remnants of whatever had affixed the bookcases to the wall with an electric sander. He didn't hear me enter, because he was whistling along to a recording of "Boulevard of Broken Dreams," a classic rock song by Green Day.

I knocked again. "Patrick!"

He switched off the sander, shoved his goggles on top of his head, and closed the app playing the music on his phone. "Morning." The sleeves of his work shirt were rolled up, exposing his massive forearms. His chinos were covered with dust.

"I've got treats," I announced.

"Wow. Cool." He accepted the box of goodies from me. "You're a saint. I didn't have time to swing by Ragamuffin. Sorry for the mess."

"Doesn't bother me. I'm not staying here. Where's your crew?"

"Two are on a break. My project manager is outside with Noeline." He hooked his thumb over his shoulder. "In addition to revamping the kitchen, she wanted to discuss adding a gazebo in the yard."

I noticed a sizable scratch on his forearm. It wasn't bleeding, but it was caked with blood. "Whoa. Pretty nasty scrape. Do you need a bandage?"

"Nah. It'll heal naturally. Got it when I went caving last night."

"Caving?"

"I went to Linville Caverns to see bats."

The subterranean, four-thousand-square-foot site, located deep inside Humpback Mountain in the Pisgah National Forest, was one of North Carolina's most mysterious attractions. Visitors had to hike down about thirteen hundred feet to view it. I'd visited once. On a tour.

"A bat scratched you?" I pointed at his arm.

He guffawed at my shocked expression. "Nah. The bats didn't do this. Don't worry. I'm not gonna get rabies or anything, and I'm not turning into a vampire anytime soon. I slipped on a rock." He lowered his voice. "Please don't tell anyone I was there. Between you and me, it's against regulations to sneak into the caverns at night, because it's dangerous, but I like a challenge. I get a real rush being in touch with nature in the pitch dark. Bats don't mind someone going solo. They're much friendlier one on one."

"Friendlier?" I shivered. Bats gave me the creeps. Sure, they didn't attack people. Usually, they swooped in because they were pursuing a bug, and apparently, they ate their body weight in insects each night, according to the tour guide. But their screeching could send fear spiraling down my spine. "When did you become interested in them?"

"My dad and me, we researched them. Learned their habits. I didn't like living on a farm much, but we had bats, so I stuck around."

"Allie!" Noeline rushed into the room, looking like a model in a *Town & Country* magazine—ecru shirt, tan chinos, her hair secured by a bandanna, her makeup understated. "Tegan contacted me. She said you were on your way here, and Helga said—" She crossed to me and hugged me. "I'm so sorry you had to see another dead body."

"Dead," Patrick said. "Who's dead?"

"Jason Gardner," Noeline replied over her shoulder.

"What? Whoa." Patrick ran a hand along the side of his head. "Really? I was supposed to meet with him today."

"You?" I freed myself from Noeline and regarded Patrick.

"He wanted me to do some repairs to the back porch of his estate before his gala event. You know, shore up everything to prevent accidents."

"He doesn't own the place."

"The owner gave him permission."

"And he hired you?" I asked, incredulous.

"Why is it hard to believe?" Noeline asked.

"Patrick and Jason were at the bookshop yesterday," I said, "and he accused Jason of doing some shoddy work, and they—"

"We made amends." Patrick ran his callused fingers through his hair. "When I ran into him at town hall later, clearer heads prevailed. I apologized and told him I was out of line and said I'd be happy to work with him on any project. He told me to stop by the estate today." He whistled with wonder. "He's dead? What happened? Did he have a heart attack, Allie?"

"He was stabbed in the back."

"Geez!" popped out of him. "He was murdered? Who did it?"

I shook my head. "The police don't know yet."

"That bites." Patrick lowered his gaze.

I noticed mud on his boots for the second day in a row. "Were the caves wet?" I gestured to the shoes.

"Yeah." He tilted the toe of his right foot up, as if inspecting it. "There's always water leaking somewhere. It can be a muddy mess. Why?"

"No reason."

CHAPTER 9

For a while these reveries provided an outlet for his imagination; they were a satisfactory hint of the unreality of reality, a promise that the rock of the world was founded securely on a fairy's wing.

—Nick Carraway in F. Scott Fitzgerald's *The Great Gatsby*

After making the remainder of my deliveries, I swung by the house, switched into leggings and a billowy-sleeved blouse, and headed to Feast for the Eyes. I'd promised to help rearrange bookshelves. Tegan liked to tackle the task once a month. She said readers spent more time scanning the aisles and often, upon finding themselves in a new realm, were willing to try the genre or a new-to-them author.

In the office Darcy was as pleased as punch to get out of his carrier. He immediately launched himself to the top of the rare books bookshelf.

"Careful," I reminded him. "Your toenail isn't healed."

He flicked his tail as if to chide me for worrying. After all, he was Super Cat. He settled on his haunches and peered through the office window, which provided a view of the bookshop's main room. From his perch, he could keep track of all the activity until he tuckered out and snoozed.

I returned to the sales counter while dusting my hands on my thighs and thinking about Patrick and the condition of his work boots. Had he lied about going caving? His set-to with Jason had been quite contentious. Had he gone to Jason's place, seen him outside, chased him through the wet soil, and tracked mud inside before stabbing him? Would anybody at town hall be able to confirm that he and Jason had reconciled?

"Morning," Tegan crooned as she entered the shop from the stockroom, her arms laden with additional copies of *The Great Gatsby*. "The next shipment came in. I'll text everyone who preordered. The list is over there if you'll tag them." She motioned with her chin.

I took the books from her, stacked them on the counter and, referring to the list, began affixing Post-it notes with customers' names to them.

"Allie!" Chloe emerged from the stockroom, wiping her hands on a paper towel. She tossed it into the trash beneath the desk, then bear-hugged me and released me. "I heard about the murder. I can't believe it. How are you?"

"Hanging tough."

"Was it gruesome?"

"Yes."

"Who would want to kill him?"

One person came to mind—Patrick—but I said, "Let's talk about brighter subjects. How was your audition?"

Chloe blew a raspberry. "Not important."

"She did a good job." Tegan silently applauded. "She won't hear about callbacks until tomorrow."

"Callbacks. Not a chance. I stank up the room." Chloe made a face. "Anyway, we're not talking about me right now. I mean, c'mon. Jason Gardner is dead, and the police suspect you? Why—"

"Because he was stabbed with a spearpoint," Tegan cut in.

"What's that?" Chloe asked.

"An artifact," Tegan replied.

Quickly, I enlightened Chloe about the Clovis culture and their hunting methods.

Tegan regarded me. "You know, Reika Moore is savvy about artifacts. You've seen the ones she has hanging in her home, including spears, axes, knives, grinding tools, and bowls."

Tegan and I'd been to Reika's home on two occasions to attend events in support of the history museum.

"Her ancestors unearthed most of them with their own hands," Tegan went on. "She might have a clue about who else in town owned or collected them."

Besides Detective Bates, I mused.

"But the murder weapon was mine." I affixed the final Post-it note.

"You aren't certain," Tegan countered.

"Yours? No!" Chloe looked astonished. "Why do you have spearpoints?"

I explained how the previous owners had left everything in the house to my parents.

She shook her head. "The whole affair is awful. Murder. It's senseless. Jason was so vibrant. I think the mall he planned to build might have been good for Bramblewood. I know you didn't want him to build it, Allie—"

"Don't say that."

"But you didn't. You were against it."

"I got over myself," I assured her. After all, we couldn't stop progress. "And you're right. He was vibrant and smart, and he didn't deserve to die."

Tears welled in Chloe's eyes, and she fled to the stockroom. Like Vanna, she'd clearly had a crush on Jason.

"Tegan"—I clapped my hands together, eager to put the whole thing out of my mind—"where do you want me to start with our shelf swap?"

"Let's move the romance section to the nonfiction section, and vice versa."

"Do you think it's wise?" I asked. "I mean, we're talking completely different kinds of readers. How about romance and fantasy instead?"

"Good idea."

Together, with me on the rolling ladder and Tegan manning the book trolley—I was dressed more casually, and she'd worn a summery blue dress and wedge sandals she'd bought on sale Saturday—we took the fantasy titles off the top shelf. They weren't in alphabetical order. By design, they were the most requested titles. *The Bookseller of Inverness, The Dragon Queen, Chain of Thorns.* Tegan had read all of them and had gushed over *The Keeper Chronicles* trilogy. If I'd let her, she would have told me the entire tale of how the storytellers, historians, and magic-wielders—aka the Keepers—fought Mallon the Undying.

When I'd said, "Too much information," she'd countered, "The blurb will have to suffice."

After we removed the entire row of books, we carted them to the romance section and repeated the action, removing the top row of romance titles, which included the Bridgerton series, *Ransom* by Julie Garwood, and *Love at First Book* by Jenn McKinlay. I'd read and enjoyed the latter, because I'd devoured many of McKinlay's mysteries. *Love at First Book* was about a librarian who traveled to the quaint Irish village where her favorite novelist lived, and lo and behold, she fell for the guy's son. Talk about a fantasy! But it was fun.

Tegan said, "Back to Jason . . ."

I groaned.

"Hear me out. I've been thinking about who would've wanted to frame you for the murder." She led the way to the fantasy section, where I situated the romance novels on the top shelf and tackled the removal of the second row of titles. "All kidding aside, who hates you so much?"

Patrick didn't, as far as I knew. Did that rule him out?

"I've been wondering the same thing." Chloe rounded the corner with two bottles of water. Her makeup was streaked, and her eyes were puffy. She must have cried hard. "Thirsty?" she asked.

I thanked her for the water and immediately downed mine. I handed the empty bottle back to her.

Tegan noticed Chloe's tear-stained face. "Kiddo, take a break. Walk around the block or something."

"And miss the two of you theorizing? Not a chance."

I flashed on Tegan dubbing anyone who helped me solve Jason's murder a member of hashtag AlliesClueCrew and tamped down a smile. My friends were stalwart, if nothing else.

"So, who hates you?" Chloe asked.

"I can't think of anyone other than Sissy Martin from high school."

"Ha!" Tegan snorted. "Yep. Pip-squeak Sissy wanted to play point guard on the basketball team, but you earned the position."

"She wasn't a pip-squeak."

"She was four feet ten and as vicious as a hurricane."

"Remember how she pulled my hair and elbowed me in the stomach?" I flinched at the memory of how brutal her attacks were.

"And did she ever have a mouth on her."

"No kidding." The vile words she'd hurled at me? Ouch!

"Where is she these days?" Tegan asked.

"She's saving elephants in Africa." In her senior year Sissy started seeing a psychologist, who prescribed some medication. Anger issues resolved, it turned out she had a benevolent nature. "There's one other person who might hate me. Your ex, for being your moral support."

Winston Potts had not been pleased when Tegan mustered the courage to start divorce proceedings. He had threatened to do so but had never pulled the trigger. It had taken Tegan's aunt's death and the subsequent inheritance, plus a kick in the rear end by me, to make her realize she could be independent.

"Yeah, he does, but no." Tegan wagged her head. "He's not living here any longer. He relocated to Ohio to head up some big tech project."

"Good riddance," Chloe said.

"How's the divorce going?" I asked. "Everything moving along with the attorney?"

"The wheels of justice turn slowly, and serving papers is tricky." She sighed. "Hey, I've got an idea about the murder. What if a woman with a thing for Jason saw you two together at the Brewery last night? Women were crazy for him. Chloe and my sister both pined for him."

"I didn't pine," Chloe argued.

"You both had your claws out," Tegan joked. "Jealousy is a powerful motivator."

I frowned. "Why not kill me instead?"

"Good point."

"Hold on." I swung around so abruptly I nearly toppled off the rolling ladder. I clutched a shelf to anchor myself. "I remember seeing Reika at the Brewery last night. She was already seated when I arrived. But she didn't have a crush on Jason."

"I'd hope not. He was twenty years her junior," Tegan stated.

"No, I mean she wasn't happy he was negotiating to purchase the historical houses."

"Which gives her motive, I suppose."

"Jason's neighbors told Zach they heard a woman scream and a dog bark around the time of the murder. Granted, the sounds were distant and, therefore, muted, but the concurrence of events seems relevant, and Reika has a dog." I offered Tegan a stack of books.

"But Reika likes you." She accepted the books and positioned them on the trolley. "No, I can't see her as a killer. She's too . . . cultivated."

Cultivated individuals had murdered—a number of serial killers, including Hannibal Lecter came to mind—but I pushed the notion aside. "I also saw Ignatius Luckenbill."

"Who's he?" Chloe asked.

"A developer who, like Reika, was not pleased Jason was going to take ownership of the historic properties, but for a completely different reason." I explained.

"Why would he have it in for you?" Chloe asked.

Good question. I'd never catered for Iggie or his wife. Neither frequented the bookshop.

"Why was everyone in town dining at the Brewery on a Monday?" Tegan asked.

"The Charlotte Knights were playing. All the TVs were tuned to the game. You know, I've seen Iggie walking a German shepherd. Doesn't he live near the estates?"

"I think you're right." Tegan swatted the handle on the trolley, as if landing on a new theory. "Let's circle back to Reika. What if the murder weapon isn't yours? Suppose Reika swiped a spearpoint from the museum."

"Or the killer did, meaning whoever killed him didn't sneak into my place and steal it, but then why is it gone?" I stewed over the coincidence. "And what about my earring? One was definitely planted at the crime scene for the police to find." I brought Chloe up to speed regarding the evidence.

"Is it possible Reika saw you lose it?" Chloe asked.

"Good question. If I were you"—Tegan pointed at me—"I'd have a chat with her."

* * *

Bramblewood History Museum was situated in a two-story frame house built in the 1800s, across the street from the Congregational church and catty-corner to the sites Jason was going to purchase. The house was covered with beaded weatherboard and featured two brick fireplaces. Black shutters around the windows gave the building a distinguished look.

The museum didn't officially open until eleven, but the front door was unlocked, so I entered. The interior was well maintained, with recently refinished hardwood floors and beautiful Persian runners. To the left, a visitor could grab a map and view a display board pinned with details about upcoming events. The main hallway held a timeline of the development of Bramblewood and the Asheville area. Visitors could view all the artifacts, which were mounted or displayed in glass cases.

The kitchen to the left was always decorated as if dinner was about to be prepared. The rustic wooden table held antique pottery and tools. The fireplace was artificially aglow, and cookware stood at the ready. The living room to the right was similarly decked out, but the meal would be much fancier, served on a maple table fitted with dishes and glassware and a gorgeous lace tablecloth.

I peered into the glass case holding spearpoints to see if one of the spearpoints was missing, but I didn't notice any empty spots, which didn't mean anything. Reika might have a cache of items not on display. I recalled she'd come across all sorts of décor for the *Gatsby* party in the attic.

"Allie, hello." Reika passed through the archway leading to the kitchen. Her jacket, blouse, and skirt today were a dull beige. She'd added a chunky natural stone necklace for color. The aroma of her pungent perfume arrived before she did. "What brings you in? Do you want to see where we'll be setting up the tea on Thursday?"

"No, I came because . . ." I stammered, unable to bring

myself to grill her. "We're friends, right? I mean, you come to the book clubs, and you're helping with the *Gatsby* party."

"Yes, of course. Why do you ask?" The way she tilted her head reminded me of the plump nonmigratory songbird known as the Carolina wren.

"Because . . ." I scrutinized Reika's face for any hint of malice but found none, making me hopeful she wasn't the killer.

"Allie, are you all right?"

I forced the tension in my shoulders to ease before continuing. "Jason Gardner was killed."

"Heavens." She struggled for breath. "What a one-eighty from asking me if we were friends."

"I didn't want to blurt it outright."

"How did he die?"

"He was stabbed with an artifact. A crystal quartz spearpoint particular to the Clovis tribe."

"His death hasn't been on the news. None of the staff has mentioned it, either. How do you know so much?"

"I found him."

"My." She covered her mouth with her fingertips. "You poor dear."

"Zach . . . I mean Detective Armstrong will probably be asking you some questions."

"About spearpoints?"

"Yes. Have you noticed any missing?" I didn't mention mine could be the actual weapon.

She moved along the displays, assessing them as I had. "Each cabinet appears to be intact. Only the janitor and I have the keys to them."

I trailed her. "Are there more in the attic?"

"There could be. My grandfather was a terrible hoarder. There are dozens of unmarked boxes, which I keep promising to sort through, but I never find the time." She moaned softly. "I worried something like this might happen to Mr. Gardner.

He was making enemies left and right. I hoped the town would see the light and prevent him from getting the properties, and then it would—"

"Cede the properties to the preservation society."

"Yes." She lowered her voice. "Who killed him? Do the police know? The vitriol from the likes of Ignatius Luckenbill toward him was intolerable."

From you, as well, I thought.

"Come with me." She guided me into the living room and ushered me to the right, out of earshot of anyone who might work at the museum. "I know I was rather vocal about my desires at Ragamuffin on Sunday, and I'm ashamed to say I locked horns with Jason Gardner publicly after that. He'd come into the museum, probing for answers about the Yeagers, the family who previously owned the houses."

"They owned all of them?"

"All." She sighed. "He asked direct questions until his curiosity began to irk me. You see, Cora Yeager happened to be my mother's best friend. When I asked him why he wanted to know, he shrugged and said, 'No reason,' but I could tell he was fishing."

"She might have been a friend of his parents."

"I doubt it. They would've been at least two decades apart. But possibly she had been his parents' nemesis. Cora had a way about her, Mother said. She irked a lot of people. I kept thinking Jason might intend to trash Cora's name, thus pitting the town against the need to protect the properties. If I'm honest"—Reika toyed with the centermost bead of her necklace—"I didn't want him, in particular, to have the property, because he wanted to build a mall."

"I know."

"In fact, I was so dismayed by his plan, I sent him vicious texts and emails."

Texts and emails didn't kill people.

"How I wish I could erase them from the stratosphere." She swiped the air with a hand. "Wouldn't it be magical if we could? You know the kinds of messages I'm talking about, like the ones you send at two a.m. and rue until the day you die?"

I'd sent a few of those to my ex-fiancé.

"But there are all sorts of people I disagree with," she went on, "and they've received the same kinds of messages from me. I can be quite prickly. At least I'm consistent in that regard." She shook her head. "Poor, poor Mr. Gardner."

"Jason," I murmured. The title Mr. Gardner didn't fit him. It sounded stuffy.

"Where did he . . . ?" She didn't finish.

"In his house."

"When did you . . . ?" She fanned the air, evidently flustered by her own curiosity.

"Around eleven thirty."

Her mouth dropped open. "Why were you there so late?"

I explained.

"Urgent. He wrote it was urgent?" She blinked, as if trying to unearth more from the term. "I wish I could have accompanied you. I was home with my sweet dog, reading an Elizabethan spy novel, *The Course of All Treasons*. Do you know the book? By Suzanne B. Wolfe? In the story, the royal retinue is thrown into chaos when the queen's youngest and sweetest lady-in-waiting is—"

"Murdered. Yes, I know. We read the novel in book club last year, don't you recall?"

Her expression shifted. "Did we? I've read all sorts of books multiple times. By the way, you are a gem at the bookshop." She tapped her temple. "So knowledgeable. So polite." She clasped both hands. "What has come over me? I'm prattling as if I didn't have a care in the world. A man, a real man, not a fictional being, has been killed. Do the police have any suspects?"

The door to the museum opened, and Zach strode through. He gawked at me. "What are you doing here?"

"Going over a menu for the tea Reika has hired me to provide on Thursday," I said, feeling my cheeks warm from the lie. "But I'm leaving. Bye."

I hightailed it out of there and didn't look back.

Chapter 10

"Let us learn to show our friendship for a man when he is alive and not after he is dead."

—Meyer Wolfsheim in F. Scott Fitzgerald's *The Great Gatsby*

On the way back to Feast for the Eyes, feeling edgy and hungry, I swung by Ragamuffin and picked up a trio of pita sandwiches packed with curried chicken salad. When I walked into the bookshop and announced I had lunch, Chloe blessed me and jumped off the rolling ladder. Noeline had stopped in earlier with sixteen-by-twenty framed quotes from *The Great Gatsby*. Chloe was posting them. Tegan was too busy slamming cabinets to notice my entrance.

I hurried to her, plunked the bag with our lunches on the counter, and grasped her arms. "Stop!"

She wriggled free and smacked a few more cabinet doors.

"Really, stop," I ordered. "You'll scare the customers."

"We don't have any."

"We will in five, four, three, two . . ."

The door to the shop opened, and the pair of women I'd stood ahead of in the queue at the coffeehouse entered. They'd told me their destination.

"Welcome!" I cried.

They waved and made a beeline for the romance aisle, paused, and looked back at me.

"We swapped shelves," I informed them. "For a change of pace. Third row for romance."

They smiled and disappeared down that aisle.

I said to Tegan, "Why are you so mad?"

"Because I'm ticked at my mother for wanting to purchase another property. She's in over her head. And getting older."

I smiled. "She's not old. She's sixty, which is the new forty."

"What does that make us? The new ten?"

"You're acting like it."

She shimmied off her anger. "What happened with Reika?"

"Zach showed up and curtailed my conversation. He wasn't pleased to see me. I'm sure he thought I was inserting myself into his investigation. Which I wasn't. I was merely gathering evidence to share with him, but knowing he wouldn't believe me, I lied and told him I was there about the tea Reika had hired me for on Thursday." I groaned.

"Why did you make that sound?"

"Because I lied." I plucked three sandwiches from the bag, handed one to her, kept one, and placed the last one and empty bag on the counter. My stomach gurgled in anticipation as I unwrapped the top half of my sandwich and bit into it. Around a mouthful, I added, "To Zach."

"OMG. Chloe!" Tegan shouted.

Chloe scuttled to us. "What?"

"Alert the press. Allie lied." Tegan sniggered.

"I don't lie." I huffed. "I never lie. I hate liars."

"And I hate that you might be framed for murder." She handed the third sandwich to Chloe and bit into her own. "Perfection."

As I enjoyed the curried goodness, Finette strolled into the store in a black pantsuit and a silver-gray silk blouse fitted with a bow. Why had she put on such a somber getup? Had she heard the news? She'd liked Jason. Was she in mourning? She glanced in my direction and frowned.

If looks could kill. Ouch! Did she know I had found Jason's body and was a suspect?

"I got your message, Tegan," Finette said, ignoring me. "I'm here to pick up my copy of *The Great Gatsby*." She perused the few quotes Chloe had hung up. "That's one of my favorites." She pointed to the one above the fiction endcap and recited it. "'Let us learn to show our friendship for a man when he is alive and not after he is dead.'" She faltered. Her face drained of color. "Oh, no!" She covered her mouth. Her eyes brimmed with tears. "I . . . I . . . I'm sorry. How insensitive of me to utter those words aloud when Jason Gardner's dead. You must have heard he was murdered."

"Yes," Tegan acknowledged as she wrapped Finette's copy of the book and inserted it into a shopping bag.

"I will truly miss him." She pulled a tissue from her purse and dabbed her eyes. "He and I were as close as brother and sister. We thought the same way. We spoke with the same cadence. Each of us was an Internet nerd. We loved history. And books. And building things from the ground up. K'nex kits were my favorite toys as a kid, and they were his, too. Can you believe it?" She sighed. "The mall he wanted to build was going to be fabulous, filled with gadgets and interactive experiences, and now"—her face pinched with anger as she balled the tissue in her fist—"I suppose the vultures are salivating to offer a bid."

"Couldn't the town council choose not to allow anyone to build on the historic properties?" Chloe suggested.

"Yes." I was glad she'd come up with the idea and not me. "Those houses are representative of the town's first homes. The preservation society would like to offer a tour—"

"We shall see," Finette interrupted. "We shall see." She teared up again.

"Why were you and Jason so close?" Chloe asked. "He'd been here such a brief time."

"On this trip. True." Finette sighed dramatically. "But I met him months ago, when he made a previous trek to scout out Bramblewood. He was quite the talker. I discovered so much about him. He had to earn everything himself, as did I."

No, he didn't, if what Jason had told me at dinner was correct. His father had been a successful businessman, meaning Jason had probably inherited much of his wealth when his parents died in the avalanche.

"My parents didn't have any pull," Finette continued. "They couldn't get me into the finest colleges. Couldn't help me secure my first job. Don't get me wrong. I didn't mind starting at the bottom. I made peanuts, but it built character. Jason said the same thing."

Interesting how he'd cozied up to her with a comparable story. Had lying been his way of courting a favor from her?

"As a child, I never regretted not having money, because my parents were such good people. They gave readily to charities. They took in my great-aunt when her husband died. They made me proud."

That would explain why she was selflessly helping her great-aunt now. To carry out her parents' wishes.

"Did Jason's parents donate to causes?" Tegan handed Finette the bag and accepted her credit card for payment.

"He didn't mention it, but he and I often talked about the similarities of our youth. The way we had to create our own identities. Actually, he likened himself to Jay Gatsby, saying he'd been misunderstood all his life." Finette fixed her gaze on me. "Allie, I heard you discovered the body, but Zach let you walk out scot-free."

Scot-free? No wonder she was staring daggers at me.

"I didn't kill him," I said. "When I got there—"

"Allie is innocent." Tegan handed Finette her credit card and a receipt to sign.

Finette waved her hand dismissively. "Zach has his favorites, of course."

I bridled at the implication that it was purely a matter of time before he realized I was guilty.

"What has he discovered so far, Allie?" Finette asked while signing the receipt and pocketing the card. "Seeing as you have his ear."

I didn't have his ear. I wasn't even sure I had his friendship any longer. "It's his investigation. He hasn't shared any clues. I'm sure he'll follow wherever the trail of evidence leads."

"*Mm-hmm*," she added sarcastically.

My left eye started to twitch. I rubbed it with a finger. What was up with her? Why was she being so nasty to me? Had she been in love with Jason, and not Zach, as I'd presumed? Was she suffering, because she was unable to utter the words out loud, and taking her sorrow out on me?

"Who do you think did it, Allie?" she asked. "You're the murder mystery expert."

"No, I'm—"

"You solved Marigold's murder."

Solved was a stretch. *Helped solve* was more accurate. "I don't have a clue."

"Did anything stick out to you at the crime scene?"

"Not that I can share."

"Good for you," she said. "Zach would want you to keep mum."

Yes, he would. He'd also like me to butt out, truth be known.

The door to the shop opened, and Lillian swept inside carrying a dress bag. "I have costumes," she trilled. She was so buoyant, she must not have heard about Jason. I was reluctant to tell her. "Finette, hello, sugar." She joined us at the sales counter and slung the dress bag over a ladder-back chair. "How is your great-aunt doing?"

"Not well." Finette's eyes brimmed with tears again. "She's so frail, she can barely take care of herself. With Mom and Dad gone and my older sister living in Arizona, it's all falling on me. I have to consider whether to ask a judge to appoint me my great-aunt's conservator, so I can force her to move into a retirement facility before she falls and hurts herself. Did you know I had to take her car and keys away last year?"

"No," Lillian said, a fervent audience.

"She was livid."

"I'll bet."

"She can be so intractable," Finette went on. "Like all the women in my family." She made a dismissive sound. "I saw her last night to discuss other possibilities, but of course she won't even remember I was there, reading to her until midnight. I read her favorite book, too. *Great Expectations*. Why she loves the story astounds me."

"But you do it," Lillian said.

"Yes, I do it because . . ." Tears leaked from her eyes. She swiped them away. "Because I love her."

"It's tragic," Lillian said. "We shouldn't have to outlive our due date, should we?"

"*Ooh*, Lillian!" Finette squealed. "How could you be so callous?" She pressed the wadded tissue to her eyes, collected her bookshop bag, and hurried out.

Lillian watched her go and turned back to us. "What did I say?"

"Jason Gardner is dead," Tegan said.

"What!" Lillian exclaimed.

"Murdered," I added. *Before his due date*, I thought morosely.

Chloe jutted a hand toward Finette's retreating figure. "She's taking it very personally."

"Who killed him?" Lillian asked.

We filled her in with as much as we knew, each of us providing a piece of the story.

"Poor Finette," Lillian said. "She adored him. I know some folks in town didn't appreciate him, but I think he would've grown on all of us in time. He was so debonair." She eyed the dress bag. "Why don't we review costumes another time, when the mood is a tad brighter?"

"What a good idea," Tegan said.

Lillian hoisted the dress bag and left.

As the door swung shut, I wondered if I should reach out to my parents. They were pushing seventy, not old-old, but they were always traveling. How many more years did they have on this earth? The last time I'd seen them was at Marigold's memorial. They'd made a special visit because of my relationship with her.

While Chloe and Tegan tended to the customers who were ready to check out, I took my sandwich to the office, sat at the desk and, using my cell phone, dialed my mother. Darcy joined me, nestling into my lap. I could feel his heart beating against my thighs.

My mother answered after one ring.

"Hi, Fern." Neither of my parents liked to be referred to as Mom or Dad. They'd believed I would grow up faster if I used their formal names. Friends had always questioned me about it. I'd shrugged and said my parents were stubborn in their ways.

"Hello, Cookie."

Over the years, Fern had used only one nickname for me. She preferred calling me Allie. Although she and my dad had taught me to be in charge of my fate at an early age, they had been adamant I not eat too much sugar. They'd indulged me with a single cookie a week. One. *Big whoop.* Doesn't it figure that later on I would adore sugary treats and, of all things, would become a baker?

"Where are you these days?" I asked. They enjoyed traveling to exotic places.

"Machu Picchu."

I was familiar with the area because I'd done a report in high school about the fifteenth-century Incan citadel, often referred to as the Lost City of the Incas. Point of fact: Most archeologists believed the citadel was the estate of the Incan emperor Pachacuti.

"How's the weather?" I asked.

"Temperate, because the Urubamba River flows past the citadel and cuts through the Cordillera Mountains, creating a tropical mountain climate."

"Are you reading the words off a brochure?"

She chuckled. "You caught me. This trip was your father's decision. Next one's mine. I'm thinking Antarctica. I'd love to see penguins in their natural habitat. Oh, to be at the end of the world, where there's absolutely no permanent human habitation." She sighed dreamily. "So . . ." She dragged out the word, as if expecting me to speak. When I didn't, she said, "Why are you calling? Are you okay?"

"I'm fine."

"Liars never prosper," she cautioned.

"I don't lie." *Or rarely do*, I mused. If only I hadn't to Zach.

"Then you're stretching the truth. Spill. Don't tell me there's been another murder."

"Mom." I didn't regret using the term. "How did you guess? Yes. A man. A developer. I found him."

"Heavens, Allie, you stumbled upon another body? Your karma is totally out of whack."

I couldn't disagree.

"Bramblewood is so dangerous," she added.

"Every place in the world has its issues. Even Machu Picchu."

"Why haven't I read anything about the murder?"

Why would you have? I mused. She read newsletters like *Abstract and Applied Analysis* and *Duke Mathematical Journal*. Those kinds of publications kept her up-to-date about scientific and statistical discoveries. She'd always hoped I'd follow in her footsteps, but math and I were not friends. Chemistry, yes. Math, no. I'd needed Tegan's help to get me through calculus.

"When did it happen?" she asked.

"Last night. He was new to town. He was working on securing the right to build a mall on the four historic properties across the street from the Congregational church."

"The nerve. Those are sacred homes. Originals." Her fevered pitch surprised me. She didn't care a fig about Bramblewood. She'd never enjoyed living here, hence the reason she and my father were in constant motion, spending their life savings, of which they had plenty. My father, a knowledgeable and successful venture capitalist until he retired, had invested wisely. "Did you know your nana's best friend lived in the blue Victorian with white trim?"

"She did?"

"Yes. Her name was Cora Yeager."

"Interesting. Reika Moore, who runs the history museum, said Cora was her mother's best friend, too."

"Everybody knew Cora." Fern chuckled. "She was a rascal. And quite wealthy."

"I heard the Yeagers owned all the properties."

"Yes. Four in a row. Her family were original settlers. After they passed on, she rented the homes but never divested herself of them. When her daughter was a teenager, the girl wanted to move north to pursue a career on Broadway, but Cora put her foot down." She took a deep breath. "'Absolutely not. You will live and die in Bramblewood,'" Fern said in an emotive, actressy way, contrary to her own steady voice. "Years later, her daughter married and had a child. When the girl was four, Cora's daughter and her husband relocated to New York. After they moved, Cora declined, went into a nursing home, and, still upset with her daughter, left all the properties to Bramblewood as a gift."

"Did Cora have any skeletons in the closet that might have pitted the town against preserving the properties?" I mean, why else would they want to sell the properties, unless Bramblewood needed the cash?

"I haven't a clue." Fern cleared her throat. "Allie, what are you going to do?"

"About?"

"You solved Marigold's murder. Will you dig into this one? After all, you stumbled upon the body. Do you have any theories?"

"Fern . . ." I paused, choosing my words carefully. "I should mention I'm a suspect."

"Wh-what?" she stammered. "How in the world . . . ?"

I explained the circumstantial evidence—the spearhead, the Celtic knot earring, my presence, the missing text messages. "Also, I objected to Jason destroying the historic sites. Detective Armstrong—"

"The good-looking man your father and I met at the memorial? I remember him well. What a charmer. Are you two still dating?"

"No. It didn't work out." Was Zach holding a grudge about our breakup? Was it even a breakup? After all, we'd dated such a short time.

"Is he the lead investigator? He'd better not be railroading you so he doesn't appear to be biased in your favor."

"He's not." At least I hoped that didn't factor into his reasoning. "He's not one to jump to conclusions, but finding my missing earring at the site is pretty damning."

"As is the weapon the murderer used. I always hated those artifacts," Fern said. "Your father was enamored with the idea of having something original to the land hanging in the house."

"Really?"

"His father was into historical things, although he wasn't himself. I think your grandfather would have loved to have been an explorer and discovered new worlds. He often visited archaeological digs to get a preview of what scientists were unearthing."

I hadn't known my grandfather well. I was four when he

died. But I remembered my father telling colorful stories about him.

"You do what you need to, to exonerate yourself," Fern cautioned. "I presume Tegan will help you. She's a smart girl."

"Yes. She'll help, as will a few others." I smiled at the notion of Allie's Clue Crew. "I should get back to work."

"Keep me in the loop."

When I ended the call, Darcy leaped onto the desk and mewed. Was he hungry, or was he telling me he, too, was one of my staunch supporters?

I inspected his toenail, which looked a whole heap better, and pulled him into my lap. "Who did it, sir?" I asked. "Who killed Jason Gardner?"

Chapter 11

"*I hope she'll be a fool—that's the best thing a girl can be in this world, a beautiful little fool.*"

—Daisy Buchanan in F. Scott Fitzgerald's *The Great Gatsby*

At the end of the day, Vanna begged off helping me bake. She'd scored a gig preparing dinner for the mayor. How could I tell her to pass it up? So rather than go to Dream Cuisine, I went home, preferring to be in a cozy environment while I made the goods for tomorrow's deliveries and tested a couple of the recipes I wanted to serve at the *Gatsby* party.

On my cell phone, I selected a Spotify playlist of 1920s-era music that included jazz, swing, and ragtime and channeled it through the Bluetooth speaker. The bouncy "Maple Leaf Rag" started playing.

I pocketed my cell phone and released Darcy from his carrier. He bounded across the living room. "Hold on, mister. I need to check your surroundings."

I picked him up, set him in the alcove by the dining table to observe, ordered him to stay put, and strode to the fireplace. He must've realized I was serious, because he sat as still as a statue. I got down on my knees and ran my palms across the flooring and the stones of the hearth. I didn't find anything that might snag his toenails or pads.

I peered at him over my shoulder. "Where did you hurt yourself?"

He mewed, clueless, it seemed.

I bent lower to peer under the armchair. At the same time my cell phone rang. I pulled it from my pocket. Tegan was calling. I answered.

"Help me!" she pleaded.

I scrambled to my feet. "What's wrong?"

"I have to do an intervention with Mom."

"Oh, geez." Relief swept over me. She wasn't hurt. She hadn't been mugged on the way home, not that she would be in Bramblewood. Purse snatchings weren't common. "Is that all?"

"Is that all?" She sounded half hysterical.

"I have to bake."

"Pretty please? Afterward, I'll help you."

I laughed out loud. "As if." Like Chloe, Tegan wasn't much of a cook. Too wrapped up in a book or a tech project, she'd lose track of time. "I'll give you an hour."

"Bless you. Would you bring cookies? Mom's favorites are—"

"Double-chocolate chip. Yes, I'll bring some." I always kept a stash in the freezer. They defrosted well without losing any flavor or texture.

I fed Darcy, checked his water, told him to behave, and headed to the B&B.

Helga met me in the foyer and instantly wrinkled her nose when she saw I was carrying a white pastry box with my signature label. "We have had dessert already," she said stiffly.

"Yes, but these are for Noeline. Tegan is worried about her."

Helga folded her hands. "All right. I will allow it. She did not taste the chocolate cream pie I made." She lowered her voice. "Between you and me, Noeline is losing weight. I am not sure if it is because of that man."

That man was the one Noeline had been dating until things soured.

"I try to get her to eat more," Helga said, "but she waves me off."

Tegan could be right about her mother doing too much. The anxiety might be squelching her appetite. "I'll make sure she eats at least one."

"She is in the kitchen with Tegan. Also, if you will stop in the office first and tell Patrick to mute the noise. It bothers the guests." She proceeded into the nearby parlor.

What noise? I wondered. I didn't hear anything overt. And why was Patrick here so late? Was he falling behind, or had he hung around in hopes of seeing Tegan?

I swung by the office and paused at the doorway. Patrick was buffing the wall with a flat piece of sandpaper, whistling "American Idiot," another Green Day song. Clearly, he had a favorite band. The whistling wasn't loud. Helga was being a curmudgeon.

"Hi, Patrick. Sorry to bother you."

He glanced over his shoulder, and his eyes narrowed. Had dust flown into them? He wasn't wearing goggles.

"Helga requested you whistle softer." I pinched two fingers together to signify the words *Mute it*.

His glower morphed into a grin, and he gestured as if locking his lips.

I continued on to the kitchen. Tegan and her mother were standing on the far side of the center island. Noeline's arms were folded. Tegan's were spread wide.

"All I'm saying, Mom—" She caught sight of me. "You talk to her, Allie." She huffed and mirrored her mother's posture.

"Hi, Noeline. Is Tegan being bossy?"

"You might call it that." The right side of Noeline's mouth quirked up with humor.

"Some wingman you are," Tegan groused at me.

"I didn't promise to take your side." I popped open the box of cookies. "Double-chocolate chip."

Noeline snatched one and hummed as she bit into it. "Yum."

"All I'm saying," Tegan continued, "while your mouth is full and you can't respond, is owning and operating two bed-and-breakfasts seems like a major undertaking."

"I heard you the first time," Noeline said around a second bite of cookie.

"Will you hire another manager? Who will you hire as the housekeeper and cook? Helga can't be in two places at once. You're not being reasonable, Mother."

Noeline swallowed and brushed a crumb from the corner of her mouth. "And you're not listening to my explanation, Daughter. I told you before, Helga has a friend who is equally efficient and talented, and she will be available. As for an additional manager, I can oversee both."

"All the extra registrations? All the additional requests for tour suggestions?"

Noeline blew a raspberry. "I can do it in my sleep."

"What if something breaks? Like a water heater or the stoves or—"

"The place is in mint condition."

"Or the roof falls in?"

"Patrick or one of his crew is perfectly capable of reroofing it. End of discussion." She took another cookie and left the room.

Tegan sank onto a stool by the island. "Well, that went well. Not."

I sat on the other stool, our knees nearly touching. "Can you imagine if I told Fern what to do? You have to honor your mom's wishes. She's a grown woman. She's capable. She's made this place into a destination spot. And she's been a tad despondent ever since . . ." I paused.

"Ever since he-who-shall-not-be-named left the picture. Yeah, don't remind me." She grunted.

Not long ago Noeline dated a financial consultant and hoped he would become the next love of her life. She hadn't fallen for anyone since Tegan's father died. The consultant raised money for the hospital and seemed nice enough, but he turned out to be a rotter. He had never loved Noeline. He'd used her. Since their breakup, she had devoted herself to work and had vowed she would never date again. As a result, Tegan and Vanna had been highly protective of her.

"Too much idle time can mess with one's mind," I went on.

"'Idle hands are the devil's playground,' Helga says."

"So did Benjamin Franklin." I peeked over my shoulder. "By the way, why is Patrick here so late?"

"He promised Mom he'd make his completion date come hell or high water."

"A sense of responsibility. Good to hear."

"Helga doesn't like him."

I grinned. "I know. She asked me to tell him to keep the noise to a minimum."

"He is quite the whistler."

"And ruggedly handsome."

"Ahem." She cleared her throat. "Might I remind you he and Jason went at it at the shop? Patrick worried Jason would trash up the place. Jason shot back with his own snipe, something about Patrick having a sketchy past. If Patrick is the kind of person to hold a grudge, he could be a killer."

I gasped. She'd thought the same thing I had? "Yes, they fought, but they reconciled, and Jason hired Patrick to repair the back porch at the estate."

"Says who?"

"Patrick. They bumped into each other at town hall and worked out their grievances."

She raised an eyebrow skeptically. "And you believed him?"

"Well . . ." Did I? I hadn't swung by town hall to investigate whether anyone had witnessed their ceasefire.

"Yeah, I knew it. You're as curious as I am." She squinted one eye. "He should definitely be on Zach's suspect list."

"But he couldn't have killed Jason. This morning, when I brought him and his crew muffins, with no prompting, he told me he went caving last night."

"Yeah?" Tegan sniggered. "He just happened to tell you his alibi?"

She was right. He could have been covering his tracks. "I noticed his shoes were muddy, and mentioned it. He said the caverns are always wet."

"Hold on! You saw mud on his shoes? Meaning he might have been the one to track mud into Jason's foyer?" She leaped off her stool. "Let's ask him about it." She purposefully strode down the hall.

I raced to catch up. "Don't attack him."

"Moi? Je ne l'accuserai pas." She swatted the air.

My French was nearly nonexistent—I'd taken Spanish in high school—but I recognized the word *accuse* in her sentence and knew that *Je ne* meant "I won't," so I breathed easier.

"I'll be charm personified," she added and shimmied her shoulders.

"Hello, Patrick," she crooned as she entered the room.

He was stretching. The hem of his work shirt had risen above the waistband of his jeans, revealing a firm set of abs. Quickly, he lowered his arms. "Hi, ladies." He shifted the gum he was chewing to the inside of his cheek. "I stopped whistling."

"Not on our account, I hope." Tegan used a lusty come-hither voice. "I like when you whistle."

Patrick's cheeks flushed pink.

"Actually," she continued, "I wanted to talk to you about your specialty diet. You're a raw-food omnivore, I hear."

Phew. She didn't lead with mud.

"Meaning you eat raw eggs and raw meat and raw vegetables, but cooked foods and processed grains are a no-no, right?"

He nodded.

"And yet you eat muffins." She winked at him, and I had to marvel at how perfectly she was acting, having never taken to the stage.

"I have a weakness." He chuckled shyly.

"Allie tells me you went caving last night," she said.

Sheesh. Too direct. I held my breath.

"What's it like?" she continued. "I've never been caving."

His nervousness eased, and he became animated. "It's, like, so cool. I could take you sometime." His hands soared through the air. "The bats are amazing."

"Bats? I love bats."

Liar. She didn't like spiders or anything creepy-crawly. Once when we were tweens, we sneaked into an abandoned house. We'd ridden our bikes to get there. Someone had told us ghosts inhabited it. We didn't encounter any, but we ran into so many cobwebs, our hair was covered with spiders. Tegan screamed and screamed. After I batted the spiders off her and made sure my hair was spider free, we raced home... and never told a soul.

I grinned. "What she means is, she likes Batman."

"Yeah? Me too." Patrick's mouth curved up on one side.

"The comics, not the movies."

"Ditto. And I like goblins and ghosts—"

"Allie has a ghost kitchen." Tegan motioned to me.

"I've heard of ghost kitchens. Is there really a ghost in yours?" Patrick made an eerie *ooh* sound and wiggled his fingers.

"I sure hope not."

As if roused by spirits, the bookcase that was separated from the wall to my right pitched forward. I pushed Tegan out of the way. Straight into Patrick's arms. A split second later the bookcase crashed to the floor. Dust billowed. Tegan eeked.

"Whoa!" Patrick said, holding her tightly. "Did not see that coming. You okay?"

"Y-yes," she stammered, but she wasn't. She was shaking like a leaf.

Tegan was so spooked, she didn't press Patrick further about the mud—neither did I—and she elected to stay the night at the inn, supposedly to protect her mother, though I was pretty sure she wanted her mother to comfort her.

After assuring her ghosts didn't exist at the B&B, nor did any spiders or bats, I went home. But, admittedly, the event had freaked me out. For a long while, I cuddled Darcy to calm myself. Once my nerves were steadied, I started in on the scones and muffins for tomorrow's delivery to Whispering Winds, a rival bed-and-breakfast to the Blue Lantern. The inn rarely ordered from me, only when their live-in cook was sick or on vacation.

When two dozen of each were in the ovens and I'd set the timers, I decided to tackle a couple of vintage 1920s dessert recipes.

While researching the era to create the menu for the party, I discovered orange-drop cookies had been in fashion. Why? Due to the war and the inaccessibility of traveling to Europe and the Mediterranean, Florida had come into fashion, as had California, with its burgeoning movie industry. Both states boasted gigantic citrus groves, and with the development of refrigerated railroad cars, citrus fruits became popular. Suddenly, fresh-squeezed orange juice at breakfast was in demand.

Orange-drop cookies were easy to make. For a twist on the standard, I decided we'd also offer blood-orange crinkles.

While I squeezed oranges and prepared the dough for the orange-drop cookies, I couldn't stop thinking about Jason and Delilah and Jay Gatsby and Daisy. Though Gatsby, because of his idealism, was worthy of honor, he had a fatal flaw. He erred when loving Daisy, and when he heroically defended her after the car crash, he received his own unjust punishment. Jason had also been an idealist. Had his love for Delilah weakened him? I recalled mentioning to Zach how Jason had uttered a syllable of Delilah's name as he lay dying. What if, as Tegan had theorized, Delilah was in town, and Jason had been trying to tell me he'd let down his guard and invited her into his home and she'd stabbed him? Was Zach considering this possibility?

Who else might be on his radar, other than me? I started to text him about Delilah, but before pressing Send, I erased the text. He wasn't going to reveal anything. He was troubled by me. Why? Did he really believe I was capable of murder? Had he focused on me as the main suspect because the weapon used to kill Jason was, indeed, my spearpoint? Could two spearpoints be identical?

"Crud," I murmured. If I hadn't mentioned that the spearpoint resembled mine, Zach might never have thought—

Stop, Allie. You had to tell him. You did the right thing.

"Double crud," I muttered.

Darcy mewed from the other side of the Plexiglas door and pawed it.

"It's okay, sir. I'm all right." I caught sight of my laptop computer on the island. If Zach hadn't researched Delilah, I should. And perhaps I should do an Internet search on others I suspected of murder.

After preparing a sheet of orange-drop cookies and removing the scones and muffins from the oven, I opted to take a fifteen-minute break and opened the computer. The screen came to life with a picture of Darcy sitting atop the head of his llama cat-scratching station.

I clicked on the Word icon and created a new blank document. For a header, I typed the words *Jason Gardner Murder*.

Once an English major, always an English major. Before

writing any thesis, I created an outline, laying out the points of my introductory paragraph, which then led to the orderly body of the thesis and ended with a well-supported conclusion, in this case, the identity of a killer.

"These are my top three suspects," I said to the cat. "Patrick, Reika, and Iggie."

I designed a three-column grid and typed each of their names in a column. Patrick, because he thought Jason would ruin the ecosphere of Bramblewood, not to mention Jason had humiliated him at the shop. Reika, because she was ardent about wanting the properties to be ceded to the preservation society. Iggie, because he had wanted to build on the properties and begrudged Jason's ability to waltz in and seal the deal.

"And possibly Delilah, if she's in town," I added.

Darcy sat on the other side of the Plexiglas door, staring at me and listening with rapt attention.

"Can you think of anyone else, sir?"

He tilted his head.

I added a column on the right, entered Delilah's name, and then opened an Internet browser. I typed Delilah's married name into the search bar. Images of her popped up, as well as links to her social media accounts. She was no longer an art curator, it appeared. She was an in-demand personal shopper, who shared everything she purchased with her viewers. That gave me pause. Patrick had accused Jason of building the mall to lure Delilah to town. At the time, I couldn't fathom why he'd have thought a mall would be enticing. This new twist made sense. If she was an influencer, building an upscale mall with her tastes in mind might be the ticket.

I scrolled down and stopped on one of the images showing her at a gala that took place last night in Hollywood. She was on the arm of a very handsome man and was glowing with happiness. The caption cited the man as her husband, who was, as

Jason had stated, a vintner and renowned art collector. Dozens of eyewitnesses were grinning in the background. Something felt off about the picture. Studying the image harder, I realized Delilah wasn't merely glowing. She was pregnant. The baby bump was small and fairly hidden under the Empire-style dress she had on, but I was certain I was right.

Had learning of the pregnancy stunned Jason and caused him to abandon the project in Santa Monica?

No matter what, the photo gave Delilah a verifiable alibi, so I left her column empty and proceeded to research the others.

Patrick Hardwick's alibi of going caving by himself was, as Tegan had suggested, flimsy. No witnesses. No proof. His claim that he'd muddied his shoes at the site sounded reasonable, but he'd looked nervous when I'd raised the issue.

"What did Jason mean when he said, 'Memories of one's mistakes rarely fade'?" Did Patrick have a criminal record? An illegitimate child? I doubted he and his parents were in WITSEC.

I typed the phrase *What's his secret?* in Patrick's column.

Darcy leaped to the top of the llama and immediately bounded down to peer at me through the Plexiglas.

"Didn't that hurt your toenail?" I asked.

The cat whisked his tail, signifying it did not, and looked from me to the top of the llama and back.

"Aha! Yes. Smart cat. A deep dive is necessary." He wasn't really implying anything of the sort. He wanted me to play. "First, however, we should learn a tad about Jason, don't you think?"

I typed his name into the search bar. A number of projects he'd built appeared as images. Most were beautiful in design. In Seattle. In San Francisco. In Aspen, Colorado. His style was akin to I. M. Pei's. I discovered a few links to articles that described his work. I skimmed them and couldn't find one person who'd claimed a design was shoddy. A link to an article about the building he hadn't completed in Santa Monica, California, popped up. I clicked on it. The image of the shell of a building was front and center. The lede read, *Builder dumps mall project, leaves pristine area in shambles.* Reading on, I learned Jason hadn't explained why he'd abandoned the mall, but it had occurred about four months ago.

"Delilah," I whispered. "It had to have been because of her."

Next, I researched Patrick and found dozens of images of him going caving and engaging with bats. Others showed him at eco-warrior events. At one, he'd encountered former Vice President Al Gore, possibly the most high-powered eco-warrior in history. On his Facebook page, Patrick had posted videos explaining, close up and personal, what a raw diet consisted of. The same videos were published on his YouTube page. I viewed the Yelp page for Hardwick Construction and hit upon dozens of positive reviews touting his work ethic, skill, and honesty. An interview in the *Bramblewood Times* provided a detailed biography of one of Bramblewood's most eligible bachelors, with images of Patrick, first as a boy on the farm, then as a senior in high school presented with running back awards, and lastly as an adult pounding nails into walls and repairing rooftops.

In a recent photo of him at Raven's Roost, a beginner's cliff that offered incredible views, he was mugging to the camera while dangling off the cliff, holding on by one hand. I recalled my theory—he could climb Mount Everest one-handed—and figured this baby cliff was a snap for him. I smiled when I viewed a video of him at a karaoke bar, rocking out with two of his crew. The song was "When I Come Around," another Green Day hit. All in all, he seemed like a nice guy, and most likely was not guilty. Plus I couldn't figure out how he would've known about my spearhead collection . . . until I remembered he'd come to a book club event at my place about six months ago.

I copied links from images and articles into Patrick's column.

Darcy thwacked the kitchen door with his paw.

"Stop. You might hurt your—" I paused. Was that how he'd injured his toenail? No, there had been drops of blood on the hearth, not by the kitchen.

He yowled. Not in pain. In irritation.

"Yes, I know. It's getting late. But I'm not done."

I fetched his favorite mouse toy, opened the door, hurled the toy into the living room, and shut the door. Then I slipped the cookie sheet of orange-drop cookies into the oven, switched on the timer, and prepared the blood-orange dough.

While it rested, I considered Ignatius Luckenbill II, who had adamantly wanted the properties Jason had been trying to secure. Why those properties? Were his other projects failing? Did he think building homes at such a visible site would drum up more business?

A Wikipedia page revealed he'd worked on construction crews while attending college, meaning not only did he know how to run a company, but he also would be familiar with tools. He had never been to my house. Had he learned from someone else about my spearpoints? Might he have a collection of his own? His father had been an adventurer. I continued browsing. During college, Iggie had earned degrees in law, business, and architecture. *Wow. A triple threat.*

Afterward, he took over his father's business, which he'd inherited because his father died of a heart attack at the age of fifty. *Young,* I thought and whistled. I didn't realize how long ago he'd passed. I quickly researched the man's demise and discovered that over the years, he'd had fainting spells. When he learned he had bradycardia, he was fitted with a pacemaker. An autopsy was performed after his death, and the coroner determined Senior had thick heart muscles, which made it difficult to pump blood out of the ventricles. No foul play had been involved.

I jotted notes in Iggie's column and dove deeper into the *Bramblewood Times* archives, where I landed on a couple more articles about him. One featured an interview in which he bragged he had a Biltmore-sized deal coming up. Had he been referring to the four properties in Bramblewood? Had he intended to build a hotel there? No, the property where the inn on Biltmore Estate was located consisted of eight thousand acres. At most, the four properties comprised ten acres.

I revisited Iggie's Wiki page and scrolled down to details of his personal life. He was married to Shayna, née Jensen, his second wife. His first wife, unnamed, moved to Charlotte and took the children. Neither of the grown children were in real estate or construction. His current wife didn't work. She donated her time to worthy causes in Asheville. *Worthy causes* could be a veiled way of saying she donated a lot of cash to passion projects, prompting me to wonder if Iggie needed money because his beloved was bleeding him dry. It also caused me to wonder if one of the children had composed the Wikipedia page on their father's behalf, little digs being part and parcel of a broken family.

I added links for Iggie's info into his column and eyed Reika's name.

"One of the neighbors said a dog barked," I murmured. Reika had a dog. A yappy dog.

I imagined a possible scenario. Reika didn't live far from the Sugarbaker estate. While walking her dog, she might have gotten a bee in her bonnet about how much she wanted the preservation society to have the Yeager properties, and in an effort to convince Jason not to follow through with his purchase, she headed there. She might not have been aware of the hour. She didn't wear a watch. Perhaps she saw Jason moving about in his gardens. To seem less confrontational, she tied Amira to a tree before approaching, but being tethered made the dog bark.

After all the time I'd spent with Reika, I knew a lot about her without having to search the Internet. She and her descendants had lived in North Carolina for as long as the state had been in existence. She had been married once, but he'd died. I recalled someone telling me it had been under questionable circumstances, but I couldn't remember who.

When I was talking to her at the history museum this morning, she'd offered her alibi for last night—reading the same book we'd read for book club. She said she often reread books. Her claim hadn't bothered me then, but now it did. Why? I often read books more than once. I'd devoured every Agatha Christie I owned so often the pages were worn on the corners. I'd read *Gone Girl* three times to learn which clues I'd missed. *The Thursday Murder Club* had required a couple of readings, as well, in order to understand each point of view. So, finding fault with Reika for perusing a book a second time shouldn't have nagged at me, but it had sounded like a lie.

I jotted a note in her column and reviewed my list from a distance.

"Is there another suspect?" I murmured. "What about Finette Fineworthy?"

Darcy, realizing I was nowhere near ready for bed, dropped to the dining room floor with a *thwump* and curled into a ball.

Finette was close to Jason. She might have been in love with him, which meant she probably hadn't killed him. What if she had professed her love, and he had rebuffed her?

"No. She'd have wanted him to remain alive. She couldn't win him over if he was dead."

Iggie had hinted that Jason was paying Finette. For what?

Her sway with the town council? If she was accepting a bribe because she needed money, it would be another reason to keep Jason alive. If he was dead, he couldn't make good on a debt.

I added Finette's name with a question mark, to be revisited if a stronger motive occurred to me.

The timer went off.

At the same time, the doorbell rang.

Chapter 12

Each night he added to the pattern of his fancies until drowsiness closed down upon some vivid scene with an oblivious embrace.

—Nick Carraway in F. Scott Fitzgerald's *The Great Gatsby*

I yelped, and Darcy bolted into the living room and cowered by the sofa.

"Silly cat, it's okay." I exited the kitchen. "It's not the murderer coming to kill me. He or she wouldn't ring the bell." Zach typically knocked, so it wasn't him. I peeked through the peephole and said to the cat, "Friend, not foe." I unlocked the door and greeted Vanna. "Hi."

"Why aren't you at Dream Cuisine?" she asked.

"Why aren't you home in bed after your big soiree?"

"It was so successful, I needed to burn off some energy. I'm here to help you with tomorrow's orders."

"In that getup?" She was in a sleeveless aqua sheath and stiletto heels.

"I'll go barefoot." She kicked off her heels and made smooching sounds while beckoning Darcy with her fingertips. "Here, kitty." She loved cats but didn't own one. Too much responsibility. Whenever she stopped in, she engaged in a huge lovefest. Darcy accepted the attention, purring as she scrubbed him behind the ears and under the chin.

"What did you serve tonight?" I asked.

She rose, and Darcy bounded into the barrel of the llama. "For the appetizer, I served *rucolo burrata*." She smiled smugly, adding for my edification, "Arugula with tomato and balsamic dressing. The burrata cheese was exquisite. For the entrée, I offered duck confit with pesto cream or *gnocchi al pesto* with a basil cream sauce. Two men from the town council attended, as did a few of the elders from the Congregational church and the municipal court judge." She nodded her head toward the kitchen. "What's the timer for?"

"Yipes! I almost forgot I'm baking desserts for the *Gatsby* event to taste test." I raced to the kitchen, slipped on mitts, and withdrew the orange-drop cookies from the oven. Luckily, they hadn't burned.

Vanna padded in, closed the door, and went to the sink to wash her hands. Afterward, she threw on an apron and a mesh hat. I kept plenty on hand. "What are they?" She motioned to the baking sheet.

I told her.

"They smell divine. May I?"

"Please."

She lifted one and nibbled the edge. "Yum. Light yet satisfying. But don't you want to have something more complex for dessert? Other than the pineapple upside-down cake, of course."

"We will, but these also have a significance to the era." I quickly explained their origin story.

She pointed at the bowl resting on the island. "What's that for?"

"Blood-orange crinkles."

"Love the name. Very mysterious. What other foods are you considering? My mind has been whirling. What about duchesse potatoes? And crown roast of pork with mushroom dressing?"

"A tad too fancy for the bookstore. Perfect for a sit-down themed dinner, though."

"Roasted chicken with rosemary was popular. We could do chicken wings similarly."

"Good idea."

"And sugar-glazed ham was in."

"You've been doing your homework."

She smiled at the compliment. "By the way, Tegan texted me on my way over. Holy moly, there's a ghost living at the Blue Lantern?"

"There are no ghosts at the inn. The bookshelf Patrick removed was resting unsteadily against the wall."

"And a ghost pushed it over."

I laughed. "No."

"Is Tegan concerned about Mother buying another bed-and-breakfast because she's afraid the place is haunted?"

"Hardly. She's worried your mother will be in over her head. Where will she find another gem like Helga? Not to mention managing two places can be daunting."

"Tegan should give it a rest," Vanna said. "Mother is capable. At worst, she'll hire an assistant manager."

"She intends to manage both herself."

Vanna scoffed. "Ha! She'll learn soon enough she can't do that. What if a fire needs to be doused at one while the pipes burst at the other?"

What dire scenarios, I mused but said, "Tegan feels the same."

Vanna wagged her head. "I'll have a chat with Mother. Hiring a second-in-command is vital."

I coughed, knowing her advice would fall on deaf ears, like Tegan's had. Noeline's mind was made up. And she, like her daughters, could be mighty stubborn. "FYI, Patrick took full blame for the bookshelf mishap. He was talking about caving and bats and began moaning like a ghost when *blam*"—I clapped my hands—"the thing fell. The timing of it was eerie."

"Patrick," Vanna said dismissively as she prepared a cookie sheet for the crinkles. "It's inappropriate for him to be working at the inn when he's obviously interested in Tegan."

I tilted my head. "Why is that inappropriate?"

"Because he'll drag the work out so he can catch glimpses of her and, therefore, overcharge Mother for his services."

"He won't. After all, he could go to the bookstore to see Tegan. Better yet, he could ask her out."

"Would she say yes?"

"I'm not sure." I smiled, remembering how comfortable Patrick had looked holding her in his arms. Though she'd been trembling, she hadn't seemed to mind his embrace. On the other hand, he was still on my suspect list, and pairing my best friend with a murderer was not the best idea. "I wouldn't worry about him price gouging your mother. He was working steadily both times I saw him today, and his business profile on Yelp has earned rave reviews."

I eyed the laptop computer, still open, with my deep-dive notes scrawled on it.

Vanna peeked in that direction. "Oho, what's this?" She scanned my suspect list. "Do you really think Patrick is the killer?"

"It's all conjecture."

"If he is, he'd better not date my sister."

"Noted." I appreciated her taking Tegan's side.

"You know, he has a sketchy past."

"Really?" My ears perked up.

"Back in high school, he made all sorts of prank calls to a girl he was hot for. She was scared out of her wits."

"You were in school together?"

"He was a senior. I was a freshman."

"You knew what he did, yet you were interested in him at one time?"

Her cheeks flushed pink. "I reasoned he was a kid then. Kids make mistakes. But let's face it. I was attracted because he's a hunk with a thriving business." She wrinkled her nose. "However, the raw-food omnivore thing really does turn my stomach."

Using a two-tablespoon scooper, she plunked twelve mounds of crinkle dough onto the cookie sheet, placed the sheet into the oven, and set a timer.

As she busied herself, I couldn't help recalling how Jason had taunted Patrick. *Memories of one's mistakes rarely fade.* A mistake sounded way worse than a prank. What else might Patrick have done as a child? Bullied someone? Cheated on an exam? Harmed an animal, heaven forbid? And how had Jason learned of it when I couldn't dredge it up on the Internet? Jason was a few years older than Patrick. I doubted the two had known each other as boys.

"As for Reika," Vanna said, reviewing my notes, "she's a gem. Surely, she's not the killer."

I told her about the dog and the scream and Reika hedging about her alibi.

"It does sound iffy," Vanna said. "I never read a book twice if I can help it."

I smiled.

"Did the neighbor say how the dog bark sounded?" she asked. "They all have distinctive yips."

"He imitated it, like a throaty bark." I wondered if Zach had followed up.

"And the scream, was it high-pitched or guttural, like someone yelling in fear or rage?"

"The witness said it was distant but shrill." I wriggled with unease.

"As for Iggie . . ." Vanna tapped the island with a fingernail.

"He's a jerk. He has maligned so many of his competitors and ruined their reputations. He even forced a few out of business."

"That seems like a better reason for him to be dead than Jason."

"True. Should we box these?" She gestured to the cooled muffins and scones.

"Good idea."

I fetched some cardstock boxes, and we folded them into containers. I tended to the scones. Vanna managed the muffins.

"You know..." She attached labels to the boxes she'd filled. "I wouldn't put it past Iggie to have killed a competitor. I mean, from what I heard, his father's death was suspicious."

"The coroner labeled it a natural death."

"Humph."

I cringed. Was she right? Had Iggie somehow helped his father along to the next world in order to inherit the business?

Vanna smiled. "I'm starting to like being a member of hashtag Allies, no apostrophe, ClueCrew."

"Stop."

"It's making my little gray cells work. Isn't that what Hercule Poirot says? I've never read Agatha Christie's books, but I've seen a couple of the movies. I particularly like the ones starring Ewan McGregor. He's dishy. But the mustache, ugh." She wriggled her nose.

I frowned, wondering how I could entice this woman to read more than cookbooks and chefs' bios. Maybe having a blind-date-with-a-book event at the shop, where we would wrap books in brown paper so readers wouldn't know the title or genre of the book they selected, would get her hooked. Somehow I'd make sure she chose *Murder on the Orient Express*, *The Mysterious Affair at Styles*, or *The Murder of Roger Ackroyd*, so she could get to know the real Poirot.

"Did you know Aunt Marigold, may she rest in peace"—Vanna pressed a hand over her heart—"had a run-in with Iggie years ago? He wanted to buy a bunch of properties on Main Street."

"He did?"

"Yes. Auntie was firmly against it and went to the town council to protest. Thanks to Finette Fineworthy, who put her foot down—Auntie and Finette collaborated to thwart him—Iggie was forced to set his sights on properties to the east of North Mountain Road, a prospect that didn't come to fruition, either."

His relationship with Finette was even more contentious than I'd imagined. *Interesting.*

Vanna yawned and covered her mouth with the back of her hand. "My, it's late. I've got to get some sleep. I'll be back first thing to deliver all of these. You did all the heavy lifting tonight."

I gawked at her, truly surprised by her largesse. Who was she? Why was she making nice? Had going into partnership with me and helping with the literary parties tapped into her deep-seated need to be part of a team? Whatever had instigated the change, I was loving it.

First thing in the morning, Vanna texted she was on the way. I'd barely slipped out of my nightshirt and wriggled into a pair of leggings and a T-shirt before she arrived with a to-go cup in hand.

"Here's hot coffee. Colombian roast. Medium-bodied, with citrusy acidity and hints of caramel." She thrust the cup at me and edged past. "I made it in my French press."

I took a sip and hummed my thanks. "Delicious."

"Hello, Darcy." She bent to pet him and stood up. "Are all the deliveries ready to go?"

"They are."

"Let's load me up." She'd dressed casually in jeans and a long-sleeved blouse. Nothing frou-frou. She'd even thrown on tennis shoes. She caught me eyeing her shoes and grinned. "Yes, you're having an effect on my style. Comfort is in."

As we carried boxes to her Nissan NV Cargo van, which was gleaming white in the morning sun, she said, "By the way, don't expect me to do all the deliveries every day."

"I would never—"

"A girl like me needs her beauty sleep."

"Of course."

"You, on the other hand . . ." She hesitated, as if doing her best to tamp down a snarky comment. "You, on the other hand, look good at any time of the day. You rock the no-makeup look."

It wasn't entirely a compliment, but it was better than "You look like garbage," which, in truth, I knew I did. I might have been able to slip on clothes before her arrival, but I hadn't had time to run a comb through my hair.

"Don't worry. I don't expect you to do all the deliveries. In fact, I like making the rounds and seeing the customers. But I appreciate you doing them today. We have a lot to arrange for the upcoming *Gatsby* party. Stop into the shop later, and we'll bring you up to speed on what we've got planned. Oh, and get excited! We're going to have a blind-date-with-a-book event soon."

"A what?"

I explained how it worked. "Will you come?"

"Sure, why not?"

"You might get hooked on a new genre."

"Don't count on it. I'm pretty particular."

Close-minded, I mused but kept mute.

After she drove off, I polished off my coffee, downed a protein drink, and fed Darcy. Then I showered and changed into black jeans, a short-sleeved silk blouse, and ballet slippers—I liked to dress up a tad for the bookstore crowd—and headed to Feast for the Eyes with Darcy.

Tegan and Chloe had arrived ahead of me.

"Morning," I chimed, breezing through the shop and situating the cat in the office. When I returned, I told them about the blind-date-with-a-book plan.

Tegan applauded. "Love it! Auntie used to do those all the time."

"It's precisely why I came up with the idea. I'm going to make sure Vanna gets a Poirot mystery."

Tegan chuckled. "She won't read it."

"She will if I make her promise. She's a woman in transition."

"Dream on."

Noeline entered the shop, a bag from Ragamuffin in one hand. In linen slacks and a floral camp shirt, she appeared blissful. Summery clothing suited her. "Tegan, I want to talk."

"Can't, Mom. How about lunch?"

"Please, darling."

"Sorry. We're busy."

Frowning, Noeline pivoted to leave, but the door opened, and Iggie plowed in, forcing Noeline to dodge into an aisle so she wouldn't be run over.

"I'm here to buy the new Patterson book." The flaps of Iggie's suit jacket flew open as he strode to the sales counter.

Tegan whispered to me, "He reads three bestsellers a year. Nothing else."

"*Aha.* He's one of those," I remarked. Lots of people did what Iggie did. They weren't real readers. They were the ones who liked to chat about bestsellers at work, around the watercooler, so they could appear well read and hip.

"Hurry up," Iggie said, spanking the sales counter.

"It's right there." Tegan pointed. "On the first endcap you passed. See it?"

"Go get it."

Tegan grunted softly, then signaled to Chloe to fetch it.

As Chloe was reaching for it, the front door opened again, and Finette whisked in, nearly ramming into Chloe.

I bit back a laugh. What was up with everyone? In a hurry? In a snit? Was a full moon on the rise? Maybe it was the heat.

"Sorry," Chloe said, though she wasn't at fault.

"Not to worry." A green Bottega Veneta tote dangled from Finette's right hand.

Seeing the bag surprised me. How could she afford such a pricey item on a councilperson's salary? On the other hand, lots of women saved up to buy one valuable accessory. Her shoes were simple. Her slacks and blouse looked off the rack.

"Good morning," Finette trilled, proceeding toward the sales counter. "I was wondering—" She halted in her tracks when she spotted Iggie. "You!" she said accusatorily.

"Me?" He whirled on her. "Don't you mean you? What is going on? Why did you curtail my bid on the Hanson Hotel?"

The property in question was the abandoned boardinghouse at the east end of town, which he'd been trying to acquire. The adult children, who all lived out of state, had agreed to cede it to Bramblewood in honor of their parents.

"You know I've wanted the property for years."

"Well, you snooze, you lose. Another buyer bid higher than you." Finette peered down her nose at him. "Your Realtor was informed. You didn't counter."

"I never saw a request."

"Then your Realtor isn't doing her job."

Iggie wagged a finger. "It's all Jason Gardner's fault."

"Whatever are you talking about?"

"He messed with your head. He . . . he pitted you against me and anyone who wants to build in Bramblewood. I want to preserve our town. I want to make it shine."

Give me a break. Iggie wasn't someone who wanted to preserve anything.

"Gardner made you careless," Iggie added.

Finette bridled. "I'm far from—"

"What happened between you two? Did you profess your love to him, and he rejected you?"

Finette gasped and pressed a hand to her chest. "Love?"

"Yeah." Iggie sneered. "You did, and he did, and his rebuff hurt your fragile ego. If I didn't know better"—he aimed a finger at her—"I'd say that gives you motive for murder."

"How dare you! How. Dare. You! I was friends with Jason. Friends," she snarled. "Murder him? Not on a bet."

"Where were you Monday night?" he demanded.

I watched the two of them like a tennis match, shocked by their public altercation, as if neither realized the rest of the world was tuning in.

"With my great-aunt," Finette said.

"Yeah? Did she remember you this time?"

"She never remembers me, you pig!" She raised a hand, as if ready to slap him. Thinking better of it, she raced from the shop without explaining the purpose of her visit.

Iggie, rousing as if from a drunken stupor, darted after her. "Finette, wait! I didn't mean it. Finette!"

Through the plate-glass window, I saw the councilwoman climb into her blue BMW coupe, which she'd parked on the street, and slam the door. Iggie reached the car and tried the passenger door. Locked. He pounded on the window. Finette made a rude gesture and screeched away.

Exasperated, Iggie swatted the rear of the car, a move that by sheer force swung him around. Realizing all of us were gawking at him, he marched to the shop's front door, whipped it open, and poked his head inside. "Hold the Patterson book for me. I'll be back."

Noeline emerged from the aisle into which she'd retreated and said, "Well, criminy! What a tornado of bad energy."

We all tittered nervously.

After a long moment of silence, Tegan said, "I can't believe they went at it. You'd think Finette, respecting her elevated position on the town council, would have some decorum. And Iggie? What a jerk. Accusing her in front of all of us. As if she could've killed Jason. Allie, you heard her extolling his virtues."

Noeline joined us. "Tegan's right. Finette's a good soul. She looks after her great-aunt. Iggie is a cretin."

"Iggie might have wanted to cast suspicion on someone else," Chloe suggested, plunking the Patterson novel onto the sales counter.

I said, "Vanna says he ruined a couple of his competitors' reputations."

"Indeed. An aspiring contractor, for one," Noeline said. "He built the small homes division to the east of Asheville." She wiggled her fingers. "You know the one I mean. Starter homes, each about three bedrooms. It was a huge hit. Half of the houses sold within six months. But then Iggie put out the word that the houses were cookie-cutter styles and lacking imagination and made of cheap wood, siding, and flooring. The remaining houses didn't sell, and the ones which had sold went back on the market. Presto!" She snapped her fingers. "The builder was ruined and left town with his tail between his legs. Last I heard, he went to Raleigh to live with his sister." She fanned the air. "And don't get me started about what happened to Stella Burberry's brother. It was appalling."

I knew Stella well. She was an accountant and an avid book club attendee. I occasionally prepared personal meals for her. She hated to cook. So, of course, I couldn't help asking, "What happened?"

"Her brother bid on three apartment complexes," Noeline said, "and each time, Iggie outbid him."

Apparently, Iggie did close some of the deals he negotiated.

"Outbidding another builder isn't unheard of, Mom," Tegan said. "Lots of people—"

"He paid the Realtor to get the inside scoop so he'd know how much to outbid!" Noeline growled.

"And the Realtor told him? Isn't that actionable?" I asked.

"Maybe. I don't know." Noeline sighed. "Even if it is, Iggie is despicable and deserves to die."

"Mother!" Tegan cried.

Noeline clamped a hand over her mouth. "I didn't mean it. No one deserves to . . . I didn't mean . . . Oh!" She sucked back a sob and hurried from the shop.

CHAPTER 13

I wasn't actually in love, but I felt a sort of tender curiosity.
—Nick Carraway in F. Scott Fitzgerald's *The Great Gatsby*

Around half past ten, I needed a snack. "Does anybody want something from Ragamuffin?"

Noeline had hurried off without leaving the goodies she'd brought in, and I was craving a raspberry scone. The sugar influx wouldn't be good for my overall sagging energy, but I didn't care.

"Cinnamon bun," Tegan requested.

"Ditto," Chloe chimed.

I grabbed my purse, told Darcy to sit tight, and left. As I drew near to my favorite coffeehouse, I saw Zach exiting the shop, a to-go bag in hand. He veered left.

I kicked up my pace and shouted, "Hey, Zach, wait up!"

He caught sight of me, and his brow puckered with a peeved expression.

"It's a beautiful morning," I said when I caught up to him.

He forced his face to go neutral. "It is."

"Listen, about me being at the history museum . . ."

"You have every right to visit our town's establishments." He started to pivot.

I tapped his arm. "Hold up. How is the investigation going?"

He swiveled back, the peeved look replanted on his face. "Allie, look, I can't talk about it."

"Because I'm a suspect?"

"I can't talk about it," he repeated like a robot on auto-repeat.

"Would you at least tell me whether you consider Patrick Hardwick a suspect?"

He didn't answer.

"What about Ignatius Luckenbill?"

"Ignatius Luckenbill is dead."

"I meant Junior, and you know it. Iggie the second. Is he on your radar?" When he didn't respond, I continued. "I heard him say to Finette if anybody was going to develop the historic properties Jason was bargaining for, it would be him."

"I'll bet lots of developers have said something similar."

"According to Noeline and Vanna, Iggie has a bad reputation for maligning his competitors."

"It is not against the law to malign another person as long as no action occurs. You've heard of freedom of speech. Nor is it against the law to crow about one's intentions."

His curt responses were getting under my skin, but I pressed on. "Did you ask about his alibi for Monday night?"

"I knew it."

"He has an alibi?"

"No." He sighed. "I knew you wouldn't be able to help yourself. You'd poke into things and come up with theories, like you did last time."

"Last time, my best friend was your main suspect. This time, I am."

"As a matter of fact, you are. You've got means, motive, and opportunity, and there was evidence of a struggle."

With my missing earring to show for it, I thought miserably. "Look, if you want to arrest me, arrest me." Brazenly, I jutted out my arms, wrists together. When he didn't latch cuffs on them, I breathed easier. "I'm not going to sit idle and let you do all the investigating when my neck is on the line. I told you, as a caterer and baker, I'm attuned to details. If I come across a clue, I'll share it."

"Allie..." He scrubbed one side of his head with his fingertips, clearly reluctant to say more.

"Go on. Something is eating at you. Speak. I'm tough. I can take it." I folded my arms, waiting.

He shifted feet and switched the to-go bag to his other hand.

"It's the kiss, right?" I blurted. "You're upset we kissed. Well, I'm equally disturbed. We shouldn't have done it. I wish we hadn't. We had a good friendship going. But now you can't even talk to me or look me in the eyes. I'm sorry. I'm to blame. I was too forward. I—"

"Stop." He rested a fingertip on my lips and, probably realizing how intimate an act it was, quickly lowered it. "When this investigation is over—"

"When you find the real killer, who is not me."

"When that happens, we'll talk. Until then—" He squinted one eye. It wasn't a wink. It was a warning. "Let me do my job."

I entered Ragamuffin in a foul mood. Did Zach really think I was a killer? He couldn't. No way. If only I hadn't mentioned the darned kiss!

When I reached the front of the line, I shook off my unease and ordered a latte with an extra pump of caffeine, treats for Tegan and Chloe, and a chocolate scone for me. After the tussle with Zach, a raspberry one didn't hold the same allure.

As I was paying, the ponytailed barista said, "Allie, I was about to call you. If you have time, the boss said we could use two dozen lemon cheesecake bars pronto. Like three hours from now. Can you do it? The Potter's Palette next door wants to have them on hand for this afternoon's art party for adults."

"They could've ordered directly from me."

"Yes, but the boss didn't clue them in. She said we might as well make a profit."

I laughed at her candor.

"Besides, we're providing all the beverages for the affair."

I agreed to help out and took our treats back to Feast for the Eyes. After explaining to Tegan that I had a rush order, I hoofed it to Dream Cuisine. It took me less than ninety minutes to bake, cool, and slice the lemon bars. I dusted them with powdered sugar, stowed them in a container, and delivered them to Ragamuffin, slightly out of breath.

When the barista received them, she said, "Next time, bring us more business cards."

I smirked. "Will you really hand them out?"

"You bet. But not to anyone who needs a same-day order. They have to go through us. Deal?"

"Deal."

On my way out, I caught sight of the young woman I'd seen outside Jason's house Monday night, the one who said she'd heard a woman scream, the one I'd dubbed Pinkie, because she'd reminded me of my favorite stuffed bunny. Today she was in a pink light-weave sweater over white jeans and was chatting with none other than Lillian's grandmother Magda, who was dressed to impress. I wished I could drape a scarf the way she had, but I'd look foolish. The scarf—it was a blue floral Hermès, if I wasn't mistaken, one I'd seen in an ad in a recent edition of *Elle* magazine—was stunning.

I drew near. "Hello, Magda."

"Well, I'll be!" she cried. "If it isn't Allie Catt."

"It's you!" Pinkie said, startled.

"It's me," I replied. "Do you know me?"

"Allie's a caterer," Magda said.

"No." Pinkie shook her head.

"Yes," Magda countered.

"No, I mean, this is the person who found the body." Pinkie shot a hand in my direction.

"She's also part owner of Feast for the Eyes," Magda added. "I was telling Pearl—"

"That's me," said Pinkie, aka Pearl.

"I was telling Pearl she must start reading more." Magda regarded her young friend. "I'm a devoted romance reader. Heat meter one, thank you very much." *Heat meter one* in the romance world meant a gentle, Hallmark-style encounter. No bodice ripping. "But I'll read anything, truth be told, except nonfiction."

"I like paranormal romance," Pearl said. "Especially with sexy vampires."

"Oh, you." Magda giggled.

Pearl chuckled but quickly sobered. "Allie, I was talking to Magda about the murder. What is this world coming to?"

Magda said, "And I was about to tell you I knew Jason Gardner."

"You did?" Pearl's eyes widened.

"He was a boy." Briefly, she recapped how her daughter—Lillian's mother—used to babysit him.

I studied Magda and Pearl, trying to figure out why they were friendly, considering their age difference.

Pearl said, "He seemed sad to me and my mom. Whenever we walked our dog Moose, we often saw Mr. Gardner lingering in his gardens, mumbling to himself as he inspected the roses and flower beds, as if it all had to be perfect, but for what?"

Delilah, I guessed.

"Allie," Magda said, "I'm so sorry it was you who found him. It's morbid to ask, but what was it like seeing a dead body?"

I felt my cheeks warm. "He wasn't dead when I arrived. He died seconds later." A pang cut through me as I pictured him struggling for his last breath. I wouldn't describe the scene to the women. Not because Zach wouldn't want me to, but because it had been gruesome. "Pardon my asking, Pearl, but you said the scream you heard that night was distant but shrill."

"Uh-huh. Like something you'd hear in a horror movie."

Magda tapped her arm. "Like how Shelley Duvall screamed in *The Shining* or Jamie Lee Curtis in *Halloween*?"

"More like Jenna Ortega in the *Scream* movies or Sadie Sink in *Stranger Things*." Pearl shot her hands wide and mimed screaming.

Magda shivered. "You poor dear."

The *poor dear* had been Jason, but I didn't feel the need to point out the obvious. "Are you sure it was a woman?"

She bobbed her head.

"Could it have been a scene in a movie playing on TV at a neighbor's house?"

"I suppose."

"And who heard a dog bark?" I asked.

"Mr. Smith, but how he heard anything is beyond me. The old coot is as deaf as a post." She covered her mouth. Her cheeks blazed hot. She lowered her hand. "I'm sorry. I shouldn't call him an old coot. Not nice. But you know who I mean," she said to Magda. "He's the guy with the sort of bald head who plays bingo on Fridays at the church. The loud one."

"You're the loud one," Magda teased. She said to me, "Pearl is the caller at the bingo games, Allie. You should hear her bellow out the letters."

Aha. That explained their connection.

Pearl tilted her head. "You know, Mr. Smith might be lying. He doesn't like dogs. In particular Moose."

Before returning to the bookshop, I swung by town hall, which was located on East Main, beyond the Bramblewood Park and Rec Center. Patrick said he and Jason had bumped into each other there Monday morning and had reconciled. Would anyone in the vicinity remember their meeting?

Town hall was an imposing building with classic columns and a grand façade. A circular drive surrounded an impressive three-tiered fountain featuring four winged leonine creatures that had the heads and wings of eagles known as griffins. According to town hall's history, the founders had chosen the griffins because they symbolized prosperity, bravery, and wisdom.

People were walking quickly in and out of the building. Most were viewing their cell phones.

I approached a gardener who was cleaning up the planted areas in front of the building. The black tub to his right was filled with discarded weeds. "Sir, can you help me?"

The weathered fifty-something man stood, brushed his hands off on his overalls, and raised a flattened palm to the bill of his cap to block the sunlight from searing his eyes. "Sup?" he asked in short.

I explained the problem. He scratched his chin and said he recollected seeing a couple of dudes chatting on Monday. He jutted an arm toward a spot near the entrance. When I asked if he could pick either man out of a lineup, he shook his head, claiming all he remembered was that both were good looking. He said one man had wavy, shoulder-length hair. The other was a brawny mountain man with dirty blond hair.

Those simple descriptions confirmed to me he'd seen Jason and Patrick together.

"Thank you." I turned to leave.

The gardener cleared his throat. "Hold on, missy. I can't say they were chatting nicely. The brawny one poked the other dude in the chest, and he backed away, both hands raised."

I thanked him again but left the area no more certain than when I'd first arrived. Had Patrick and Jason made amends? Was the final poke good-natured or malevolent?

I proceeded to Feast for the Eyes. When I arrived, Tegan and Chloe were inundated with teenaged girls. I rounded the sales counter and whispered, "Are you giving away free copies of *Powerless*?" It was the first in a series featuring a romance between a prince and an ordinary girl as they tried to survive their kingdom's punishing laws.

Tegan smiled. "A teacher's assignment is the culprit. Students must choose something in a genre they don't usually read. Most of those girls are sci-fi or romance readers. With some cajoling, we've suggested they try the Enola Holmes mysteries or John Grisham's Theodore Boone series."

Chloe unloaded a stack of books on the counter and called over her shoulder, "I'll be right back," to a trio of young customers waiting in the romance aisle. She whispered to Tegan and me, "If I hear someone use the word *like* one more time"—she emphasized the word—"I'm going to scream."

We laughed.

"*Psst*, Allie," Chloe whispered. "Tegan likes Patrick Hardwick."

Tegan swatted her. "Cut it out!"

"She couldn't stop asking about his taste in books while you were gone."

Tegan huffed in exasperation. "I want to know more about him because . . ." She let the sentence hang.

"Because you aren't sure if you suspect him of murder," I finished.

"He could be the murderer?" Chloe gasped. "But how? He's so nice and handsome and, well, down to earth."

"Nice, handsome, down-to-earth people kill," Tegan said.

"I suppose you're right. James Bond does."

I thwacked her arm. "What is it with you and James Bond, Chloe?" She loved thrillers.

"I like his suave style."

"He's a trained killer."

"Yes, but he makes women swoon. Wouldn't you like to swoon some time in your life? I mean, really swoon? I know I would." She crossed her arms melodramatically over her chest and moaned in a dreamy way. "Just because I believe in romance, the kind that occurs in classic literature, doesn't mean I can't also believe in the fantasy of a huge, over-the-top, world-shattering love affair."

"With a killer!" I laughed, until the notion sobered me.

Was Patrick a killer? Was Iggie? How could either of them have stolen into my house and swiped the spearhead? I wished I'd installed a Ring camera, and made a mental note to invest in a security system soon.

"Ladies!" Lillian swept through the front door with three spangly dresses on hangers draped over one arm. "I have a couple of clients who want getups for the *Gatsby* party, and I need your opinion."

"Sorry. Not now." Tegan gestured to the activity in the shop. "We're swamped."

Lillian raised the dresses by the hangers. "A quickie opinion, then. Thumbs-up, thumbs-down."

"Fine," Tegan replied.

Lillian selected a red one with a plunging neckline and glorious gold beads.

Tegan held up two thumbs. "Stunning."

Lillian displayed a blue one that tapered tightly at the hem.

"A mermaid might choose it," Tegan wisecracked. "A very skinny mermaid."

"And this, Allie?" Lillian raised a brown gown. "Your turn to chime in."

I wrinkled my nose. "It's sort of drab."

"What do you think, Tegan?" Lillian asked.

"For a person who wants to be under the radar, it's perfect."

"It's a classic," Lillian said.

"Classically drab," I joked.

Tegan laughed. "I've gotta get back to work."

Lillian proceeded toward the exit.

"Lillian, hold up." I scurried to her. "Before you go, I've got to ask . . . You know Iggie Luckenbill pretty well, right? I mean, your family does. They've invested in a couple of his property developments."

"Funny you should mention him. He's at the shop right now. What do you want to know about him?"

"Tegan's mom said Iggie bad-mouthed a couple of people in town, in particular Stella Burberry's brother."

Lillian and Stella were good friends. In fact, Stella had encouraged Lillian to start volunteering at the children's ward at the hospital, as if she didn't already donate enough time to the community theater and had more hours to spare.

"I heard similar rumors." Lillian clucked her tongue. "He swooped in like a hawk and outbid him. If you ask me, he's got no couth, but I won't turn him away. I always need customers. What does that make me?"

"A smart businesswoman."

"Did you know Iggie was not in favor of Jason Gardner getting the historic properties?" Lillian asked. "He wanted it for his own developmental purposes."

"I mentioned as much to Zach, but Zach isn't taking an interest."

"Are you sure? He holds his cards pretty close to the vest. He doesn't reveal a whit to anyone."

She was right. Zach hadn't said he wasn't interested. He'd shut down any further questioning on my part to curtail me from poking into the details of the crime. "What else do you know about Iggie?"

"He's dogged. Determined. A bit of a dilettante."

"How so?"

"He drinks too much. Plays too much golf. Doesn't follow through on promises to buyers. But"—she clasped my arm—"to think he'd kill Jason to clear the way so he could bid on the properties? How cold."

"Murder isn't warm and fuzzy." I heaved a sigh. "If only Zach knew Iggie's alibi for Monday night."

"He hasn't asked?"

"I don't think he suspects him."

"Hmm. Why don't we question Iggie? He can't make up his mind about what to wear to the *Gatsby* event. Gangster or

Dapper Dan. Gangster is all the rage. Pin-striped suit. Wool fedora." She flapped a hand. "And you know men. They want to think they're tougher than they are. But I keep trying to tell him dressing gallantly would be—"

"Hold on. Iggie told you he's coming to the party? He hasn't preordered a book."

"Why would he waste his time? He can learn everything there is to know about *The Great Gatsby* from his wife. Shayna is the reader in the family. She's as smart as a CliffsNotes study guide."

"She's a reader? How come I've never met her?"

"She strictly borrows from the library. She came from nothing, like Finette, and refuses to ever purchase a book. *Evah!*" Lillian pronounced the final word with a phony accent as she flourished a hand. "Shayna can be quite dramatic."

Also like Finette, I mused.

Lillian tugged my arm. "Come with me. Tegan and Chloe have this place under control. I'll ask Iggie where he was Monday night."

"You can't ask him point-blank."

She winked. "Watch me work my wiles."

Chapter 14

They were careless people, Tom and Daisy—they smashed up things and creatures and then retreated back into their money or their vast carelessness, or whatever it was that kept them together, and let other people clean up the mess they had made.
    —Nick Carraway in F. Scott Fitzgerald's *The Great Gatsby*

I told Tegan where I was going, and followed Lillian.
Puttin' on the Glitz was one of my favorite shops. Despite its modest size, with its gold-and-glass décor, plush velvet curtains, and ornate chandelier casting a warm, inviting glow on the racks holding high-end clothing, it exuded luxury and taste and drew customers from as far away as Charlotte and Raleigh. Soft classical music was playing through speakers as we entered. A hint of Shalimar, Lillian's favorite fragrance, lingered in the air.

"Allie," she said upon entering, acting as if we were in the middle of a conversation, "I do hope you can manage a dinner party for twenty women. Stella wants to join in the fun. We're all volunteers somewhere, and we'd like to honor each other with a special evening."

"Of course I can. At your place?"

"Where else?" Lillian lived in a modest house her family had given her. It had high ceilings, gorgeous hardwood floors, and lots of windows, through which she could view her carefully cultivated gardens.

We moseyed to the sales counter, where Finette was waiting to pay a clerk struggling to insert two jackets into a garment bag.

"May I attend?" Finette asked. She appeared forlorn and in need of a boost. "I love women get-togethers, and I volunteer. I'm in charge of Friends of the Bramblewood Fire Department."

"May I come?" Candace Canfield peeked from behind a dressing room curtain to our left. "I donate time at the animal shelter." She was a soft-spoken woman in her forties with huge, round eyes. She played guitar and sang folk songs for a living. When I'd first heard her perform at a coffeehouse, I'd thought she had to be related to the owner, because she was so shy and reserved. Recently, I'd learned she booked lots of gigs around town, because unobtrusive, unflashy music was in demand.

"Of course." Lillian laid the spangled dresses on the sales counter. "You may both attend. I'll send you the deets."

Giddily, Candace whisked her blond curls over her shoulders and ducked back into the dressing room, but she reemerged immediately. "I almost forgot. Will you all come to a sing-along Thursday night at Blessed Bean? Lots of folks are going to attend. We're raising money for the library."

"Sure, I'll come," I said. "Wouldn't miss it. Anything for a worthy cause."

"Yay," Candace chimed and disappeared.

"Nice choices, Finette," Lillian said as she offered to help the clerk fit the jackets into the dress bag.

"Thank you. Both were on sale. You know how much I love a good bargain."

Lillian said, "Iggie, I'm back."

Iggie, who was standing atop a riser by a trifold mirror, was admiring the pin-striped suit he'd slipped on. He swiveled toward us and frowned. At me, I feared.

Finette muttered, "Iggie. What a slug."

Apparently, they hadn't resolved their differences.

"Iggie," Lillian continued in full voice, "Allie's throwing a dinner party for me. I want your wife to come. She will, won't she? After all, she's such a do-gooder."

"She'd be delighted."

Lillian said in a hushed tone, "Shayna helms a number of art society events, plus she reads to the children at the library. She hasn't any of her own. It's a sad story but not mine to tell." Returning to full voice, she said, "Iggie, come on over here. Let me see what you've got on."

He stepped off the riser and sauntered toward us. His rotund belly pressed at the seams of the suit's vest. He took off the wool fedora and patted his thinning hair into place. "Shayna can't eat gluten," he said to me.

"Not a problem," I replied.

"Or nuts or sesame, and she doesn't do well with legumes and shade plants."

"I've got many clients who have rigid diets. I'll make sure I mark all the items we'll be serving with the ingredients." I offered a reassuring smile.

"But that's not the real reason you're here, is it?" Iggie's eyes narrowed.

"It isn't?" Finette asked.

"Actually"—Lillian gently clasped my elbow—"Allie had a few moments, so I cajoled her into peeking at some of the *Gatsby* costumes. She wants to be the party hostess with the mostest. Don't you, Allie?" She gave me a push.

Quick thinking, I thought, seeing as I'd already selected a costume.

"Mind you, most are copies," Lillian went on, "but there are a few vintage ones."

Taking her cue, I moved toward a nearby freestanding rack

that held a variety of 1920s-style clothing—everything from flapper dresses to gorgeous ball gowns. Where had Lillian procured them all? She must have raided more costume departments than merely the community theater's.

"Check out all the green-toned beauties in the mix," Lillian said. "Have fun." She faced Iggie, clutched the lapels of his jacket, and gave a firm tug. "I like it, but I want to check the inseam and hem, handsome."

Handsome? I had to hand it to my friend. She was acting up a storm.

"Fits pretty good," Iggie said, "as far as I'm concerned."

"Yes, well, we might want to loosen it a tad," she said judiciously. "We don't want any of those buttons to pop off and hit someone in the eye. It could cause a lawsuit." She thwacked him playfully on the arm and steered him toward the riser.

"Lillian." Candace emerged from the dressing room and held up two frocks. "May I take both of these home and see which one Quinby likes?" In her monotone clothing, Candace looked nerdy and in need of a makeover. Perhaps Lillian would take her under her wing. In addition to knowing which styles customers should wear, Lillian had an eye for which makeup to apply to render even the ugliest swan prettier. Candace wasn't ugly. She simply lacked confidence.

"Yes, of course."

A month ago Lillian might have questioned her decision to let Candace walk out with not one but two dresses. After all, the Canfields had been struggling financially, but recently, Stella Burberry had given them strategic financial advice, and Quinby, like his wife with her career, was turning his flagging landscaping business around.

Candace beamed and strode to the sales counter to wait while the clerk finished up with Finette.

"Iggie, you sing, don't you?" Lillian said, loudly enough for all to hear.

"I was a choirboy," he admitted.

"In his dreams," Finette said under her breath.

I bit back a laugh.

"I started out as a tenor," he said. "Now I'm a baritone."

Lillian crouched to insert straight pins into the hem of the trousers. "I wish you had auditioned for the upcoming musical at the theater. You have such a melodic voice."

"Which show are you doing?" he asked.

"Miss Saigon."

Iggie grunted. "I saw it. There isn't a part for me."

"The engineer," Lillian cooed. "He's the owner of Dreamland."

"He's half Vietnamese and half French."

Lillian trilled out a fake laugh. "Silly man. You don't think we can cast perfectly in a town the size of Bramblewood, do you? No, it's all about the costumes and makeup." She rose and, using a stick of tailor's chalk, marked the vest near the buttonholes. "I think we'll let it out this much. Okay?"

"Yeah, might be comfier."

"Auditions were held Monday night. Would you have been able to make it?"

"No. I was at a poker game with my buddies."

Did his lack of hesitation mean it was the truth?

"Which buddies are those?" Lillian asked.

"My golfing guys."

"Are any of them single?" she said in a flirtatious manner. "I might be interested."

He guffawed. "Not a one. All happily married. And way too old for you."

Finette signed for her purchase and said sotto voce to me, "She's incorrigible."

"How'd you do in the game?" Lillian asked Iggie.

"I lost my shirt."

"Well, you've come to the right place, then. I'll sell you a new one. Go change, and I'll show you a few that will look really good with your complexion."

When he disappeared into a dressing room, Lillian gave me a thumbs-up.

I mirrored the gesture, because honestly she'd done a superb job, but I left the shop frustrated. I'd really wanted Iggie to be the killer. Given his alibi, I had to cross him off my suspect list.

Feast for the Eyes was bustling with even more teenagers when I returned. I spotted Darcy in the office window, peering at everyone. He wasn't anxious. He was curious, as if wishing he could join the fun.

I went to the office and cuddled him. "Yes, sir, I know. You're like the shy kid who thinks he wants to dance, but when the chance arrives, he runs to the bathroom to hide. Lest you forget, teenagers are not your favorite people."

Tegan rushed into the office and left the door ajar. "How did it go with Iggie?"

I filled her in.

"He could have lied about his alibi," she suggested.

"He didn't falter. Didn't even grope for words." I supposed he could have practiced a pat response, should the police question him. On the other hand, the police could corroborate his whereabouts.

"You should follow up. A few of his cronies are customers. One might know if he's lying. I'll give you a list. But right now, I need a break."

"We can't leave Chloe with a jumble of people." I motioned to the main room of the shop.

"When they clear out, I'll close for a couple of hours, and you and I will go on a hike and have a picnic."

"You hate exercise, not to mention, you're wearing a skirt."

"Culottes. And I do like to eat." She pointed at a picnic basket sitting on the desk. "Vanna brought us lunch. Turkey, bacon, and avocado subs."

"Yum. She is really going overboard at making nice."

"I think she likes you, as in she admires you a ton. She was so ready to hate you because you were a fellow caterer, but I think she realized hating you was a lost cause. You're sweet and kind, and she needs friends."

A while back Vanna had admitted that she and Tegan had never been warm to one another, which made her jealous of anyone who was Tegan's friend—i.e., me. Of course, I felt sorry for her, and I vowed if she truly didn't have friends, I would work harder at enjoying her company.

"Okay," I said. "Hike, it is."

"And a picnic! I'll drive."

"Knock, knock." Finette appeared at the door, her purchase from Puttin' on the Glitz draped over one arm. "Who's going on a picnic?"

Darcy startled and snarled. I cooed to him. "Cool it, macho cat."

"Customers aren't allowed back here," Tegan stated.

"I know, and I'm sorry to bother you." She seemed as despondent as she had at Puttin' on the Glitz. "Chloe was swamped, and I saw you through the window and thought . . ." She jutted her chin toward it. "This'll take a second. I'd like to order another copy of *Gatsby*. For my great-aunt."

"We have extras." Tegan motioned toward the main room of the shop. "Go to the sales counter. I'll be out in a sec and will ring you up."

Finette smiled. "Where are you going on your picnic, Tegan?"

"It's a secret, but it'll be a fun trek."

"Does *trek* mean you're going hiking, too? I love to hike. How I wish I had more time, but work comes first. Enjoy."

When she left, I said to Tegan, "Do you have walking shoes?"

"In my car."

I followed her into the main room and was surprised to see Iggie at the sales counter, paying for the Patterson novel. Chloe was running his credit card. She must have finalized Finette's purchase already, because Finette was walking out the front door with a gift bag. Iggie lasered me with a look. Had he figured out why Lillian had questioned him about his alibi? Did he blame me for the intrusion?

"Iggie," I whispered to Tegan.

She said, "I'm on it. Why don't you help those teens in the mystery aisle?"

I did. And survived.

Once the lull in activity resumed, Tegan lifted the lunch basket Vanna had delivered, withdrew a sub sandwich, gave it to Chloe, and declared we would be back in two to three hours. Chloe said she'd be happy to hang out and watch Darcy. She loved the little rascal.

"Hey, Allie, did you ever figure out how he hurt himself?" Chloe asked.

"I haven't. I need to address the issue when I get home. Thanks for reminding me."

I followed Tegan to her MINI Clubman, its bumper filled with feisty stickers. I noticed a sassy new one, which read: I DON'T HAVE THE TIME OR THE CRAYONS TO EXPLAIN IT TO YOU.

I laughed. "Good one. Crayons. Hysterical."

"Glad you like it."

We both climbed in and strapped on our seat belts.

"It shouldn't take too long to get to Linville Caverns." Tegan cranked the car into gear.

"What?" I glowered at her. "You want to go to the caverns? You couldn't have mentioned that?"

She cackled. "You would've given me guff."

"The caverns are over an hour away."

"Not the way I drive."

"They're closed on Tuesdays and Wednesdays," I reminded her.

"Good. We won't run into any tour groups or guides." She veered east, out of town.

"What have you got up your sleeve?" I asked, rolling down my window to allow in the fresh summer air.

"I want to rule out Patrick as a suspect."

"Because you like him."

"Get real."

"You do. I'm not blind. The way you clung to him after the bookshelf toppled..." I comically fanned myself.

She blew a raspberry.

For centuries, the Linville Caverns weren't known to humanity. In the early 1800s a local fisherman who was heading up an expedition in this area of North Carolina was shocked to see fish swimming in and out of what he thought was solid rock. Surprise! The limestone caverns were filled with fascinating formations, including stalagmites and stalactites. To me, many resembled the baleen inside a whale's mouth.

"What do you hope to discover?" I asked.

"I want to know if he was really caving Monday night," Tegan answered.

"Who's going to tell you? The bats?"

Like a demon, she sped along the roadway, zooming past cars, keeping watch for highway patrol vehicles. "Did you know a recent bat survey confirmed that six bats out of the hundreds that dwell in the Linville Caverns are infected with white-nose syndrome?"

"What the heck is that?"

"It's a fungal growth around a bat's muzzle and on a bat's wings."

"Eww." I wriggled in my seat. "You remember so much trivia, you really should have become a librarian."

"Back to Patrick and what I hope to find," she said, her gaze fixed on the road. "I believe everyone leaves a footprint."

"Not him. He's not a litterer. You heard him. He loves the environment."

"There are other kinds of footprints. The man has huge feet. His Timberlands will leave a distinctive print."

"Lots of people wear Timberlands."

"Go with the flow."

She quieted when she merged onto Highway 221. We sailed past Woodlawn. Then Ashford. For the remainder of the drive, I took in the beauty of the Pisgah National Forest, which was part of the Blue Ridge Mountains, one of the oldest mountain ranges in the world, having been formed over two hundred and fifty million years ago. Time, weather, and erosion had given these mountains a graceful, rolling hills–type feel. I would never grow tired of looking at the lush green vegetation.

Soon a large sign reading LINVILLE CAVERNS ENTRANCE and painted with arrows directed us to turn in. Tegan parked in the small lot. The welcome building, where I'd purchased my ticket for the tour the last time I visited, was closed. The gift shop was, too. Delicate flowers jutted from the rock face of the caverns. It was illegal to pick them.

Tegan hopped out of the car and through the opened window said, "Let's leave the lunch here and do some exploring first."

I was hungry, but I wouldn't argue. She was a woman on a mission, and I could tell she was eager for answers. I climbed out of the MINI Clubman and stretched. Though I spotted a Chevy Tahoe and a couple of mountain bikes parked in the lot, I didn't see a soul.

Tegan popped the trunk of the car and swapped her pumps for tennis shoes. When they were snugly tied, she said, "Let's go. Look for anything. Footprints. Gum remnants."

"Gum remnants?"

"He chews gum like a fiend."

For a half hour, we scoured the entrance and fifty yards in either direction. Birds twittered, undisturbed by our presence. Squirrels and other frisky creatures darted in and out of the nearby vegetation. We didn't find any empty bottles, trash, or food wrappers of any kind. Not even discarded wads of gum. I peered into the public garbage receptacles, but they had been recently emptied.

"Ahem, Miss Researcher, I can't find squat, and these footprints are useless." I pointed to the ground, where dozens of footprints, none of them definable, went right and left. "Next?"

Something shrieked. We both stopped in our tracks.

"Was that a bird?" Tegan asked.

"Human, I think."

She blanched. "Is someone in trouble?"

A young woman in jeans shorts, a tank top, walking sandals, and a sun hat burst through a stand of bushes and squealed again. But she wasn't frightened. She was laughing in between heavy panting. "You can't catch me!"

A man in his twenties, also in jeans, as well as an I LOVE ASHEVILLE T-shirt, stumbled after her and then bent over, heaving. He clasped his thighs to catch his breath. "You're too fast, and I'm carrying the gear. Not fair." The camping backpack he toted, complete with sleeping bag, looked heavy.

"Loser," the woman teased, then spotted us. "Oh, babe, there are people here."

He raised his chin and gazed at us. "So there are. Hi, people," he said amiably, moving to the pair of bicycles chained to a bicycle rack. He unlocked the chain that held them together and slung the chain across the handlebars. "Caverns are closed, ladies."

"We know," Tegan replied.

"Have you been here all night?" I asked.

"Nah," he said. "You can't sleep here. We were up at the campgrounds by the falls for the past couple of nights."

"Since Sunday," his companion said.

"We thought we'd stop here, take one last look at the river, and have lunch before we headed back to Asheville on our bikes."

"I was starved," the woman said.

"Seen anybody else lately?" I asked. "Say, Monday night? A

single guy? Yea high?" I gestured with a flat hand a foot above my head. "Outdoorsy, powerful arms, unruly blond hair?"

"Nah, but maybe the other couple did."

"Other couple?"

"They're down by the river." He motioned with his thumb. "They were at the campground, too. I'm not sure if they were there Monday. We weren't paying attention to anyone else. It's our honeymoon." He slung his arm around the woman. She giggled. He released her and pushed her bike toward her, after which he straddled his own, the backpack making him a little wobbly until he stabilized it. "Have a great day."

"You too. C'mon, Allie." Tegan trekked toward the river.

I followed.

Minutes later, we encountered an ultra-fit man and woman in hiking gear. The man had no facial hair and was wearing an outback-style hat. The woman sported a sun hat with a floppy brim. Sizable binoculars hung on lanyards around their necks, and their faces were slick with sunblock.

Tegan waved. "Hello!"

The guy grinned. "Hiya."

Tegan introduced the two of us, then added that we worked at Feast for the Eyes in Bramblewood and that we were doing some research. Boldly, she asked what we'd asked the previous couple. Both said they hadn't seen Patrick, but a non-sighting didn't mean he hadn't been there, the woman added. They weren't very observant of humans. They were bird-watchers.

Disheartened, we returned to the car. I fetched the picnic basket, and Tegan laid out a blanket she kept in the trunk on the ground. We sat and pulled out the sandwiches and other goodies Vanna had prepared.

"What do you think?" Tegan asked around a mouthful of sandwich. "Did Patrick lie about being here Monday night?" She brushed a crumb from the corner of her mouth with her pinkie.

"It's hard to say."

"Guilty or not guilty? Your gut feeling."

I sighed. "I'd like him to be innocent."

"*Psst!*" The ultra-fit man emerged from the bushes and beckoned us. "I've got two seconds until she realizes I split. The name's Zorro."

"Zorro?" Tegan scoffed.

He crossed his heart. "My mother had a thing for the masked vigilante. Anyway, I didn't want to talk in front of my girlfriend, but I know who you're talking about. Patrick Hardwick, right?"

We nodded.

"Yeah, me and Patrick go way back. He loves these caverns. The bats." He chuckled. "Years ago, when we were kids, we got pulled in with a couple of other guys for eco-trashing."

"Eco-trashing?" I asked.

"Throwing away items that can harm the environment or animal life." Zorro ticked the list off on his fingers. "Tossing junk, which could wind up in waterways. Leaving barbecue crap or broken glass around, which might injure animals."

"Got it."

"We both had chips on our shoulders. We thought the world owed us. His stepfather was so ticked, he forbade Patrick to ever see me again."

I'd forgotten Patrick's mother had remarried. Patrick and his stepfather seemed so close.

"Long story short, we did community service, which reformed us, and Patrick became a zealot when it came to eco-trashing."

Was that why he'd pounced on Jason regarding the trash his mall might produce? Had Jason learned of his childhood prank? Had Patrick killed Jason to keep it a secret? I couldn't wrap my head around it.

"However, it's the other thing that left a black mark on his record," Zorro went on. "It prevented Patrick from getting a grant to attend college."

"What other thing?" Tegan asked.

Zorro hesitated. "Uh, sorry, it's Patrick's story to tell, but suffice it to say, he was really—"

"Zorro!" his friend cried.

"Coming." He waved good-bye to us and hustled back to her.

"Interesting," I said after his departure. "I know Patrick's stepfather, and I've never gotten the feeling he and his stepson were at odds about eco-trashing or anything else, but the 'other thing' Zorro alluded to might be worth exploring."

The way Zorro had ducked the issue had sounded more dire than making prank phone calls in high school.

Chapter 15

"God knows what you've been doing, everything you've been doing. You may fool me, but you can't fool God!"

—George Wilson in F. Scott Fitzgerald's *The Great Gatsby*

On the way back to the shop, Tegan took the turns at high speed. She'd never had an accident, but I had to admit I was nervous.

"Slow down, pal," I cautioned.

"We didn't get answers."

"But we got a tip. Something to go on. You know all murders aren't solved in a matter of days."

At the next bend, she cried, "Oh, no!"

"What?"

"The coolant level is down. How is that possible?" She tapped the glass covering the control panel, as if the action would help. "I recently had the car serviced."

"Pull over."

She did, then set the car in park, switched off the engine, and yanked the latch inside the vehicle to open the hood. We both scrambled out. She propped up the hood. Steam billowed from beneath it. She batted away the moisture.

"Don't touch the cap." I was no expert, but a boyfriend in high school had taught me a lot about engines—like valves, pistons, and spark plugs. Yes, he had also shown me what the backseat was for, which had ended our relationship. I wasn't a prude, but I wasn't easy, either. "You could get burned."

"I know." She leaned forward and gasped. "The radiator hose has been cut."

"Cut? You mean, it tore off?"

"No, I mean cut, as in it was sliced. On purpose. Look."

I peered in and agreed. The edges weren't frayed. It was a smooth cut. Who would've done something like that? Had one of the campers or one of the bird-watchers tampered with the car while we were fifty yards away in one direction or the other? They'd all seemed friendly. I doubted any were responsible.

It dawned on me that Iggie had been in the bookshop earlier. "Tegan, when did you tell Chloe our plans to go hiking?"

"The moment we came out of the office."

"While she was ringing up Iggie." I groaned. "Do you think he overheard you?"

"OMG." Her face went pale. "And he did this because you were asking questions at Puttin' on the Glitz and . . . and . . . he hoped we'd crash or something?"

"I wasn't doing the asking. Lillian was. But the timing is unnerving. And the way he glowered at me when he was buying his book . . ." I pulled my cell phone from my pocket and dialed the Auto Club for roadside assistance.

While we waited for a tow truck to arrive, Tegan phoned Chloe and said that we'd be delayed. At the same time, I received text messages from Fern. Four, in fact. The first was to touch base. The second was because she was concerned I hadn't responded to the first. The third was a dozen question marks. The fourth was frantic, saying she was worried to distraction, and I had to contact her immediately. My mother was not the hysterical type. In fact, she was calmness personified. I texted her that I was only now receiving all her messages and would call soon, adding everything was fine. I added a thumbs-up emoji and two kisses.

After I sent the text, I wondered again about the messages I'd received from Jason. "Where could they have gone?" I muttered.

"Where could what have gone?" Tegan asked.

I told her about my phone not displaying the text messages after Jason wrote me the night he died. "Zach didn't *not* believe me about receiving them, but he was skeptical. I suggested Jason had deleted them via his phone, but Zach said Jason wouldn't have been able to delete them on mine."

"Aw, geez, I meant to mention this earlier. I did some research this morning, and . . . tech lesson two hundred and twelve . . ." In high school Tegan had been a nerd. She'd learned coding and how to build and take apart computers. She wasn't a major geek any longer, but over the years, she'd provided all sorts of tips that had helped me understand how to navigate the Internet, utilize social media, and access apps on my phone. "I discovered there's an app that can erase text messages."

"Really?"

"Yep. It's new. It allows you to delete messages from other people's phones. You know, for those people who make the huge mistake of drunk texting at three a.m. and wish they hadn't. They're able to reach into the stratosphere and hit delete, delete, delete. On both of their platforms."

"Wow. It sounds illegal and like you'd have to be super-savvy to do so."

"I could master it. I'm not sure you could." She grinned. "You know, Jason didn't have to be the one to delete them. The killer might have."

I shuddered as a new theory occurred to me. "Building on that premise, what if Jason didn't text me at all? What if the killer posed as him to lure me there and deleted the texts to destroy the trail and make me look like a liar?"

"Whoa." She palm slapped her forehead.

I couldn't see Patrick being a techie, but I didn't know him well. Looks could be deceiving. Lots of brawny guys could probably do rings around me when it came to this kind of stuff. I recalled a conversation the other day at Ragamuffin between Finette and Iggie. They'd chatted about keeping up with Burt the Cyber Buddy's blogs, meaning they might be up-to-date with new creations in the tech world. Reika had said she was familiar with Burt's work, too.

"Reika," I murmured.

"What about her?"

I explained how she rued sending mean texts to people and wished she could rescind them. "What if, to toy with me, she was hinting that she'd mastered the send-and-delete skill?"

A tow truck from Garth's Garage pulled ahead of Tegan's MINI Clubman and parked. A guy in overalls hopped out. His grin was crooked but sincere. "Trouble?"

"We reached out to the Auto Club," Tegan said.

"Yeah, that's me. I'm an independent contractor for them. Garth's the name."

Tegan quickly described the problem.

Garth checked under the hood. "Yep. Yep. The hose does appear to be cut, but it's not. The normal life for one is up to ten years. When they crack, it can look like a knife cut."

"This car is three years old," Tegan argued.

"Yep, yep, but sometimes hoses are bad when installed. You might've gotten a rotten hose, not to be confused with a rotten apple. Had one of those once. Yuck. Knew it after the first bite." He pulled a face. "Where do you want me to tow this puppy?"

"Bramblewood."

"Whewie!" He ran a hand down the back of his neck. "B-wood? What a haul."

"Yes, but it's where we live."

"Okay. Yep. Yep. The Auto Club is here to serve. Hop in

the truck. I gotcha." He hooked up the car by extending a hydraulic arm underneath the front of it. Once the wheels were raised, he climbed into the cab and secured his seat belt.

"Good thing you're a club member." As he cranked the truck into gear, he rattled off how much it would have cost Tegan otherwise. "B-wood sure is pretty. You like it there?"

On the drive back, while Tegan and Garth chatted about the beauty of living in Bramblewood, I phoned Zach, but he wasn't in. I started to leave him a message about the incident and my concern Iggie might have tampered with the radiator hose, but I stopped short. It was merely a theory, and nothing untoward had happened to us. It might have been a coincidence.

Instead, I said, "Hope we can talk soon," and hung up.

Tegan broke off her conversation and gawked at me. "What was that about?"

I whispered, "I want to be friends with him again. As long as I'm a suspect, it's impossible."

"We'll figure this out." She patted my knee. "Don't worry."

We arrived at the bookshop around four thirty, and I retreated to the office, deciding it was time to do another deep dive on the three people I suspected of murder—whether they had an alibi or not and, more importantly, whether I liked them or not. I didn't kill Jason. I needed to prove who did.

Darcy leaped onto the office desk and purred.

"Hello to you, too."

He began pacing along the far edge, as if he wished he could take away my angst.

"Cool it, cat. I'm fine."

First, as I had done at home, I created a Word document on the office computer. I generated a three-column grid and added the names Patrick, Iggie, and Reika.

Next, I reached out to three of Iggie's cronies from the country club using numbers Tegan provided. None answered their phones, so I left cryptic messages saying they had won a free private meal from Dream Cuisine. I didn't think they would call me back without knowing me or the reason for my call, and I didn't want to say I was investigating their buddy.

Following that, I checked out Shayna Luckenbill online. I didn't know whether she would talk to me about her husband, but we were kindred spirits. Like me, she was an avid reader. After I knew more about her, I would reach out as a part owner of Feast for the Eyes and encourage her to come to the shop and join our book clubs. Images of her popped up everywhere, ones of her donating time to the theater, to the art society, to the children's group at the library. In each she was decked out in what appeared to be expensive clothing. I phoned Lillian and asked if Shayna was a regular at Puttin' on the Glitz. She said she was and had one of the deepest pockets she'd ever seen, adding she wasn't sure how long Iggie could afford to keep her in so much finery.

One picture of Shayna and Iggie at a formal event gave me pause. Iggie was fixing his cuff link, as he had at Ragamuffin the other day. I zoomed in on it and gasped. A cursive capital *I* was etched on the cuff link, a capital *I* that, because of the serif, could've been mistaken for a capital *J*. Could the cuff link found at Jason's belong to Iggie?

I jotted the tidbit in his column, and then, because I couldn't help myself, texted Zach about the discovery. Not unsurprisingly, he didn't respond. By now, he might have learned Iggie's alibi and ruled him out.

"Let's get to know Reika better."

Darcy stared at me, waiting for more.

"I know she reads historical fiction, like the Elizabethan Spy Mystery series by Suzanne B. Wolfe and the Wrexford & Sloane mysteries by Andrea Penrose. She also tunes in to Burt the Cyber Buddy's blog. Does she have any actual tech experience? If she does, why doesn't she read techno-thrillers, like *The Gomorrah Gambit* or *Kipper's Game*?"

Because I hadn't researched Reika online last time and had

simply jotted down what I'd already known about her, I typed her name into the search engine bar. Up popped links to articles about her, most particularly in regard to the history museum. Upon nabbing the position of curator, Reika was interviewed at length by the *Bramblewood Times*. She had earned a doctoral degree in history and had served as assistant curator for thirty-five years. Now, with her guidance, she had persuaded the museum to shift away from merely displaying artifacts and strived to present the objects in a social, cultural context. In addition to acquiring new objects, Reika enjoyed writing exhibit scripts, preparing grant applications, and having teas to raise funds.

All in all, she sounded like a model citizen. I scrolled through pages of articles and paused when I saw one in the *Charlotte Observer* with a photo of her. Not a flattering photo. Her hair was a mess; her face slack. Apparently, she'd been arrested for disorderly conduct after attending a conference for the American Alliance of Museums. In a drunken stupor, she'd taken down an entire exhibit. *How embarrassing*, I reflected, but the incident had nothing to do with Jason Gardner.

I moved on to Patrick. I still wanted to know what Jason had been referring to regarding his childhood. It couldn't have been about Patrick making prank calls as a teen or about him and his buddy Zorro being hauled in for eco-trashing. Leaking information about those mild offenses wouldn't affect Patrick's current business.

Using the Internet search engine again, I learned Patrick's name was quite popular. Lots of links appeared. I narrowed it down by city and state and landed on an article referencing Patrick S. Hardwick and featuring a picture of him and a few other guys at the top of Mount Kilimanjaro.

Moving on, I spied a link to a person-in-the-spotlight article in the *Bramblewood Times*. The text next to the link read: *Hardwick's sealed record for assault remains secret.*

My adrenaline kicked up a notch. I clicked on the link, which led to a blank page with a picture of a miracle cure for belly flab.

"Crud," I muttered. "A broken link."

Was the assault the "other thing" Zorro had alluded to? I doubted Patrick would discuss the matter. Hoping to track Zorro down and press him for answers, I was about to type his first name in the search bar—how many Zorros could there be?—when I caught sight of a disturbing image of Patrick lower down on the server page. "Age ten," the caption read. He was standing at a graveside, staring solemnly at the coffin of his father, who had passed away in prison.

Holy moly.

The two-line explanation below the caption went on to say that Patrick's father went to jail for killing a man, but it didn't mention whom he killed. Had Patrick inherited his biological father's bad genes? Had Jason learned about this and, to keep Patrick in line, threatened to expose him?

Given his history of assault, I could see Patrick wanting to squelch the story of him being the son of a known murderer.

I pulled a blank thumb drive from the top drawer of the desk and saved my grid document. Then I hurried out of the office to inform Tegan of my findings.

At the same time, Finette sauntered through the front door and made a beeline for the sales counter. Tegan and Chloe were assisting customers who were looking for specific books, so I went to help her. "What brings you in?" I asked pleasantly. "You picked up your second copy of *The Great Gatsby* earlier."

"I ran into a friend and was telling her about your darling shop, and she mentioned a series I should start. Juliet Blackwell's Haunted Home Renovation mysteries. I don't know the title of the first."

"*If Walls Could Talk*. We happen to have it on hand. Let me show you." I escorted her to the mystery aisle. "In the story Melanie Turner, the protagonist, is a remodeler in San Francisco. There are eight books in the series. I've read all of them. They're terrific." When she didn't respond, I mustered the courage to say, "How are you doing, by the way?"

"Why do you ask?"

"Earlier at Lillian's shop you . . . I mean . . ." I groped for the right words. "How are you doing with Jason gone?"

"Ooh." She fanned the air, as if willing herself not to cry. "I'm devastated and also stressed out. Even though his murder hasn't been solved, the town council wants to go forward with the project with Iggie at the helm."

"No!"

"Yes. He circumvented me and pressed the others for an answer. That man makes me so . . ." She hissed between her teeth.

I pulled the Blackwell book from the shelf and gave Finette a quick recap. "In this story, Mel is visited by the ghost of a colleague who recently met a bad end with power tools."

"Talking about meeting a bad end, I wouldn't put it past Iggie to have killed Jason to get rid of the competition. You know about his father, don't you? They say he died of a heart attack and left all his wealth to Iggie, but his demise sounds suspiciously convenient to me."

"I heard." I didn't say more, loath to reveal I'd done my own research. "But from what I hear, nothing untoward happened. He had heart issues."

"Ha! I have read enough mysteries to know there are ways to cause heart attacks. As for killing Jason, Iggie—"

"Has an alibi. He was playing poker."

"*Pfft.* He could've paid his poker buddies to lie about his whereabouts. They're always in cahoots about one thing or another. However, I suppose he might have been gambling. He's not careful with his money. My father—"

"Do you and Iggie have a history?" I interrupted, the question eating at me. Their relationship was complex.

She frowned and pursed her lips. After a long silence, she said, "We dated. Years ago. He was between wives. It didn't work out."

Did she blame him for the botched relationship, which would explain why she was throwing shade on him? Out of spite, had she pitted him against Jason and vice versa?

"As I was saying," Finette continued, "my father used to tell me, 'Do not save what is left after spending, but spend what is left after saving.'" She placed a hand over her heart. "He was always uttering witticisms and quoting great men. I shared a few quips with Jason. He wished he'd met my dad." She sighed and pointed to the book I was holding. "Ring that up for me. I've got a meeting to attend."

When she left with her purchase, I replayed our conversation and her insinuation that Iggie wasn't to be trusted. Was it a diversion to mask her own guilt? I revisited the theory that she might have killed Jason because she'd been in love with him, but he'd rejected her. What would her beloved father have told her to do? Eighty-six him? No, he would have channeled Winston Churchill. "Success is not final, failure is not fatal: it is the courage to continue that counts."

Allie, you're on the wrong track. Finette hadn't killed Iggie after they'd broken up. Therefore, she wouldn't have killed Jason, either.

Tegan sidled to me. "What's going on in your cleverly devious brain?"

I sighed. "I wish I could read minds."

Chapter 16

> *He had thrown himself into it with a creative passion, adding to it all the time, decking it out with every bright feather that drifted his way. No amount of fire or freshness can challenge what a man will store up in his ghostly heart.*
>
> —Nick Carraway in F. Scott Fitzgerald's *The Great Gatsby*

"Go over the crime scene again with me." Tegan dragged me to the endcap of James Patterson books to have a private conversation. "Let's see if talking it out will trigger new ideas."

I did, piece by piece, shuddering as I did so, unable to shake the desolation I'd felt at the time. The spearhead. My missing earring. Dirt on the floor. Mud clinging to Jason's shoes. Him reaching for his cell phone. A shrill scream. A dog barking. "I've been wondering what Zach has learned. He won't share diddly with me."

"And rightly so." She elbowed me. "Hey, do you think he could compare the mud on Patrick's shoes to the mud found at the crime scene? We should tell him about it. Or did you already? The coincidence of it is suspicious, and now we know Patrick was a young eco-trasher—"

"It gets worse." I told her about his sealed record for assault and his father's crime.

"His biological father was a killer?" Tegan shimmied her shoulders, as if ridding herself of bad juju. "So much for contemplating dating him."

"Now hold on. The sins of the father are not necessarily the sins of the son."

"But Patrick attacked someone."

"We don't know who or what provoked the attack. The truth would be nice to learn."

"Geez, Allie." She scrubbed the back of her neck. "Sometimes you can be a pain about not jumping to conclusions."

"Get the specifics. That's all I'm saying. We're fact finders."

The door to the shop opened, which caused a breeze at the back of my neck.

"I get the feeling he's a good guy," I continued. "We simply can't prove otherwise right now. Iggie Luckenbill, on the other hand—"

"Ladies." Evelyn Evers paraded past us like she owned the shop. Was her confidence feigned or a natural gift? I didn't think I could ever command a space the way she did. It didn't hurt that she was rocking a tropical green-and-blue cocktail dress similar to the one Michelle Obama had worn at a gala. I was barely a tween at the time, yet I'd begged my mother to buy me a dress exactly like it. When she'd said no, she'd sealed my fate as a non-fashionista. "Where's Chloe?"

"Here I am." Chloe emerged from the back holding Darcy, who was in a state of nirvana, his head lolling over the crook of her arm. She sidled to us. "What's up?"

"Your audition, young lady, was quite good," Evelyn announced. "We want you to come back for a callback tonight."

"Tonight?" Chloe eeked. Darcy startled.

I took the cat from her.

She clapped her hands. "You mean it? You're not kidding?"

Evelyn grinned. "I never kid."

Tegan said under her breath to me, "Swell. We're going to lose her to the theater."

"No we're not. Chloe is a true bibliophile."

"Seven sharp," Evelyn said. "Wear what you wore the other night. It was perfect."

Chloe frowned. "It's at the dry cleaners."

"Then something in the same color."

"Oh, I can do that. Almost everything I own is red." The smile on Chloe's face was priceless.

Evelyn started to leave and swiveled back. "Allie, I couldn't help hearing you and Tegan mentioning Iggie Luckenbill's name as I was entering."

She'd heard us? No way. I was sure we'd been whispering.

"He's a rogue," she said, "who doesn't deserve an ounce of your attention."

Perhaps her frank opinion was the real reason why he hadn't auditioned for the musical, I mused.

"Allie was theorizing about whether he killed Jason Gardner," Tegan responded.

I elbowed her.

"Girls, girls. You needn't worry yourself about the murder. It's the police department's job."

Tegan said, "Except Allie is a suspect."

"She is," Chloe chimed.

Evelyn regarded me. "Very well, then. Carry on. I'm all ears. Why would Iggie want to kill Jason?"

"Because," Tegan inserted, "he wants to develop the historic properties Jason was prepared to acquire."

"Yes, I see." Evelyn pursed her lips, pondering. "It is a viable motive. Iggie has made some questionable deals over the years."

"Except Iggie has an alibi for Monday night," I added. "He was playing poker with his friends. On the other hand, his cuff link might have been the one I saw at the crime scene."

"What!" Tegan exclaimed. "Why didn't you tell me?"

"I just came up with the theory." I explained the cursive capital *J* that might be a capital *I*. "I texted Zach."

Evelyn arched an eyebrow. "You'll want to talk to Ulla to confirm Iggie's alibi."

"Isn't his wife's name Shayna?" I asked.

"Correct." Evelyn smiled. "We've tried to entice Shayna to join the troupe. She can be quite dramatic. But she's too busy. She and Iggie have no children, so she occupies herself with the arts and such. In fact, she attended an art exhibit Monday night."

"Then who's Ulla?" Tegan asked.

Chloe said, "Ulla Karlsson is an actress. She performs in lots of the plays."

I'd seen her unusual name in the program for the community theater's musical *Young Frankenstein* and learned she was Inga, the Swedish bombshell. She'd brought down the house with her version of "Roll in the Hay."

"Ulla is very talented and sultry," Evelyn said. "A sensualist, one might call her. A bon vivant." She made a grand gesture. "Shayna is her good friend. However, though they are friends, I believe—don't quote me—I saw Iggie leaving Ulla's house the night of the murder."

Chloe coughed out a yelp.

"I wasn't snooping," Evelyn said. "Ulla lives three houses down from me. I was on my way home from auditions. It was close to midnight. And, well, all I'm saying is I doubt they were playing cards or rehearsing lines."

"They're having an affair?" Tegan gawked.

Evelyn nodded once. "It was the good-bye pat on her bottom that gave them away."

"If true and your time frame is correct, I doubt he could've gone to the Sugarbaker estate, killed Jason, and split before I got there."

Evelyn clucked her tongue. "He won't own up to the affair. If he does, Shayna might take him for every penny. She's shrewd."

"His buddies won't support a phony alibi, or they could be in hot water," Tegan stated. "He'll have to come clean."

"True," Evelyn said. "Very true."

Wow, wow, wow. I'd really wanted Iggie to be guilty. The cuff link. The motive. *Dang it.*

Evelyn turned to leave and said, with her hand on the doorknob, "How's your mother, Allie?"

"She's fine. Traveling with Jamie."

A month ago Evelyn had made a snide remark about Fern being a vagabond and never being able to put down roots, let alone raise a child. Then at Marigold's memorial, the two had passed one another, and my mother had snubbed Evelyn. What was their full story? I had to know.

"You don't like my mother, do you?"

She didn't respond.

I pressed. "Why?"

"Let's say I have my reasons." She aimed a finger at Chloe. "Tonight. Seven sharp."

As Tegan and I were closing the shop—Chloe had already left to prepare for her callback—Tegan invited me to join her and her mother for dinner.

"Why? Do you want me to be your wingman again when you discuss her new venture?"

"No. I want support in case Patrick is still there working."

The car repair guy touched base at a quarter to six to inform Tegan her car wasn't going to be fixed until tomorrow, so I gathered Darcy, stowed him in his cat carrier, and drove Tegan to the Blue Lantern in my Ford Transit.

When we arrived at the bed-and-breakfast, the sun was setting, and the brass lanterns flanking the entryway were glowing softly. Tegan entered first. I followed. Guests were mingling in the parlor, chatting about their activities for the day. A wine tasting was in progress.

Helga was offering hot mini quiches. "Welcome, ladies. I have made an excellent dinner tonight, Allie. Your favorite meal.

Honey-baked chicken, roasted potatoes, and fresh green beans, with apple crumb cake for dessert."

I eyed her slyly. "How do you know it's my favorite?"

"I have spies." She cackled and continued offering hors d'oeuvres to guests.

Tegan hitched one shoulder. "Yes, I told her. She likes to know everyone's weaknesses."

"And you assured her I was coming tonight? Before even asking me?"

"I knew you wouldn't say no." She gave me a one-armed hug. "Let's plant Darcy in the garden room off the kitchen and enjoy our wine outside." She nabbed two glasses of the Biltmore estate chardonnay and led the way out. "Today was fun, despite the car trouble and the failure to find evidence of Patrick being at the caverns. It reminded me of a hike we took when we were twelve. Remember going off the trail and getting lost? Thank heaven we had cell phones. What did people do before those were invented?"

"Asked directions."

"I meant in the wilds, you goon." She would've thwacked my arm if her hands weren't full.

We were walking past the office as Patrick and Noeline were exiting. They pulled up short.

"Hey, you two," Noeline said. "Helga is making a feast. You'll stay, Allie?"

"Yes."

"Patrick, would you like to join us?" Noeline asked.

"Can't. I agreed to have dinner with my folks."

Tegan glanced at Patrick and quickly lowered her gaze. Was she afraid if she made direct eye contact, she'd blab everything we'd learned so far? "We're going outside for a glass of wine, Mom."

"I'll join you in a sec. Patrick and I are finishing up. One more wall to do." She silently applauded. "Take a peek. Doesn't it look great?"

Removing the built-in bookshelves made the space look so much bigger. I said, "I love the soft blue color and the dark blue accent wall."

"Patrick's suggestion." Noeline breezed down the hallway to the kitchen.

Patrick peered into Darcy's cat carrier. "Hi, kitty. What's your name?"

"Darcy," I replied.

"As in Mr. Darcy in *Pride and Prejudice*? I read the book way back when."

"Willingly?" Tegan asked.

He chuckled. "Nah. I had to do it in order to pass freshman English. Say, Tegan"—he slipped one hand into a jeans pocket—"I heard you're a hiker."

"Who told you?"

"An old friend of mine touched base. He said he saw you at Linville Caverns."

Uh-oh. We'd been caught in the act. Why had Zorro reached out? He said he hadn't seen Patrick in years.

Hold on, Allie. That's not what he said. I replayed the conversation in my mind. He'd stated that Patrick's stepfather had forbidden Patrick to see him ever again, but he hadn't said they'd complied.

"We did go there, Patrick," I said. "After you shared your adventure, I had the urge to see the caverns. I hadn't visited in years."

"Allie told me about the bats. I was fascinated," Tegan replied, crafting a reasonable excuse. "We were hoping to figure out what time the furry critters were at their peak."

"The caverns aren't open on Wednesdays," Patrick said.

I groaned. "Yeah, we found out. Dumb. But it was a pretty drive."

"Zorro said you asked about me." Patrick's gaze narrowed.

"We did." I opted to take the direct approach. "We hoped one of the hikers we questioned would know how you got in. We wanted to sneak in ourselves. Alas, none did."

Darcy meowed.

"Yes, buddy." I cooed. "I'll let you out in a sec."

Tegan raised the two glasses of wine. "Allie, our drinks are getting warm. See you, Patrick. Nice job on the office."

As I was unpacking Darcy from his carrier—he'd visited the inn before and knew to stay put in the garden room—Noeline sauntered in.

"I meant to tell you, ladies, I've received yeses from all the invitees for the *Gatsby* event."

"I figured," Tegan said. "We sold out of the second batch of books."

"Also I scored the most romantic flapper dress ever," Noeline continued. "Lillian discovered it among the theater costumes. Cobalt blue with lots of sequins and bling." She used her hands to describe it. "How are your plans coming along?"

"I did some taste testing." I listed what I'd made so far. "I have more to do tonight, meaning I'm not staying after dinner."

Tegan tapped my arm. "Give me a ride home when you leave? I need to tend to the snails in the garden."

"Snails?" her mother exclaimed.

"Yes, the garden needs tweaking." When Marigold died, Tegan had inherited half of her house. She'd purchased the other half from Vanna. After starting the divorce proceedings, she had moved into the house and now was spending as much time as she could sprucing up the garden and the interior. Marigold had kept her home in pristine shape, but Tegan was updating the bathrooms and the counters in the kitchen. "Who knew I was such a DIY person?"

"Are you overextending yourself?" Noeline asked, concerned.

"*Moi?* No! You, on the other hand—"

"No. Uh-uh." Noeline wagged her head. "You are not going to talk me out of buying another bed-and-breakfast. Aren't you the one who's always telling me I need more joy in my life? Well, a new project will bring me great delight. End of discussion." She marched away.

"Sheesh." Tegan exhaled. "She can be so stubborn."

I bit back a smile. I felt the same about Fern. And hadn't Finette said all the women in her family were intractable?

We retreated to the garden and sat on a bench beneath a blossoming white crape myrtle to enjoy our wine. The aroma from a stand of roses to the left was heady.

After a long moment, Tegan said, "Patrick . . ." but didn't continue.

"What about him?"

"He clearly didn't swallow that we'd asked his friend about the bats or the secret entrance to the cave. Do you think we should be worried?"

"Why?"

"If he's the killer and he thinks we're nosing around . . . I mean, he went to jail for assault, and . . ." She sipped her wine. "Will he go after us?"

"Relax. He doesn't know we discovered all that."

"But he might have guessed we didn't find evidence of him being at the caverns, meaning we know he lied."

"Yoo-hoo." Vanna swanned outside, her heels digging into the grass, making it impossible for her to make a smooth entrance. She was carrying a glass of wine, which was sloshing over the rim. When she reached us, she sipped her wine and shook off her wet hand. "I had such a fruitful day."

"What did you do?" Tegan asked.

"I met with the mayor to talk about another private party, because the one I threw was such a success."

"Congratulations," I said.

"Afterward, I met with the alderman on the town council, who also wants me to hostess a party. It sure pays to know people in high places."

Tegan and I exchanged a look. Vanna couldn't help herself. She liked to crow about her accomplishments.

Vanna eyed me. "That doesn't mean I can't help you do all the things you need me to do for the *Gatsby* event, Allie. The mayor's party isn't for another month, and the alderman's is in two months." She inspected the heel of her left shoe. "*Ooh*, mud. Why does Mother water so much?" She slipped off the shoe and, balancing with her barefoot toes on the wet ground, wiped off the mess using a tissue from her purse. "Hopeless." She inserted her foot into the shoe and balled up the tissue. "Following those meetings, I delivered an early dinner to Katherine Fineworthy, Finette's great-aunt."

"You did?" I asked.

"Yes. I go every Wednesday. Finette hired me to do so."

Aha. That made sense. Vanna had been paid. She wasn't entirely altruistic.

"She likes macaroni and cheese. I made it extra special with a three-cheese blend."

I grinned. "I make it the same way."

"Aunt Marigold and Katherine were such good friends," Vanna went on. "She is . . . was an avid reader. She lives in the darling blue house with the yellow shutters on the corner of Oak Knoll, not far from Auntie's . . . I mean *your* house, Tegan."

"I know the one."

"Finette mentioned her great-aunt was ailing." Actually, she'd intimated that her great-aunt was slipping mentally. I took a sip of my wine. "She's deliberating about applying for a conservatorship."

"Yes." Vanna bobbed her head. "She wants to coerce her great-aunt into moving into a retirement facility. To be truthful, sometimes the poor dear can't even walk to her mailbox without forgetting why she went outside. I bring it to her whenever I visit and sort through it with her. She gets quite a lot of junk."

"Don't we all?" I joked.

"She enjoys flipping through advertising mailers," Vanna said. "As if she'll ever buy another item in her life. Now is the time to sell what she's got, Finette tells her. I don't think Katherine agrees. Finette doesn't press. She doesn't want to upset her." She leaned forward. "Speaking of upsetting someone you love, did you tick off our mother, Tegan?"

"What do you mean?"

"She was muttering, 'Stubborn, stubborn, stubborn,' to herself when I arrived. I asked if she meant me, and she said no. You were the bullheaded one."

"Me! Ha! She's the—"

"Dinner!" Helga called from the back porch.

Tegan, Vanna, and I rose and convened at a table in the dining room with Noeline. Inn guests occupied the other tables.

To my surprise, Helga served something akin to a Waldorf salad to start. She'd used pistachios instead of walnuts, and chunks of green apples instead of red. The dressing was slightly different, too. Although she had used mayonnaise and lemon juice, which was typical, she'd added maple syrup rather than honey.

"Wow," I mumbled around a mouthful. "Helga, this is so tasty."

"Thank you." She was filling glasses with tap water. "Vanna gave me the recipe."

Vanna beamed with pride, leaving me to wonder what other secret delights she might be harboring. I supposed I should rope her in to help with the rest of the *Gatsby* party taste testing.

"Mother"—Tegan sliced a flaky biscuit in half and buttered each side—"I really do want to discuss your plans."

Give it a rest, I tried to telegraph mentally, but my ESP suggestions never worked on my headstrong pal.

"There's nothing to discuss," Noeline said.

"But—"

"No."

Helga bussed the salad plates, replaced them with dinner plates, and returned with platters of entrée choices.

I whispered to Tegan, "I've got to leave soon."

"I'll ask Helga to make us dessert to-go plates. You can't pass up her apple crumb cake." She polished off her biscuit, brushed off her hands, and leaned forward on both elbows, hands folded. "Mother, how much is the new place going for?"

"Tegan, drop it," Vanna ordered. "Honestly, you're like a dog with a bone. Now is not the time."

"When is the time?"

"Mother has plenty of money."

"I don't want her to be taken to the cleaners. Do you remember how she put her heart and soul into opening this place?" Tegan stabbed the table to make her point. "Do you remember how tired she was all the time?"

"Girls, I'm right here," Noeline said. "I can hear you. Relax. I've got it under control."

"You say that now." Tegan thwacked the table with her fingertips. "But how about a year from now, when the roof caves in or the staircase gives way? Have you forgotten all the things you had to repair or replace here? Do you have long-term memory loss?"

Vanna gasped. I held my breath.

"Enough, young lady," Noeline said. She pushed back her chair. The feet screeched on the floor. She rose to a stand and dropped her napkin on her plate. "Do not diss me. For your information, no, I haven't forgotten a thing. I relished every step of the process of making this place beautiful. Even the snags and pitfalls. I look forward to bringing another dinosaur to life. Now, leave me be." She stomped away.

"You heard her, Tegan," Vanna said under her breath. "Leave her be." I doubted Vanna disagreed with Tegan, but I figured she was defending their mother because she knew it would irk her half sister.

Which it did. Tegan gave her sister the evil eye and marched out of the room.

Chapter 17

"Well, I've had a very bad time, Nick, and I'm pretty cynical about everything."

—Daisy Buchanan in F. Scott Fitzgerald's *The Great Gatsby*

I talked my pal into coming back to dinner and finishing her meal. Over the years, I'd learned ways to cajole her when she was out of sorts. After all, what were best friends for? Noeline did not reappear.

Later, on the way to her house, Tegan asked if she had been in the wrong.

"Your mother is not old. She's very smart and capable. If I were you, I'd ease up. Allow her to spread her wings."

"And if she fails?"

"You'll swoop in to help her then. Remember, you are not the mama bird. You are the baby bird." I was pretty sure Noeline wouldn't ever need Tegan's help. She was a live wire.

"Fine," she grunted. "I hear you."

I pulled in front of her house and idled. "By the way, your garden looks good. Even in the dark. Happy snail hunting."

She stuck out her tongue and climbed out of the van.

As I was turning around, I peeked at the blue house with the yellow shutters. How difficult it must be for Finette, having to manage her great-aunt all by herself. I doubted I'd ever need to assist my parents. They were so vital.

Driving along Main Street, it dawned on me I'd promised Fern a phone call. She hadn't texted after I'd assured her everything was fine. Seeing as Machu Picchu was an hour earlier than our time, I dialed her.

She answered after one ring. "Thank heavens. You're alive."

"Yes, I'm fine. Did you get my message?"

"I did, but hearing your voice, Cookie, makes all the difference."

"Gee, Fern, how do you think I feel whenever I can't reach you and Jamie?"

"You know we're stalwart, and we have each other. You—"

"Have a cat." I chuckled. "I've taught him how to dial nine-one-one."

"Very funny."

"Relax. I have a good support system. Tegan, her mom, Chloe, Vanna."

"Yes, I know, but there's a murderer on the loose. Anything new regarding the investigation?"

"The police do not have a suspect in custody. It can be a long process. And, no, I haven't been exonerated, if that's what you're asking." The notion made my head ache. "But I have some ideas about who did it, and I've been sharing them with Zach."

"Is he listening?" She said away from the phone, "No, Jamie, it's not the maître d'. It's Allie. Yes, I'll tell her." To me, she said, "Your father sends his love and is telling me it's time for dinner."

"It's late," I replied.

"You know we're night owls. Keep me in the loop. And check your text messages more regularly. Ta-ta." She ended the call abruptly.

"Bye. Love you," I said into the stratosphere. "Love you, too, Cookie," I added snarkily and regarded my cat. "My mother is not fuzzy and cuddly like you. FYI, I prefer you."

He meowed his approval.

The moment we were in the house, I locked the door and switched on all the main lights. Without thinking, I also checked the walls to see if any other art or artifact was absent. Everything seemed intact. Why hadn't I noticed the spearhead missing before? A shiver ran down my spine. Having one's personal space violated was unnerving. From this moment on, would I feel secure? Would solving Jason's murder put an end to my anxiety?

I shimmied off my unease and said to the cat, "I've got to prep." I fixed him a bowl of food and placed it on the floor by the dining nook. "You can snooze."

After closing the Plexiglas door, I scrubbed my hands, secured my hair, uploaded the information from the thumb drive onto my computer—merging the new suspect notes with the previous notes—after which I focused on a plan for tomorrow. Yes, I was burning the candle at both ends, but I wanted my business to thrive as much as I wanted the bookshop to flourish, and I really wanted to see a murderer brought to justice. I was young. I could multitask without getting eight hours' sleep.

While I was gathering items for the assorted cookies and muffins I would make for the museum tea in the morning, like cocoa, macadamia nuts, and white chocolate—ingredients I was running low on at my ghost kitchen—I noticed Darcy in the living room, scraping under the armchair.

"Stop, mister." I pushed through the door. "Knock it off. I know I need to redo the jute straps and fix the springs on the darned thing. It's older than Moses. You don't have to remind me. Out! Now!"

Sufficiently reprimanded, Darcy bounded to the top of his llama cat-scratching station and sat stock-still.

Mortified by my negligence not to have figured out the reason for his sore toenail, I crossed to the fireplace to recheck for rough edges. I ran my palm along the surface. It was as smooth as it had been the last time I'd examined it.

"Darn it. What did you hurt yourself on, sweet thing?" I didn't see any splinters jutting from the flooring. No protruding nails required hammering back into place.

My cell phone pinged. I pulled it from my jeans pocket and scanned the readout. Talk about timing. The vet had sent a message asking how Darcy was doing. I smiled, not surprised she'd contacted me. She'd once told me she made all her follow-up calls after hours. I was grateful for how dedicated she was. I texted back that he had pulled off his bandage, but I was checking diligently to make sure his toenail didn't get infected, adding, **So far, so good.** She suggested I bring him in on Friday for a follow-up. I agreed.

I returned to the kitchen, washed my hands again, and after stowing the nonperishable ingredients I'd amassed in a large plastic tub and setting it by the front door, I slogged to bed.

Thursday morning the alarm trilled before dawn, and I was disinclined to get up, but as always, I did. I was a creature of good habits. To burn off the mental fog, I decided to take a quick jog. I donned workout clothes and reflective shoes and headed off.

I enjoyed running in the dark. I'd been doing so ever since I'd started track in junior high. The hour before dawn was peaceful and invigorating. I could process thoughts in my muddled brain with no distractions, despite the sound of critters skittering in trees.

Before long, I was thinking about the murder. If Iggie was truly innocent, then only Patrick and Reika were left as suspects. Was I missing someone? Did Zach have more names on his list? Was it possible someone on the town council had been against Jason's plan? What about the neighbor named Ed Smith, who Pearl had said might have lied about hearing a dog bark?

C'mon, Allie. How in the heck would he, or anyone on the council, for that matter, have known to implicate you?

A nagging feeling gripped my insides. Suppose Finette had mentioned my spearpoint collection in passing, which had given the killer the idea to steal one.

Frustrated, I went home and screamed in the shower à la Janet Leigh in *Psycho* while letting the hot water pummel my tired body. Refreshed, I stepped out, dried off, put on a tad of makeup, slipped into comfy blue jeans and a white button-down shirt, and drove to Dream Cuisine. I left Darcy at home with kibble and water and warned him not to fool around. He seemed content with the plan.

After drinking my first cup of coffee, I addressed the assorted cookies for the museum tea. I knew each recipe by heart. I started with the triple chocolate chunk cookies; then I tackled the white chocolate macadamia ones and the dark chocolate raspberry cookies. Not everyone was a fan of the latter, but I adored them. Next, I threw together four dozen peanut butter cookies, each topped with a chocolate kiss. I'd take extras to the bookshop.

While I was baking the sugar cookies, I thought of Zach. He hadn't responded to my text. How I missed bouncing ideas off him and wished I could tell him so, but I couldn't and shouldn't reach out again until the murder was solved. He might snap off my head, and I needed it.

As the cookies were cooling, I decided to make a batch of deviled eggs as well as a pineapple upside-down cake. I'd take them to the bookshop for a taste test. I could make deviled eggs in my sleep. The secret ingredient was white vinegar, so I tackled those first.

Then I addressed the cake. I had made it in the past and had struggled with having a soggy cake. However, while researching which foods I wanted to serve at the *Gatsby* party, I'd read on a fellow baker's website that using creamed butter instead of melted butter could make a difference. She'd also suggested using cake flour instead of sifted all-purpose flour and egg whites in place of whole eggs.

On top of the melted butter and brown sugar I'd combined in the bottom of a cake pan, I arranged the topping of pineapple rings, which I blotted dry, and deposited a maraschino cherry in the middle of each. I stowed the pan in the refrigerator to chill and focused on the batter.

A pineapple upside-down cake meant exactly that. You layered the batter on the topping, which was on the bottom, and when the cake was turned out of the pan, the topping was now on the top. Once I poured the batter over the topping, I slid the cake into the oven. Reika's order was next on the list. I mixed the batters for the muffins she'd requested—chocolate as well as apple. Afterward, I assembled the batters for the items I had to deliver to Jukebox Joint, Ragamuffin, and Blessed Bean.

Sometimes I was amazed by how quickly I could produce all my orders. To make sure I hadn't missed anything, I checked the to-do list on my Notes app. I'd written a duplicate list on the whiteboard on the wall. Big Mama's Diner wanted sourdough bread for the weekend, but I could handle the task tomorrow.

While everything cooled completely, I brewed a second cup of coffee, and though I craved a cookie, I opted for a protein bar from the walk-in refrigerator. To make it through the day, I'd need sustenance, not a sugar rush.

An hour later I loaded the items into the Ford Transit.

First on the delivery schedule was Jukebox Joint, Zach's mother's place.

The diner's entrance was adorned with a flashy turquoise-and-red neon sign with the words *Jukebox* squarely upright and *Joint* on a slant. Inside, large turquoise vinyl booths lined the walls, while tables with red vinyl chairs filled the open floor space. Yellow stools brought a pop of color to the curved counter. Red, yellow, and turquoise accents abounded, from the sugar containers to the coffee mugs. At the far end of the diner stood a walnut-paneled jukebox sporting neon bands. Though retro in style, it had been updated with LED-powered Bluetooth, so a diner could connect to it with any Bluetooth device. The popular Elvis song "Blue Suede Shoes" was blasting through overhead speakers.

There were no customers. It was way too early. The diner's hours were noon until nine.

"Morning!" Jenny Armstrong waved to me from behind the counter as I entered. She rounded it quickly, wiping her hands on her red-checked apron. "Lovely to see you."

"You, as well."

A petite woman in her mid-fifties, Jenny, like her son, Zach, was the kind of person who instantly made people feel comfortable. She had an easy gait, a warm smile, and bright eyes twinkling with humor. Her soft brown hair was secured in a snood.

I crossed to her with two pastry boxes. "I have your order."

Though Jukebox Joint was known for its barbecue and its burgers, Jenny had decided to add sweets to the menu for those who ventured in for a late afternoon coffee and treat.

"Bless you." Her voice was raspy, as though she shouted orders all day every day . . . or sang along with whatever song was playing. I'd caught her on a recent delivery crooning into a spatula. "I can't tell you how much my customers are loving these goodies." She took the boxes, set them on the counter, and tucked a stray lock of hair into the snood before pulling a wallet from the pocket of her apron. "Here you go." She paid me the full amount, as I requested of all my customers.

The door opened, which made the overhead chimes jangle. Jenny beamed. "Hello, handsome."

I pivoted and saw Zach entering. He frowned, which made me feel *sooo* welcome. *Not.* I mustered a smile, said I was leaving, and started past him.

"I got your message about the cuff link," he said. "You could be right."

"Even if I am, I learned Iggie has an alibi."

"Playing poker."

"No. He was dallying with his wife's best friend."

Jenny coughed out a laugh. "He's stepping out with Ulla? My, my."

"Mom, you did not hear any of this," Zach warned.

"But I can't unhear it, sweetheart."

"Go sing, Mom," he chided. "Shoo!"

She cackled and returned to her spot behind the counter.

Zach addressed me. "Who'd you hear this from?"

I told him. "Who else is on your radar?"

He didn't respond.

"You wouldn't say the other day, but Patrick Hardwick's alibi is iffy, and he and Jason had a run-in at the bookshop."

"I heard."

"Who told you?"

"Chloe let it slip to a friend, who mentioned it to Detective Bates. Word gets around. Care to give me the specifics?"

I did my best. "In the end, Jason held Patrick down and said, 'Memories of one's mistakes rarely fade.'"

"'Memories of one's mistakes.'"

"Mm-hmm. Well, get this, Tegan and I learned Patrick went astray a few times in his past."

Zach folded his arms, but he didn't order me to be quiet. Maybe he didn't want to snap at me with his mother present.

"Before I tell you more," I began, "I want you to know I like Patrick, and I don't want him to be guilty."

One side of his mouth twitched, as if he was tamping down a smile. "Go on."

"We ran into an old friend of his at Linville Caverns."

"What were you . . . Never mind. Continue."

"The friend told us he and Patrick did some eco-trashing when they were young." I quickly explained the term. "The friend—"

"Got a name?"

"Zorro. I didn't get a last name. I don't know where he lives. It was pure coincidence to run into him. Anyway, he said the stunt hurt Patrick's relationship with his stepfather."

"Which has nothing to do with Jason Gardner."

"Right, and having a reputation for eco-trashing probably wouldn't hurt Patrick in the long run. Kids do silly stuff." *Like make prank calls*, I mused. "But get this. Zorro started to share something more about Patrick and stopped. He said, 'The other thing was what prevented Patrick from getting a grant to attend college.'"

"What other thing?"

"I was curious, too, so I did a bit of evidence searching on-line."

His mouth twitched. "You mean investigating?"

"I landed on a person-in-the-spotlight article about Patrick and his business. He assaulted someone."

Jenny appeared at my side, a spray bottle of cleanser in one hand, a rag in the other. "Did the article say who he assaulted?"

"Mom," Zach said.

She squirted the cleanser at him, missing on purpose. "I'm here. I'm listening." She turned back to me. "Did it?"

"No," I replied. "The article didn't pop up. The text next to the link read, 'Hardwick's sealed record for assault remains secret.' When I clicked on it, it led nowhere."

"I hate broken links," Jenny said. "They're maddening. You

always end up on a page for some miracle cure, or you wind up on a bogus site eager to eat your computer's brain."

I nodded.

"But an independent business operator must learn to navigate the Internet if one is to thrive," she said. "What else did you learn?"

Zach's gaze remained fixed.

"I saw a picture of Patrick, age ten, by his father's grave, and the caption mentioned his father had killed someone, but it didn't elaborate. Around twenty-seven or twenty-eight years ago, I figure."

"I remember that!" Jenny exclaimed and regarded her son. "I was pregnant with you at the time." She said to me, "What was the man's name? Gil... Gil... Gil... Killagher." She swatted her leg with the wet rag. "Remember the Killaghers?" she asked Zach. "They owned a one-hundred-and-fifty-acre ranch north of here. No, you wouldn't remember. It was bought by another operation by the time you were a toddler. Gil was a drunk. He started a knife fight with Patrick's father. I'm surprised the photograph you saw said Patrick's father murdered the man. It was self-defense. He went to prison, though, and died a year later. In a knife fight, of all things. How ironic."

Zach said, "Just because his father killed someone doesn't mean Patrick would have."

"Of course not," I said. "I'd hate to be judged by my parents' faults." Which were few. Lack of interest in pursuits other than their own was their worst. "But doesn't it make you wonder? What if Jason knew all this and somehow got his hands on the sealed record? What if he threatened to expose Patrick?"

"Good point," Jenny said.

"Mother, please."

"Your father always said—"

"I know what Dad said. You quote him often enough."
She glowered at her son.

"Patrick said he ran into Jason outside town hall after the fracas," I went on, undeterred. "He said they mended fences, and I checked. A gardener did see them there."

Zach made a dismissive sound with his tongue.

I ignored him and continued. "But the gardener didn't know what they discussed, and said the two men did some finger-pointing. Patrick told me Jason had hired him to do some repairs to the back porch of his house, but what if he lied so he could claim he'd visited the estate and gotten mud on his shoes?"

Except he said he'd muddied his boots at Linville Caverns.

"What mud?" Zach snapped.

"Tuesday morning, when I saw Patrick at the Blue Lantern, he had dried mud on his boots. He said he'd acquired it at Linville Caverns, thus, the reason why Tegan and I drove up there. To see if he'd left evidence of having been there."

Zach groaned.

"Have you tested the dirt from Jason's foyer floor?"

"We're awaiting results."

"You might find remnants to test in Patrick's truck or at his house. Also, there's one more person you should consider. Reika—"

"Allie, enough," Zach said, a stern warning in a tone, which, to be truthful, I was beginning to hate.

"She has a dog. The neighbor, Mr. Smith, heard a dog barking Monday night. What if—"

Zach swatted the air. "Thank you for your information. Bye. And, Mom, don't say a word."

She mimed locking her lips.

When he left, I didn't move, angry with myself. Over the years, my parents had cautioned me about being impulsive.

Mostly, I'd learned to curb this bad habit. Why hadn't I been able to today? I'd crossed the line with Zach without blinking an eye.

Give it a rest, I thought. *Everyone's entitled to act stupidly once in a while. On the other hand, you really abuse the privilege.*

CHAPTER 18

So we beat on, boats against the current, borne back ceaselessly into the past.

—Nick Carraway in F. Scott Fitzgerald's *The Great Gatsby*

When I arrived at the history museum, Reika was on the front porch, sweeping with a besom broom. She'd wrapped a bandanna around her hair. Her denim overalls were filthy with dust. Her bulldog was lying on the porch swing, a silly-looking Covid mask covering her mouth.

"Hi." I climbed the steps, carrying bakery boxes. "Hello, Princess."

The bulldog yipped in greeting.

I pointed to the dog's mask. "For the dust?"

Reika replied, "I'm free to roam inside the museum without her attending to my every move, but when I go outside, she refuses to leave my side. She gets clogged up and coughs incessantly if I don't mask her. Are those our goodies?"

I nodded. "Where would you like me to put them?"

"Let's go to the kitchen." She propped the broom against the wall, removed the dog's mask, scratched the pup's ears with affection, and ordered her to follow us.

Amira loped behind, her tongue lolling from her mouth.

"Here we are," Reika said, entering the kitchen.

"I love this room." As a girl, I'd wanted to live in a Victorian house. I'd imagined myself in a room on the top floor, isolated from the rest of the world and letting my hair grow so long Rapunzel would be jealous. "It's charming."

"Thank you. I had a hand in the redo."

The space was in keeping with the design of the original house, though the appliances had been updated and the dark woodwork had been refinished.

"Is the white tile original?" I asked.

"No, but as close as it could be. Put the boxes there." She indicated the island's marble countertop, which was definitely new. "I'll plate them later."

I obeyed and then leaned my back against the counter's edge. "Read any good books lately?"

"Too many to count."

"How about *The Falcon at the Portal*?"

"Of course. One of Peters's best. I read it for the fifth time last year."

"And *The Course of all Treasons*?"

"I haven't browsed it in quite a while. Not since book club."

I gawked at her. "Um, you said it was the book you were reading last Monday night."

"Did I?" Her face pinched with concentration. "Did . . . I . . . Ooh . . ." She paled and faltered.

I gripped her elbow and guided her to a chair by the vintage dining table. "Do you need water?"

"Yes, please. I'm . . ." Tears flooded her eyes. "Allie, I'm so embarrassed."

Amira hurried to her human and nudged her knee. Instinctively, Reika petted the dog's head.

I fetched the water and brought it to her.

She drank greedily and plunked the glass down. "So very, very embarrassed," she muttered.

"Why?" I took a seat and placed both hands on the table as a gesture of trust.

"Thirty years ago, after I was attacked, I started drinking heavily. Before I knew it, I was an alcoholic. It took me ten years to break free. My ESA dogs have been my saving grace." A tear leaked down her cheek. "Books, too, of course. They are my greatest refuge. As for my weakness, years passed before I went to AA, but I did, and I beat the addiction, and I was doing fine until Monday afternoon, when my boyfriend . . ." More tears slipped from her eyes. She swiped them with her knuckles. "When my boyfriend of three years ended our relationship. Rather than call my sponsor, I succumbed. I got so drunk, I went to bed and stayed there with the covers over my head, hating myself for being weak."

I reflected on the article I'd read about the inebriated incident at the conference in Charlotte.

"When you came here Tuesday, I noticed you staring at me," she said. "I brushed off your concern and claimed I had a sour stomach. I didn't want to admit what I'd done."

I recalled the aroma of her pungent perfume wafting to me. Had she donned the scent to cover the noxious odor of a binge?

Reika sighed. "I've never been one to need a man. I've always stood on my own two feet."

"Weren't you married once?"

"Yes. He died over twenty years ago. He overdosed."

That was the piece of information I couldn't remember. Tegan had told me after book club one night. No one had known he was addicted to pills. Rumors had abounded about whether he'd taken his life or someone had helped him along.

"We were quite a pair." Reika chuckled with self-deprecating sadness. "*Days of Wine and Roses* had nothing on us." She rubbed Amira's scruff. "After he passed, I started going to AA. His parents had money. They helped me financially and buried the story about his addiction. I never thought I'd fall in love again, but getting sober helped me greet the world with open arms. Fast-forward to three years ago. I met Roy when he brought his history class to the museum for a field trip, and he and I hit it off, but on Monday he . . ." A sob caught in her throat. "I can't go on."

"Reika, if you have an alibi for that night, the police will need to hear this."

"Why?"

"Because you have a strong motive to have killed Jason. You wanted the Bramblewood Historical Preservation Society to secure the properties he was bidding on."

"Heavens. I wouldn't kill him for such a shallow reason."

"You said you sent him vicious texts and emails."

She didn't respond.

"Also . . ." My voice trailed off.

"Also what?" Her gaze hardened.

"A dog was heard barking Monday night, around eleven thirty, near the estate where Jason was staying. Amira has a very distinctive growly yip. If you and she were out walking—"

"We weren't. We were home. I swear."

"The police are searching for the source of the barking." It was a fib. I didn't know if it was true.

"Hold on. Roy can solve this." She fetched her cell phone and tapped in a text message. She showed the text to me. It read: **Please answer.** Then she typed in his phone number and pressed speaker.

"What now?" a man asked with a surly edge to his voice.

"It's me," Reika said. "I'm sorry to bother you, but a friend is with me—she's listening in—and I need you to verify I was drunk Monday night and could barely talk to you when you phoned me."

He sighed.

"Please, Roy. This friend . . ." She regarded me. "She's questioning whether I killed Jason Gardner."

"You couldn't have," Roy said. "You were totally plastered that night. Who's the friend?"

"Allie Catt."

"Of Dream Cuisine?"

"The same."

"You're good at what you do, Miss Catt," he said. "I attended a benefit you catered last year. Best desserts I've ever tasted."

"Thank you." I'd helmed at least six benefits, so I wasn't sure which one he meant.

"Reika is telling the truth," he went on. "She was in bed Monday night."

"Because you broke it off with me."

He grunted.

"Roy, tell her why," Reika pleaded. "Every sordid detail. She needs to believe me."

"Fine." His voice softened. "Now that I'm retired, I asked Reika to retire so we could sail the world. She refused."

"I'm afraid of water," she argued.

"You could get over your issue with hypnosis," I whispered.

"The real truth," Roy continued, "is you're married to your work, and you chose it over me, and I blew up. I never wanted to see you again. I called you selfish and a big tease. I'd hoped to spend my best years with you, but obviously, I wasn't good enough."

"You are," Reika said meekly. "You're more than enough. You're wonderful."

"Yeah," he muttered.

"An hour later, I sought comfort in a bottle of vodka," Reika said to me.

Roy made a dismissive sound. "Starting around eleven, she drunk texted me every three or four minutes for nearly an hour. I finally phoned to make her stop. She answered and was slurring her words."

After a long silence, Reika said, "Thank you, Roy. For what it's worth, I'm sorry."

"Sure."

"I am," she stressed. "And I'm already back at AA and working on the issue."

"Glad to hear it. I wish you well." He ended the call.

Reika pressed her cell phone to her chest, clearly heartbroken. "Do you believe me, Allie? Do you believe him?"

"Yes." I squeezed her arm and offered a supportive smile. "Give him time. He'll come around. At the end of the call, I heard longing in his voice."

She sucked back a sob. "Let me cut you a check for the goodies you brought." She hurried from the kitchen and came back in a matter of minutes.

I left the museum, still pondering who had killed Jason. If both Iggie and Reika were absolved, only Patrick was left with a strong enough motive.

For the next two hours, I visited the places where I purchased all the ingredients I'd be needing over the next few days. Eggs from Garden Greene Farm. Butter from Butting Heads Farm. Fruits and veggies from the farmers' market, which convened on Thursday mornings.

By the time I breezed into Feast for the Eyes, I was ready for a snack. I set the pineapple upside-down cake on the desk behind the sales counter, ate one of the deviled eggs before placing a platter of them beside the cake, and then waved to Chloe, who was assisting a pair of women I didn't recognize.

"Where's Tegan?" I asked.

"In here," she cried from the stockroom.

I followed her voice and found her bent over a huge box, unpacking even more copies of *The Great Gatsby*.

"Mom texted and said ten more people responded." Tegan

paused to catch her breath. "This event is going to be huge! I hope Lillian has enough costumes on hand."

"I'm sure she'll figure out how to accommodate everyone. She knows theater people all over North Carolina."

If I was honest, the stockroom was one of my favorite places in the shop. The delicious aroma of hardcover and paperback books held the promise of adventure for all our customers. New books, as well as remainders—books that would be returned to publishers because they didn't sell—filled the additional freestanding metal shelving we'd added a couple of weeks ago. A beverage station, a refrigerator, and a microwave abutted another wall. The employee washroom stood to the left. The exit door to the alley was straight ahead. The door to the office was on the right.

"Hey, I was thinking..." *About murder and mayhem*, I mused but didn't utter the words out loud. "I was thinking about doing the blind-date-with-a-book promotion right away. Like today. We need to drive sales. I'll arrange some wrapped books in the display window as a lure. What do you think?"

"Superb idea. We have plenty of packing paper in the closet in the conference room." She jutted an elbow. "I'll join you in a few seconds to help."

"By the way, I did a bit of cooking for the *Gatsby* taste testing. Pineapple upside-down cake and deviled eggs are on the desk out front."

"Yum."

"Also, we can rule out Reika Moore as a suspect in the murder. I corroborated her alibi." I didn't elaborate. Reika didn't need me revealing her weakness now that she was on the mend. If I had to corroborate her conversation with Roy for Zach, I would do so privately.

I headed to the modest conference room, an important place because it was where we brought buyers who were interested in viewing rare books and first editions. I fetched the packing paper, tape, and two sets of scissors from the cupboard and went to the front of the bookshop. More customers had entered and were browsing the aisles and endcaps.

Making a tour of the shop, I pulled ten mysteries from the shelves and carried them to the sales counter, after which I fetched a number of romance, thriller, historical, young adult, and women's fiction novels. I began wrapping each, adding cryptic Sharpie notes to the paper.

For the women's fiction novel, *Beautiful Disaster*, I wrote: *Blind date with a masterpiece you probably haven't read yet. Good girl drawn to bad boy.* For Agatha Christie's *The Murder of Roger Ackroyd*, I wrote, *Blind date with one of the most important crime and mystery works of all time.* For *The Eyre Affair*, I wrote: *Blind date with time travel, cloning, and an outlandishly resourceful literary detective.* Bibliophiles would love that story. For *The Princess Bride*, which was popular with YA readers, I wrote: *Beautiful girl, handsome prince. What could go wrong?*

"Whatcha doing?" Chloe asked after ringing up her contented customers. She looked flirty in a red dress with puff sleeves and a flare skirt, which complemented her flawless, fawn-colored skin.

"Feeling clever." I showed her the most recent book I'd wrapped. "You look lovely. Wasn't your callback last night?"

"There's a final callback tonight. I'm so nervous."

"Don't be. Evelyn will make you feel comfortable."

"As if. She's intimidating!"

"She's a pussycat," I said, though I wasn't so sure, since I still couldn't figure out why she and my mother were at odds.

"Ooh, what's all this?" Chloe was gazing at the food on the desk.

"A taste test for the *Gatsby* event." I explained what each was. "Want to try?"

"Yes, please. I adore pineapple. May I do the honors?"

"Sure. That way I can keep wrapping with clean fingers."

She dashed into the stockroom and returned with plates, napkins, forks, and a cake knife. She cut a slice of cake for herself and another for me and dove in. "Wow. Not too soggy. Not too dry. Just right." She giggled. "I sound like Goldilocks." She took another bite. "I've always wanted to try my hand at making this, but you know me. I can't cook worth a lick."

Tegan emerged from the stockroom, her arms filled with copies of *The Great Gatsby*. "Done." She set the books on the counter. "I'll tag them after I eat dessert."

"It's delish," Chloe said. "I'm going to wash my hands. I'll be right back." She disappeared.

The front door opened, and Vanna strode in, all dolled up, her hair in a messy twist, tendrils cupping her face. I preferred her in jeans, sans makeup, but I'd never say so. She took such pains to put herself together.

"Which political big wheel did you meet today?" I asked.

She skirted the display table, her mouth quirked up on one side. "What makes you think I met with anyone?"

"Well, those are not delivery togs," I joked.

She assessed herself all the way down to her spiked heels. "The governor took me to lunch. He's thinking of running for president and wanted to talk to me about becoming the personal chef at the White House if he wins."

My mouth dropped open. "Really?"

"No, silly. Get real." She swatted the air. "The governor would never deign to come to Bramblewood. I met with the bank manager who handled all of Aunt Marigold's affairs. She wanted me to meet with an investment guy. He's very nice." She eyed Tegan. "You should meet with him, too. Sooner rather than later."

Vanna and Tegan had inherited a sizable amount of money, stocks, and jewelry when their aunt passed away.

"I will," Tegan promised. "But first I need to finalize divorce proceedings. Serving my ex papers has been a challenge."

"I think the bank manager wants you to get advice first," Vanna said. "But don't quote me on that. Call her. What're you doing, Allie?"

I handed her the wrapped version of *The Murder of Roger Ackroyd*. "Here. Enjoy a blind date with a book."

"Which book is it?"

"That's the point. You don't know until you accept the blind date."

As she read the caption, her mouth screwed up, making her look like she'd tasted something tart. "I don't read mysteries."

"Yes, I know, but you want to be part of Allie's Clue Crew, don't you? You have to read a few to understand how a detective's mind works."

She sighed dramatically. "Fine. I'll read it. But I won't like it." She unwrapped the book and frowned. "*The Murder of Roger Ackroyd*? Well, I guess I know who's going to die."

"There's a good twist."

Tegan leaned in. "Maybe we should've given her a culinary cozy, like one of the Domestic Diva mysteries. She'd relate to snooty Natasha, don't you think?"

"Or what about the mysteries set in Key West?" Chloe suggested, rejoining us. "The protagonist is a food critic."

"Next time," I said. "Vanna, try this book first. If you like it, we've got plenty of other suggestions."

"I'll read it after I read *The Great Gatsby*."

Tegan applauded. "Mother talked you into it? Hooray!"

"She bribed me," Vanna said. "She promised no dating advice for a year if I did."

I chuckled.

She peered past me at the cake. "Allie, is that what I think it is?"

I nodded.

"It's yummy." Chloe handed Vanna the plate she'd dished up for me. "Have some."

"I've got to watch my figure."

"One bite," Chloe said.

Vanna tasted it, and her eyes lit up. "Oh, my. I had no idea. It's really good. What's on top of the pineapple and cherries?"

"Butter and brown sugar."

"Divine." She forked in another mouthful.

"Gee, Sis, didn't you say you wanted to watch your figure?" Tegan chided.

"Eat dirt."

Chapter 19

A stirring warmth flowed from her, as if her heart was trying to come out to you concealed in one of those breathless, thrilling words.

—Nick Carraway in F. Scott Fitzgerald's *The Great Gatsby*

By the end of the day, half of the blind-date books had been sold, and I was already adding witty sayings to more wrapped books.

"Success!" Tegan closed the register and deposited the day's take into the safe. "I'll bring this to the bank on Monday when I meet with the manager." She scanned the shop. "Hey, Chloe!" she yelled.

Chloe was pacing the bookshop and humming nervously.

"Do you want me to go with you to your final callback?"

"No," Chloe replied. "Enjoy the sing-along. Mrs. Canfield is expecting you."

Lillian had phoned a half hour ago, reminding us of our promise to attend.

"You sure?" Tegan asked.

"Yes." Chloe's cheeks were flushed as red as her dress.

"Okey-doke. Allie, I've got to go home and change."

"Me too," I replied. "Chloe, break a leg."

"What does that mean?" Chloe's voice wavered.

I chuckled. "Curtsy when you get a standing ovation."

"You're kidding."

"No. I read it somewhere. Do like this . . ." I showed her my feeble attempt at a curtsy. "You're thanking the audience for its applause."

Chloe pulled a face. "Okay, I'll break a leg, but I'll probably stink."

Tegan clasped her in a hug and whispered something in her ear, which made Chloe laugh. Then she pushed her toward the door. "Be brilliant."

Chloe exited, and I turned to my pal. "What did you say to her?"

"She is adorable when she's nervous."

I swatted her arm. "You're shameless."

"See you at Blessed Bean."

I raced home and checked Darcy's toenail, which was healing nicely. Then I fed him, and I slipped into a pair of skinny black jeans and a soft blue short-sleeved silk top. I added a dab of mascara and a touch of lip gloss and hurried on to the coffeehouse. Lillian had advised us the owner would be serving appetizers to show her support for these sing-along nights, which thrilled me, because my stomach was growling. Like a dolt, I hadn't eat any of the cake.

"Wow," I murmured as I entered Blessed Bean.

The place, which was a rustic mishmash of tables, fairy lights, and hanging plants, was packed. One wall was filled with local art, and another lined with used books. Colorful signs reminding everyone to deposit library donations in the baskets on the coffee and wine bar were posted all over.

On the impromptu stage—a parquet square with a microphone and a karaoke screen scrolling the words to the current song—Candace was singing and bopping to Journey's "Don't Stop Believin'." For a soft-spoken woman who usually strummed her guitar while crooning folk songs, I was blown away by the way she was rocking it. She was outfitted in a jeans skirt, a jeans shirt, and cowboy boots and was twirling her hand in the air, as if prepared to lasso a calf. Her long blond tresses swished to and fro. I didn't see her husband in the crowd. Maybe she had forbidden him to come so she could let loose.

"Allie!" Tegan called from across the room. She was sitting at a long table with Stella Burberry and Lillian.

I wove through tables to join them.

"Hi, Allie!" Stella waved from the far end of the table. A dollars-and-cents kind of woman, she admittedly wasn't a fashion guru and said coming up with getups taxed her brain, so single-color ensembles, like the all-lavender one she had on, were the solution.

"What a crowd!" I exclaimed. "Who else is joining us?" I noticed a number of empty chairs at our table.

Lillian said, "Lots of ladies. Finette's at the counter, ordering a glass of wine. The waitress . . . Wallis from the Brewery . . . Did you know she was working here?"

I nodded.

"She was a tad overwhelmed by the crowd, and Finette was getting edgy. She got her loan, but she's had a long day of putting out fires."

"What loan?"

"To renovate her house. She mentioned she's thinking of hiring Patrick."

Seconds later, Finette appeared carrying a small tray arranged with empty wineglasses and a carafe of chardonnay. I was surprised to see her dressed in jeans and a simple white blouse. The outfit took years off her age. She placed the tray in the center of the table and lifted the carafe. Wallis trailed her and deposited a plate filled with mini grilled cheese sandwiches on the table. I thanked her and selected one.

"Who's thirsty?" Finette asked. "I thought everyone might like to indulge."

Lillian said, "You come into money, and suddenly you're graciousness personified."

Finette laughed. "Raise your hand if you want a glass."

Everyone did, with no reservations. I wondered about Reika and her addiction and whether she was remaining sober through another night, especially after Roy had rejected her a second time. To show my support, I decided to call her. It was too loud inside, so I slipped out the front door and tapped her contact on my cell phone.

She answered after one ring. "Hello?"

"It's Allie." It dawned on me that she might think I was being intrusive, and so I improvised. "I was, um, calling to ask how the tea went."

"It was lovely. The muffins and cookies were divine. Everyone raved. And lots of attendees opened their pocketbooks and gave sizable donations."

"Excellent."

"You'll be happy to hear I'm with a neighbor, and we're feasting on hot chocolate and s'mores."

I gathered she was assuring me she wasn't imbibing. "Excellent. Have fun. G'night."

When I rejoined my friends, I noticed another singer was onstage. Candace had joined us at the table. She was steering the conversation.

I reclaimed my chair next to Tegan and whispered, "I like your getup."

"It was easy." She'd thrown on a light sweater over leggings. "But shh, and pay attention." She jutted a finger at Candace. "She's telling us how she knew Jason. When they were young. They went to elementary school together."

Candace laughed, her eyes glinting with humor. "I remember chasing him in the yard—we were five—and I wanted to kiss him behind a tree."

Tegan said sotto voce, "Apparently, once his family relocated, she never saw him again. She didn't even know he was here until she heard about his murder."

"When I chased him, he didn't fight me off," Candace said

wistfully. "Probably because I had pretty blond curls, and he loved girls with blond curls."

Delilah had beautiful blond hair. Had Jason been obsessed with it? Had Finette added highlights to her tawny hair hoping to entice him?

"I didn't mind when he touched them," Candace continued, clearly enjoying sharing the memory. "Whenever he did, I could stare into those gorgeous eyes. His lashes were so long."

Finette said, "What was he like as a boy?"

"A bit of a braggart." Candace mimicked him. "'I can run faster than you. I can read better than you. I'm smarter than you.'" She tittered. "You know how it goes. My boy is pretty much the same. A lot of hot air." Her twenty-year-old son was living at home and attending junior college. "But Jason was sweet, too. Very kind and gentle."

"Aw," Finette said, misty-eyed. "Tell us more."

"He loved animals, and he dreamed of traveling the world and building skyscrapers. When he moved away"—she pressed a hand to her heart—"I was heartbroken. I dreamed we'd marry one day."

"Why didn't you keep in touch?" Finette asked.

"Back then, we didn't have the Internet, plus we were ten. It wasn't like we were going to become pen pals. Write a letter? Gag me." She giggled. "He lived in California. I lived here. End of story."

Except it hadn't been the end of the story. He'd returned.

"Allie," Finette said, "do you know if Zach is close to finding out what happened?"

Candace said, "My husband said Jason was engaged, but it didn't work out, and the breakup was what prompted him to come back to Bramblewood."

"I don't believe that was the case," I said. "Delilah married her husband thirteen years ago." Seeing her pregnant must have been the impetus.

"I wish we had closure for him," Finette said. "Zach is usually so good at solving things. Allie, is he close?"

"Detective Armstrong won't discuss the case."

"Do you have theories of your own?" she asked. "After all, you cracked Tegan's aunt's murder."

I hadn't cracked it per se. I'd come up with viable clues.

"Tell her who you suspect." Tegan prodded me with her fingertip.

I threw her the side-eye.

Tegan said to the rest, "Allie suspected Reika Moore because she wanted the properties Jason was bidding on for the Bramblewood Historical Preservation Society."

"But she didn't do it," I stated. "She's in the clear. She has a solid alibi."

"What is it?" Lillian asked.

I shook my head. "It's private but confirmed."

"Ignatius Luckenbill didn't kill him, either," Tegan offered. "He—"

I elbowed her.

She scowled at me. "It's going to come out. Gossip doesn't stay buried forever."

Her choice of words troubled me.

Lillian chimed, "He played poker on Monday."

"Monday may be the night for his regular game, but he didn't attend," Tegan said.

Finette's eyes widened. "He didn't?"

"No, however, an eyewitness gave him another alibi."

"Like . . ." Finette, eager for details, rotated a hand to urge Tegan to continue.

Tegan mimed sealing her lips.

"Poker is his passion," Finette went on, "so if he didn't play that night, why not? What could be more important?" She tapped her chin with her fingertips, and I could see the wheels in her brain working feverishly. "I've got it. He's having an affair!"

Tegan tried to remain stoic, but she blinked.

"I'm right!" Finette whooped. "With Ulla Karlsson? Of course it's her. He slobbers around the woman. She's sexy beyond all get out. And single. What a skunk he is. Behind poor Shayna's back. She's such a kind soul. He doesn't deserve her." She blew a raspberry. "He must have met up with Ulla at her place so they could keep the affair quiet." She regarded me for acknowledgment.

I maintained a neutral expression.

"Which *means*"—Finette dragged out the word while making eye contact with everyone at the table like a lawyer summing up her case to a jury—"his alibi isn't solid, because he could've sneaked out the back of Ulla's house, gone to Jason's, killed him, and doubled back to Ulla's before anyone was the wiser."

I gasped. She was right. Evelyn hadn't seen him enter Ulla's place. She'd caught sight of him exiting the front of her house after the time of the murder.

"Iggie is a weasel," Stella muttered. "Do you know what the rat did? He paid a Realtor to reveal how much my brother bid on three apartment complexes, and then he outbid him."

"Deplorable." Lillian tsked.

Again, I dredged up the conversation between Iggie and Finette at Ragamuffin about Burt the Cyber Buddy. What if Iggie, not Reika as I'd theorized, had the wherewithal to clone Jason's phone, and he sent me the texts Monday night to lure me to the estate? If so, he might be tech savvy enough to know how to erase them from my phone. I pictured the cuff link at the crime scene. Was it his? Had Zach pinned down that fact? If Iggie and Jason had scuffled, the cuff link could have come loose and fallen to the floor. But how could Iggie have known about my spearpoint collection? And where would he and I have crossed paths the day I lost my Celtic knot earring?

Someone tapped on the microphone.

"Hi, everyone. I'm Candace Canfield."

I hadn't realized she'd left the table.

"Let's give a round of applause for the library," she said. "We've raised over five thousand dollars this evening."

The crowd cheered.

"Now, let's get all of you singing this next song by Green Day, 'At the Library.'"

Candace pivoted toward the redheaded man queueing up the tunes. He gave her a thumbs-up. She twirled back and launched into song.

The crowd began bellowing out the words along with her, the lyrics on the karaoke screen telling the story about Billie Joe, who was too shy to talk to a girl at the library.

"I can't hear you!" Candace beckoned everyone to sing along with the raucous refrain.

We all chimed in at the top of our lungs.

Suddenly, the sound crackled, sparks flew, and the amplifier exploded.

Finette and Lillian shrieked.

And I bounded to my feet. "Call nine-one-one."

Chapter 20

"[Daisy has] got an indiscreet voice," I remarked. "It's full of—" I hesitated. "Her voice is full of money," he said suddenly.

—Nick Carraway and Jay Gatsby in conversation in F. Scott Fitzgerald's *The Great Gatsby*

The electrical glitch didn't trigger a fire. Blessed Bean didn't burn down. Nobody got hurt. But my nerves were still on edge when I arrived home. I cuddled Darcy for a long time before heading to bed.

Friday morning, bright and early, I rose, stretched, threw on a pair of black capris and a white camp shirt, and fed the cat, and together we hurried to Dream Cuisine. I had bunches of sweets to make, as well as a couple of party platters for Legal Eagles.

I hadn't had time to make myself a cup of coffee when Vanna swept into the ghost kitchen.

"Morning, Sunshine!" she said jauntily.

"Why are you in such a good mood?"

"Because I was up all night reading the best book."

"I enjoyed *The Murder of Roger Ackroyd*, too."

"Not that one, silly." She tossed her purse and silk cardigan on the table, strapped on an apron, slipped her hair into a chef's cap, like I had, and washed her hands. "Hey, kitty," she said to Darcy, who was lazing in his cat carrier. He meowed.

"Are you going to the bookshop? You lucky thing. Freedom will be yours soon."

He warbled his assent while butting his head against the zippered mesh cover.

"I read *The Great Gatsby*," she continued. "I couldn't put it down. In addition to promising no dating advice for a year, Mother said it was imperative I read it if I was going to participate at the event. She said people would be asking my opinion on the story and theme."

What a smart way to engage Vanna. Noeline knew her daughter would want to pontificate.

"What're we making?" She eyed the ingredients I'd assembled on the island.

"Let's taste test pasta pomodoro before we do all the baking for deliveries. Are you game?"

"Pasta for breakfast?" She wrinkled her nose.

"It contains all the food groups. Starch, fruit, and protein."

"What protein?"

"Cheese."

She jutted a hip. "Fine. Let's do it."

I brought the water to a boil and chopped the garlic while she blanched, peeled, seeded, and diced the Roma tomatoes I'd picked up at the farmers' market.

"What did you think of Daisy?" I asked.

"Daisy was ridiculously stupid. How could she let Gatsby take the blame for running over the woman? Didn't she realize her silence would be the end of him?"

"She didn't let him take the blame. Her wicked husband insinuated it was Gatsby, and—"

"Whatever." Vanna huffed. "As for Jay Gatsby, where do I begin? His sole motivation for making money was to win Daisy back? Honestly? She wasn't worth it."

I recalled how Patrick had taunted Jason, inferring that the notion of building a spectacular mall wouldn't woo Delilah into his life. Had Jason truly believed she'd return? I clacked the knife on the cutting board.

"What's wrong?" Vanna asked.

"I can't figure out why Jason Gardner moved to Bramblewood. The woman he loved was living in Los Angeles."

"I'd bet his happiest moments were when he was a young boy, and he hoped to rekindle the memory."

Her insight surprised me, and I recalled Candace talking about Jason being a dreamer when he was a child.

"The tomatoes are ready," Vanna said. "Want me to grate the cheese?"

"Yes, please."

I grew quiet as I browned the garlic in oil in a large sauté pan. I added the tomatoes and sauteed them to deglaze the garlic from the bottom of the pan. When the tomatoes were the right texture, I mashed them into a paste and boiled the angelhair pasta. After rinsing the pasta, I tossed it with the tomato sauce, freshly chopped basil, and half of the Parmesan cheese. When it was ready, I dished up two portions, dusted each with more grated Parmesan, and handed a serving to Vanna. "Taste."

She did and hummed her approval. "This is simple yet absolutely delicious. I'm hooked." She polished off her meal, washed both of our plates, and reviewed the orders we needed to prepare. "I'm so nervous," she mumbled.

"About today's deliveries?"

"No. Don't be daft."

"About the *Gatsby* party? Don't worry." I swatted the air with a spatula. "You do not have to opine about the story or the overarching theme of trying to achieve the American dream—a dream in which each man or woman should be able to attain greatness, regardless of the circumstances of their birth or position."

She gawked at me. "That's the theme?"

"One of them."

"No. I'm not . . . I mean, discussing the book doesn't worry me. It's . . . I'm going to the town council meeting tonight and . . ." She took a deep breath. "Don't get me wrong. I love working with you. But I would like to grow my business, and the mayor said he'll introduce me around. He knows all the bigwigs in town. I'll have to be on my toes."

"You'll be great. No one pitches *you* better than you." I smiled. "What're you wearing?"

She told me.

"You'll wow them. If for any reason you don't feel comfortable going alone, ask Tegan to accompany you."

"Why?"

"You're always saying you'd like to bond with her. What an ideal time."

"My sister at a town council meeting? She'd rather die."

I made deliveries to Ragamuffin, Perfect Brew, and Big Mama's Diner. Vanna was handling all the deliveries on the east side of town. My last stop was Jukebox Joint. Before entering, I peered in the windows to see if Zach was chatting with his mother. He wasn't. I didn't know why I was nervous to run into him, but we still hadn't resolved our issue. Would we ever? Jenny was over the moon with the sale of the last batch of goodies and asked if I'd ever considered making homemade hamburger buns. I hadn't and told her I had to pass. Doing so would be a full-time job. The Joint served over five hundred burgers a day.

At ten, when I arrived at Feast for the Eyes, Tegan was whizzing around like a crazy woman.

"What's up?" I asked.

"Chloe's running late, and a women's group wants to hold their book club here today. You won't believe who the group's leader is. Last night her ears must have been burning."

"Who?"

"Shayna Luckenbill."

"Iggie's wife?"

"The same."

"She has never come to Feast for the Eyes in her life. She's a library person."

"Yes, well, her house flooded because a pipe burst. The other participants weren't prepared to hostess. The library has two events and couldn't accommodate her. She begged and pleaded, saying they absolutely have to discuss Liane Moriarty's *Nine Perfect Strangers*. 'Have to,'" Tegan said, mimicking a breathless voice when she said the last words. "So I said yes."

If only the book club leader were Ulla Karlsson, we might have been able to cajole the truth out of her regarding Iggie's whereabouts Monday night. Shayna, who'd attended an art exhibit, would be useless.

"They're due in less than an hour." Tegan consulted her watch. "Fifty-two minutes, to be exact."

"Do they have snacks?" I asked.

"She said they don't need any, but of course, they'll be hungry. Got any on hand?"

"Actually, I made some lemon bars for you to taste test. I'll bring them in, and I'll put on a pot of coffee."

"We got rid of the machine, remember?"

I smiled. "I cater, did you forget? I have an urn and ground coffee in the van. You have tea. Let's get cracking. I'll handle the food prep."

At ten minutes to the hour, the door opened, and a forty-something man who appeared ready to blaze a trail from here to Oregon strode into the shop. He was broad-shouldered, with ruddy skin, shaggy gray hair, and salt-and-pepper stubble on his chin. His Pendleton shirt hung unbuttoned over a blue T-shirt and jeans.

"Hi. Welcome. I'm Allie."

Tegan was arranging chairs in the reading nook area.

"Name's Ott." His voice was gruff yet friendly.

"How may I help you?"

He scrubbed the back of his neck. "Not sure, but my buddy said I should come to town and speak to someone who works here."

"Are you looking for a specific book?"

He glanced around, as if surprised to find himself in a bookshop. "Uh, no, ma'am."

"Allie," I corrected.

"Yeah, see, my buddy is Zorro Vega. You know him?"

Honestly? Zorro's last name was Vega? I tamped down a smile. The literary Zorro's real name was Diego de la Vega. "Yes, I met him."

"Yeah, he asked if I was camping around Linville Caverns Monday night. I was, and, see, he asked if I saw anybody else. I did. I can't say I saw the guy's face, but I spied someone exploring with a flashlight." He grinned. An attractive dimple cut his right cheek. "He was cupping his hand over the flashlight, as if he didn't want anyone to notice him, so it was dim. By then the caverns were closed."

My heart began pounding against my rib cage. Had he seen Patrick? "Go on, Mr. Ott."

"Yeah, well, see, he was walking sort of sneaky like, but he wasn't being too quiet. In fact, he was whistling a tune. Soft and low. I recognized it because it's one of my favorites. "When I Come Around."

"By Green Day?"

"You know it?" He whistled a bar.

"I do." It was the song Patrick was singing in the video I'd landed on when I'd done the deep dive.

"I figured the guy must be looking for bats. I'm a bat guy. Do you like bats?"

"I can't say I do."

"They're cool. Did you know bats can naturally produce multi-harmonic tones that can be heard up to a hundred meters away? They don't attack whistlers. I figured that was why the guy was tootling." He spread his rough and chapped hands. "Anyways, that's the reason I came in to see you. Zorro asked me to do him a solid and share what I knew about his friend. If it was his friend."

"About what time was this, do you remember?"

"Close to eleven. I'd finished dinner. Hot dogs over an open fire. My favorite."

In view of the distance between the caverns and Bramblewood, Patrick couldn't have made it back in time to kill Jason. If the killer wasn't him and it wasn't Reika, maybe Finette was right—Iggie was the killer.

Ott jutted a thumb. "Hey, is that James Patterson's latest?"

"It is." I took one off the endcap and handed it to him. "Here. It's yours. A gift."

"You mean it?"

"Yes. I appreciate you taking the time to share what you knew. The guy you heard whistling will thank you, too."

Ott tossed the book into his other hand and raised it. "Mighty nice of you." He scanned the shop with one long sweep. "Nice place. Wish I was more of a reader."

"One can always start." I smiled. "Say, if the police need you to tell them what you saw and heard, would you be willing to do so?"

"Yeah, sure. I got nothing to hide. I live off the land, but I don't break any laws."

What an interesting guy.

"Do you have a cell phone?" I asked.

"Nah. I hate anything requiring plug-in batteries. But Zorro knows where to find me."

As Ott was leaving, Tegan appeared. "Who was the dude?"

"A guy who exonerated Patrick of murder."

Chapter 21

"Do you ever wait for the longest day of the year and then miss it? I always wait for the longest day of the year and then miss it!"

—Daisy Buchanan in F. Scott Fitzgerald's *The Great Gatsby*

After arranging the lemon bars, coffee mugs, sugar, and cream on a table in the reading nook for the impromptu book club, I phoned Zach and left a message, telling him what I'd learned about Patrick. Yes, he would chastise me for intervening, but I hadn't lured Ott to the shop. I hadn't asked him to verify Patrick's alibi. I was purely a helpful conduit for the police, right?

At four p.m., when the book club concluded, Shayna Luckenbill joined Tegan and me at the sales counter. She was quite a dramatic woman, using her hands and alto voice to great effect. Her silk scarf dress with its playful balloon motif was colorful and a testament to her love of art. For at least two minutes, she gushed about how wonderful the bookshop was. She questioned why she'd never popped in before—*popped* being her word.

"Thank you so much for letting us hold the meeting here," she said. "You are a lifesaver."

"Say, Shayna," Tegan said, offering me a sly wink, "we often host book clubs on Monday nights. Maybe you'd like to attend."

"That would be lovely."

"You would've enjoyed last Monday's event," Tegan lied, seeing as we hadn't had one. "We read and discussed Liane Moriarty's *Apples Never Fall*. Would you have been able to make it?"

"Sadly, no. I was at the library, hosting an aspiring new artists exhibition."

"Was your husband with you?" Tegan asked. "I heard he's so proud of what you do for the arts community."

Shayna blushed. "How kind of you to say. No, Iggie has a standing poker game. Heaven forbid I ask him to skip that. *Men!*" She cackled. "Allie, I have a friend who works at Legal Eagles who raves about Dream Cuisine's food. I should have you cater a future exhibition. Call me." She held up her cell phone and rattled off her number. "This way I'll have your contact."

I did as requested.

She pressed the cell phone to her chest. "Superb. Absolutely superb. By the way, my friend Ulla is sold on your shop, and she'll be telling everyone about your beautiful displays."

"Ulla Karlsson is h-here?" I stammered. Of course she was. She was Shayna's best friend. *A duplicitous best friend*, I mused.

"She's over there. The one in the tent dress." Shayna pointed toward the reading nook area.

The woman—Ulla—was wearing a shapeless dress. Her ash-white hair was secured in a claw-style clip, and she hadn't donned a stitch of makeup. Was that how she snowed her friend into believing she was as innocent as a lamb and not a husband stealer?

"She said she wants to start investing in books so she can expand her library. Maybe you ladies could steer her to the next best read."

"I'll say hello," I offered and strolled over to Ulla before she could depart with the other women, who were filing out. "Hi, Ulla. I'm Allie. Nice to meet you. I enjoyed you in *Young Frankenstein*."

"Thank you," she replied. "It was a fun show to do."

"Shayna said you enjoyed the bookshop."

"Not merely enjoyed. I love it here. The layout is so friendly. The nook area is warm and inviting. Did I hear right? You have first editions for sale?"

"Indeed. Most have been written by prominent North Carolinians." Using Tegan's tactic, I added, "We often have book clubs on Monday nights. You should join us."

"I'd love to, but I can't on Mondays. I have a standing appointment."

"With?"

She glanced at Shayna, who had begun talking to Tegan, and returned her gaze to me. "With my trainer."

"Gee, I had no idea Ignatius Luckenbill was a trainer."

Her face drained of color. "He . . . no . . . he's not—"

"Weren't you with him last Monday?"

"He . . . we . . . How do you know . . . ?"

"Someone saw you."

"It's o-over." Her voice cracked. "We—" She hiccupped a sob. "We ended it that night. I swear. We both love Shayna too much. If she discovered we were . . . we'd never forgive ourselves. We—"

"Did he leave before eleven thirty?"

"Why?"

"It matters."

"He was with me until midnight."

That confirmed what Evelyn had said.

"Did he go out alone at any time before then? Maybe he used the back door?"

"No." She clutched my hands. Hers were trembling. "Please don't tell Shayna. It was a mistake."

She looked so mortified, I agreed to keep the secret. She'd cleared Iggie. Verifying his whereabouts had been my solitary goal.

"Tegan!" Chloe whizzed into the shop, the skirt of her dress wafting up. She skidded to a stop by the sales counter, and the skirt settled down and clung to her thighs like saran wrap. "I'm not going to be an actress."

Tegan rounded the counter and grasped Chloe's shoulders. "Breathe."

Chloe inhaled sharply. She wheezed like a deflated balloon.

"Tell us why not." Tegan released her.

"I learned rehearsals might go well into the wee hours of the morning. With regularity. I can't handle such a commitment. Why, last night, callbacks ran until midnight." She repeated the word. "Midnight! That's why I overslept today." She clapped a hand to her chest. "I never oversleep."

"Poor thing," Ulla mumbled to me. "She needs a pep talk." She strode to Chloe. "Sweetheart, I saw you at your first callback. Don't quit. You're too good."

I joined them and petted Chloe's shoulder.

She shimmied from my touch, her eyes misting with gratitude. "Thank you, everyone, for your support, but my mind is made up. I don't want to split my time between the shop and the theater. Besides, rehearsals would cut into my reading time. I love to read. I live for reading!"

Shayna sidled to Ulla and linked arms with her. "We all do. Books are magical. Books bring friends together. It's the reason we started our book club, right?"

"Absolutely," Ulla chimed. "Literary friends forever." She winked at Chloe and said, "Good luck." Then she guided Shayna toward the door. At the threshhold, she peeked over her shoulder.

I gave her a thumbs-up. I wouldn't reveal her secret. I believed she really was ending things with Iggie. As for him, however, he would step out on Shayna again, but his deceitfulness wasn't my business. Unless Shayna and I became friends.

Chloe tilted her head. "Those were new customers."

Tegan filled her in on the impromptu book club.

"I'm sorry I wasn't here to help," Chloe said.

"Allie and I managed."

Chloe touched her cheeks. "Oh, I must look a mess. I'll be right back." She rushed into the stockroom.

At the same time, the door to the shop opened, and Lillian's grandmother Magda strode in. She pivoted decisively toward the display of blind-date books.

I nudged Tegan. "Go tend to Chloe. I'll help Magda." I sauntered to her, and as I drew near, I gasped. "Magda, what happened to your arm?" She was clad in a summery sleeveless dress. Her right arm was blotchy with black and blue bruises. "Did someone attack you?"

"Heavens, no. If they did, I'd hurt them. I know karate." She snorted. "No, dear, I'm a klutz. I was on the porch, changing shoes—one my age shouldn't wear wedges—and the laces on one snarled, and the shoe refused to come off, and, well, I teetered and fell. Down the stairs. Onto my shoulder." She laughed at herself. "Yes, it hurt, but I hobbled up the stairs to go inside for some ice. That was when I realized I'd locked myself out." She knuckled her temple. "I'm brain dead lately, I'm telling you. But I absolutely had to get inside to fetch my purse before going to tea with my friend, so I crawled through my schnauzer's doggy door and caught my arm on the edge."

I winced, imagining the pain. On the other hand, I couldn't believe scraping the doggy door would cause so much bruising. "Magda, is it possible you broke your arm or shoulder when you fell?"

She tsked. "I made a poultice to treat it. I'll be fine. Don't give it a second thought." Lillian had told me her grandmother was a naturalist who refused to take medicine.

"But maybe going to a doctor and getting an X-ray—"

"No, sirree. The last time I did such a ridiculous thing, I ended up having a hip replacement. I'll be fine. I didn't come in for sympathy. I want a blind date with a book. I can't wait to see what he looks like." She giggled and motioned to the array of new books I'd wrapped with brown paper. "And I'll need one for Lillian. She said it would be great fun to chat about them, and once we finished, we'd swap."

How sweet of Lillian to engage her grandmother in this way. I missed my nana and wished she was still here to talk about books and food and life.

"Stop staring at my arm," Magda said. "Drat it all. I should have worn long sleeves, but it's so warm out."

"Fine. No more staring." I made a mental note to text Lillian and give her a heads-up. "I know you love to read romance. What else appeals to you?"

"I also love a good murder."

I flinched, thinking of Jason, but quickly recovered and picked up the wrapped book that I knew was *Into the Night*. I handed it to her.

She read aloud: "'A gilded cage, a shocking murder. Riveting suspense. A high-profile celebrity.' This sounds good. I really enjoyed the movies Hitchcock made."

Next, I handed her *Every Summer After*.

She recited the words I'd written on the wrapping aloud: "'A radiant debut. Six summers in the making. A man who can cook.'" She squinted at me. "I believe I've read this one, but I'll bet Lillian hasn't. She prefers historical novels and nonfiction works about theater."

Chuckling, she headed toward the sales counter. I followed to ring her up.

"You know," she said, "ever since I saw you the other day, I can't get Cora Yeager out of my mind."

"Why?"

"Well, I told you I knew Jason as a boy, but I didn't mention Cora was my friend and Cora's daughter and son-in-law were friends with Jason's parents. I didn't omit it intentionally, mind you. It merely slipped my mind. I'm forgetting all sorts of things lately. Age . . . it's a real thing." She chuckled. "Anyway, I was telling Lillian about Cora's connection to Jason—remember my daughter babysat him?—and she said I had to tell you, because I happened to know that for years, Cora's daughter kept in touch with the Gardners via postcards and the occasional Christmas card. You know how it goes." She leaned in, as if she was imparting a well-guarded secret. "I think they were hoping to appease sweet Delilah because she and Jason—"

"Delilah!" I exclaimed. "Was that the name of Cora's daughter?"

"Yes. I told you."

"No, you didn't. Jason was in love with a woman named Delilah. Could it be the same person?"

"Heavens, I don't know. It's a rare name, to be sure, but Delilah was six years younger. A bitty thing. She and Jason horsed around, of course, when the parents would get together for weekend barbecues. Cora's daughter had dogs, and Jason loved playing with them. Delilah followed him everywhere. She revered him like an older brother." She snorted. "When he and his family journeyed west, Delilah was inconsolable." Magda inhaled to refill her lungs before continuing. "That's why a few months later, Cora's daughter and son-in-law moved lock, stock, and barrel to New York."

"Not to spite her mother?"

"Well, I'm sure it was part of the equation."

Wow! I couldn't believe it. Delilah and Jason had an actual historical connection? Having known her as a child might explain why he'd been so adamant about owning the Yeager properties. If there had been bad blood between Cora Yeager and her daughter, and if Delilah had grown up hearing about their rift, and in the process realized her grandmother was the reason she no longer saw Jason, she might have delighted in seeing the properties destroyed and converted into a mall.

If he built it . . . she might come.

Chapter 22

And so with the sunshine and the great bursts of leaves growing on the trees, just as things grow in fast movies, I had that familiar conviction that life was beginning over again with the summer.

—Nick Carraway in F. Scott Fitzgerald's *The Great Gatsby*

A half hour later, as Chloe and Tegan were tending to customers, I reminisced about the conversation with Jason at the Brewery and decided I needed to fill in some blanks. I retreated to the office, where I gave Darcy a good cuddle, sat at the desk, and awakened the computer.

An hour later, the mystery was solved. When I'd asked Jason where he and Delilah met, he'd slyly said they'd "hooked up" at UCLA, not "met." After he left the army, he must've tracked down her whereabouts, discovered she was enrolled at the University of California, Los Angeles, and applied. I leaned back in the chair, wondering how their first reunion might have taken place. At a party? A mutual class? The library? Had he reminded her of their playful association as kids? Had the cute meet rekindled their friendship? Had Delilah taken pleasure in the notion he'd pursued her? Their history didn't change what had happened to him, but it explained so much about who Jason was and how obsessed he'd been with a girl with pretty blond curls.

At two p.m., after a quick bite to eat, I gathered Darcy. We left the bookshop for the day and drove to the veterinarian's office for the cat's follow-up appointment. The vet gave him a clean bill of health, after which I warned my cat with a sweet tap to his nose to stop scratching the brick around the fireplace.

The vet said, "I doubt this toenail snag was from encountering a raised or rough surface. I believe he caught it on wire."

"He's been playing under an armchair. There's loose strapping."

"I don't think strapping would have caused this, either. Perhaps a spring is broken and hanging down. I'd check it out. I also found some skin beneath the toenail."

"You didn't mention that before."

"I figured he scratched you when you tried to treat him."

Huh. If he had, I hadn't felt a thing, and I hadn't bled. I thanked her, then added we'd see her in six months for his annual checkup, and we left.

On the drive home, as much as I wanted to talk to Zach and tell him what I'd learned about Jason—it probably wouldn't impinge on the investigation—I opted not to leave him another message. "Less is more," a high school teacher used to tell me when it came to explaining things. I had a tendency to write really long thesis papers to make sure everything I believed was essential made its way onto the page. When I listened to the teacher's "less is more" advice, my theses became pithier and, therefore, better, which earned me repeated A's.

As I was nearing Oak Knoll, the street on which Tegan lived, I called her at the shop and asked if she was free for dinner. I'd cook. She wasn't, and she sounded distraught. She had to meet with the divorce attorney due to a snag in her case. Good old Winston, who had yet to be served, had decided to sue her for spousal support. I told her to call me after the meeting. She promised she would.

While ending the call using the steering wheel's speaker icon, I caught sight of the blue house with the yellow shutters at the corner. Finette Fineworthy's great-aunt's house. The lights were dim. No cars stood in the driveway. I noticed mail jutting from the mailbox, as Vanna had described, and decided to take it in to her. Finette . . . and Marigold, rest her soul . . . would want me to do so.

I parked the van and opted to bring Darcy with me. Unless Katherine Fineworthy was allergic, I doubted she'd mind.

First, I gathered the mail and reviewed it as I walked to the door. Katherine must have donated to a number of women's causes over the years, because much of the junk mail was pleas to support breast cancer research and Equality Now. In addition, I saw plenty of other items, including pink and yellow envelopes, as well as flyers with ads for upcoming summer sales.

On the porch I picked up what sounded like a game show playing on TV. I rang the doorbell, but I didn't hear footsteps inside. I knocked and waited. The volume of the television didn't lower.

Darcy mewed.

"Yes, sweet boy, you're right. We have to check on her."

I tiptoed to the living room window and peeked in. Through a break in the curtains, I saw a vintage Sony television on a middle shelf of a wall of books. *Wheel of Fortune* was playing. A frail, silver-haired woman in a recliner faced the screen. Her eyes were closed. Was she asleep?

Deciding I should conduct a wellness check—I prayed she hadn't died—I returned to the front door and tried the handle. Locked. I searched the porch for a fake rock holding a key but didn't find one. I recalled Magda crawling through the doggy door of her house and scanned the area for one, but I didn't see a pet door of any kind. I noticed the porch swing was tilting a tad to the right, and once again thinking of Magda, I crouched down. I peered beneath the swing and let out a whoop.

Success! A metal hide-a-key box was affixed to the chain dangling below the seat. I retrieved the key, inserted it into the front door lock, and twisted it.

I stepped into the foyer. "Katherine," I called in a muted tone. I didn't want to startle her by yelling. The house was rife with the scent of lavender. A vase of dried flowers stood on the entry table, as did a basket of either unread mail or discarded mail. I deposited the stack I was carrying beside it. "Katherine, it's Allie Catt," I continued. "Your grandniece's friend. I'm coming in."

I set Darcy's carrier on the floor, tiptoed through the archway, and glimpsed the old woman on the recliner. Her hands rested prone on the armrests. I noticed her fingers twitching ever so slightly, which made me breathe easier. She was alive.

Skirting the worn sofa and walnut coffee table as quickly as I could, I said, "Katherine, I've come to check on you. Finette . . ." I mentioned her name in case the woman might waken. "Finette asked me to bring in today's mail."

Darcy yowled.

Katherine flinched. Her eyes snapped open. She peered at me with fear. "Who are you?"

"My name is Allie. Don't be frightened. I'm Finette's friend."

"Don't know any Finette." She pulled the tie of her pink robe tighter around her waist. A pair of slippers lay on the floor at an odd angle, as if they'd fallen off her feet.

"I was concerned when you didn't answer the door, so I located your key and used it to enter. I know Finette would want me to—"

"Don't know any Finette."

"Sure you do. She's your grandniece."

"I have two."

At least she'd gotten that fact right. She was probably foggy after falling into a deep sleep. I grabbed the remote control and muted the television.

"I'm thirsty." Katherine pressed a button to raise the recliner to a more suitable sitting position.

"Yes, ma'am. On it." I fetched a half-drunk glass of water from the side table by the sofa and handed it to her. "Here you go."

She held it in two hands and bent her head to the rim of the glass rather than raising the bottom of the glass to help the flow. "It's empty," she said.

"No, ma'am. You have to tip the glass a bit more." Was she senile? Had she forgotten how to drink from a cup? "Let me help." I reached over to assist. A small amount of water spilled into her mouth.

"Thank you."

"Yes, ma'am."

Darcy mewed again, eager to make Katherine's acquaintance.

"Is that a cat?" Katherine blinked.

"Yes. It's Darcy, my tuxedo cat."

"I love the name Darcy. Marigold did, too. Did you know Marigold? She died."

"Yes, ma'am, I did. She was a dear friend."

She hummed. "Fitzwilliam Darcy was so handsome." She extended her arms. "May I hold him?"

I took the glass from her, placed it on the side table, and retrieved my cat. I told him to be gentle and set him in her lap. "Here you go."

"Nice kitty. Nice Darcy." She petted him slowly, head to tail. "I had a tuxedo cat. He died a few years ago. My nephew hated cats, but I didn't care. I wanted his girls to have one. Pets are important. They show humans how to be more loving."

"That's true. Your grandniece Finette—"

"No!" She said it so sharply Darcy quaked and leaped to the floor. "You do not pronounce it in such a fashion."

"You don't?"

"It's Finette. Accent on the first syllable, long *i*. Not Finette like Annette."

I repeated the word properly, showing her I was listening, while wondering why Finette had changed the pronunciation. Perhaps her parents had said it that way, and it had been a bone of contention between them and her great-aunt.

"Is this your family?" I pointed to the multiple photographs of Katherine and the man I presumed to be her husband. I regarded one picture in which an angelic thirty-something woman was standing beside a young fireman. They were flanking a pair of teen girls. The girl closest to the fireman was clearly Finette. The other had to be the older sister, who'd relocated to Arizona. "Very attractive."

"Mm-hmm."

"I brought in your mail. Would you like me to go through it with you?"

"Please." She eased herself out of the recliner and shuffled barefoot to the sofa. She patted the cushion beside her, suggesting I sit.

I collected the mail from where I'd left it in the foyer, and placed it on the coffee table. Katherine patted the sofa again.

I sat beside her. "My friend Vanna visited you on Wednesday. She brought you dinner. Do you remember her?"

"Yes. Good cook. Likes ads about electronics. Ovens are her specialty."

I smiled. I could picture Vanna prattling about the differences between Wolf and Viking ovens. The heat variances. The quality of craftsmanship.

"What did you eat that night?" I asked.

"Can't remember."

"Vanna said mac 'n' cheese."

"Maybe." Katherine picked up the stack of mail and began sorting through it. She tossed piece after piece on the table. She viewed a pink envelope, grunted, "Another one?" and pitched it onto the messy pile. On the front were the words *final notice* in bold black print. "If it's not final, why mark it as final?"

She flung the yellow envelope, too. On it was the single word *foreclosure*. Heavens. Was the poor woman going to be kicked to the curb? Did Finette know? A foreclosure gave the owner ninety days to either pay off what was owed or sell the property. Had Finette wanted to talk her great-aunt into moving to a retirement facility so she could unload the house and get out from under the burden?

"I'm tired," Katherine said abruptly. "Leave."

I didn't think I should. She was clearly upset. "Vanna said Finette asked her to cook for you on Wednesdays."

"No!"

"Finette." I pronounced it correctly this time, accent on the first syllable.

"Yes."

"She's your grandniece, ma'am."

"Yes."

"The president of the town council. She reads to you. She was here last Monday and read *Great Expectations*. Do you remember her being here?"

"That's my favorite book."

"She said so."

"She didn't read it."

I stared at her.

"She didn't read it, because she wasn't here."

Chapter 23

"Of course she might have loved him just for a minute . . . In any case . . . it was just personal."

—Jay Gatsby in F. Scott Fitzgerald's *The Great Gatsby*

Clearly agitated, Katherine said she didn't want company or any further help with the mail and, in no uncertain terms, told me to get out. Darcy, understanding the old woman's wishes, bounded into his carrier and warbled loudly, as if to say, *Let's get cracking.*

Though I wished I could help the older woman find peace, reluctantly I left.

The moment Darcy and I arrived home, I released him, and he dashed under the armchair.

"Uh-uh, buster. No." I crossed the room. "The vet told us no more messing around where you might tear another toenail. I have to get the chair fixed." I bent and waved to him. "Come out."

He didn't budge.

Growling, I lowered myself to my knees and, feeling like Magda crawling through the doggy door, sans the possibly broken shoulder, lasered him with an evil eye. "Come out."

He backed away.

"What the heck? C'mon, sir. Please . . ."

He yowled.

I noticed jute straps and broken springs weren't the only things hanging from the underside of the chair. Something gold was dangling. A dainty piece of jewelry.

"Oh, my, have you been trying all this time to draw my attention to it? Got it. I'm on it. I'm reaching in. Not for you. For your plaything. Ready? Three . . . two . . ." I stretched my arm and wrapped my hand around the chain. I couldn't pull it loose. "Darcy, I need to turn the chair upside down. Please don't be upset." I rose to my feet.

He dashed out, bounded to the top of the cat-scratching station, and glowered at me like an angry toddler.

"Tough beans."

I gripped the chair's roll-style arm and laid the heavy piece of furniture on its side. Extending my hand between the turned-wood legs, I unhooked a bracelet from the offending loose spring. It wasn't just any bracelet. It was an infinity ankle bracelet. Like the one Finette sported when she'd visited my place at the neighborhood watch party a few weeks ago. She'd worn one of her classic skirt suits, and I'd noticed the bracelet and commented on how pretty it looked. I also remembered Iggie pointing it out at Ragamuffin.

I perched on a chair at the dining table and studied what I was holding as another thought occurred to me. Was it possible the bracelet had a faulty clasp and had wound up in my house when an intruder, say Finette, sneaked in and stole the spearhead from my collection?

No way. She wasn't a thief. She wasn't a killer, either. She had loved Jason. At least that was the vibe I'd gotten. They'd teased. They'd cajoled.

But her alibi of reading to her great-aunt was questionable.

I recollected Lillian asking Finette how her great-aunt was doing. She had bemoaned her great-aunt's frailty and intimated that Katherine "wouldn't remember" her being there Monday, even though Finette claimed she had read to her until midnight. Had she offered up the tidbit to make us believe her great-aunt was losing it and therefore couldn't be counted on to corroborate her alibi?

Finette's buddy-buddy relationship with Jason had been unusual. The first time I saw them interact was at Feast for the Eyes. He swaggered in, and she cozied up to him. Their playful banter was light and easy. In an English accent, Jason said, "Hello, ducky, old sport." She laughed and explained to us he'd dubbed her "Duckworthy" because he had a friend in college with that last name. She feigned umbrage because she was a Fineworthy of *the* Fineworthys, and—

I gasped. *Duckworthy.* Before dying, Jason had uttered the single syllable "Duh." I thought he was calling for Delilah, but "Duh" could also be the beginning of Duckworthy. Had he been trying to tell me she was the one who stabbed him?

Earlier, I'd considered Iggie a tech-savvy person because of his interest in the tips Burt the Cyber Buddy offered. Finette was equally enthused. What if she, not Iggie, had cloned Jason's phone and sent me the texts? What if she had the expertise to erase them from my phone? I recalled seeing her the day I lost my earring. At Ragamuffin, waiting for her latte. She could have nabbed the jewelry and planted it at the crime scene.

I paused. Why would she want to frame me? Because she was interested in Zach? Was she jealous of my relationship with him? Did she want him, not Jason, and think by pinning a murder on me, he would be available?

I pictured the cuff link I had seen at the crime scene, etched with the cursive letter *I*. The other day at Ragamuffin, Finette had helped Iggie when his cuff link had come loose. Had she, like a magician, swiped it and swapped it for another—difficult to do, but not impossible—and taken his to the crime scene to frame him, as she had me? A twofer, as it were. If Zach didn't believe I committed murder, he might believe Iggie did. I recalled how Finette had latched on to Iggie's affair with Ulla at the sing-along. If she'd been keeping tabs on him after their breakup, she could've learned he was fooling around with Ulla, and realized he couldn't or wouldn't be able to verify his alibi, lest he destroy his marriage, and therefore would be an easy target to frame. Also, she needn't have palmed the cuff link that day. She could have devised the plan to frame us long before and stolen one from his house.

A niggling notion cycled through my mind. What if Finette wasn't even a blip on Zach's radar? What if he deemed only me and Iggie suspects, and Iggie was now cleared for the second time, thanks to me? After all, I'd left Zach the message about Ulla's confession.

Tag. You're it, Allie.

But why would Finette kill Jason? When I had first tried to come up with suspects, I'd given her a feeble motive: she professed her love to Jason, but he rebuffed her. I'd ditched the theory, thinking she couldn't win Jason over if he was dead. She would want him to remain alive. However, if she did have a thing for Zach, her interest in Jason was moot.

Darcy clawed the llama cat-scratching station with intensity, and I harkened back to the vet saying there had been skin under Darcy's toenail when I'd brought him in for treatment. She hadn't mentioned it on our previous visit, assuming he must have scratched me, and since I hadn't complained, she'd believed it wasn't a big deal.

But he *hadn't* hurt me. Had he defended our home and clawed Finette?

Come to think of it, I hadn't seen her ankles in a while. She'd taken to wearing slacks. For a woman who liked to show off her legs, her donning slacks seemed unusual, especially considering how hot it had been lately.

I revisited her motive for wanting Jason dead. If not rejection . . .

I snapped my fingers. "Darcy, yes! This is about money. Iggie intimated that Jason might have been paying Finette for her sway with the town council. If she was hard up for cash, she might have demanded Jason pay her more money than they'd first negotiated. What if he'd refused? At her wit's end, distraught with her financial situation, she'd lost all reason and plotted his death."

Darcy tilted his head, listening.

"Last night at Blessed Bean, Lillian talked about Finette having secured a loan. What if she was in charge of managing her great-aunt's finances, and because of her elaborate tastes—jewelry, designer handbags, and expensive hair highlights—she messed up and missed payments on the house loan, thus launching the house into foreclosure?"

I flashed on the other day, when Finette jokingly rushed into the bookshop, out of breath—I'd feared she needed CPR. She was fanning a pink envelope similar to the one I'd seen at her great-aunt's house, the one marked Final Notice. She said she was overwhelmed with business meetings, as well as with talking to citizens and going to the bank. Had she met with the lenders in an attempt to rectify her financial situation, but the loan officer had denied her any assistance? Was the official end to the ninety-day foreclosure period at hand?

On another occasion, Finette had asserted that she never regretted not having money growing up, because her parents were such good people. According to her, they donated readily to charities, and they kindly took in her great-aunt and cared for her. When they passed on, did Finette opt to leave her great-aunt in the family home to honor her parents? Did she buy herself someplace new, ultimately stretching her pocketbook to the max? Supposedly, her father had said, 'Do not save what is left after spending, but spend what is left after saving.' Was it possible she hadn't heeded his words?

I mulled over Jay Gatsby's obsession with money. With class.

With status. When Finette first met Jason Gardner, did she believe she could climb the social ladder with him on her arm? Did she think she'd be able to abandon her meager lifestyle, give up working, and become a lady of leisure? When a love affair didn't ignite, did she resolve to press him for money to end her financial woes?

I fished my cell phone from the pocket of my capris and pulled up Finette's contact. Tegan had shared an entire roster of regular bookshop customers when I'd taken part ownership. I dialed Finette, but when she didn't answer, I recalled Vanna mentioning that a town council meeting would take place tonight. No doubt Finette would be there. She never missed a meeting, not even for illness.

I waited for her message to finish and, after the beep, said, "Hi, Finette. It's Allie. I . . ." I paused. Taunting her about finding the bracelet would be foolish. Outright accusing her of murder would be, too. "I'm coming to the town council meeting. I'll bring cookies. See you there."

I ended the call and stared at the phone's screen. Yes, contacting her had been rash. Luckily, I'd put on the brakes in time. I slipped her ankle bracelet into my pocket and texted Zach.

Me: **I know you're ticked at me. Sorry. A girl's gotta do . . .**

I erased the text, muttered, "C'mon, Allie. Use your brain," and I started over.

Me: **I wish you would return my call. I have some news you'll want to hear. I promise I won't be wasting your valuable time.**

I moaned softly, admitting it was a sarcastic use of the word *valuable*, and erased the message.

Me: **I hope you'll be at the town council meeting tonight. I'm bringing sugar cookies. Maybe we could chat afterward. Get caught up.**

Good. Friendly and bland. So be it. Heaven forbid I texted my intention to confront the woman I suspected of killing Jason.

The Bramblewood Park and Rec Center was located at the intersection of Main Street and North Mountain Road. It housed a gymnasium for sporting events; an auditorium, where the town held concerts and indoor festivals; and a few smaller rooms, one of which was where the town council convened.

Before entering the room, I drew in a deep breath. *You can do this, Allie.*

The meeting was already in session. All fifty chairs were filled. A few onlookers were standing by the right-hand wall, including Vanna and Tegan. Vanna was rocking it in a cream-colored suit and a soft blue blouse, but I could tell she was nervous, because she kept checking her fingernails. Tegan caught sight of me and offered a supremely bored face. I was wound too tightly to laugh. She eyed me, concerned, and tapped something on her cell phone.

I felt my phone ping and scanned the screen. Tegan had sent a text.

Tegan: **Meeting with divorce attorney went well. Winston is handled.**

Me: **Good. Talk later.**

I pocketed the phone.

At the front of the room, Reika Moore was standing at the lectern, speaking into the microphone as she discussed her role in the Bramblewood Historical Preservation Society. Three councilmen sat at each of the tables positioned on either side of the lectern. In front of the men sat white placards scrawled with the particular person's name. To the left stood Finette, in profile. She was clad in the white skirt suit she'd worn earlier in the week and came across self-assured and serene. Was I mistaken about Darcy and her getting into a squabble? Wrong about the ankle bracelet belonging to her? Wrong about her need for money?

No. I didn't think I was, but my gut was roiling with doubt. Tamping down my angst, I strolled to the beverage and treats station in the rear right corner. I placed the platter of cookies I'd brought beside the coffee urn, removed the saran wrap, and tossed it into the garbage pail.

Reika said, "The preservation society has a long-standing relationship with this town. Because of the work we do . . ."

A few people were checking their watches. Finette looked itchy to move on.

"We are prepared to offer top dollar for the Yeagers' historic properties," Reika said. "The town will reap the benefits. There will be no loss."

"Hold on!" Patrick, who was sitting beside the mayor in the front row of chairs, jumped to his feet. "I want to make a bid. I secured the financing."

I wondered if he knew Mr. Ott had vouched for him and he was no longer a suspect. Maybe he had never thought he was under suspicion.

"Not so fast," Iggie said, bounding to a stand. "I've already been told I won the bid."

"Gentlemen, decorum!" Finette bellowed. "You'll have your turn to make a pitch. Sit, please."

Iggie spotted me, inched out of the row, and moseyed to the food table. He picked up a cookie, ate half, and wiped his mouth free of crumbs. "Evening, Allie. I heard the bookshop hosted my wife's book club at the last minute."

"We did."

"She was very happy."

"Glad to hear it."

"I also heard you chatted with Shayna's friend Ulla."

Interesting segue. "Did Shayna tell you?"

"Ulla did. Every detail. She wasn't lying to you. We're through. Neither she nor I will be telling Shayna about the affair. What's past is past."

"I think you should inform Detective Armstrong."

He cocked his head. "Why does he need to know?"

"Because he's wondering if you had motive to kill Jason Gardner."

"Me? Murder Gardner? Get real."

"The police came across your cuff link at the crime scene."

"What the blazes are you talking about?"

"A cuff link with a cursive capital *I* on it, to be exact." I still didn't know if Zach had verified the letter was an *I* or a *J*, but I figured a small distortion of the truth was allowable.

Iggie's cheeks puffed up. Warm air leaked from his mouth. "I was never there."

"So you say."

"My friend Ed Smith heard a dog that night."

"Yes, I know."

"I don't have a dog."

"The murderer didn't necessarily bring a dog to the scene. It could have been one of many in the neighborhood."

Iggie worked his tongue along the inside of his cheek. "Yeah, fine, I'll talk to Armstrong. Please . . ." His gaze was filled with remorse. "Please keep my relationship with Ulla on the down-low."

I murmured, "Okay."

Reika completed her pitch and left her post at the lectern. Finette jumped into the spot Reika had vacated. The audience applauded politely as Reika collected Amira, who was sitting dutifully at the end of the first row, and she took a seat beside a weathered, silver-haired man in the middle of the row. He pecked her on the cheek, making me wonder if he might be Roy.

Finette spoke into the microphone. "Ladies and gentlemen—"

"My turn." Patrick leaped to his feet again.

She shot him a dirty look but quickly forced a smile. "Yes, Mr. Hardwick. Please come forward. You have three minutes." She left her post, caught sight of me, and lasered me with a look.

Because I'd brought cookies? Or because she'd learned I'd visited her great-aunt?

Remaining the object of her wrath, I proceeded along the right side of the room. Vanna still seemed nervous. Why hadn't she made an appointment at the mayor's office, where she wouldn't have dozens of other people pleading for a moment of his time?

I sidled to Tegan. "How's your sister doing?"

"I've never seen her so edgy. I'm not sure what the whole story is."

"And you? Winston is handled?"

She brushed her hands together. "Done and done. His attorney made him realize he was grasping at straws. When my attorney threatened to sue him, he caved. He signed papers this afternoon and FedExed them. As of tomorrow, I'm free!" She studied my face. "What's up?"

"You won't believe what I learned."

"Tell me."

I whispered in her ear and pulled Finette's bracelet from my pocket. She gazed at it and whistled softly. Out of the corner of my eye, I saw Finette approaching. Quickly, I stuffed the bracelet into its hiding place.

"Allie," Finette said, "thanks for calling and leaving a message. Given your kind visit to my great-aunt, I was hoping you would show up. A word."

"After the meeting."

"Now."

Chapter 24

He smiled understandingly—much more than understandingly. It was one of those rare smiles with a quality of eternal reassurance in it, that you may come across four or five times in life.

—Nick Carraway in F. Scott Fitzgerald's *The Great Gatsby*

Finette hitched her chin, insisting I follow her.

I did and glanced at her ankles. The one that usually sported an infinity bracelet had a wide flexible fabric bandage on it.

Tegan trailed me. "I'll come, too."

"No, Tegan," Finette said. "This is a private matter. Stay here." She flicked a finger. "Allie, outside."

"It's okay," I assured my pal. "When Zach gets here, tell him where we are."

Finette said, "Let's go," and passed through the archway into the vestibule. She made a beeline for a door leading to the rear patio and exited. She strode to the cast-stone fountain, which stood about twenty feet from any walls or windows.

The air was cool, but I didn't dare wrap my arms around my torso. I might need them to defend myself.

"For your information, Zach won't be coming," Finette said. "He's on a call. It appears there's been a disturbance near the Sugarbaker estate."

My stomach wrenched. Had she killed someone else? Did she hope Zach would think a serial killer was at large? "What kind of disturbance?"

"A vicious dog named Moose is on the loose." Her eyes glinted with malice.

Oh, no. After learning I'd spoken with Katherine and intended to attend the council meeting, she must have let the dog out to distract the police.

"What's in your pocket, Allie?" she demanded.

"Nothing."

"You're lying. You showed Tegan a piece of jewelry."

"Oh, that." Man, she had eagle eyes. I pulled the ankle bracelet free. "I came across this at my place. Could it be yours?"

"It is. I lost it the night of the neighborhood watch party." She opened her palm. "Hand it over."

"Now who's lying? You had it on at Ragamuffin on Sunday. Iggie commented on it."

Her eyes flickered, as if she was trying to work out a better explanation.

I gestured to the bandage on her leg. "What happened to your ankle? Did you catch it on a nail or, to be specific, a cat's toenail?"

"No."

"Many cat scratches heal within a few days, but a deeper one can take longer. It could even get infected. Want me to take a peek? I'm an expert at treating wounds."

"A cat didn't scratch me."

"After a few days, if you start noticing swollen lymph nodes or fever, you really need to contact your doctor."

Automatically, she swallowed hard. "Give me the bracelet."

"I can't. It's evidence."

"Of what?"

"Of you breaking into my house and stealing an artifact."

"I did no such thing."

"Darcy wasn't happy about your intrusion. That's why he attacked you. I figure you raced out in pain and didn't realize until later his assault unlatched the bracelet. It must have been some tussle. The bracelet wound up clinging to a loose spring beneath the armchair. When I didn't mention finding it, you thought you were in the clear."

She studied me with loathing. "Why did you go to my great-aunt's house? Who gave you permission?"

I cocked my head. "I didn't think I needed permission to show kindness to a woman who's housebound."

"She's not house—"

"You're out of money. You can't afford to keep your great-aunt in the home any longer and are so desperate to move her, you do your best to convince people she's losing her marbles."

"She is."

"She seemed perfectly sane to me. In fact, she seemed with it."

"*With it.* Right." She scoffed.

"You've been diligent about giving the impression that you're doing fine financially. New hair highlights. New jackets. New handbag. You even told everybody you secured a loan to renovate your house."

"I am doing fine."

"Yeah. *Not.*" I plowed ahead. "Here's what I think happened. Weeks ago, when Jason came to town and asked for your help to get the town council's approval of his project, you dunned him for money."

"I didn't dun him."

"He paid. He really wanted those properties. But when the final notices about the foreclosure started to appear, and you pressed him for more—"

"What foreclosure?"

"Finette, can it!" I barked, tired of our little dance. "I saw the bank notices at Katherine's. When Jason realized you had no extra sway with the council members, and believed he could get any or all of them on his side without forking over another dime, he reneged on your arrangement. You acted all cozy with him, but in truth, you were livid. You were going to go bankrupt if you didn't do something. You figured if you got rid of him, you could put the squeeze on some other chump. Someone like your former lover, Iggie Luckenbill."

She didn't respond, which had to mean my guess was right.

"Why did you frame me, Finette?" I pronounced her name the way Katherine preferred.

She repeated her name the way she liked it, with a short *i*, accent on the second syllable.

"Finette," I echoed to appease her. "Why did you want me to take the fall for Jason's murder? Because of your infatuation with Zach Armstrong?"

"I'm not infatuated with him."

"Sure you are. Did you think once I was out of the way, you could swoop in and win his heart? When did you come up with the idea?" I snapped my fingers. "Hold on! I know exactly when. The day I lost my Celtic earring, a scenario came to you—a way to get rid of Jason and me at the same time."

She glowered.

"Soon after, on the night of the neighborhood watch party, you got the clever idea to steal the spearpoint. How did you get into the house without alerting—" I halted as a light bulb clicked on in my mind. "You saw me using the spare house key I kept in my van."

"Who needed a key?" She smirked. "My father taught me how to pick a lock. He was adamant I know how to save myself in all sorts of situations."

"He must've been a stand-up guy."

She frowned.

"No? He wasn't all he was cracked up to be?" I asked. "Did you blame him for your current circumstance because he was such a do-gooder and never saved a dime, as he'd recommended? Not to mention he took in his aunt—your great-aunt—and then died, leaving you to foot the bill?"

"He was a saint. He taught me everything I know."

I inhaled sharply as another realization struck me. When

Tegan and I were making plans to go to the caverns, Finette had appeared at the office door. She'd asked about our picnic. Tegan mentioned we were going on a hike and she would drive. "Did your dad also teach you how to mess with a car's coolant system so the car might have trouble on a steep country road?"

A vicious smile pulled at her lips.

I continued. "You came to the bookshop, not because you actually wanted another copy of *The Great Gatsby* for your great-aunt—why would you spend another dime on her?—but because you heard Lillian questioning Iggie about his alibi, and you believed I'd put her up to it."

"You must have. She is not a self-starter."

She was, but I wouldn't quibble. "You worried that in time, I'd figure out you were the killer, so you targeted Tegan's car, hoping it would fail and I'd die."

She didn't respond.

"For the longest time, one thing stumped me," I went on. "I couldn't fathom how the killer could have sent me messages from Jason's phone and erased them, until I recalled overhearing you and Iggie talking about Burt the Cyber Buddy. His fans are techies, which means you're one. My guess? On one of his blogs you read about an app that could help the user delete messages from a cell phone. You followed instructions and made it impossible for me to prove to Zach that Jason—actually you—had summoned me to his house."

"Burt is wise beyond measure, but no, I didn't learn how to reconfigure phones from him."

I hissed. "It doesn't matter how you figured it out. My guess is the idea came to you when you and Iggie were facing off Sunday morning."

"Facing off?"

"At Ragamuffin he threatened to press for your dismissal." I clucked my tongue. "Poor Iggie. You weren't content to simply frame me. You wanted to entrap him, as well. Ever since he dumped you, he's been a bur in your side, hasn't he?"

"What a quaint expression."

"I'm assuming when you helped him with his cuff link that day, you got the inspiration to leave one at the crime scene to make it seem like he'd argued with Jason, as backup in case Zach couldn't possibly believe I was guilty. Did you have a duplicate made by the jeweler who sells you your infinity pieces? The police will find out."

She didn't answer.

"As for the mud—"

"What mud?"

"At the crime scene. It baffled me. For the longest time I thought it was a clue proving Patrick Hardwick killed Jason. His boots are always dirty. But in the end, I realized Jason tracked it in. No one else. Neighbors often saw him tweaking his gardens, trying to make them perfect for Delilah."

"Delilah. Spare me. What a fool he was for that woman." Finette faked a yawn. "She didn't love him. She would never love him. How he went on and on about her. It was pathetic." She checked her watch. "And now, although this has been a lovely exercise in deduction, Allie, I must go."

"One more thing before you do. Tell me the truth. When you stabbed him, did you scream with fury?"

She huffed. "I will be more than gracious and not cite you for harassment with that accusation. I will chalk up your mistakes to your impulsiveness. You should work on that aspect of your personality. It's a nasty habit." She started to leave.

"Hold it, Miss Fineworthy," Zach said. He and Bates emerged from the shadows, along with Tegan and Vanna, and I breathed easier. "After listening in on your chat, I'd like you to accompany my partner and me to the precinct."

"Whatever for?"

"For the murder of Jason Gardner, as well as for animal cruelty. Moose's owners' security cams caught a perfect photograph of you unlatching the gate to the outdoor dog run."

"Did you find Moose?" I asked.

"He is safely home with his people," Zach said, after which he read Finette her rights.

CHAPTER 25

A sudden emptiness seemed to flow now from the windows and the great doors, endowing with complete isolation the figure of the host, who stood on the porch, his hand up in a formal gesture of farewell.

—Nick Carraway in F. Scott Fitzgerald's *The Great Gatsby*

Zach wasn't pleased with me for putting myself in harm's way, but fortunately, because the text I had sent him was bland to the max, which was very unlike me—his words, his compliment—he had determined something might be up. Concerned, he'd dispatched another officer to deal with the loose dog situation, and he and Bates had come directly to the recreation center.

During the course of the next week, Finette claimed I was wrong on all counts. She had plenty of money. She was flush. She had no reason to want Jason Gardner dead. But the facts proved out. She was in foreclosure. She had received final notices. Her bank account was empty. Also, after the police canvassed the neighborhood around the Sugarbaker estate, a witness came forward who'd seen Finette exiting the property through the rear gate last Monday night. The witness hadn't said anything until now, because she'd gone to Charlotte to take care of a sick sister. According to her testimony, the intruder had dressed in all black and was hunched over and limping on her right leg, the leg Darcy had attacked.

"Are you ready?" Tegan asked me. She'd come to Dream Cuisine at noon to supervise the final preparations for the *Gatsby* party.

Vanna and I had started cooking at five a.m.

I tamped down a yawn. "Ready as we'll ever be. Deviled eggs." I gestured to a platter filled with one hundred portions. "Fixings for Waldorf salad." Each was prepared in a bento-style box. Difficult to transport but easier for service. "Five dozen orange-drop cookies and five dozen blood-orange crinkles. Ten pineapple upside-down cakes. Bowls of marinated olives and platters of cheese, as well as grilled shrimp. Four lemon-filled coconut cakes. Seventy-five salmon mousse cups. A hundred roast chicken wings with rosemary. Three sliced sugar-glazed hams. Five strawberry ladyfinger icebox cakes." My back was aching, but I had to admit I was beyond pleased with the results.

"Stop!" Tegan pleaded. "My mouth is watering. I'm putting on pounds thinking about the feast." She turned to her sister. "Vanna, did you bring your dress along, or are you going home to change?"

"I'm going to the bed-and-breakfast. I'll get ready there and drive Mother over when we're both ready."

Tegan helped us load up the van and then left to let us finish up.

As the door to the kitchen closed, Vanna said, "Allie, we have to talk about something."

"Your meeting with the mayor. Of course. I apologize for not asking how it went."

"It went so well, um . . ."

I cocked my head and waited for her to continue. Vanna was rarely at a loss for words.

"I'm not sure I want to partner with you any longer," she said in a rush. "I'll continue to do the literary dining parties, but not the day-to-day stuff." She motioned with her arm at the array of pots and pans needing cleaning. "Would it be okay? I mean, you probably want to say I'm more disappointing than an unsalted pretzel—"

I snorted. "Good one."

"Your one-liners are rubbing off on me." She grinned. "But please know that simply because I want out doesn't mean I don't love you. I do."

My eyes widened. She what? I thought she barely tolerated me.

"And I love books, mysteries in particular."

Okay, now she was scaring me. Who was this woman, and what had she done with Vanna Harding?

"But I'm sort of a one-woman act, you know? All these early mornings are, well, messing with my routine. I need more sleep. I need my beauty rest." Frantically, she motioned to her face. "I've got bags under my eyes!" she wailed, after which she took a deep calming breath. "Besides, I like doing nighttime soirees. Are you okay with my decision?"

Honestly, I was relieved. I'd decided recently that I didn't want to expand the business. I was enjoying catering and working at the bookshop. If Dream Cuisine continued to grow, I would have to curtail my time at Feast for the Eyes or give up reading . . . and that wasn't going to happen.

"Of course I'm okay with it," I assured her.

"Really? Thank you for understanding." She grabbed my hands and squeezed. "By the way, I loved the Agatha Christie book *The Murder of Roger Ackroyd*. Who knew mysteries could be so much fun to read?"

"Glad to hear it." I tamped down a laugh. I didn't want her to think I was mocking her.

"Hercule Poirot is really clever. However, I must tell you I found a number of misspelled words. Like *organise* with an *s*, instead of *organize* with a *z*, and *marvellous* with two *l*'s, instead of *marvelous* with one *l*. You'd think the publisher would've caught the mistakes."

"Some British English words are spelled differently from Americanized English versions."

"Really? I had no idea." She mimed her head exploding.

Three hours later I whisked home and grabbed my flapper dress. I would change into it after we arranged the food at the bookshop. However, I twisted my hair into a loose updo with tendrils, put on red lipstick—gloss simply wasn't authentic for the period—and then plunked Darcy into his carrier. I was bringing him along so he could observe from the office. After all, being a tuxedo cat, he was already dressed for the party.

We arrived at Feast for the Eyes two hours before the party was to start. Tegan and the servers we'd hired were in full swing, prepping tables, moving our modest lectern into place, and transporting "on hold" books to the stockroom. Chloe, clad in a red tiered-tassel dress that swished with every step, was tweaking all the printed quotes from *Gatsby* that were tilting.

I studied one of Nick's quotes, the one referring to wealth and class inequality, and thought of Finette. *In my younger and more vulnerable years my father gave me some advice I've been turning over in my mind ever since.* "Whenever you feel like criticizing any one," he told me, "just remember that all the people in this world haven't had the advantages that you've had." I believed Fitzgerald wrote it to remind us, the readers, that much of a person's success might be due to their wealthy upbringing and not their skill. Certainly Nick had struggled with the principle.

Chloe rounded an endcap and stood beside me. She pointed to a different quote. "I love this one. 'Reserving judgments is a matter of infinite hope.' It's so Nick. It sets him up for the reader as a truthful narrator. We can trust he'll continue to tell us the real story throughout." She sighed. "If only life were that way and everyone was honest."

"If only," I echoed.

Lillian and a team of designers from the community theater had come in earlier in the morning and arranged the décor. Three brass torchiere lamps dripped with strands of pearls. A number of oversized black vases boasted huge white plumes. Lamé drapes adorned the front door and the stockroom entrance. Each of the tables was covered with a gold tablecloth and set with platters of food. Lillian had acquired exquisite Art Deco tiered cookie and cake stands. On the sales counter stood a pair of gorgeous candlesticks fitted with white candles.

A bartender with a knack for mixed drinks stood at the bar near the sales counter, prepared to make old-fashioneds and sidecars. Those particular cocktails were all the rage in the 1920s. In addition, we were offering champagne, lemonade, and sparkling water.

To the right, in the open space, we'd laid out a ten-by-ten parquet floor in case anyone wanted to "cut a rug." No longer thinking we should erect a coffee bar there, I began to fantasize about making the unused section of the bookstore a mini gift shop. We could sell specialty bookmarks, book-themed jewelry, mugs, and other paraphernalia. I hadn't mentioned the idea to Tegan yet. It could wait for now.

Tegan moseyed to me. "We're ready to go."

"I love the music."

"Me too."

We hadn't agreed to Vanna's idea of hiring a band, but Tegan had had the brilliant idea of putting her sister in charge of the playlist. She'd embraced the responsibility. "Rhapsody in Blue" was playing through the speakers at the moment.

"I'm going to change into my gown," she said.

At a quarter to three Reika strolled into the shop, looking bright-eyed and eager. Her elegant floor-length burgundy gown adorned with black beads and fringes swished as she walked. While adjusting the cap sleeves of the matching dress cape, she said, "Allie, it looks fabulous."

"We couldn't have done it without all the finishing touches the museum and the theater provided."

She motioned to someone outside.

The weathered, silver-haired man I'd seen sitting at the town council meeting pushed a beverage cart into the shop and paused. On the cart were dozens of Prohibition-style glasses.

"Roy, this is Allie," she said, confirming my suspicion.

"Pleased to meet you, miss." His voice was filled with warmth. The quaint way he said *miss* was genteel. He smoothed the lapels of his pin-striped jacket and gave the hem a tug.

"Push the cart over to the beverage table, Roy," Reika said. "Thank you, love."

Roy fondly cupped Reika's chin and pecked her on the cheek before following her directions to the letter.

I stepped closer to Reika and slipped a hand around her elbow. "He's back?"

"Yes. We're going to couples therapy."

"Wonderful. Um, are you going to be okay around liquor?" I motioned to the bar area.

"I am. I'm completely back on my program. I've already seen a hypnotist. It's working. I have no cravings whatsoever. No feelings of self-loathing, thanks to your suggestion. I even think I can manage a trip on the water. And . . ." She twirled. "You'll notice I'm sans Amira."

"How is that possible?" Her bulldog went everywhere with her.

"I'm feeling confident. Strong. Mind you, that doesn't mean I won't take my sweet girl to work and such, but if I'm going to sail with Roy, I need to be able to be dog free. My assistant is eager to give her a temporary home."

"I'm so happy for you."

Vanna and Noeline entered the shop, and I excused myself to Reika.

Tegan, who looked sassy in her navy blue-and-silver flapper dress—the floral beading was exquisite—beat me to her family and hugged them. "Go change," she whispered to me.

"On it. But before I go, ladies, you look fabulous. I love hot pink on you, Vanna. It really lights up your face."

"It does, doesn't it? I never wear this color, but Lillian convinced me."

Noeline scanned the shop. "This is impressive. I'm so proud of you girls for pulling it off. I feel like I'm in a 1920s bookshop, right down to the pearls. By the way—Vanna, I didn't want to tell you until we were all together—I've decided not to buy the other bed-and-breakfast."

Tegan let out a happy squeal.

"Why not, Mother?" Vanna asked. "You can't let Tegan bully you."

"She didn't. As it turns out, Helga's friend is no longer available to help me with the enterprise. She got a gig at Whispering Winds, of all places, for a paycheck much higher than I could afford. Of course, she had to accept."

"Helga can find someone else," Vanna protested.

"She could, but for now, I'm happy with one place. The renovations are done. I'm booked for an entire year. I can't wait to mount the special Christmas celebration."

During the holidays, Noeline dressed up the bed-and-breakfast in the same fashion as the inn on Biltmore Estate, though on a much smaller scale. It was magical.

"Go, Allie." Tegan nudged me. "Time's a-wasting."

I hurried to the office, closed the blinds, and changed into my dress. Darcy mewed his approval. Before returning to the shop, I checked my makeup and hair in the mirror on the stockroom wall. Still good. Setting up the party hadn't marred a thing.

Tegan greeted customers as they entered. Chloe directed people to the food stations and beverages. All the guests embraced the Roaring Twenties style. Not one was wearing everyday clothing. Happy chatter abounded.

Zach strode through the entrance with Brendan Bates. Bates had donned a very dapper beige suit. Zach, who'd dressed in black trousers, black vest over white shirt, black tie, pocket watch, and bowler hat, gave the impression of a gentleman gangster. All he needed was a sly mustache to complete the look. Both men admired the lamé drapery, after which they began scanning the quotations.

I sauntered to them, a glass of lemonade in hand. "Welcome, boys. If you're thirsty and you're not on duty, the bar is thataway." I hooked a thumb over my shoulder.

Bates strolled away. Zach stayed put.

"You look stunning," he said. "Your emerald green is something else."

"Beats my typical black-and-white getups, right?" I grinned. "Is the case settled? All t's crossed and i's dotted?"

He nodded.

"I've been meaning to ask, were you able to determine whether the initial on the cuff link we found was an *I* or a *J*?"

"Definitely an *I* and made by Finette's jeweler. Good guess. Finette told them it was a gift to replace the one her father lost." He smirked. "Guess they didn't know her history. Her father never wore a suit in his life, let alone cuff links."

The door swung open, and Evelyn Evers swept in, dressed in a ruby-red, floor-length gown, elegant red gloves, a feathered headband, ornate gold-and-pearl dangling earrings, and strands of pearls. She looked ready to launch into song à la Bessie Smith. She paused by Zach and me.

"Wow!" I cried. "Double wow!"

She smiled. "I love a little drama. If you have a moment, Allie . . ."

Zach excused himself and joined his partner at the bar.

I eyed her expectantly. "Are you hoping I'll volunteer more often, as thanks for all that the theater did for our party?"

"Yes, and . . ." She drew me into one of the book aisles. "It's time you know what happened between your mother and me."

My lungs tightened. Did I want the truth?

"I was once an actress," Evelyn said.

"Well, you don't have that in common with Fern," I said lightly, attempting a joke.

"No, we don't, because she could never commit to anything."

"Except math and Jamie," I countered.

Evelyn glanced to her right. No one was listening in. I waited patiently. She regarded me again. "We were good friends. No, we were great friends."

Wow. I hadn't seen that with binoculars.

"Best buddies. We played together. Studied together. Attended the same college. She was going to be the best mathematician in the world. I was going to become a world-class actress, and then . . ." She drifted off again.

"She met my father and forsook you."

"No. Never mind. It's not mine to divulge."

Before she could escape, I nabbed her elbow. "Uh-uh. You do not get to drop a bombshell and walk away. Fern likes me to know the truth. If she hasn't told me, it's because she didn't think it was important. What happened?"

"She met my boyfriend."

I gasped. "You called her a vagabond. Did she run off with him?"

"They traveled the US for one summer. He was head over heels for her. But when the autumn semester began, she dumped him, and he was never the same. I blamed her for his downfall. I reproached myself for ever trusting her. Looking back"—she sighed heavily—"I realize it wasn't her fault. She was alluring and funny."

Fern, alluring? Funny? I rolled my eyes.

"Alluring," Evelyn continued, "because she was so knowledgeable and could speak rings around anyone."

"And funny?"

"In a math genius kind of way. Do you know what mathematicians do after it snows?" She waited for a response. When I didn't reply, she said, "They make snow angles." She guffawed. "Angles, not angels!"

"That's a genius joke?"

"It's dumb, but it made her so relatable." Her eyes crinkled. "I've held a grudge for far too long. I owe her an apology. She was a good mother to you."

"She didn't teach me how to cook."

She pulled a face. "There are other lessons a parent can instill."

"Like how to not put down roots?"

"What a horrible comment that was. I never should have uttered it at Marigold's memorial. Forgive me?" She tilted her head. "If you'll give Fern my number, please tell her I'd like to make amends. Maybe coming from you, she'll call me."

"I'll be glad to." I caressed her arm. "Why didn't you become an actress?"

"I was a basket case. Heartbreak showed up in every performance. I needed to pursue something more administrative, something less emotionally taxing. It was the best decision." She pecked my cheek and crossed the room to chat with Chloe.

Tegan waved to me and gave me a questioning look. I gestured with a thumbs-up.

Zach saw I was free and rejoined me. "Got a sec?"

"More than a sec." I licked my lower lip. His gaze followed

my tongue. I felt my cheeks burn. "You keep avoiding me. It's because I brought up the kiss, right?"

"Shh," he urged. "Let me speak. It is about the kiss. I'd wanted to kiss you for the longest time. I was so nervous about it. When you leaned forward, I froze. I know it wasn't a good kiss. A proper kiss. Then when you said you shouldn't have kissed me and rued having done so, I thought, *Well, that's that. We're done. Friends going forward.*"

I tugged his tie and pulled his mouth to mine. We kissed sweetly, eyes open. It was better than the first. Way better.

The front door opened and nearly hit me in the rear end. Laughing, I released Zach and apologized to the newcomer. Then my jaw dropped, because I recognized her.

"Delilah," I whispered. "You came."

"Yes," she said in a dulcet voice. "I came."

I'd tracked her down via her online presence and told her what had happened to Jason, unsure whether the news of his death would have reached California. She'd been shocked to hear. She hadn't a clue where he'd gone. Never knew why he'd left. I'd confided what I believed to be true. Upon learning she was pregnant, he'd abandoned his project and fled California. She'd cried, saying because he never wrote, she thought he might have died.

She was as pretty as she was in all her pictures. A natural beauty. Gorgeous blond curls. Her soft pink Empire dress matched the color of her cheeks. But her eyes were filled with sadness. She noticed me eyeing her pregnant belly and pressed a hand to it. "It's a boy."

"Congratulations."

"We're going to name him Jason."

My eyes welled with tears.

"I've come for the funeral."

Magda had decided to host the funeral, seeing as Jason had no family, and because she and his family had been friends with the Yeagers. It was to be a small affair at the cemetery. She had ordered the headstone and had told me it would read: *Dreamer. Builder. Gone too soon from this world.*

Delilah surveyed the room and returned her gaze to me. She clasped both of my hands. "Jason would have loved this party. He always appreciated the past."

"Yes, but he was hopeful for the future."

Recipes Included

Broccoli and Cheddar Cheese Quiche
Chocolate Crinkle Cookies + Gluten-Free Version
Deviled Eggs
Easy Lemon Cheesecake Bars
Orange-Drop Cookies + Gluten-Free Version
Pasta Pomodoro
Pineapple Upside-Down Cake + Gluten-Free Version
Simple Blueberry Tarts

Broccoli and Cheddar Cheese Quiche

Yield: 1 pie, 6 servings

¾ cup finely chopped broccoli, florets and stalks *
2 teaspoons olive oil
1 cup shredded Cheddar cheese
One 9-inch pie shell (homemade or frozen; gluten free is fine)
4 large eggs
¾ cup whole milk
¼ cup cream of chicken soup (use gluten-free soup for a gluten-free quiche)
½ teaspoon dried *herbes de Provence* or Italian seasoning
½ teaspoon salt
¼ teaspoon ground pepper

Preheat oven to 375°F.

Blanch the broccoli (*you may use stalks and florets or only florets) in boiling hot water for 2 minutes. Then drain and rinse with cold water.

In a small sauté pan, heat the oil over medium heat. Add the broccoli and sauté, stirring once or twice, for 1 minute.

Sprinkle ¼ cup of the Cheddar cheese over the bottom of the pie shell. Spread the broccoli over the cheese in an even layer.

In a medium bowl, beat together the eggs, milk, soup, *herbes de Provence* (or Italian seasoning), salt, and pepper. Slowly pour the egg-milk mixture over the filling in the pie shell. Sprinkle the remaining ¾ cup cheese on top.

Place the quiche on a baking sheet and bake for 35 to 40 minutes, or until it has set and is lightly brown on top.

Tip: If you have any egg-milk mixture left over, butter an individual soufflé dish (ramekin), and pour in the remaining mixture. Bake in the oven for about 20 minutes, or until firm and lightly brown on top. Delish!

Chocolate Crinkle Cookies

Yield: 4 dozen

1½ cups granulated sugar, plus ½ cup for rolling
1½ cups brown sugar
8 ounces (1 cup) unsalted butter, melted
4 ounces unsweetened chocolate, melted
4 large eggs
2 teaspoons vanilla extract
2 cups all-purpose flour
1 cup cocoa powder
2 teaspoons baking powder
½ teaspoon salt
½ cup powdered sugar

Heat oven to 350°F. Line 2 cookie sheets with parchment paper.

In a large bowl, mix together the 1½ cups granulated sugar, brown sugar, butter, and chocolate. Add the eggs one at a time and mix well with each addition. Next, add the vanilla extract and mix until combined. Set aside.

In a separate large bowl, whisk together the flour, cocoa powder, baking powder, and salt. Add the flour mixture to the reserved sugar-butter mixture and mix until incorporated.

Pour the remaining ½ cup granulated sugar and the powdered sugar into separate shallow bowls.

Roll a tablespoon of the dough into a walnut-sized ball. (You might need to moisten your fingers to prevent the dough from sticking to your hands.) Repeat until all the dough has been rolled into balls.

One by one, coat the balls with granulated sugar and then with powdered sugar. Place them about 2 inches apart on the prepared cookie sheets.

Bake the cookies for 10 to 12 minutes. When you remove them from the oven, the "cracks" in the cookies will look slightly gooey. That's fine. Do not overbake.

Chocolate Crinkle Cookies
Gluten-Free Version

Yield: 4 dozen

1½ cups granulated sugar, plus ½ cup for rolling
1½ cups brown sugar
8 ounces (1 cup) butter, melted
4 ounces unsweetened chocolate, melted
4 large eggs
2 teaspoons vanilla extract
2 cups gluten-free flour
1 cup cocoa powder
1 tablespoon whey powder
2 teaspoons baking powder
½ teaspoon xanthan gum
½ teaspoon salt
½ cup powdered sugar

Preheat oven to 350°F. Line 2 cookie sheets with parchment paper.

In a large bowl, mix together the 1½ cups granulated sugar, brown sugar, butter, and chocolate. Add the eggs one at a time and mix well with each addition. Next, add the vanilla extract and mix until combined. Set aside.

In a separate large bowl, whisk together the flour, cocoa powder, whey powder, baking powder, xanthan gum, and salt. Add the flour mixture to the reserved sugar-butter mixture and mix until incorporated.

Pour the remaining ½ cup granulated sugar and the powdered sugar into separate shallow bowls.

Roll a tablespoon of the dough into a walnut-sized ball. (You might need to moisten your fingers to prevent the dough from sticking to your hands.) Repeat until all the dough has been rolled into balls.

One by one, coat each ball with granulated sugar and then with powdered sugar. Place them about 2 inches apart on the prepared cookie sheets.

Bake the cookies for 10 to 12 minutes. When you remove them from the oven, the "cracks" in the cookies will look slightly gooey. That's fine. Do not overbake.

Deviled Eggs

Yield: 12 deviled eggs

6 large eggs
¼ cup mayonnaise
1 teaspoon white vinegar
1 teaspoon yellow mustard
¼ teaspoon freshly ground pepper
⅛ teaspoon salt
Paprika for garnish (optional)

Let 6 eggs come to room temperature.

Bring 6 cups of water to a boil in a large saucepan. Reduce the heat to medium low and lower the eggs slowly into the water. (If you put them in too fast, the eggs will crack.) Boil the eggs for 9 minutes and then remove them immediately from the water. Set them aside to cool.

When the eggs have cooled, slice them in half lengthwise. Scoop out the egg yolks, place them in a small bowl, and set aside. Next, arrange the egg-white halves on a serving plate.

Mash the reserved egg yolks. Add the mayonnaise, vinegar, mustard, pepper, and salt to the yolks and blend well.

Pipe (with a piping bag fitted with a star tip) or spoon about 1½ teaspoons filling into each egg-white half. Dust the deviled eggs with paprika, if desired.

Easy Lemon Cheesecake Bars

Yield: 9 to 12 bars

1½ cups crushed graham crackers (gluten free, if desired)
2 tablespoons unsalted butter, melted
Two 8-ounce packages cream cheese
½ cup granulated sugar
1 tablespoon freshly squeezed lemon juice
1 teaspoon lemon zest
½ teaspoon vanilla extract
2 large eggs

Preheat oven to 350°F. Line an 8" square pan with parchment paper and spray with nonstick spray.

Prepare the crust. Pour the crushed graham crackers into the prepared pan. Drizzle with the melted butter and stir with a spoon. Press the graham cracker mixture firmly into the bottom and up the sides of the pan to form an even layer. Set aside.

Next prepare the filling. In a large bowl, whisk together the cream cheese, sugar, lemon juice, lemon zest, and vanilla extract until well blended. Add the eggs and mix until incorporated.

Spoon the cream cheese filling into the prepared crust. Bake for 20 to 25 minutes, or until the center is almost firm. Remove the cheesecake to a wire rack and cool completely. Next, refrigerate the cheesecake for at least 3 hours, though it is best when refrigerated overnight.

Cut the chilled cheesecake into small bars and serve.

Orange-Drop Cookies

Yield: 2 dozen

4 tablespoons unsalted butter
¼ cup freshly squeezed orange juice
2 tablespoons freshly grated orange zest
2 cups all-purpose flour
1 tablespoon + 1 teaspoon baking powder
½ teaspoon kosher salt
2 large eggs
1 cup granulated sugar

Preheat the oven to 375°F. Line 2 baking sheets with parchment paper.

In a small bowl, soften the butter in the microwave by warming it for 15 to 20 seconds on high. Fold the orange juice and orange zest into the butter. Set aside.

In a large bowl, whisk together the flour, baking powder, and salt. Set aside.

Using a stand mixer fitted with the paddle attachment or a hand mixer and a large bowl, beat the eggs on medium speed. Add the sugar and mix until incorporated. Next, add the reserved orange-butter mixture and beat well. Finally, add the reserved flour mixture and beat until just combined.

Drop the dough by teaspoonfuls onto the prepared baking sheets. The cookies will spread in the oven. Bake one sheet at a time until the cookies are a light golden brown, about 9 to 10 minutes.

Remove from the oven and allow the cookies to rest for a few minutes before transferring them to a wire rack to cool.

Store the cookies in an airtight container for up to 3 days.

Orange-Drop Cookies
Gluten-Free Version

Yield: 2 dozen

4 tablespoons unsalted butter
¼ cup freshly squeezed orange juice
2 tablespoons freshly grated orange zest
1 cup sweet rice flour
¾ cup + 2 tablespoons tapioca flour
2 tablespoons whey powder
1 tablespoon + 1 teaspoon baking powder
½ teaspoon xanthan gum
½ teaspoon kosher salt
2 large eggs
1 cup granulated sugar

Preheat the oven to 375°F. Line 2 baking sheets with parchment paper.

In a small bowl, soften the 4 tablespoons of butter in the microwave by warming it for 15 to 20 seconds on high. Fold the orange juice and orange zest into the butter. Set aside.

In a large bowl, whisk together the sweet rice flour, tapioca flour, whey powder, baking powder, xanthan gum, and salt. Set aside.

Using a stand mixer fitted with the paddle attachment or a hand mixer and a large bowl, beat the eggs on medium speed. Add the sugar and mix until incorporated. Next, add the reserved orange-butter mixture and beat well. Finally, add the reserved flour mixture and beat until just combined.

Drop the dough by teaspoonfuls onto the prepared baking sheets. The cookies will spread as they bake. Bake one sheet at a time until the cookies are a light golden brown, about 9 to 10 minutes.

Remove from the oven and allow the cookies to rest for a few minutes before transferring them to a wire rack to cool.

Store the cookies in an airtight container for up to 3 days.

Pasta Pomodoro

Yield: 4 to 8 portions

One 28-ounce can whole peeled tomatoes
3 tablespoons kosher salt
4 garlic cloves, peeled
3 tablespoons extra-virgin olive oil
3 basil sprigs, plus more for garnish
1 pound dried spaghetti (may be gluten free)
4 ounces Parmesan cheese, finely grated (about 1 cup)

    Start the sauce. Drain the whole peeled tomatoes in a colander over a large bowl—you want to catch the liquid. Use a fork to poke holes in the tomatoes so that all the liquid drains. Set aside the bowl with the liquid. Place the drained tomatoes in a separate bowl and remove the seeds and any tough parts where the stems were attached. Set aside.
    Fill a large stockpot with water, add the salt, and bring to a boil. No, the amount of salt is not a mistake. It's a lot, but it helps season the noodles throughout.
    Crush the garlic cloves with a knife or garlic press. In a large skillet, heat the oil over medium heat. Add the garlic and cook, stirring often, until it is golden, about 3 minutes. Add the reserved drained tomatoes. Increase the heat to medium-high and cook, stirring occasionally, until the tomatoes start to break down, about 8 to 9 minutes. The tomatoes will caramelize (become sort of brownish). Mash the tomatoes with the back of a spoon. This will help form a paste.
    Next, add half of the reserved tomato liquid to the skillet and stir. If the sauce is too thick, add a little more liquid. Toss in the basil sprigs and reduce the heat to a simmer. Cook approximately 8 to 10 minutes to thicken the sauce.
    Meanwhile, add the pasta to the boiling water—you didn't

turn it off, did you?—and stir to prevent clumping. Cook according to the directions on the package, stirring occasionally, but reduce the time by 1 minute. You want what is known as al dente pasta, meaning slightly underdone, because the pasta will continue cooking once you add it to the sauce. Before you drain the pasta, ladle out ½ cup of the cooking liquid and set aside.

Next, add the drained pasta to the skillet and stir. Increase the heat to medium-high, and cook the pasta in the sauce, stirring often, until the sauce clings to each noodle, about 1 minute. If the sauce looks dry, add a tablespoon or two of the reserved pasta cooking liquid. If it looks too wet, cook a tad longer. That will thicken it.

Remove the skillet from the heat. Sprinkle ½ cup of the Parmesan cheese on top and toss until it has melted. Divide the pasta among serving bowls, top with the remaining ½ cup cheese and basil sprigs, and serve at once.

Pineapple Upside-Down Cake

Yield: 12 slices

Note: This is an intensive recipe! Also, before you begin, all the ingredients should be at room temperature.

Topping:
4 tablespoons (¼ cup) unsalted butter, melted
½ cup packed dark brown sugar
8 to 10 canned pineapple slices in pineapple juice, drained (reserve the juice)
16 maraschino cherries, drained (whole or halved)

Cake:
1½ cups cake flour (make sure it's level)
1 teaspoon baking soda
½ teaspoon salt
6 tablespoons unsalted butter, softened, not melted
¾ cup granulated sugar
2 large egg whites
⅓ cup full-fat sour cream
1 teaspoon vanilla extract
¼ cup pineapple juice (reserved from the can)
2 tablespoons whole milk

Preheat oven to 350°F.

First, make the topping. Pour the melted butter into an ungreased 9-inch deep-dish pie dish or a 9-inch round cake pan. Sprinkle the brown sugar over the melted butter.

Blot the pineapple slices with a paper towel. You don't want wet fruit! Arrange 6 pineapple slices in the bottom of the pan. Halve the remaining pineapple slices and arrange them around the sides of the pan. Place the cherries around the pineapple slices. Set the pan in the refrigerator so the topping firms up.

Meanwhile, make the batter. In a medium bowl, whisk together the cake flour, baking soda, and salt. Set aside.

Using a stand mixer fitted with the paddle attachment or a hand mixer and a large bowl, beat the softened butter on high until creamy. Add the sugar and beat on high until incorporated. Scrape down the sides of the bowl with a spatula, add the egg whites, and beat until combined. Next, add the sour cream and vanilla extract and beat on high for 1 minute.

Add the reserved flour mixture and mix on low speed. Pour in the pineapple juice and milk and beat just until combined. Scrape the sides of the bowl with the spatula to make sure all the ingredients are incorporated. You don't want any lumps. This is a thick batter.

Remove the pan from the refrigerator and pour the batter over the pineapple slices. Bake for 42 to 46 minutes, or until a toothpick inserted in the middle comes out clean. If necessary, tent the cake with foil halfway through baking so it doesn't over-brown. Don't be surprised if your cake takes longer or even rises and sticks to the foil. It's going to be flipped, and any imperfections will vanish from sight.

Remove the cake to a wire rack and cool for 20 minutes. Then carefully turn the cake out onto a serving plate. This cake is best when cooled completely before serving.

Pineapple Upside-Down Cake

Gluten-Free Version

Yield: 12 slices

Note: this is an intensive recipe! This cake will not be as "light" as a cake made with cake flour. Before you begin, all the ingredients should be at room temperature.

Topping:
4 tablespoons (¼ cup) unsalted butter, melted
½ cup packed dark brown sugar
8 to 10 canned pineapple slices in pineapple juice, drained (reserve the juice)
16 maraschino cherries, drained (whole of halved)

Cake:
1½ cups sweet rice flour (make sure it's level)
1½ tablespoons whey powder
1 teaspoon baking powder
1 teaspoon baking soda
½ teaspoon xanthan gum
½ teaspoon salt
6 tablespoons unsalted butter, softened, not melted
¾ cup granulated sugar
2 large egg whites
⅓ cup full-fat sour cream
1 teaspoon vanilla extract
¼ cup pineapple juice (reserved from the can)
2 tablespoons whole milk

Preheat oven to 350°F.
First, make the topping. Pour the melted butter in an ungreased

9-inch deep-dish pie dish or a 9-inch round cake pan. Sprinkle the brown sugar over the melted butter.

Blot the pineapple slices with a paper towel. You don't want wet fruit! Arrange 6 pineapple slices in the bottom of the pan. Halve the remaining pineapple slices and arrange them around the sides of the pan. Place the cherries around the pineapple slices. Set the pan in the refrigerator so the fruit topping firms up.

Meanwhile, make the batter. In a medium bowl, whisk together the sweet rice flour, whey powder, baking powder, baking soda, xanthan gum, and salt. Set aside.

Using a stand mixer fitted with the paddle attachment or a hand mixer and a large bowl, beat the softened butter on high until creamy. Add the sugar and beat on high until incorporated. Scrape down the sides of the bowl with a spatula, add the egg whites, and beat until combined. Then add the sour cream and vanilla extract and beat on high for 1 minute.

Add the gluten-free flour mixture and mix on low speed. Pour in the pineapple juice and milk and beat just until combined. Scrape the sides of the bowl with the spatula to make sure all ingredients are incorporated. You don't want any lumps. This is a thick batter.

Remove the pan from the refrigerator and pour the batter over the pineapple slices. Bake for 42 to 46 minutes, or until a toothpick inserted in the middle comes out clean. If necessary, tent the cake with foil halfway through baking so it doesn't over-brown. Don't be surprised if your cake takes longer or even rises enough to stick to the foil. It's going to be flipped, and any imperfections will vanish from sight.

Remove the cake to a wire rack and cool for 20 minutes. Then carefully turn the cooled cake out onto a serving plate. This cake is best when cooled completely before serving.

Simple Blueberry Tarts

Yield: 12 tarts

1 dozen frozen tart shells (may be gluten free)
3 cups fresh blueberries
½ cup granulated sugar
2 tablespoons cornstarch
Pinch of salt
2 tablespoons lemon juice
Whipped cream, if desired

Preheat the oven to 375°F. Line a baking sheet with parchment paper.
Arrange the tart shells on the baking sheet and bake for 10 to 12 minutes, or until golden. Remove the shells from the oven and place on a wire rack to cool.
Next, pour 1½ cups of the blueberries into a small saucepan. Do not turn on the heat on the stove yet.
In a small bowl, stir together the sugar, cornstarch, and salt. Add the sugar mixture and the lemon juice to the berries in the saucepan and stir. Next, bring the blueberry mixture to a simmer over medium heat and cook for 2 to 3 minutes, or until the berries burst and soften, and the juices thicken. Then allow the mixture to come to a boil, and cook for 1 minute more to thicken it further. This also removes some of the "starchiness" of the cornstarch.
Remove the saucepan from the heat and stir in the remaining 1½ cups blueberries. Let the blueberry filling sit for 1 minute, and then spoon it into the reserved tart shells. Allow the tarts to cool for 10–20 minutes so that the filling firms up.
Serve the tarts with whipped cream, if desired. Refrigerate any leftover tarts.

ACKNOWLEDGMENTS

"The world needs dreamers and the world needs doers. But above all, the world needs dreamers who do."

—Sarah Ban Breathnach

Thank you to so many for your wonderful support while I take this creative journey. Without all of you, I would not have nearly as much fun.

Thank you to my talented author friends, Krista Davis, Hannah Dennison, Janet Bolin (Ginger Bolton), Kaye George (Janet Cantrell), Marilyn Levinson (Allison Brook), Peg Cochran (Margaret Loudon), Janet Koch (Laura Alden; Laurie Cass), and Roberta Isleib (Lucy Burdette). You are a wonderful pool of talent and a terrific wealth of ideas, jokes, stories, and fun! I treasure your creative enthusiasm.

Thank you to my early readers and reviewers. You have been so encouraging. Thank you to all the bloggers who enjoy reviewing mysteries and sharing your thoughts with your readers. Thank you to Lori Caswell for leading the pack when it comes to virtual book tours.

Thanks to those who have helped make this second book in the Literary Dining Mystery series come to fruition: my publisher, Kensington Books; my editor, Elizabeth Trout; my copy editor Rosemary Silva; my agent, Jill Marsal; and my cover artist, Patrick Knowles. Thanks to Madeira James and Xuni for maintaining constant quality on my website. Thanks to my virtual assistant, Christina Higgins, for your clever ideas. Thanks to my family for all your love and care. And many thanks to my lifelong cheerleader and sister, Kimberley Greene. You are the best!

Last but not least, thank you librarians, teachers, bookstore owners, and readers for sharing the fun and colorful world of a caterer who owns part of a bookstore and loves to celebrate books with themed parties.

Bless you all.

Learn more about me on my website and join my newsletter: https://darylwoodgerber.com/contact-media/